THE WORLD STOOD STILL

The voice, so familiar, so haunting, made Jenny whirl around in disbelief. Standing in the doorway was Luke Sheridan, the man who had given her so much joy, so much heartache, so much anger.

Why now? Why did he have to come back now?

Luke's face was grim and stern. His attention was focused solely on Jenny, as if he could see right through to her soul. Luke had always read her so well. She didn't want him to read her now, didn't want him to know how strongly he affected her.

He smelled like her youth, like warm summer days and hot, sultry nights. His voice took her back to bonfires on the beach, to love songs played on an old guitar. Her gaze traveled down to his hands, to the strong, capable hands that had played her like a fine instrument.

Jenny closed her eyes and felt dizzy. Her body swayed. It was too much to take in. Danny's accident. Now Luke.

Daniel's Gift

BARBARA FREETHY

AVON BOOKS ◆ NEW YORK

DANIEL'S GIFT is an original publication of Avon Books. This work has never before appeared in book form. This work is a novel. Any similarity to actual persons or events is purely coincidental.

AVON BOOKS
A division of
The Hearst Corporation
1350 Avenue of the Americas
New York, New York 10019

First Avon Books Printing: March 1996

AVON TRADEMARK REG. U.S. PAT. OFF. AND IN OTHER COUNTRIES, MARCA REGISTRADA, HECHO EN U.S.A.

Printed in the U.S.A.

RA   10   9   8   7   6   5   4

*To my husband, Terry,
and the two best kids in the world,
Kristen and Logan*

ACKNOWLEDGMENTS

Special thanks to my editor, Ellen Edwards, for bringing out the best in me; to my agent, Natasha Kern, for her unending support; to my writing friends, Melissa Martinez, Lynn Hanna, Sheila Slattery, Carol Culver, and Barbara McMahon, for asking the tough questions; to my father, George Beharry, for his medical expertise; and most importantly to my mother, Pat Beharry, who taught me to love books.

"I WANT TO MEET MY DAD." TWELVE-YEAR-OLD Danny St. Claire stood in the doorway to the kitchen, his blond hair tousled from sleep, his eyes drowsy but determined.

The glass of orange juice slipped from Jenny's fingers and crashed to the floor. "Your father?"

"I want to talk to him, Mom."

"Danny—"

"I want to ask him if he ever played shortstop. I want to know how tall he was when he was my age. I want to know when he started to shave." A curl fell down over Danny's right eye, and he flipped it back off his face in disgust. "I want to know if his hair is straight now."

"Danny, please." Jenny shook her head in despair. "We've talked about this before. I know it's difficult for you to understand that a man might not want to have a child. Maybe when you're older . . ."

"I'm old enough. I'm his kid. He should know me."

Danny stuck out his chin in a show of stubbornness that was exactly like his father—if he only knew it. A sudden pain cut across Jenny's heart.

She walked over to the counter, giving herself time to think. The toaster popped up two slices of wheat bread. She buttered them, set them on a plate, and returned to the table with a pleading smile. "Eat your breakfast. We'll talk about this after school."

"You won't have time after school. You'll be at work. You're always at work."

"I'm sorry, but I do the best I can, Danny. I think you could be a little more understanding."

"Rob's mother stays home all day. And his dad is taking him camping this weekend," Danny said, throwing out a challenge that was impossible to beat.

"Are you deliberately trying to make me feel guilty? I'm doing my best. What do you want me to say?"

"Nothing. Forget it." Danny slid out of his chair.

"Aren't you going to eat?"

"I'm not hungry."

Jenny sighed as Danny left the room. She hated to disappoint him, but lately that's all she seemed to do. Working eight hours a day at McDougal's Market, trying to build a jewelry-making business on the side, then keeping up with the house, the cooking, and the cleaning didn't leave much time for play.

Picking up a sponge, she cleaned up the mess on the floor and packed Danny's lunch. When she went into the living room, Danny was stuffing his homework into his backpack with an expression so woebegone he looked more like six than twelve.

His drooping mouth caught at Jenny's heart. It reminded her of simpler times, when Danny hadn't thought beyond his next cookie. He was growing up fast, too fast, asking questions she didn't want to answer, wanting things he couldn't have—like his father.

She was losing her child, her baby, and she couldn't bear the thought.

"Runner on first," Jenny said.

Danny looked up. "Huh?"

"Runner on first. Two outs. Two strikes, one ball. What's the pitch?"

A reluctant smile spread across Danny's face. "The heater."

"No curve?"

He shook his head. "Blow some smoke, Mom."

Jenny drew back her arm, Danny's sack lunch clutched in her hand. "The runner steals. The pitcher turns. She throws." Jenny hurled the bag across the room.

Danny caught it and dropped to the floor, tagging an imaginary runner. "You're out."

"Nice play."

"Nice throw—for a girl."

Jenny walked over and pushed the cowlick down at the corner of Danny's head.

He brushed her hand away. "Aw, Mom."

"Hug me good-bye?" she asked hopefully.

Danny rolled his eyes, but did allow her one quick squeeze. It wasn't enough. She was lucky to get that much.

Danny paused at the front door. "Can we go to the mall this weekend? I want to buy a gift for your birthday."

Jenny looked at her son for a long moment, not sure if she should be touched by his thoughtfulness or impressed by his ability to manipulate her. The quirk at the corner of his mouth gave him away. "Nice try, kiddo. Is Sportsworld having a sale?"

"Come to think of it . . ."

"We'll see."

"That means no."

"That means, we'll see. Maybe Alan can go with us."

Danny made a face at the mention of Jenny's boyfriend. "Forget it."

"Come on, Danny, give Alan a chance. He's trying."

"Yeah, right." Danny hiked up his too-big blue jeans under his too-big sweatshirt and placed his San Francisco Giants baseball cap on backward.

Jenny sent him an affectionate look. Even though his clothes were atrocious, his attitude worse, he was still her kid, and underneath all that adolescent armor beat a tender and loving heart. She just had to remember that.

"You do understand about your father, don't you?" she asked.

Danny looked her in the eye. "No, I don't understand. I have a right to know my father. Kids are supposed to have two parents."

"I wish it could have been different."

"Don't you want to know what happened to him, Mom? Don't you care about him at all?" Danny didn't wait for an answer. He ran down the steps, across the grass, and disappeared from view.

Jenny walked out to the sidewalk to pick up her morning paper. The street was quiet and peaceful, just a block from the Pacific Ocean. It was a working-class neighborhood with small one-story homes, neatly kept yards, and plenty of bikes, skateboards, and soccer balls to keep the kids happy. There wasn't a lot of money in this part of town, but there was a lot of pride and a lot of love.

As she turned to go back to the house, Jenny saw her elderly neighbor Gracie Patterson digging in her garden.

Gracie was wearing a wide-brim straw hat to protect her aging skin from the sun and a pair of strong, dirty gloves over her thin hands. Despite her advanced age, somewhere in her seventies, Gracie still worked in her garden, baked cookies for the neighborhood kids, and kept an eye out for Jenny and Danny. She was one of the reasons Jenny liked living in Half Moon Bay, a small coastal community just south of San Francisco. People cared about each other here. They weren't just neighbors but friends.

"Morning, Gracie," Jenny called.

Gracie looked up and waved. "Good morning. How are you today?"

"Late."

"Same as always." She tipped her head toward the street. "Danny ran by in an awful hurry. Everything okay?"

"He's almost a teenager."

"Don't say another word." Gracie laughed as she got to her feet and walked over to the chain-link fence that separated their two yards. "Anything I can do to help?"

"Not this time, but thanks for the offer."

"Just remember that all children do grow up."

"I'll hang on to that thought. Have a good day."

"You, too."

Jenny returned to her house and got ready for work, hoping that Gracie was right, that the problem of Danny's father, Luke Sheridan, would simply disappear, given enough time.

Tonight she would come home early from work and surprise Danny. They'd go for pizza, a movie. He'd forget all about his father—and so would she.

It was past five that night when Jenny returned home. She called Danny's name as she set her purse down on the kitchen counter. There was no reply. When she turned, she saw the note.

The paper was clamped to the refrigerator door with an orange pumpkin magnet left over from Halloween. It was next to the two-dollar-off coupon for pepperoni pizza and the PTA newsletter. The word scrawled across the front in red crayon read simply, "Mom."

There was nothing threatening about the piece of paper, but as soon as Jenny saw it, she knew something was wrong.

If there was such a thing as mother's intuition, she had it now. Every nerve ending in her body tingled. Goose bumps ran down her bare arms, producing a shiver that racked her thin body. In the distance she could hear the sound of sirens growing closer, louder, reinforcing her sense of disaster.

Danny never went out after school, not without asking first. Forcing her feet to move, Jenny walked over to the refrigerator and peeled off the note. Slowly, she unfolded the paper.

Mom,
I've gone to find Dad.

The words were simple, stark, horrifying.

I know he didn't want me when I was born, but maybe now he will. I'm a pretty good ballplayer. Don't be mad. Christopher's sister is giving us a ride. I'll take the bus back.

Danny

His father? Going to see his father? How could that be? Danny didn't know where Luke lived. Unless—

Jenny dashed out of the kitchen and down the hall to her bedroom. She threw open the closet door and stood on tiptoe so she could reach the shoebox in the back. Her hands touched nothing but air. The shelf was empty.

In desperation, she ran to Danny's room. On the middle of his unmade bed, next to a pile of baseball cards and a half-eaten chocolate donut was her box of memories.

It had been stupid to keep any reminder of Luke, but she had found it impossible to throw away the past. She had pictures from their days at the beach, love letters, and her diary, the pages on which she had poured out the joy of her love, the panic of her pregnancy, and the sorrow of her breakup.

Danny had found it all, including the newspaper clipping she had cut out last month, announcing Luke's return to the Bay Area. It wouldn't take Danny long to get the exact address. Her child was as smart as he was determined.

Damn! She should have known this was coming. During the past month, Danny had asked endless questions about his father, begging her to call Luke. She had refused, hoping Danny's interest would wane, until he was more mature, less vulnerable— until *she* could handle meeting Luke again.

Danny had taken the decision out of her hands.

Jenny sank down on Danny's bed and hugged his pillow tight to her chest. It smelled like her son, like Oreo cookies, sweaty socks, and old baseballs. No matter how grown-up Danny thought he was, he was just a child.

What if Luke rejected Danny? Would Danny cry, or pretend to be a big kid who didn't care?

Jenny stared at the ceiling and listened to the quiet.

It was an eerie, spooky silence. Danny wouldn't like it. He hated being alone in the house, and he was often alone, because he'd been a latch-key kid the past two years.

Guilt, anger, and fear raced through Jenny, each emotion twisting her stomach into a tight knot. Danny was the most important thing in her life. She couldn't lose him—not even to his father. He was hers, and hers alone. She just had to find Danny and convince him that he didn't need anyone but her, certainly not Luke Sheridan.

"The Bay Area welcomes home Dr. Luke Sheridan, most recently the head of Research and Development for McAuley Perkins. Sheridan will take over the reins of Sheri-Tech, the biotech company founded by his father, Dr. Charles Sheridan. Sheri-Tech is expected to introduce a new drug this year that will rebuild damaged skin tissue in burn patients."

Malcolm Davis tossed the newspaper down on the desk with a flourish. His round face beamed with excitement at his success in placing such a delicious tidbit in the *San Francisco Review*.

"Nice job, Malcolm." Luke raised his bottle of Perrier in a silent toast.

"What can I say? The press loves your long list of degrees and your success at McAuley. The tie-in with your brilliant father makes this story impossible to resist."

Luke leaned back in the oversized, leather chair behind the desk. The chair had been his father's, like everything else in Luke's office and home. It was too big, too stiff, too unforgiving in texture. He made a silent vow to get rid of it come Monday.

Luke changed positions as he looked at Malcolm. "How long have you worked for my father?" he asked.

"Almost eight years. Why?"

"Do you think you're going to like working for me?"

Malcolm sent him a funny look. "I certainly hope so."

"I'm not my father."

"I never thought you were."

"Really? You're probably the only one."

Malcolm gathered his papers together, and Luke swiveled his chair around so he could look out the window. The Sheri-Tech building complex sat on the edge of the San Francisco Bay at Oyster Point, a few minutes south of San Francisco. From his vantage point he could see the Bay Bridge in the distance and the lights coming on in Oakland across the bay, reminding him that it was time to go home and celebrate his wedding anniversary.

Still, he hesitated. In the past few years, he'd begun

to feel more comfortable at work than at home. It was easier to focus on concrete business problems than deal with the inescapable feeling of restlessness that pervaded his family life.

Happiness was found in the black figures on the profit and loss statement, not in his wife's arms, not in the huge house that his parents had passed on to him. Something was missing. Something important, vital. Damned if he knew what it was. Everything he had planned for was now his. He should be ecstatic. Instead, he felt—lonely.

Malcolm walked around in front of him and leaned against the wall. He was a short, balding man, filled with energy. Even now he tapped his fingers against the wall in a restless beat as he studied Luke through sharp, perceptive eyes.

"Okay, what's wrong?" Malcolm asked.

"Nothing." Luke shrugged.

"Try again."

"All my life I've been cursed with the desire to want more than I have. I want to be content."

"Content? That sounds like old socks and game shows on television. You're living the good life, Luke. You're running the game. The world is at your feet."

"Right." Luke pulled at the tie around his neck.

"I'm bringing Stan Polleck from Genesys to your party tonight. He's very interested in selling his company to us. I hope Denise doesn't mind mixing business with pleasure."

"Not at all. She's more ambitious than I am. In fact, Denise would like to see Sheri-Tech acquire Genesys. It would certainly make us a major player in the area of gene research. Of course, she'd also like the company to go public." Luke smiled cynically. "She thinks a public offering would enhance our bank account."

"It would certainly do that. But you'd lose some control."

"Exactly."

The phone on the credenza buzzed. Malcolm picked it up. He held out the receiver to Luke. "Scott Danielson."

Luke took the phone. "Scott. How are you?"

"Fine. I got worried when Denise missed her appointment today. I hope she's not feeling any side effects."

The muscles in Luke's body tightened as he tried to decipher the words he was hearing from Denise's gynecologist. "I didn't know Denise had an appointment with you today."

"Follow-up appointment for tubal ligation is standard procedure, old buddy, or have you been out of the practice of medicine so long you've forgotten?"

Tubal ligation? Follow-up? Denise had had a tubal ligation? That was impossible. When?

At the back of his mind, Luke remembered Denise's unexpected trip to her mother's house a month earlier. She'd been gone four days.

No. Denise would have told him. They would have discussed it. He would have said absolutely not. He wanted children, of course he did. In fact, just the other day he had decided it was time to add a baby to their lives.

"Luke, are you there?"

"Yes. I'll tell Denise to phone your office."

"As long as she's okay."

"She's fine." Luke hung up the phone.

Malcolm sent him a concerned look. "Everything all right?"

"I have to go home."

"An hour early? Did someone die?"

"Not yet." Luke picked up his briefcase and walked out the door.

2

"**L**UKE, COULD YOU ZIP THIS FOR ME?" DEN-
ise Sheridan struggled with the zipper
on her black evening dress. It wouldn't
budge, and she was not about to risk her fifty-dollar
manicure on a reluctant zipper. "Luke?" she asked
with irritation as she watched her husband in the mirror. "Did you hear me?"

Luke tossed his suit coat on the bed. "I heard you."

"Then help me."

"Why should I?" He looked up, his cold blue eyes
daring her to answer. His face was hard, his jaw set,
as if he were going into a battle, not dressing for a
party. "You don't seem to need my help in anything,"
he added.

Denise turned to face him. "Don't start with me,
Luke. Tonight is important. It's our wedding anniversary, eight wonderful years together."

"I know how long we've been married."

"It's not just our anniversary, it's our homecoming.
All of our friends will be here tonight to help us celebrate. Please don't ruin it for me."

"What exactly are we celebrating, Denise?" Luke

asked as he walked over to her. "Happiness? Joy? Passionate love? I don't think so."

Denise stared at the man who in recent months had become a stranger to her. "You're not talking about children again, are you?"

"Of course, I am." Fury drew his brows into sharp, angry lines. "When the hell were you going to tell me you got your tubes tied? Did you think I wouldn't find out? Scott Danielson is a very good friend of mine."

Denise sucked in a breath, then let it out. "He's also my doctor. What happened to confidentiality?"

"What happened to truth? How could you do such a thing without talking to me first? This was not your decision to make alone."

"It's my body."

"It's our future, our family."

"We're a family, Luke. You and me, and your parents. We're adults, free to travel, to play, to enjoy our lives." She reached out to touch his cheek in a consoling gesture. He flinched and stepped away. Denise tried not to panic. "Maybe I should have told you first, but when we married, you said you didn't want children. I believed you."

"That was eight years ago. I was in the midst of starting my career. We were newlyweds, for God's sake." Luke ran a hand through his hair in frustration.

"How was I to know you'd changed your mind?"

"You could have asked."

"When, Luke?" Denise looked at him and shook her head. "I hardly see you. At breakfast, your face is buried in the newspaper. When I call your office, your secretary says you're unavailable. At night, you take papers into your den and don't come out until after midnight."

"I've been busy taking over my father's company. Don't try to sidetrack me, Denise. We've been together. We've made love. The last time, I asked you not to use your diaphragm, you said you wouldn't. What a joke. Obviously, you didn't have to use a diaphragm at all."

Denise swallowed hard, hating when the truth caught up with her. But she could talk her way out of this. She had always been able to convince Luke that her way was the best way. She tried one last time.

"You don't want a child, Luke. You're going through an identity crisis, taking over your father's business, moving into your parents' house. That's the problem. Having a child, however, is not the answer."

Luke placed his hands on her shoulders and spun her around. With rough fingers, he yanked the zipper into place.

Denise sighed and walked back to the mirror. She carefully applied her lipstick while Luke finished dressing. Although she pretended not to look at him, she was aware of his every movement, and she wished she could say something to ease the tension between them.

Luke would not give an inch. He was a hard man, tough, unyielding, closed off. He had a brilliant mind, a gorgeous body, honed by miles of running every morning in the cold, dark dawn—without her. But then he did so many things without her. As they grew older, they grew further apart.

They weren't on the same wavelength anymore. Her workaholic, ambitious, money-making husband was turning soft. Although Luke was a rising star in the world of biotech, he seemed to be questioning his decision to take over Sheri-Tech. It was that kind of wavering that would destroy him. She had tried to tell him that he had to stay focused, that he couldn't quit— not now, not until he was a proven success story.

Sometimes, Denise didn't think Luke cared about his career as much as she did. And it wasn't just business that came between them. It was their social life, too. Luke avoided parties she desperately wanted to attend, parties where he could make valuable contacts. He turned down opportunities to travel to Paris and London. Now, he wanted children, of all things.

What in the hell did she want with a child?

There was no way she was going to change dirty diapers and burp a baby when she could be drinking a daiquiri on a beach in Maui. No, thank you. She had no desire to recreate herself. Luke would just have to get past this fatherly urge of his. And he would. She would see to it.

"Your mother said we could join them in Maui after Christmas if you like," Denise said persuasively, looking at Luke in the mirror.

Luke pulled on a clean shirt. "I don't think so."

"Maybe Aspen with the Willoughbys then. We'll talk about it later." Denise walked to the door. "Are you ready?"

"I'll be down in a minute."

"Luke, please."

"Go, dammit!"

Luke walked over to the window and looked out at the view, wondering why he felt compelled to stare into space every chance he got. From his hilltop vantage point, he could see the planes landing at the airport. The sight was peaceful, comforting. He had stood at these windows before, reassuring himself that everything he wanted was out there.

Now, Luke wasn't sure. Maybe he was having an identity crisis. Coming home had triggered old feelings. As soon as he had driven down the Eucalyptus-lined street of El Camino Real and up the hills toward his parents' Spanish-tiled, three-story home, in the exclusive community of Hillsborough located on the San Francisco Peninsula, he had been swept back in time. He was no longer a confident, brash scientist with a keen mind and deep pockets; he was a young man with ideals, with romance in his soul, with thoughts of—Jenny.

Luke closed his eyes and sighed, envisioning her

sweet face. Jenny, with the laughing brown eyes, and hair the color of dark chocolate. Jenny, with the tender hugs, the sexy smile, and legs that wrapped tightly around his waist. Jenny.

The memories came back as if they had happened yesterday instead of thirteen years earlier.

The lights from the airport in front of him grew hazy, turning into the orange flames of a fire, a bonfire on the beach. Through the flames he saw her.

Jenny held a can of Diet Pepsi to her lips and laughed as the wind from the ocean whipped long strands of hair across her wide, generous mouth. She tried to pull her hair away from her soft, pink lips, but it was a futile struggle. Finally, she gathered her hair into a ponytail and tucked it into the back of her sweatshirt.

Someone told a joke, and Jenny smiled. The man standing next to her, a guy named Frank, leaned down to kiss her. Jenny playfully pushed him away.

Another laugh. Another smile.

Jenny was magic, flitting around the group like a firefly, drawing people out, completing the circle with an effortlessness that made Luke feel a sharp pang of envy.

He didn't belong here, not to this group, not to any group. They suffered his presence, because he was rich, smart, and drove around town in a Mercedes. Even his supposed girlfriend, Diane, was now snuggling under a blanket with Gary Burroughs, another of his supposed friends. Did they care that he was watching? No.

Luke turned away.

Jenny stood in front of him, a wispy, slender girl bathed in moonlight. He caught his breath. Up close, he could feel the magic.

"Why aren't you singing?" she asked.

For the first time it occurred to Luke that everyone was singing, off-key and half drunk.

"I don't sing." He attempted to move past her.

"Neither do I." Jenny fell into step alongside him.

The sand was moist between his toes. Her arm brushed

against his. Goose bumps teased his skin at the innocent motion. His heart began to pound.

"Do you swim?" Jenny asked.

Luke looked at the dark waves breaking against the shore. The ocean appeared more than a little dangerous. "I can swim." He raised an eyebrow as he turned to her. "You don't mean now, do you?"

Jenny grinned, her lips curving delightfully. A dimple creased her cheek, her brown eyes lit with excitement. Luke felt an immediate response, a magnetic force that pulled him closer to her, even when he wanted to walk away.

"Now," she whispered, taking his hand.

Her hand felt small, warm, and soft, but he could feel a callous along her thumb. He wondered where it had come from, how it had the nerve to light on a body and a spirit so pure, so giving.

He had seen Jenny before this night, but always in the distance, always in the center of a circle of people. He had never been alone with her, until now.

They stumbled down the beach in the shadowy moonlight. At least Luke stumbled; Jenny seemed to float, like a vision. For the first time he wondered if she was real or a figment of his imagination. He turned his head, hoping to anchor reality with the sight of the bonfire. It was gone. The cliff behind them blocked everything from view.

They stood in a small cove where a circle of rocks created a pool protected from the ocean. Jenny pulled her sweatshirt over her head. Then her shirt. She slid her jeans down long legs, while he watched and waited. Her body was slender, graceful, strong. Her panties and bra were hot pink. A bright flower in a sea of darkness.

There was no self-consciousness to Jenny's movements, no humility or vanity, just a calm acceptance of who she was and what she wanted to do. He, who was terrified of letting out his real feelings, was intensely jealous of her ability to be so direct, so uncaring of his opinion. Or was she?

Luke's gaze moved up to her face. She was looking at him, waiting and watching.

Awareness. Connection. Desire. Each emotion hit him with the same force as the waves crashing on the beach.

"Are you coming?" she whispered.

Oh, he was coming all right, here and now.

"Why me?"

"It's not safe to swim alone."

"Being safe is high on your list of priorities?"

"I don't have a list of priorities," she said with a smile.

Luke dug his hands into the pockets of his trousers. "I'm leaving at the end of the summer. Medical school at USC."

"I know."

"My parents both went there."

"I heard."

"I'm following in their footsteps."

"I hope they wear the same size shoes."

Luke's mouth curved up in a reluctant smile. "I shouldn't be here tonight. This isn't really my thing."

"Are you finished?" Jenny held out her hand to him. "Come on, a little water won't hurt you."

"It's not the water I'm worried about."

"You think too much." She stepped into the ocean with a delighted squeal of joy. It was the most innocent, most appealing, most irresistible sound he had ever heard. Without another thought, Luke stripped off his shirt and pants and followed her into the water.

The ocean was so cold his heart missed a beat. Jenny splashed water at him. He shivered with anticipation.

"Isn't this great?" she said. "I feel alive, free."

Luke felt exactly the same way, for the first time in his entire life. That was the only reason he walked toward her, the only reason why he cupped her face with wet hands, and kissed her until a wave crashed over their heads.

Luke clenched his hands as the memory faded away. The flames from the fire, the dark pool were gone. Jenny was gone.

That summer had been the best summer of his life.

Like a thief, he had stolen precious moments with a woman he knew he would eventually leave.

His plans for the future had been set in stone. Every member of the Sheridan family for three generations had gone into the field of medicine. It was his duty to carry on the tradition. When Jenny came to him with the news that she was pregnant, he panicked. Thoughts of disappointing his parents, his family, future generations of Sheridans made it impossible for him to stay with her.

In the end, he'd given her five hundred dollars and suggested an abortion. He'd never seen her again.

Now he was married to Denise, a woman who didn't want children. The irony of the situation hit him hard. He had had his chance to be a father and had walked away. It was too late to wish things were different.

"Ring the doorbell," Christopher Merrill urged Danny as he glanced furtively around the yard. "We don't have all night. My mom gets off work at eight, and if I'm not home by then, I'm in big trouble."

"Maybe I shouldn't." Danny tilted his head to one side as he considered the matter. His father's large home in the ritzy town of Hillsborough was a far cry from Danny's house by the beach. Even the doorbell looked intimidating, a solid square of gold. Who wasted gold on a doorbell?

"Come on, Danny, do it."

"What if he isn't home?"

"Then he won't answer the door. Stop chickening out."

"I'm not."

"Bawk, bawk, bawk," Christopher said, waving his arms like a chicken.

"I'm taking my time, okay?"

"You don't have any time left. We still have to get down the hill and catch the last bus to Half Moon

Bay." Christopher checked the sports watch on his wrist. "Come on, it's almost six-thirty."

"My mom is going to be mad." Danny drummed his hands restlessly against his legs. He wished he knew what to do. It had all started so easily, finding the newspaper article, looking up the address, taking the bus over the hill. But now that he was here, Danny wished he were home.

"Your mom's gonna be mad even if you don't ring the bell," Christopher said.

"You're right. We're here. Let's see if he's home." Danny pushed the doorbell and held his breath.

After a moment, he heard the sound of someone unlocking the door. Danny turned to Christopher, suddenly panicked at the thought of seeing his father face-to-face. He started to back away. Christopher put a hand on his back and shoved him up the steps.

The door opened, and Danny stared into the face of a beautiful woman wearing a tight black evening dress. Her hair was a dark shade of red, her eyes green, like a cat. Her smile faded the instant she saw him. In fact, she looked downright mean.

"What do you want?" she snapped.

"We're—I'm—" Danny licked his lips.

"Whatever you're selling, I don't want any." She started to close the door.

"Wait. Wait." Danny stuck his foot in the way of the door, wincing as the wood bounced off his toe. "Is Luke Sheridan here?"

Her eyes narrowed. "Who wants to know?"

"Me."

"And who are you?"

"I'm—I'm—" Danny looked desperately at Christopher, who simply shrugged. "I'm his kid."

Her mouth dropped open. "What? What did you say?"

"I'm his son, Danny. Danny St. Claire."

"Mr. Sheridan isn't here," she said quickly. "And

you must have the wrong man, because this Mr. Sheridan does not have a son, nor does he want one."

The words hit Danny like a baseball in the gut. Mom was right. Luke hadn't wanted him to be born and still didn't want him. "But—"

"Who's at the door?" a man's voice demanded from somewhere behind the woman.

She shifted as she looked over her shoulder. "Just kids selling candy."

As the woman moved, Danny looked straight at Luke. Stark blue eyes. Blond hair. Just like his. Oh God!

Time moved in slow motion, broken by the sudden slamming of the door in Danny's face. The abruptness took him by surprise. He glanced over at Christopher, still dazed. "What happened?"

"She told us to get lost," Christopher replied.

"That was him. That was my dad. I saw him."

"I didn't see him."

"He was behind that lady. He looked at me."

Christopher shrugged. "If you say so. But he didn't want to talk to you."

"He didn't know it was me. She closed the door too fast." Danny reached for the doorbell, then paused as the roar of an engine drew his attention to the driveway. A car pulled up in the semicircle drive, its headlights pinning Danny and Christopher like thieves in the night.

"Come on, let's get out of here," Christopher urged. "He's got company."

"I want to see him. I want him to tell me to my face that he doesn't want to be my father."

The headlights faded into black as two couples got out of the silver BMW. They looked inquisitively at the boys.

"You can't do it now," Christopher said. "He's having a party. We'll have to come back."

Christopher grabbed Danny's arm and pulled him

down the steps, past the two couples, their fancy car, and the iron gates at the end of the driveway. When they reached the street, Christopher let go. They turned and looked back at the brightly lit house.

"You know something, Chris, my dad must have big bucks. Look at this place." The house was a three-story mansion, with red brickwork, beveled windows, and a high, sloping roof. The grounds were perfectly landscaped down to the tiny lights placed discretely next to the porch and in the bushes along the driveway.

Danny felt a sudden rush of anger at his father, fury that the man didn't want him, that Luke had so much when he had so little. His mom could never afford anything extra. And his father was living in this fancy house.

"I'm going back," Danny said.

"No, you're not. That lady won't let you in."

"It's not fair."

"Yeah, well, as my mom says over and over again, who ever told you life was fair? Move it, dude, we've got a bus to catch."

"Who were those boys?" Luke asked, pulling Denise aside as she motioned for their guests to go into the living room.

"Just kids, selling something for their school. Did you see Lily's mink? Must have cost a fortune."

"What were their names?" Luke persisted, driven by a curiosity that he couldn't begin to explain. There was something about the boy on the step—something disturbing.

"I don't know their names." Denise raised an eyebrow. "Why are you so interested?"

"The blond kid—he looked familiar."

"All kids look the same to me, dirty hair and fingernails, food smeared across their faces, and a strange smell coming from the direction of their tennis shoes."

Luke sighed, her cutting tone beginning to irritate him. "I get the picture."

"I hope you do," she said pointedly.

"Sometimes I don't think I know you at all, Denise."

"Maybe you don't. I've let you call the shots in our marriage. I've been very accommodating, but not on this point. Not ever."

"What do you have against children?"

"Nothing. I just don't want any of my own. I grew up in a houseful of sniveling brats. Those brothers and sisters you think I'm so lucky to have got in the way of everything I ever wanted to do. I always had to stay home and babysit or change a diaper." Her voice trembled with emotion. "I won't do that again, Luke. Not even for you."

"You should have told me this before."

"I didn't think I needed to."

She had a point. He had never considered having a child—until now—now that it wasn't possible. Maybe that was his problem. He always wanted what he couldn't have.

"Why don't you get me a drink?" Denise suggested. "Then, come and join our guests. This is a party. I want to have a good time."

Denise moved into the living room with a graceful step and a cheerful smile. She would play the role of hostess, loving wife, and adoring daughter-in-law to perfection. No one at the party would ever suspect that they were anything but happy.

Luke walked past the foyer window and paused. At the end of the drive he could see the two boys in the shadows. They were hovering, not like kids selling candy, but kids on some sort of a mission. He looked over his shoulder at Denise. She was talking to his mother.

After a moment's hesitation, he opened the front

door and walked down the drive. When he reached the street, it was empty. The boys were gone. He wondered if they would be back. He wondered why he cared.

3

"MATT, I NEED TO TALK TO YOU." JENNY sat down on the bar stool next to her brother and yanked on his sleeve. Her action made the whiskey in his glass spill onto his hand and down the front of his brown leather jacket and faded blue jeans.

"Oh, hell," Matt said grumpily. "Can't you see I'm busy?"

"You're drinking. You're not running for President."

"Not bad, Jen-Jen. As if a worthless piece of shit like me could ever be President." Matthew St. Claire smiled through red-rimmed, tired brown eyes. He looked older than his thirty-four years. His sandy brown hair had turned gray at the sideburns. His once athletic body had gone soft with age and lack of exercise.

"Stop feeling sorry for yourself," Jenny said. "I need your help. Danny's gone."

"Young Daniel? Gone where?" Matt straightened in his seat.

"Gone looking for his father. That's where."

"Shit. That's too bad." Matt snapped his fingers in the air. "Barry, give me another shot."

"Matt, please. We have to look for him. My car is not working, or I'd go by myself."

"Go where?" Matt asked again. "I thought old Luke was in L.A. finding a cure for cancer or something."

"He was until a few weeks ago. He moved back to his parents' house in Hillsborough—with his wife." Jenny shook her head, feeling helpless rage run through her body. "Danny saw the newspaper article," she continued. "You know how he's been lately, talking on and on about his dad. I should have told Danny his father was dead. I thought telling him the truth was right, but look where it's gotten me. My son is out there alone, and I'm sitting here in this seedy bar watching my big brother get shit-faced."

"It's better than watching me try to find a job." Matt drained the whiskey from his glass.

Jenny tried to feel compassion. Matt was going through tough times, but she was tired of the same old story. Sometimes, she didn't think he wanted things to be better. Still, she tried to be sympathetic. Lord knows, out of her entire family, Matt was the only one who had ever given a damn about her.

"No luck with the broadcasting job?" she asked.

Matt shook his head. "Not even a nibble. It seems there's no market for bad-knee, washed-up quarter-backs who like to party."

"Maybe you should change your image."

"As if I could. Everyone in the Bay area knows Matthew St. Claire, the Golden Boy of Stanford University, the top draft pick for the Forty-niners, the worthless son of a bitch who spends his nights at the Acapulco Lounge getting bombed on Tequila."

"It doesn't have to be this way. You got hurt. Your career ended because of an injury. But you didn't hurt your head. You can still use it to do something worthwhile."

"Like what? I tried coaching. I hated every minute of it, watching guys who weren't half as good as I was getting a chance to play in the NFL. It sucked."

"You didn't give it a chance, one lousy job for a team you hated. There will be other opportunities, Matt. And if not in coaching, somewhere else. Don't give up. If you don't like the way things are, change them."

"I can't change. I'm too old. I'm too tired."

"You're too afraid. It's been five years, Matt. You're running out of time and running out of money. Get on with your life."

Matt took another sip of his drink. "That's what I'm trying to do."

Jenny shook her head in disgust. "We will talk about this later, but not now. Now, I have to find Danny." Jenny reached into Matt's jacket pocket but only came up with a handful of change.

"Hey, what are you doing?" Matt slapped her hand away.

"I'm looking for your car keys."

"No way. You're not taking my car. The kid's probably already home."

"He's not." Jenny shook her head. "I don't have a good feeling about this, Matt. I have to find him, now. Before something bad happens."

"Nothing bad will happen."

"How do you know? You're the one who thinks life is the pits." Jenny looked down the bar. "Barry," she called out, "can I borrow your extra car? I'm desperate. I have to find Danny."

"Sure, no problem. Just bring it back in one piece."

"Thanks."

Barry tossed her the keys, and Jenny stood up. "Oh, and one more thing, Barry. Don't let Matt drive home."

"Excuse me, but I am fine, Jen-Jen. I'm sober enough not to let you drive my car. I saw what you did to your front fender pulling out of McDonald's last week."

"That was an accident."

"Your whole life resembles an accident."

"Look who's talking."

"Why don't you get GI Joe to help you?"

Jenny frowned at Matt's nickname for her current boyfriend. "Alan is at work."

"Thank God. We can all rest easier knowing he's protecting our small city."

"Ease up, Matt. Alan is a good guy."

"He's a cop. And I don't know what the hell you see in him."

"He will make a good father. He's a man a boy can look up to." Matt stared at her in amazement, and she felt completely foolish. "Well, he is."

"If you're dating him for Danny's sake, catch a clue, Jen-Jen. Your kid hates him. In fact, that's probably why Danny is so eager to find his real father. He wants to get the hell away from Alan."

"He doesn't." But even as she made the denial, Jenny wondered if there wasn't some truth to Matt's statement.

"Why don't you ask him?"

"I will when I find him." Jenny groaned as a slinky blonde in a red jumpsuit walked into the bar and headed straight for Matt. "Not Brenda. Please, tell me it's not coffee-tea-or-me Brenda."

Matt opened one eye a little wider as he turned in his seat. He smiled, big and broad. "Baby face. You made it."

"Buy me a drink, big guy? I've got a night off, before I hop on a flight to Tokyo." Brenda slid her hand around Matt's neck. "Hello, Jennifer."

"Brenda." Jenny looked at Matt. "Are you sure you won't come with me?"

"You can't steal him away. I just got here," Brenda protested.

Matt shrugged. "Sorry, Jen-Jen. I'll call you later."

"Not that I think you will, but if you don't get me at home, try Merrilee's."

"You're going to tell Merrilee you lost your kid?" Matt shook his head. "Bad idea, Jen-Jen. You'll never hear the end of it. Our big sister can't tolerate failure."

"Well, I'll tolerate anything if Danny is sitting in her solid white living room getting yelled at for putting his feet on Merrilee's precious couch." Jenny walked out of the bar and let the door slam behind her.

The ocean was only a mile away and the air was cold and wet. The fog was drifting in. In another hour, the road between Half Moon Bay and San Mateo would be one long, dark and misty tunnel. She had to find Danny, and quickly. Hopefully, he had sense enough to go to Merrilee's instead of trying to get home on a night like this.

Merrilee St. Claire-Winston took the Cornish game hens out of the oven and set the pan on top of her stove. The hens were a perfect golden brown. She smiled proudly as she turned to her daughter, Constance. "*Voilà*," she said.

Connie, who was sixteen and depressed about everything in her life, especially the extra ten pounds of baby fat around her thighs, tossed her head in disgust. "I'm not eating that, Mother. I'm a vegetarian now."

"You're a what?"

"Vegetarian. As in, I don't eat dead animals."

Merrilee sighed as she studied her daughter. Constance was a mixture of her mother and father, with Merrilee's blond hair and bosomy chest, and Richard's brown eyes and long legs. She was at an awkward stage, not particularly thin, average in height, long arms and stringy hair that Merrilee was just itching to style.

Constance, of course, would have none of it. She hated Merrilee's short, perky hairstyle, her perfectly matched dresses and pumps. In fact, Constance took pride in looking exactly the opposite of her mother.

Constance walked over to the stove and lifted the cover on the mashed potatoes. "I really wish you wouldn't mix butter into the potatoes. We should be cutting our fat intake."

"Fine, dear. Next time you can make the potatoes."

"Oh, Mother, please. Cooking is not my thing."

Merrilee bristled in the face of her daughter's arrogance. She and Constance had been going head-to-head for the past two years, and Merrilee was not about to lose. "Nothing to do with this house seems to be your thing. You need to know how to cook if you're going to be a proper wife."

Constance made a face. "I have no wish to be a proper wife, Mother. In fact, I don't think I'll get married."

"Of course you will. You want children, don't you?"

"I don't have to be married to have a kid. Aunt Jenny isn't married."

"Your Aunt Jennifer is hardly the example I want you to live up to."

"I like Jenny. She's cool. She listens when I talk to her. She understands."

"Because she has about as much maturity as you do," Merrilee said scornfully. She hated the fact that Constance liked Jenny. It made her feel as if she was competing for her daughter's love, something a perfect mother should not have to do.

As far as Merrilee was concerned, Jenny hadn't done anything right since she had arrived two weeks late for her own birth. As a teenager, Jenny had worn makeup, neglected her homework, and ignored Merrilee's every suggestion. It got worse when their mother died. Jenny didn't listen to anyone. Then she had the nerve to come home pregnant, splitting the family even further apart.

With Thanksgiving just around the corner, Merrilee was reminded that once again she would have to beg Jenny, Matt, and their father, John, to come to her house for dinner. Then, she'd have to play peace-maker all day. But she would do it, because the hol-idays were important to her, and families should be together.

Come hell or high water, Merrilee was determined that her family would have a happy holiday this year. That was the way it was supposed to be. She could make it happen. She just had to try harder.

"Mother." Constance waved her hand in front of her face. "I asked if anyone called me today?"

Merrilee stared at her daughter as the words sunk in. "Did you check the message pad in the hall?"

"Yes, but I thought maybe you forgot to write something down. I'm expecting a call," Constance said somewhat hesitantly.

Merrilee looked at her through narrowed eyes. "It's that boy, isn't it, the one you and Cassie are always whispering about? Why don't you tell me about him?"

"Well, he's got the coolest haircut."

"Haircut? Is that all you're concerned about?" Mer-rilee demanded.

"No, but . . . oh, forget it. I knew you wouldn't un-derstand. He's not interested in me anyway."

Merrilee felt relieved at this piece of information. She didn't want to deal with dating just yet. She wasn't ready.

Constance picked an apple out of the fruit bowl on the counter, rubbed it clean with the edge of her sleeve, then bit into it. "When's Daddy coming home?"

"He's working late tonight."

"Again? Are you two fighting?"

Merrilee turned away from her daughter's inquisitive eyes. She didn't want to think about Richard's odd behavior, much less discuss it with Constance. Instead, she concentrated on lifting the hens out of the pan and onto a floral serving plate. "Your father and I never fight," she said finally. "We're very, very happy together." *If she said it often enough, it would be true.*

"Daddy doesn't seem happy lately," Connie observed. "He never smiles anymore. When he's home, he sits in the family room watching sports."

"Advertising is a tough business, and your father and I take our responsibilities as parents very seriously. You and William are going to get a good education. That costs money, especially if you go to Stanford."

"I don't want to go to Stanford. I want to go to Berkeley."

"I hardly think so, dear."

"Mother." Eleven-year-old William Winston pushed open the kitchen door and frowned at them both. "There's a bug in my computer."

"Oh, God," Constance shuddered. "I hope you closed your door."

William rolled his eyes. "Not a bug, bug. A computer bug. A virus. I think it attacked my program. Half of my math homework is gone." William pulled off his glasses and rubbed his eyes. "I'll have to reinput all my equations."

"Why don't you just tell your teacher the dog ate your homework?" Constance suggested.

"I hardly think Miss Davenport would fall for a line like that," William said. "Besides, I am the best student in the class, and I refuse to jeopardize my grade point average with an unfinished homework assignment."

Merrilee nodded approvingly. At least one of her

children was on the right track. "You're a good boy."

William smiled back at his mother, his earnest face pale from days spent inside the house, staring at his computer. For a moment, Merrilee felt a twinge of conscience. But she talked herself out of any guilt. William would be a brilliant businessman. With his high IQ and fascination with computers, she knew his future was secure.

"When is Dad coming home?" William asked.

"I don't know. But dinner is ready. Let's sit down and eat."

"I don't have time to eat," William said. "If I don't start now, I'll never get my homework done." He walked out of the kitchen, snatching a carrot off the counter.

Constance shrugged as she looked at Merrilee. "You know how I feel about dead animals," she said as she left the room.

Merrilee looked down at her game hens and felt like crying. Richard was working late. Her children hated her cooking, and nothing in her life was going right. She was supposed to be the perfect homemaker, and she would be, if the rest of her family would only cooperate.

Squaring her shoulders, Merrilee took the game hens into the dining room and set them on the table. "William, Constance. Come here," she said.

Her children strolled out onto the upstairs landing. Constance peered over the banister, and William looked through the railing.

"It's dinnertime," Merrilee said. "We're a family, and we're going to have a family dinner."

"I don't have time," William argued.

"You can do your homework after dinner."

"This is such a farce, Mother," Constance said. "Daddy isn't even here."

"Just because your father isn't here doesn't mean we can't share the news of our day together."

Constance walked down the stairs. "As if you care about what I'm doing."

"Of course, I care, I'm your mother."

The doorbell rang, and Merrilee bit down hard on her lip. "I can't imagine anyone with any sense of decorum would come calling at dinnertime."

Constance ran to the front door and opened it.

Jenny walked in, her hair frizzed with moisture from the fog, her eyes dark and worried. Merrilee felt her heart sink to her stomach. "What's wrong?"

"I'm looking for Danny."

"Looking for Daniel? Here?" Merrilee asked in amazement.

Jenny nodded, drops of water flying onto the carpet at her motion.

"Good heavens. You're wet. Look what you're doing to my rug," Merrilee said.

"I don't care about the damn carpet." Jenny paused, forcing Merrilee to meet her eyes. "Danny found out that Luke is back in town."

"Luke? Who's Luke?" Constance asked curiously.

Merrilee stared at Jenny, furious that she would mention that man's name in front of her children. "Go to your room, Constance, William," she said, noticing her son hovering at the edge of the dining room.

"You told us to come down for dinner," Constance protested.

"I said go."

"I'm hungry. Why should I have to starve because that stupid Danny is in trouble again? He's a pain in the neck. He always has been. I wish he'd never been born."

"Constance. Go to your room."

"Fine." Constance stomped up the stairs in righteous indignation. William followed quietly behind her.

When the doors slammed shut on the upstairs landing, Merrilee turned her attention to Jenny. "Tell me what's happened."

Jenny stared into her sister's hard, unforgiving face. Merrilee had always hated Luke. She hated him for what he had done to the family, the shame he had brought on all of them. For Merrilee, pride was more important than love.

"Danny has been obsessed with finding his father the last few months. I've been stalling. Unfortunately, Danny found an article I cut out of the paper last month. Luke is living in his parents' house in Hillsborough. Danny put everything together and went to find him."

"Oh, my word." Merrilee shook her head, her mouth tightening with anger. "If Danny's gone to find his father, then why are you here, Jennifer? Why aren't you at Luke's house?"

Jenny felt the blood recede from her face so quickly she thought she might keel over. Apparently, Merrilee thought so, too, because she shoved her down in a wing-backed chair in the entry.

"I can't see Luke again," Jenny whispered. "Besides, Danny left hours ago. He wouldn't still be there. I thought he might have come here."

"If he had, I would have given him quite the lecture. That young man needs a strong hand in his life. You need to be firm with him, set limits. He's growing up wild. Now look, he's gone off to find his father. If you'd done what I said years ago, you'd have told him his father was dead."

"I probably should have," Jenny admitted. Slowly she got to her feet. "You're right. I'll go to Luke's house and see if Danny is there."

"I'll go with you."

"No. I'll go by myself. You have the kids, dinner, Richard . . ."

Merrilee patted down her hair. "Of course, you're

right. Richard likes to talk over the events of his day while he has a brandy."

Jennifer smiled wistfully. "Sounds nice."

"It is. You could have had all this, too."

"Merrilee, please."

"I don't think you should see Luke. He'll talk you into something again."

"Don't be ridiculous. I'm not eighteen anymore. And he's married."

"You were a fool for him once."

"I'm not a fool any longer. He told me to get an abortion, Merrilee. I could never forgive him for that."

"Sometimes I wonder."

"Good night." Jenny stood up and walked to the door.

"Call me the minute you find out anything."

"I will."

"And Jennifer."

"What?"

"Be careful. Be dignified. Remember who you are."

"Who am I?"

"You're a St. Claire, and you're just as good as those Sheridans. I don't care how much money they have."

4

"**D**IGNIFIED," MERRILEE HAD SAID. CLIMBing onto a brick planter so she could peek into Luke's house was probably not what her etiquette-conscious sister had in mind. But Jenny had no other choice. It was obvious from the line of fancy cars parked in front of Luke's house that he was having a party. She simply could not walk up to his door and ask him if the son he knew nothing about had dropped by that afternoon.

Instead, she hoped to catch a glimpse of her son in the living room. She saw Luke almost immediately, standing in front of a large granite fireplace. He turned his head toward the window, and her breath caught in her throat. He was more handsome than she remembered, bigger, taller, stronger. A man, not a boy.

His suit was well tailored, his appearance as crisp as a new dollar bill. He looked like a man in control of his life, of his destiny, a man who had no idea he was the father of a twelve-year-old boy.

As she watched, Luke's smile turned into a frown, his head tilted slightly to the right. She wondered if he could see her, sense her prying eyes. They had always been connected, from the first moment they met, completely in tune with each other's thoughts and feelings. They had been different, yes, but deep down, they had been the same then, young, lonely, uncertain of their futures, lost in families that didn't seem to understand them, captivated by the sight, sound, and sense of each other.

Jenny sank further into the bushes, her hands shaking, her body trembling at one look from Luke. After a moment, Luke turned his attention back to the beautiful redhead standing next to him, and Jenny breathed easier. She looked at the other people in the room, at Luke's mother, who beamed like a proud mother hen. Not that Beverly Sheridan had ever been a hen in her life. The tall, blond woman was a brilliant doctor, a perfect match to her brilliant husband and her brilliant son. Beverly was one of the beautiful people, and she had hated Jenny on sight.

Luke had asked Jenny to come to the house for his twenty-second birthday party. Without his knowledge, his mother had invited a lovely debutante to join them. Throughout appetizers, dinner, and birthday cake, Beverly had made Jenny feel like an outsider.

It became clear that the Sheridans had big plans for their one and only son. Jenny was not a part of those plans. Looking back, she understood their feelings better now that she was a parent. Unfortunately, understanding didn't erase the pain of rejection. She had been eighteen, insecure, testing her wings, and they had cut her off without giving her a chance to fly.

She couldn't imagine how they would treat Danny if they knew he was their grandson. She couldn't count on any more sensitivity than they had shown her. And Luke, what would his reaction be? Would he walk away from Danny as he had walked away from her?

Jenny suddenly had to know if Danny was there, if he had met Luke, if he was inside the house at this very moment, huddled in a dark corner, waiting for her to come and take him home.

She jumped off the ledge and walked up to the front door, unconsciously smoothing down her jeans and drawing her jacket tightly about her shoulders. Then she rang the bell.

A moment later, a middle-aged woman wearing a simple gray dress answered the door, obviously a maid or one of the caterers.

"Yes?" she said, her expression less welcoming as she took in Jenny's appearance.

"I'm here to see Luke Sheridan."

"Do you have an invitation?"

"No, but it's important."

"I'm sorry, Miss—"

"Please, tell him that Jenny needs to speak to him."

The woman shook her head. "He's entertaining guests. If you come back tomorrow, I'm sure he'd be happy to talk to you."

Jenny fumed at the brush-off, then put her hand up as the woman attempted to shut the door. "Wait. Just tell me one thing. Is there a little boy inside the house? A twelve-year-old named Danny? He's about this tall." She held up her hand to the level of her chin.

The woman shook her head. "Oh, no, ma'am. There are no children at this party."

"You're sure?"

"Positive." She closed the door, leaving Jenny staring at the brass knocker.

Okay, so Danny wasn't in the house. Good. Maybe he had changed his mind. Maybe he hadn't found the address after all. He was probably at home wondering where she was. Her tension eased at the thought.

Luke was inside the house, smiling and laughing with his guests. He didn't look like a man who had just discovered a son. Danny hadn't told him. Somehow she was sure of that fact.

Thank goodness. Jenny walked down the drive and got in the car. She would go home, pull Danny into her arms and tell him never to scare her like that again. They didn't need Luke Sheridan. They had each other.

Luke watched as the housekeeper walked into the living room and began picking up discarded glasses of champagne. After a moment, he excused himself from a group of guests, who were listening raptly to his wife's tale of their trip to Cancun, and walked over to the housekeeper.

"Mrs. Collins?"

"Yes, sir?"

"Did I hear the doorbell ring?"

"Yes, you did, sir." Mrs. Collins didn't explain, and Luke felt a surge of impatience.

"Who was it?"

Mrs. Collins looked at him as if his question were completely absurd. "Why a young woman, sir. She wasn't a guest. I told her to come back tomorrow."

Luke's gut tightened. "A woman? Did she give her name?"

"I believe she said it was Jenny."

God, no. Luke backed away, shocked by the sound of one word, one name that he had thought never to hear again. He walked to the front door and threw it open. There was no one there. She was gone. He thought back to the incident earlier, to the boys.

His feeling of uneasiness grew stronger. Maybe it was a coincidence, but he didn't think so. Something was going on, and he would find out what it was— even if it meant seeing *her* again. He shut the door and walked back to the party. He needed a drink, and he needed it bad.

*   *   *

"Ninety-nine bottles of beer on the wall, ninety . . ." Matt's head rolled around on his neck as his muscles went limp. He was so drunk he couldn't even remember the words. A feminine hand stroked his neck and long fingernails raked against his skin, causing an automatic hard-on. Although what the hell he could do with his body at this moment was anyone's guess.

He turned his head and his vision blurred. "Brenda? Baby? Is that you?"

"Of course, it's me." She giggled. "Who else would it be?"

He smiled. "Dunno. Who's sitting with us?"

"All your old buds. Kenny's over there. Jody and Larry. Don. Everyone."

Matt peered across the table. "Kenny. Jesus, man. I thought your wife cut off your liquor allowance."

Kenny snorted. "I do what I want—when I want."

"Louise must be working late," Matt said knowingly.

"Yeah."

Matt raised the beer bottle to his lips. "Hey, I was drinking tequila."

"You ran out of money, babe," Brenda said with a drunken giggle. "All I could afford was beer."

Matt tipped the bottle at her in appreciation. "You're all right, sweetheart." He looked around the table at his friends. Life was getting better by the minute. He downed the bottle and reached for another.

Someone began to sing. Matt tried to join in, but the only part of his body that was feeling anything was his groin, where Brenda's hand was resting. Actually, her hand was moving. Jesus. If he weren't so drunk . . .

"Hey, Matto, we're going to O'Riley's for some pool action," Kenny said.

Brenda's hand moved away as she leaned over to whisper something to Jody. Without the pressure of her long nails against the snaps on his jeans, Matt could think a little more clearly, at least enough to see that his friends were leaving.

"You with us?" Kenny asked.

"Shit. Why not?" Matt got to his feet. "Where are my keys?" His fingers latched around the metal ring. "Right here. Let's go."

The crowd stumbled out of the bar, singing, then laughing as the fog hit their faces. "Jesus, how the hell are we going to see the road?" Matt asked, but nobody answered.

Danny looked out the window; he couldn't see a thing. He rubbed the pane with his hand, but it didn't make a difference. The fog was thick, and the bus was moving slowly. He had no idea what time it was, but it had to be late.

"My mom is going to be pissed," Danny said. He looked over at Chris, who was working the buttons on his Game Boy. "Think we'll get grounded for this?"

Chris nodded. "Two weeks, easy. What about you?"

"Same." Danny sighed. "I better get my mom a nice gift for her birthday or I'll be stuck in the house for months."

"Are you going back?" Chris asked.

"I don't know." Danny shook his head. "I thought it would be so great to meet my dad. But, man, you saw his house. Why would a rich dude like that want me as his kid?"

"Don't know. But my dad was a slime ball, and he didn't want me either."

"I don't think it's fair that he lives like that, and my mom has to work all the time. She never has any money for anything. She said she didn't know if I could play baseball this year. Registration is ninety bucks."

Danny slouched down in his seat, resting his knees

against the back of the seat in front of him. His feet swung restlessly as he kicked them against the bench. "I gotta play baseball," he said, turning to Chris. "I'll die if I can't play baseball."

"She'll change her mind," Chris said. "Moms always change their minds."

"Not if she's mad about this." And his mom would be mad. Every time he asked about Luke, she changed the subject. Even knowing that it bothered her to talk about Luke hadn't stopped Danny from asking. He had to know about his father. He just had to. He couldn't think about anything else.

Now that he had seen Luke, Danny knew that he would go back. Next time, he wouldn't leave until he had talked to his father.

The bus glided to a stop. "Finally," Danny said as Chris scrambled to his feet.

"You boys be careful now," the driver said. "It's hard to see out there."

Danny and Chris looked at each other as the bus pulled away. They were about a half mile from their houses, and they still had to cross Highway 1. It wasn't that far in the daytime, but right now it looked like a million miles away.

"Man, this was a really stupid idea," Chris said. "I am never listening to you again."

"I didn't know it was going to be foggy."

They walked for about five minutes, then Chris tugged on Danny's arm. "I see the sign for Ida's Ice Cream."

Danny nodded with relief. "Good."

"Let's cut across here," Chris suggested.

Danny took a step, then tripped on his shoelace. Chris kept going as Danny knelt down to tie his shoe. He had barely straightened when a sudden rush of headlights blinded him. He tried to run, but the car caught the edge of his body. He felt himself being lifted in the air. He heard someone scream, but he didn't know if it was him or Chris. Then there was nothing but blackness.

"Hell of a night, isn't it?" Police Officer Alan Brady looked at his partner, Sue Spencer, as they walked out of the Golden Moon Chinese Restaurant on Highway 1.

Sue shivered and zipped up her coat. "No kidding. Maybe the weather will keep the kids off the beach."

"Maybe," Alan said as they walked across the parking lot to their patrol car. They had just taken a late dinner break and had another three hours to go before they were off duty. Hopefully, it would be a peaceful night.

The coast was quieter at this time of the year, not as many beachgoers as in the summer, but the restaurants and bars along the highway produced their share of troublemakers, especially on Friday nights.

Alan liked his beat. Half Moon Bay and the neighboring coastal towns were small and cozy. He had spent ten years in L.A. and had burned out on gangs and drive-by shootings. At least here there was a semblance of normalcy.

"You and Jenny have plans for the weekend?" Sue asked.

Alan adjusted his cap, "She wants to spend time with Danny, so probably not."

"Does the kid like you any better?"

"No. In fact, lately all he talks about is finding his real father."

Sue gave him a curious look. "Where is his real father?"

"I don't know. Jenny said the guy took off when she told him she was pregnant. He didn't want to be a father. I'm the one who's around now, the one who wants to spend time with Danny. You'd think the kid would appreciate that."

"He'll come around."

Alan paused by the car. "Jenny and I aren't doing that great. I don't know what the hell she's thinking anymore. We've been seeing each other for six months. That's a long time at my age. I'd like to move things along, maybe get married. I'm turning forty next year; it's time to be settling down."

Sue smiled. "Have you told Jenny how you feel?"

Alan shook his head. He had a difficult time talking about personal things. "It's hard with Danny around," he complained. "The other night I got so mad at the kid I told him that like it or not, I wasn't leaving, and if he had a problem to get over it."

"What did he do?"

"He went to his room and refused to eat dinner. Jenny spent the rest of the night worrying about him. She blamed me, of course. Said I was too harsh. That I acted more like a cop than a friend. Maybe I do. But Danny needs rules in his life. He's spoiled. Sometimes I could wring his neck."

Sue put a gentle hand on his shoulder as his tirade came to an end. "It's okay, Alan. You're entitled to feel frustrated. Dating a woman with a child is not easy."

"Tell me about it." He rolled his neck to one side, then the other, trying to ease the tension that stiffened his body.

"Kids can drive you crazy," Sue said. "I should know. My two are a handful. Luckily, I've got Jim at home, who's solid as a rock and patient as a saint. But kids know you love them. They just like to test you. Give Danny a chance. Show him you care. He'll realize you're one of the good guys."

"That's the problem, I've always been a good guy. I know how to get respect from people, even kids. I just don't know how the hell to get them to like me."

"Just be your natural sweet self."

"Yeah, right," Alan growled. He opened his door and slid into the driver's seat while Sue got in on the other side. He had barely started the car when the call came in—an accident on Tully Road.

"That's just down the road from Ida's Ice Cream," Sue commented. "I hope it's not a child."

Alan pulled the car out of the parking lot and sped down the highway. It was incredibly difficult to see. He could only imagine what they would find when they got there.

The paramedics beat them to the scene, and another patrol car pulled up alongside them. As soon as Alan opened his door, he heard crying, wild shrieking, like that of an animal in pain.

Alan hoped it was an animal and not a human being. Instinctively he knew it wasn't. He and Sue walked through the small group of people huddled on the road, while the other officers set up a roadblock to protect whoever was lying in the middle of the street.

When Alan got to the front of the huddle, he stopped dead in his tracks. Nothing prepared him for the sight before him.

"Oh my God," he muttered.

Sue caught up to him, pushing past his shoulder so she could see. She cried out, a mother's cry, a friend's cry, an anguished cry.

Jenny's tension increased as she drove slowly through the fog. Twelve years of living on the coast had made the route as familiar to her as the back of her hand. She knew the landmarks, the incline of the road, the smell of the sea.

Tonight everything seemed different. In the past five minutes, her heart had begun to race without reason, her pulse going ninety miles an hour.

She knew every fear was greater because Danny wasn't with her. That's why her imagination was running wild. She had to think positively. Danny was probably sitting at home, eating ice cream out of the carton for dinner.

A few more minutes, and she would be with him. The nightmare would be over. A gleam of light cut short her thought. She was getting closer to the highway, where there were streetlights and businesses rather than the rural Christmas tree farms and pumpkin patches that dotted Highway 92.

Jenny came upon the accident before she saw it. She slammed on her brakes and narrowly avoided hitting the car in front of her. As she peered through her windshield, she saw the flashing lights of a police car and the rescue squad. They had completely blocked off the road. In front of her were five cars waiting to get by.

Jenny shifted into park. It took her fifteen seconds of debate before she jumped out of the car and ran down the road. She heard someone call after her, but she didn't stop. She was pulled forward, relentlessly, by something stronger than herself.

Someone caught her by the waist as she joined the throng of people standing in a circle. A body had been placed on a stretcher. The paramedics were loading the person into the ambulance. A flash of blond hair took her breath away.

A fear that was so great, so powerful, so debilitating hit her all at once. The figure on the stretcher was so slight, so pale, so fragile.

A wild cry broke from her heart. "Danny. Danny!" she screamed. "Oh God, no."

5

SOMEONE WAS TALKING TO HER. SOMEONE WAS holding her back. She had to get to her baby.

Jenny struggled against the arms that bound her. She turned in fury, attacking her captor as if he were an assailant. She pummeled her fists against his chest until her hand caught the edge of a slash of silver. A badge. A cop. Alan.

She looked into his face and saw pain and fear. "Danny?"

"He's hurt bad, Jenny. They have to get him to the hospital."

"I'm going with him," she insisted, but even as she spoke the ambulance roared into the night.

"No, no. Stop!" she screamed. "I have to go with him. He's my baby. He needs me."

"He's unconscious."

"Why did you stop me? Why did you hold me back? Damn you. I should be there with him."

"I'll take you to the hospital in the patrol car. We'll be right behind them."

Jenny stared at the spot on the ground where Danny had been lying. She saw a pool of blood that must have come from some part of his body. It looked so dark. There was so much of it. She felt faint, horror-stricken.

She looked away from the highway and saw a slight figure wrapped in a blanket, crying inconsolably as he sat on the side of the road.

A woman was talking to him, but the child wasn't listening. He rocked back and forth, his arms wrapped around his body, his eyes wide and shocked.

Jenny ran across the road to Christopher. Without a word, she gathered him in her arms and held him tight.

"I'm sorry. I'm sorry," he cried. "It's my fault. It's all my fault."

"Sh-sh," she whispered against his hair, feeling the tears streaming down her face onto the top of his head. "It will be okay. It has to be okay."

"Jenny," Alan interrupted. "Are you ready? Christopher's mom is on her way over."

"I want to go home," Christopher said, rubbing his eyes. "I want to go home."

"Your mom will be here soon."

"Danny's hurt bad," Christopher whispered.

She stared into his face and couldn't say a word. Alan pulled her away and put her in the car before she realized that her legs had moved.

They sped down the highway as fast as visibility would allow. Jenny didn't know how far they went or how long it took. She didn't know if Alan spoke to her or if she answered. She was numb, in shock. Her system shut down. The only thing that ran through her mind was that her son was hurt. He was in pain. He was probably terrified.

Not being with him hurt more than anything else in the world. Her heart felt like it was ripped in two. The pain was worse than anything she had ever experienced.

Her child. Danny, with the smile that brought her joy, with the arms that brought her warmth, with the innocence that made her believe in everything impossible. He was her life. If anything happened to him, she would die.

Alan pulled up to the emergency entrance, and Jenny jumped out of the car before he had put it in park. She was at the front window, demanding to know where her child was, when Alan came through the door.

The nurse didn't seem to understand what Jenny was saying. She was asking for insurance. She was pushing papers at her, and a pen. A goddamn pen.

Jenny picked it up and threw it back at the nurse. "Danny. Where is Danny St. Claire?" she yelled.

"Easy, honey." Alan stepped up behind her.

The badge obviously brought respect, because the nurse stopped looking at her as if she were a lunatic and straightened up.

"Daniel St. Claire," Alan said briskly. "Where is he?"

"He's in the examining room. We don't have any information yet," the nurse replied. "I do have to ask you to fill out these forms. I'm sorry," she added belatedly.

Jenny turned to Alan. "I can't."

Alan took the forms as the nurse shut the window between the waiting room and reception desk. "I'll help you. Try not to worry."

"Try not to worry? Are you crazy?" Jenny shook her head in amazement. "I'm going in there. I'm going to find Danny. She can't stop me. I'll look in every room until I find him."

Alan put his hands on her shoulders and gave her a little shake. "Stop it, Jenny. They're doing all they can. This is a good hospital. They have excellent doctors."

"He's my son. My son," she wailed. "He needs me."

"He needs medical attention more."

"I'm his mother. His mother." Her voice broke on the word. And what a horrible mother she was, letting her child get hurt. She wrapped her arms around her waist, feeling so cold she didn't think she would ever feel warm again.

Alan tried to pull her into his arms, but she resisted. She didn't want his comfort. She didn't want his arms around her. She wanted Danny's arms, only Danny's.

"What happened?" she asked finally. "Who hit him?"

Alan shook his head, his mouth a grim line. "We don't know yet. The driver didn't stop."

"A hit and run? Oh my God! How could they have left a child in the middle of the road, broken and bleeding?" Another cry broke out of her. She cut it off, trying desperately for control.

"Probably a drunk," Alan said. "I'll find him, Jenny. I promise you that. I'll find who did this to Danny."

Jenny turned away from him and stared at the solid white wall. She couldn't look at him. She couldn't look at the other people in the waiting room, who were staring at her like some object of curiosity. Her heart was breaking. Her life was ending. She had never felt so alone. So utterly alone.

Ten minutes passed, then twenty, thirty, forty-five, sixty. Every minute on the clock ticked off with interminable slowness. An hour of incredible pain, broken only by the arrival of a doctor who came to tell her that Danny needed surgery to remove a blood clot from his brain, and Jenny had to sign a release form so they could proceed. Jenny barely heard the explanation, the risks described that all seemed to end with one word, *death*.

In the end she signed the paper, knowing she had

no other choice. Danny was in critical condition.

At some point, Jenny sat down in a chair. She closed her eyes and tried to breathe. Alan paced between her and the pay phone at the end of the room. Nurses and doctors walked in and out. People were called in. People came out. Some were bleeding. Some were crying, but Jenny didn't care. Her thoughts were only for Danny.

Her child was somewhere behind the double doors. He was being cut into. All she could think of was how much Danny hated getting a shot. A big baby, he was, and the thought made her cry.

The tears streamed down her face, but not a sound passed her lips. She didn't know her face was wet until Alan handed her a handkerchief. She wiped her eyes and handed it back.

It was nine o'clock when Merrilee arrived at the hospital. She rushed over to Jenny and threw her arms around her. Jenny stiffened under her embrace.

"How is he?" Merrilee asked.

Jenny stared back at her, unable to speak. Merrilee looked at Alan.

He shrugged. "We don't know anything except they rushed him into surgery."

"Surgery? Oh God. You didn't say it was that bad." Merrilee caught herself. "Of course it isn't that bad. Danny will be fine. You'll see, Jennifer." She squeezed Jenny's hands for reassurance.

"You don't know that." The words burst out of Jenny. "You didn't see him. You didn't see all that blood on the ground."

Merrilee looked taken aback, as if Jenny had struck her with her fists instead of her words. "No, I didn't, but I have faith, Jenny. God wouldn't take Danny, not yet. Danny's a child. He'll be all right. Next week, he'll be sitting at the table on Thanksgiving, laughing and licking the whipped cream off the top of his pumpkin pie."

Jenny closed her eyes, hoping her sister would go away. She didn't want to listen to Merrilee's silly talk about holidays. She didn't want to think about anything but Danny. If she concentrated on his face, if she could remember every freckle on his cheeks, if she could hear his laugh again, if she could will him to live, he would have to live.

Danny felt a pain in his head and his chest. There was a feeling of incredible heaviness in his stomach, contrasted by nothingness in his arms and legs, as if they were no longer attached to his body. He tried to take a breath, but it hurt, so he stopped. He felt something being pushed down his nose. All around him came the sound of voices, but nothing was familiar.

He wanted to call out for help, but he couldn't open his mouth. His next attempt was to open his eyes. Nothing happened. The effort only made the pain worse, so bad he couldn't even cry. And he wanted to cry. He wanted to scream for his mother. He wanted her arms around him.

A sense of terror filled his soul. Was he going to die?

A light came in front of his eyes, growing stronger, pulling him into it with so much power that he couldn't resist going along. For some reason, his fear eased. He was more curious than afraid.

He wanted to go with the light. It beckoned him. It danced in front of his eyes like a sparkler on the Fourth of July. There were shapes in the light, figures, floating, flying, and he had the incredible sense that he was going with them to a place that was far away from everything he knew.

The pain in his head vanished. The heaviness in his stomach lifted. The frustration of not being able to open his eyes or take a breath completely faded away.

His body was as light as a feather, and he was above it all.

Suddenly Danny could see, and what he saw shocked him.

It was his body lying on a table. Surrounding him were men and women wearing baggy green pants and shirts. They had masks over their faces and plastic gloves on their hands. There were bright lights everywhere, and there seemed to be a lot of blood. They were fixing something in his head. His eyes were closed, and there was a long tube coming out of his mouth.

How strange that he felt nothing, that his body was being worked on, and he wasn't in it anymore. Was he dead? Where was his mom? Where was Christopher? A feeling of intense sadness filled him. What if he never saw them again?

Danny looked around. He wanted to move his arms, to fly like a bird, but he couldn't see his arms. The only thing he saw was the light.

It beckoned him in a new way. He could hear singing, soft, lovely voices. He wondered if the voices belonged to the angels in heaven. He wondered if that's where he was going now.

Because he was moving. Without any conscious thought, without hitting walls or doors, he left the hospital. Now, he was surrounded by whiteness, by puffy clouds that bounced beneath him like a trampoline. He couldn't resist trying to jump. He went up high, then down low. He tried a somersault in midair. He twirled around. Then a voice spoke, deep, dark, and stern.

Danny whirled around. There was a man sitting on what appeared to be a chair made out of a cloud. He was an old guy, at least fifty. His hair was black and white, his beard rough and tinged with gray. In the center of his face was a huge, red nose.

As Danny stared, the man reached up and touched

his nose. "What? You think I asked for this big ka-zoo?"

"No. No, sir," Danny stammered. "Who—who are you?"

The man moved his hand down and pointed at his clothes. Danny suddenly realized that the man was wearing an old baseball uniform, the kind that Babe Ruth had worn.

"Don't you know?" the man asked.

"Babe Ruth?"

The man laughed, long and hard. He grabbed his side as if the laughter had given him a cramp. "My name's Jacob. And I was a great ballplayer. But not the Babe."

Danny eyed him doubtfully. "Then how come I never heard of you before?"

" 'Cause I died on my way to tryouts. I was so impatient, I ran in front of a bus. Didn't even see the damn thing. Smashed me flat as a penny, I tell you. I think there were tire tracks on my back."

"That's too bad," Danny said, unsure of how he was supposed to respond. He looked around him, but it was just him and Jacob sitting on a cloud. "Am I dead?"

"Not officially."

"What does that mean?"

"They're still working on you down there. 'Course, they don't know what the Big Guy has in store for you."

"The Big Guy?"

"Yeah, you know the Big Kahuna, the Big Bucka-rooney, the Big Boy upstairs."

"You mean God?"

"Some people call Him that."

"Am I going to meet Him?"

"That depends on you, Danny boy." Jacob shook his head. "You know, I thought that mother of yours should have called you Jake. Much better name than Danny. But she wouldn't listen to me."

"You know my mom?"

" 'Course I do."

"Are you—are you an angel?"

"I sure ain't the devil. He's a mean son of a bitch." Jacob crossed his legs and picked at what looked like dirt on his spike shoes.

Danny crossed his arms in front of his chest. For some reason his body seemed to be with him again, right down to the blue jeans, sweatshirt, and baseball cap he'd been wearing when he was hit by the car. "You don't look like an angel. I thought angels were supposed to be blond and pretty."

"What? I'm not good-looking enough for you?" Jacob asked, patting down his wild, fly-away hair. "You're a choosy boy, ain't you?"

Danny shrugged. "What happens now?"

"Now? Well, that's kind of up to you. See, that car took me by surprise. I was watching an old replay of the '89 series between the Giants and Cubs, and I missed you by just a split second. The Big Guy isn't too happy."

"You mean I'm not supposed to be dead? You're my guardian angel, and you blew it?"

The old man straightened up, a look of indignation on his face. "You ain't dead. You just ain't quite alive. We've got some work to do, boy."

"What kind of work?"

"First off, we gotta see what your mother's up to."

"My mom?" Danny suddenly felt heavy again. In fact, he started to sink into the cloud.

"Now, now, don't be doing that," Jacob said, grabbing him by the arm. "There are things to be learned, choices to be made, son, and I'm going to help you make the right ones for everyone concerned. Stick with me, kid."

"Like I'm going anywhere else," Danny said as he looked around him.

Jacob laughed. "That's better. Now you got your guts back. Thought we'd left 'em on the operating table."

"Where is my mom?"

"At the hospital. Want to see her?"

Danny nodded, and suddenly they were flying again.

Alan walked over to the coffee machine and bought two cups of coffee. Juggling them carefully, he handed one to Merrilee.

"Thanks." She looked over at Jenny, who was sitting across from them, leaning against the wall with her eyes closed. "Can you tell me what happened?"

"I wish I could." Alan sat down in the chair next to Merrilee. "Danny's friend Christopher was with him. He said they got off the bus and were walking home. The fog was so thick, they couldn't see. Danny stopped to tie his shoe or something. When he stood up, a car ran him down. Christopher said he didn't see the car, and it didn't stop."

"Oh, Lord." Merrilee took a sip of coffee, drawing strength from the hot liquid. "I'll have to call my father and let him know."

Alan shook his head. "I don't think Jenny can handle seeing John right now."

"Danny is his grandchild. He'll want to know."

"Your father doesn't give a damn about Jenny or Danny."

"Of course he does," Merrilee said, shocked to the core. "We're a family. We support each other. They've had their differences in the past, but this is serious."

"Don't call him yet, okay? Not till we know more."

"I suppose. What about Matt?"

"He's probably too drunk to be of any use to Jenny."

Merrilee bit back a sharp retort. There was really

nothing she could say to combat Alan's comment, and it irritated the hell out of her. She didn't take criticism of her family from anyone. But as Merrilee glanced over at Jenny, Alan's comment faded away. Jenny looked terrible, and Merrilee didn't know what to do.

She was supposed to be the leader in the family, the one who always knew the right thing to say. But she couldn't even bring herself to attempt a word of solace. Jenny wouldn't hear her. She was locked inside of herself.

"What I can't figure out is what Danny was doing on that road in the first place," Alan said. "I'll have to talk to Christopher again."

"He was probably coming back from seeing his father."

Alan choked on his coffee. "What the hell are you talking about?"

"Jenny came by my house earlier this evening, looking for Danny. Apparently, he left her a note saying he'd gone to see Luke."

"Luke? Is that his name?"

Merrilee sensed the anger building in the man next to her, but at the moment she was more concerned about Jenny than Alan. "Luke Sheridan. He's come back to town."

"Goddammit. So he's the reason Danny's hurt."

"I don't think he ran him down," Merrilee said with a sigh. "I don't even know if Danny saw him."

The doors in front of them opened. Alan stood up. Merrilee set down her coffee cup, and Jenny opened her eyes, as if sensing the moment of truth.

"Mrs. St. Claire?" Dr. Lowenstein, the physician who had handed her a release form several hours earlier walked over to her. He was still wearing surgical scrubs, and his face was grim.

Jenny nodded dully, not even bothering to correct him about her married state. "Danny?" she whispered.

"He's alive," the doctor said, his eyes softening as

if he wished he could share some of her pain. "We were able to remove the blood clot and your son is holding his own. We've done everything we can for now. We have to wait and see what Danny can do for himself."

"Is he going to die?" Jenny asked. She stood up and grabbed the doctor's sleeve, twisting it through anxious fingers. "Is my baby going to die? Tell me the truth. I have to know."

6

D<small>R. L</small>OWENSTEIN PAUSED FOR SO LONG, JENNY thought he hadn't heard her question. Finally, he shook his head slowly, cautiously. "I don't know, Mrs. St. Claire."

"How can you not know? You're a goddamn doctor, aren't you?"

"Jenny," Merrilee said imploringly.

"It's all right," Dr. Lowenstein said. "I understand." He spoke slowly, picking his words carefully. "Danny's condition is critical. There was enormous trauma to the brain. We should know more within the next twenty-four to seventy-two hours. He's a strong, healthy boy. We have to hope for the best."

"Hope, that's all I can do is hope?" Jenny asked in utter bewilderment.

"You might also pray," the doctor said quietly.

"Oh God." Jenny put a hand to her mouth and swallowed hard. "He's going to die. I know he's going to die."

"Stop it, Jenny. He's not going to die," Merrilee said firmly. "He's not. We won't let him."

"I want to see him," Jenny said.

Dr. Lowenstein nodded. "Of course. He should be out of recovery by now. I'll take you to him. He's been moved into pediatric intensive care."

"Intensive care?" Jenny echoed.

"Yes." Dr. Lowenstein looked at Merrilee and Alan. "Just Mrs. St. Claire for now, please."

Merrilee looked as if she wanted to argue, but Alan put a restraining hand on her arm, and the doctor led Jenny away. They went up in the elevator, a silent, grim pair. Although Jenny had a million questions, not one word crossed her lips.

In some ways, she thought she was in a dream, that at any moment she would wake up, and Danny would be there, smiling, laughing, whole.

When they got off the elevator, they walked down a long corridor, past colorful murals of giraffes and zebras, past a child in a wheelchair and a parent hovering outside of a hospital room, past the beeping sounds of machines and the sorrowful cries of pain.

Jenny took a breath to ease the tension, but the pungent smell of antiseptic only made her lungs constrict. It reminded her of where she was, of what she was about to face. She wondered what death smelled like—if it smelled like this.

Stop it, she told herself. Danny was alive. The doctor had said so. She had to believe. She had to think positively.

Dr. Lowenstein led her through another set of double doors. It was quieter in this hallway, but there were more people, nurses, doctors, and orderlies, all going about their tasks with quiet efficiency. There were machines with lights and beeps, oxygen tanks, bottles of blood and other unidentified substances. The smell was stronger here, the fear of death almost tangible.

Jenny paused as Dr. Lowenstein bent his head to talk to a nurse sitting at the desk. The nurse glanced up at her and smiled reassuringly, compassionately. It didn't touch Jenny.

She looked beyond the nurse to the wall of glass, behind which lay her son. Jenny saw him in the bed, a large white bandage around the front of his head, his blond hair shaved in the front but still tousled in the back, the way it always was when he slept. But he wasn't asleep. He was unconscious. He was quite possibly—dying.

A sharp pain cut across her stomach. Nausea warred with pain. Bile rose in her throat, but she forced it back. She felt Dr. Lowenstein's hand on her arm and turned to face him.

It helped to look at the doctor instead of Danny, to focus on his square face, his bushy eyebrows, his compassionate, intelligent eyes. He was calm, and she felt calmer just having his hand on her arm.

"Are you all right?" Dr. Lowenstein asked. "If you need some time . . ."

"No, I'm okay. I want to see him. All this . . ." She waved her hand in front of her. "It took me by surprise."

Dr. Lowenstein nodded and led her into Danny's room. Jenny took a deep breath and walked over to the bed. She stared down at her son. There was an angry red cut over his eye, and tubes coming out of his arms, his mouth, his head. The bandage showed streaks of blood.

In the oversized hospital gown, Danny looked small and helpless. Her heart broke.

"Oh, Danny, Danny," she cried, touching his face with her hand, caressing his cheek as tears flowed down her face. "I'm sorry. I'm so sorry."

Danny didn't move, didn't flinch. He was still, utterly still. His face was white, as if the life had been drained from his body. His freckles stood out in stark accusation, as if they were furious at being deprived of the sun. A respirator pushed oxygen into his lungs. It was the only sound in the room.

Jenny faced the doctor. "Is he—is he in any pain?"

"No, he's heavily sedated."

"Was he conscious at all—before the surgery?"

"The paramedics said he was unconscious from the time they arrived at the scene."

"I guess—I guess that's okay," Jenny said, trying to latch on to something consoling. "At least he wasn't crying. I mean, maybe he wasn't hurting or anything."

"The mind has a way of shutting down when things get too bad," Dr. Lowenstein replied. "He has some fractured ribs. We ran a CT scan on his abdomen and pelvis as well as his head. There doesn't appear to be any internal bleeding. Right now our biggest concern is the swelling in the brain."

"What does that mean?"

"It means there's pressure on the brain, and we want to keep the pressure as low as possible, allow the wound to heal."

"How long does it usually take for the swelling to go down?"

"Every patient is different. Every head injury is different. In a trauma like this, the brain goes into a self-protective hibernation phase to allow for healing. It may be a day or two before Danny regains consciousness, perhaps longer. I wish I could offer you something more concrete, but I can't. We'll know more as time goes on."

Jenny sighed and looked at Danny. Tenderly, she plucked a strand of hair off his cheek and pushed it behind his ear. His skin felt cold to her touch. He never felt cold. In fact, he was her furnace, her blanket that she cuddled up with on winter nights. They had laughed about how hot he was, on fire for life. Now, he was icy cold.

"I think he needs another blanket," she said.

"I'll have the nurse bring one in."

"Can he hear me?"

"It wouldn't hurt to talk to him. In fact, it might help."

Another nonanswer. Jenny felt frustrated. Why the hell couldn't they tell her what was going to happen to her son? They were doctors. They were supposed to be the brilliant chosen ones in life, the people who had all the answers. Luke had always seemed to know everything.

Luke—another overwhelming surge of anger flooded her body. It was his fault. He was the reason Danny was lying in the hospital bed. God, she wished she had never met him.

Even as the thought crossed her mind, she recanted. If she had never met Luke, she would never have had Danny, and at this moment, when Danny was so close to leaving her, she couldn't bear the thought of never having had him, never having known him.

"We have a room where you can stay tonight, Mrs. St. Claire," Dr. Lowenstein said.

"I want to stay here with Danny."

"That's fine. If you want to lie down—"

"I don't."

"Okay." Dr. Lowenstein touched her arm and left.

Jenny picked up Danny's hand and squeezed it. There was no response. "Wake up, baby," she whispered as she had done so many mornings in Danny's life. "Wake up, honey. Rise and shine. It's a new day, and we've got so much to do." Her voice broke on the last word and she laid her face on Danny's bed, her cheek touching his hand, and she cried.

Danny looked over at Jacob. "She's so sad. Can't we tell her I'm okay?"

"You're not okay." Jacob pointed a bony finger at the kid in the bed. "You're barely alive."

"I'm going to get better, right?"

Jacob didn't answer.

"I'm going to get better," Danny said again, his voice rising along with his fear. What if he couldn't go back? What if he really was dead? He looked over at his mother with a heavy heart, wishing he could have the day over again, do everything differently.

"I knew this wasn't a good idea," Jacob said. "Come on. We're outta here."

"Wait, I don't want to go yet. I want to do something. I want to let her know I'm okay."

"You can't talk to her. It ain't allowed."

"Can't I do something, anything? Please." Desperation made him feel heavy, and Danny felt his body drift toward the ground.

Jacob rolled his eyes as he grabbed Danny's arm. "You're a stubborn cuss, ain't you?"

"She's my mom, and she's all alone. She needs me. I'm all she's got."

"She's got the rest of her family, her father, sister, brother."

"They don't love her like I do. Please, let me talk to her."

"Maybe later," Jacob said cryptically, and Danny felt himself being pulled from the room.

"Wait, stop!" he cried. Danny flailed his arms and legs in a desperate attempt to control his movement.

"Come on, kid. You're gonna get me in trouble."

"I'm not going anywhere until you give her some sort of a sign." Danny crossed his arms defiantly in front of his chest.

Jacob sighed loud and long. "A sign, huh?"

"Yeah. Knock over a glass of water or something."

"I'm an angel, not a ghost."

"Is there a difference?"

"Damn right there is. Oh, why not?" Jacob reached out an arm that seemed to grow longer as he extended it, until his fingers touched Jenny's arm. He did a spider crawl along her bare skin until she raised her head. It was a simple caress. It was also a game that Danny had played with his mother since the day he was born.

Danny looked over at Jacob. "How did you know?"

"I know everything, kid."

Jenny lifted her head from the bed and shivered as she looked at Danny's body. "I'm here, baby," she whispered. "I won't leave you. I'll stay right here until you wake up."

"I love you, Mom," Danny muttered, but his mother didn't hear him, because the boy on the bed hadn't moved. Danny ran the back of his hand across his eyes, feeling like crying, but there weren't any tears.

"Come on now," Jacob said.

Jacob extended his hand to Danny. Reluctantly Danny took it. The touch reassured him, comforted him in a way that no words could.

"Where are we going?" Danny asked.

"To see someone."

"God?"

"No, this time we're going to see your father."

The night was long, tormented. The minutes passed slowly, mockingly. Luke rolled over on his back and stared at the ceiling.

He had wrestled with his pillow for hours, trying to get comfortable. He had counted sheep, counted money, counted the days since he had last seen Jenny. Nothing worked. He kept thinking about her and the boys on the porch.

After the party he had asked Denise about the blond kid, about what she had said to him, and what the boy had said to her. Denise had simply repeated that the boys were selling candy.

Luke wanted to believe her. The only children who ever came to his door were usually selling something. Why should those boys have been different? But there was something about the child's face, something familiar. Then later—to have Jenny stop by—after thirteen years of nothing, no letters, no calls, no contact of any sort. Why would she suddenly show up at his door without warning?

It didn't make sense, and he was used to things making sense. One plus one always equaled two. Two halves made a whole. Logic ruled his life. He saw everything in concrete, countable terms. As a scientist, it was the only way he allowed himself to think. There was no room for maybe, if, or perhaps. Which was why there hadn't been room for Jenny in the first place.

She had always been unpredictable. Being with her had been like riding on the tail of a kite. Sometimes they soared. Sometimes they crashed. But he had to admit every day had been exhilarating.

Luke turned his head and looked at Denise. His wife was sleeping on her side, her face turned toward the wall. She looked unapproachable. There was no way he could pull her into his arms, make love to her, without drawing a cross look.

Denise was predictable. She made love in the evening, never in the middle of the night, once in a great while in the morning. She preferred the seduction of evening clothes, dim lights, and perfume, not the rustle and tustle of sweaty bodies with hair that had been slept on and teeth that needed brushing.

Luke closed his eyes. Maybe Denise was right. Maybe he was having an identity crisis, wanting to change everything, wanting to have kids. He sighed and tried to clear his mind.

Right now, he just wanted peace, a good night's sleep, a chance to wake up to a new day and forget about everything that had happened in the past twelve hours.

"Dad."

Luke twitched when he heard the voice. He opened

one eye and blinked. There was no one there. He buried his face in the pillow and tried to let go of reality.

"Dad."

He was hearing things now. Definitely going over the edge.

"Dad, wake up."

Luke lifted his head off the pillow. Sitting Indian-style on the end of his bed was a kid with blond hair and blue eyes, wearing jeans and a sweatshirt, the same kid who had rung his doorbell that afternoon.

"What the hell—"

"Hi." The kid waved at him, and gave him a half-hearted smile that was almost as wary as it was welcoming.

"Who are you? What are you doing in my room? How did you get in here?" Luke demanded, struggling to a sitting position.

"I'm Danny," the boy said, peering at him in an intense manner that made Luke want to squirm. "You're bigger than I thought you'd be, and you have a lot of hair on your chest."

"Bigger?" Luke asked in confusion, crossing his arms somewhat self-consciously. "What are you talking about? What do you want?"

"I came by to see you before, but *she* wouldn't let me in," Danny said, pointing a finger at the sleeping Denise.

"My wife said you were selling candy."

"She's a liar. She slammed the door on my toe."

"Now hold on," Luke said, then stopped himself. Why was he defending Denise? She probably had lied about the candy. "If you weren't selling candy, why were you at my door?"

" 'Cause I wanted to meet you."

"Why?"

Danny shrugged and looked off to one side as if there were someone else in the room, but Luke didn't see anyone.

"Jacob says we have to go now."

"Who's Jacob?"

"Come and see me tomorrow."

"See you? See you where?" Luke asked. Even as he spoke, the boy vanished. He didn't get up and walk out the door, he just disappeared.

Luke looked over at Denise. She was fast asleep. The clock on the bedside table read 4 A.M. Only five minutes had passed since he had last looked at it. Five minutes in which to have the strangest hallucination . . .

He fell back against the pillows and stared at the ceiling. It was another five minutes before he remembered—the boy had called him Dad. How could that be possible?

It wasn't possible. It didn't make sense. He wanted to go to sleep, and fast, because he had a feeling that if he didn't fall asleep immediately, the next person he'd see sitting on the end of his bed would be— Jenny.

Jenny jumped as a hand touched her shoulder. Her first thought was that Danny had moved, had lifted his hand and touched her. Then she looked up, saw Alan, and realized she had fallen asleep on the narrow couch in the hospital waiting room.

"Oh, it's you," she said, rubbing her eyes. "I guess I fell asleep." She swung her legs off the couch and sat up, feeling dizzy at the sudden motion.

"You've been in here all night, honey." Alan sat down next to her and put an arm around her shoulders.

"What time is it?"

"Six o'clock in the morning."

"Six o'clock? My God. I just came out for a minute when they wanted to run some tests." Jenny looked at him in alarm. "He didn't wake up, did he? If he woke up, and I wasn't there, I'd—"

Alan shook his head, cutting off her panic. "He didn't wake up. I just checked with the nurses. No change."

"Oh. I guess that's good," Jenny said. "I mean, it's only been a few hours, and Danny's probably tired from the surgery. You know he loves to sleep in. I wouldn't expect him to wake up till at least ten. It's Saturday. Maybe he won't wake up till eleven. There's no ball game to go to or anything." Her voice caught in her throat, and her lip trembled. "Oh God, Alan, what if he never wakes up?"

Alan drew her into his arms, and she pressed her cheek against his chest. He was a big man, solid as a rock, dependable, protective. Jenny took a deep breath, wanting to absorb his strength. Alan wasn't the most affectionate man in the world or the most tender, but she knew he was brave, and right now the thing she needed most was courage.

"He'll wake up," Alan said. "He's a strong kid. And tough. Too stubborn to die. You'll see."

"I hope so. I really hope so." She looked into Alan's eyes, but his gaze wasn't as strong as his words. He was afraid, too. "You've been here all night, haven't you?"

"I didn't want to leave you alone. Merrilee said she'd be back this morning. She'll probably bring Matt or your dad with her."

"My father?" Jenny shook her head. "I don't think I can handle seeing my father right now, knowing the way he feels about Danny."

"He loves Danny. He just doesn't know how to say it."

"No, I don't believe that. The way he acts isn't love. He criticizes Danny and me all the time. Nothing we do is right."

Jenny pulled herself out of Alan's arms and stood up, suddenly reminded that Danny and Alan didn't get along all that well either.

"Maybe he's just trying to help," Alan suggested.

"Everyone thinks they know what's best for Danny. But I know what's best. I'm his mother," she said, her voice rising along with her agitation.

"I'm sorry. I didn't mean to upset you."

"I'm going to find out how Danny's doing." Jenny stood up, then paused. She turned to see Alan watching her with a troubled expression, and she felt guilty. She was taking out her anger on him, and he had done nothing to deserve it. "I'm sorry, Alan."

"It's okay."

"Look, you don't have to stay here all day. You must be exhausted. Why don't you go home and get some sleep?"

"I'm not leaving you here alone."

"Alan—"

"No, Jenny, I'm staying." Alan stood up. "Let me come with you. I'd like to see Danny."

Jenny hesitated for a long moment. She didn't want Alan in Danny's room. She knew Alan cared about Danny, he just didn't get along that well with children. But right now he was complicating things, and she didn't want to deal with anyone but Danny.

"I want to be alone with him," she said. "You understand, don't you?"

"No. Yeah. I guess." Alan held out his hands in a pleading gesture. "Don't shut me out, Jenny. I want to help you through this. I want to do whatever I can to help you. Tell me what you want."

"I want Danny, happy, healthy—but you can't give that to me," she said simply.

"I wish I could."

"I know you do."

Alan put a hand on her arm as she turned to leave. "Jenny, there's something I have to ask you. I'm trying to piece together what happened yesterday. I need to know why Danny was on the highway last night."

Jenny tensed. She didn't want to answer him, but

what was the point of lying? He would find out sooner or later. "Danny went to see his father."

"His father?"

"That's right."

Alan swallowed hard, biting back words that would surely have held criticism. She could see it in his eyes. "Did he see him?" Alan asked finally.

"I have no idea."

"Maybe one of us should talk to this guy."

"Why? He wasn't driving the car that hit Danny."

"You don't know that."

"Actually I do. I saw him standing in his living room about twenty minutes before I found Danny on the street."

Alan looked at her in amazement. "You went to his house? What did he say? What did you say?"

"I didn't speak to him."

"Why not?"

"Because I didn't."

"Jennifer. What the hell is going on?"

His demand cut through her last remaining thread of control. "I'll tell you what's going on. My son is hurt. He might even be dying, and you're standing here shouting at me about Luke Sheridan. I don't give a damn about Luke. I don't want to see him. I don't want to talk to him. And right now I don't want to talk to you either."

"Jenny, wait. I'm sorry," Alan shouted, but Jenny didn't stop. She felt angry, out of control, and deep down inside absolutely terrified.

Alan slammed his fist against the wall. He wanted to hurt someone, make someone pay for the pain they were all experiencing, and damned if it wouldn't give him pleasure to knock Luke Sheridan's head against the wall.

7

L UKE RAN FASTER, HARDER, UNTIL HIS BREATH
came in gasps, and his hair began to drip from
the morning dew and his own sweat. The pave-
ment beneath his feet was rocky, uneven, as he
pushed himself up one hill, then down another.

The relentless pace prohibited him from thinking.
If he could run fast enough, maybe he could escape
his thoughts, his memories of Jenny, his hallucinations that made no sense.

The street in front of him turned and twisted. A dog
came up on his heels, barking in delight.

Luke tried to shoo it away. The dog wouldn't leave
him alone. Finally, completely out of breath, Luke
slowed down and ended his run in front of the
wrought-iron gates at the beginning of his driveway.
The dog barked again.

Luke looked down at him, hoping for a collar.
There was none. The dog looked like a mutt, a tiny
little thing with crooked ears and a yapping voice. For
some reason, it reminded him of Toto in the *Wizard
of Oz*.

"Go away," Luke said.

The dog barked and ran between his legs. Luke stumbled over his small body.

"Come on, beat it."

The dog bit through his sock with sharp, pointed teeth. Luke yanked his foot away in irritation. The dog ran into the bushes next to the fence, drawing Luke's attention to a piece of ripped paper stuck on a branch.

Luke reached for it, instinctively sensing its importance.

"Daniel S." The name was written at the top, along with a grade marked in red pen, B-, and the comment that Danny could do better if he tried harder. The paper was the beginning of an essay on space travel in the twenty-first century. Luke read the unscientific, twelve-year-old philosophy with a deepening grin, disappointed when the paper ended in midsentence.

He looked up, suddenly aware of the quiet. The dog had vanished as quickly as it had appeared. After a moment, Luke folded the paper carefully in his hand and walked into the house. He showered, dressed, and went back downstairs for breakfast.

When he got to the breakfast room, he picked up his glass of orange juice and drained it. He now felt awake, alert, in control of his body and his emotions. Yesterday had been an aberration in his highly organized life. Today, he would get back on track.

As soon as he finished breakfast, he would go to the office, bury himself in the details of his business and forget about the night before.

"Good morning, darling." Denise walked into the room, dressed in a Chanel linen suit with matching turquoise pumps. Her lips against his cheek were cool. Any thought he had of turning his mouth against hers disappeared as she moved quickly away. Luke realized in that instant that she was afraid of something, maybe his mood—maybe something else.

He watched her slide into her chair and pour herself a cup of coffee. Denise didn't start the day without a shot of caffeine, usually more than one. After a few sips, her tension seemed to ease. He offered her a tentative smile.

"Better?"

"Better," she agreed, relaxing as he offered her a silent olive branch, which she gratefully accepted. "The party was a big success, don't you think?"

"It was all right."

"Your parents aren't up yet?"

"Are you kidding? My father's already on the golf course and my mother is having her hair done. She said something about not being able to find a decent salon in Carmel."

Denise set down her coffee cup, her mood turning serious. "I've been meaning to talk to you about something."

Luke tensed, not sure he wanted to hear what she was about to say.

"I'd like to make some changes around the house, but I don't want to upset your parents. After all, this was their home for thirty years."

Luke shrugged, feeling relieved that she hadn't brought up their discussion of the day before. "Do whatever you want, Denise. This is our home now. They have their own house to decorate."

"If you're sure."

"I'm sure."

There was a long silence that went on and on, moving from companionable to uncomfortable. It seemed as if he and Denise had little to say to each other anymore. Or maybe there were just too many subjects that were taboo between them.

"What are you going to do today?" Luke asked finally.

Denise took another sip of coffee, then set the cup down, leaving a perfect pink lipstick ring around the edge. "I thought I'd go shopping."

Shopping. How wonderful, Luke thought wryly. Another dent in his bank account. Not that there wasn't plenty to go around, but he would have thought his wife would have shopped herself to death by now.

"What are your plans?" Denise asked.

"Work."

Denise sighed at his curt tone. "You're not still angry . . ."

"No. What's the point?" He looked her straight in the eye and saw her flinch, but she drew her shoulders up and faced him proudly.

"You're right. There's no point in rehashing the past. Let's look to the future. We do have a bright future together, Luke. I can make you happy. You know I can."

Denise smiled seductively, but Luke felt nothing, the same nothingness he had felt the last few times they had made love. During the past year, sex had become more of a chore than a joy.

Instead of responding to Denise's smile, he picked up the newspaper. It was a cowardly way to respond, but all he was up to at the moment.

He skimmed through the articles, his mind wandering from topic to topic, nothing capturing his interest, until his gaze drifted down to the last column on the page. The title read BOY HIT, LEFT FOR DEAD. The article went on to state that 12-year-old Danny St. Claire was crossing Tully Road in Half Moon Bay when he was struck by a hit-and-run driver. The boy was listed in critical condition. Witnesses were encouraged to contact the Half Moon Bay Police Department.

Luke caught his breath, rereading the words until they began to make sense. The name St. Claire stuck in his head, because it was Jenny's name. The fuzzy photograph of the boy, Danny, confirmed his worst fear. The boy on the step and the boy in his dream were one and the same, Danny St. Claire.

Jenny's son? His mind whirled with questions.

Of course, Jenny could have had a son in all these years, even a twelve-year-old son. He didn't remember the exact day they had parted. It was years ago. But even as Luke struggled with the implications, he remembered one word, one very important word—*Dad*. The boy had called him *Dad*.

No. No. Luke shook his head. It was impossible. Jenny had had an abortion. She had taken his money. She had left him, promising to take care of things.

"Is something wrong?" Denise asked.

He looked at her blankly, barely aware of her presence.

"Luke," she asked anxiously, "are you all right?"

Slowly he folded the newspaper, his hands shaking with the force of his emotions. A child. A son. It was entirely possible that he had a son.

A sense of joy flooded his body, immediately chased away by fear. Danny St. Claire had been hit by a car. Danny St. Claire was in critical condition. It was entirely possible that *his son* might die before he saw him.

Luke stood up abruptly. His chair fell over backward. Denise looked at him in shock. "What's wrong?"

He shook his head, too filled with his own questions to even think of answering hers.

"Luke. You look like you've seen a ghost."

A ghost? He'd seen something all right. "I have to go. I'll see you later."

Luke grabbed his car keys off the kitchen counter and sprinted through the door that led into the garage. He was in his black Mercedes, doing forty down Ralston Avenue when he realized that he had no idea where the hell he was going. A hospital obviously, but which one? Probably Peninsula, he decided.

Whatever—he was going to hit every one until he found Danny. Luke had to know if he had a son.

Merrilee entered her son's bedroom and stared down at his sleeping form. William's hand was tucked up under his chin as he lay curled in a fetal position, the covers flung off his skinny body, goose bumps dotting the bare skin on his legs where his pajama bottoms had crept up to his knees.

With a tender hand, Merrilee pulled the comforter over William's body, catching her breath as he murmured something in his sleep, then drifted off again. He looked small, innocent. Only a year younger than Danny. She couldn't imagine what Jenny was going through right now, seeing her son in a hospital bed, knowing there was a chance that . . .

No, she wouldn't think that way—only positive thoughts.

Danny would be all right. He would recover. The family would get back to normal. Next week they'd share Thanksgiving turkey and thank God that Danny had survived. It would be another blessing to count.

"Merrilee?"

She turned to find her husband in the doorway.

"Yes?"

"I have to go to work," Richard said.

"It's Saturday."

"The Hardings are only here for the day. We're going to meet this morning, have lunch, sign the contract and put them on a plane by three. It's a big account for the agency. McAllister will have my head if I don't show."

Merrilee walked into the hall and shut the door to William's room. She stared at Richard in his finely cut charcoal gray suit, crisp white shirt, and red silk tie. His hair was a dark brown with edges of silver along his sideburns, his eyes a brilliant blue. He was the handsomest man she'd ever known. And he was her husband.

A sense of possessive pride filled her soul. He was hers. He belonged to her and William and Constance. No one else.

"I'll come to the hospital as soon as I can," Richard continued.

"All right."

Richard looked at her with concern and compassion, emotions that she hadn't seen in his eyes in a very long time.

"What have you told the kids?" he asked.

"Nothing yet."

"Nothing? You ran out of the house without a word?"

"I told them I needed to help Jenny. I gave them firm instructions to go to bed at nine. They were asleep when I got home." Merrilee reached out to straighten Richard's tie and fix his collar. Richard grabbed her wrist and stopped her, forcing her to look directly into his eyes.

"You have to tell them that Danny is hurt. You can't pretend this isn't happening."

"We don't know how badly he's hurt. He could be much better by now. In fact, I was just about to call the hospital." Merrilee tried to pull her arm away from Richard, but he held on tight. "What?" she murmured, confused by his intense attention.

"I'm sorry I wasn't home last night," he said slowly.

Merrilee averted her gaze. "I understand. Work comes first."

"I should have checked in with you."

"There was nothing you could do."

Richard let go of her hand, and Merrilee walked down to the end of the hall where an antique phone sat on her great-grandmother's writing table.

"God, how do you do it?" Richard asked.

"Do what?"

"Stay so goddamned calm about everything," he said with annoyance. "You're acting like Danny scraped his knee, but from what you said last night, the kid is in critical condition."

Merrilee felt a lump rise in her throat. She didn't want Richard to remind her that Danny's injuries were serious. There was no point dwelling on negatives.

"He'll be all right."

"You don't know that."

"I'll find out." She reached for the phone.

Richard leaned against the wall, watching and waiting.

Merrilee dialed the number for the hospital. "I'm calling about Daniel St. Claire," she said. "He was brought in last night; pediatric ICU. Yes, I'll hold." Merrilee tapped her fingers restlessly against the address book lying by the phone. Finally, the impersonal voice returned. The words were crisp, unemotional. It made the news easier to hear. "I see, thank you."

Richard looked at her expectantly. Merrilee shook her head. "He hasn't regained consciousness."

"Jenny must be going out of her mind. How the hell did this happen?"

"It wouldn't have happened if Jenny had done what I told her to do twelve years ago."

Richard rolled his eyes. "I hope you didn't tell her that."

"Of course not. But if she had told Danny his father was dead, he wouldn't have gone looking for him, now would he?"

"You're right, Merrilee, but then you usually are. It must be nice to be perfect."

"I'm not going to fight with you."

"Why doesn't that surprise me?"

A door opened in the middle of the hall, and Constance walked out in a long, white Bart Simpson T-shirt that drifted down to midthigh. She rubbed one hand against her sleepy eyes then looked from Merrilee to Richard. "What's wrong?" she murmured.

"Nothing, honey," Merrilee said. "What would you like for breakfast? A waffle, French toast, eggs? Some hot oatmeal? It's important to have a good breakfast."

"Mother, what's wrong? You're acting weird, even for you."

"Why don't you just tell her?" Richard said. "She'll find out eventually."

"Find out what? You're not—you're not splitting up?" Constance's voice filled with panic.

"No," Merrilee said vehemently. "No. Goodness, why on earth would you say that?"

"Then what is it?"

"It's Danny," Richard said. "He was in an automobile accident last night. He's hurt pretty bad."

Constance stared at them with big, round eyes. "Is he going to be okay?"

Richard shrugged. "We don't know yet."

"Of course, he'll be all right," Merrilee interjected. "Danny is a strong, healthy boy. He'll come through this just fine."

Constance turned to her mother. "You went to the hospital last night?"

Merrilee nodded, hating the look of pain in her daughter's eyes. She wanted to protect her children from everything, but as they got older, it became more difficult to do.

"Why didn't you tell me?"

"I didn't want you to worry."

"That's just great. Everyone in the family knows but me." Constance put her hand on her hips. "When are you going to stop treating me like a baby?"

"This isn't about you, Connie. It's about your cousin," Richard said.

"That's right, and William doesn't know yet either. I'd appreciate it if you would let me tell him," Merrilee added. "Now, what will you have for breakfast?"

"Nothing, I'm not hungry." Constance stormed down the hall to the bathroom and slammed the door.

Merrilee sighed. "Shall I fix you some eggs, Richard?"

"No, I'm not hungry either. Have you spoken to Matt?"

"He hasn't returned my calls."

"Matt and Danny were so tight."

"Don't talk about him like he's already dead. Danny is very much alive."

"He's unconscious."

"He'll wake up," Merrilee said desperately.

"I hope so. Try Matt again—maybe he can help Jenny."

"I can help Jenny. I don't need Matt."

"Maybe you don't need Matt, but I think Jenny does."

Merrilee put her hands on her hips and glared at him. "What are you saying? That I can't take care of my sister? Because I've been taking care of Jenny since my mother died."

"Sometimes you rub Jenny the wrong way," Richard said carefully. "You criticize her instead of supporting her."

"Don't be ridiculous. I always do what's best for Jenny. Always."

"Fine. Fine." Richard held up his hand in surrender. "Call Matt anyway."

Merrilee watched her husband walk down the stairs. Call Matt—as if she hadn't already called him every ten minutes for the last twelve hours. He obviously wasn't home, or else he was in no condition to answer the phone. Either way, Matt wouldn't be much use to Jenny.

Still, he was their brother. She supposed she could give him one more try.

*   *   *

Matt grumbled in his sleep as the phone rang and rang, forcing him out of happy oblivion and back into the real world. Groggily, he tried to open his eyes, but the pain was blinding like a hundred needles poking into each nerve. Gradually, he pried his lids open and found himself staring into a white pillow case as the phone stopped ringing.

A voice came out of nowhere. His answering machine, he realized after a moment.

"Matt, where are you? Call me right away. I need to talk to you."

Matt groaned and pulled the pillow over his head, enjoying the coolness of the sheet below. Merrilee. Not a woman he wanted to wake up to. She was probably on the rag again, ready to give him hell for ditching his last job interview, the one she had set up with her boring accountant friend. He would call her later, much later.

First, he would close his eyes and dream awhile. Life was so much better when he was asleep.

The phone rang again, and he swore. Three more rings, then the machine picked up. Matt rolled over on his back, prepared for Merrilee's grating voice once again. The husky baritone did not belong to his sister.

"Matt. Alan Brady. Jenny needs you, man. Where are you?" The message machine beeped, and Matt sat up in bed. The sudden movement sent his head into a tailspin, matching the rumbling in his stomach. He rubbed a hand over his grizzly cheek and tried to figure out what was going on. He had never had a call from Jenny's boyfriend before.

A sense of uneasiness made its way through his hangover. Jenny. She had been yapping about something last night. What was it? Matt tried to remember as he swung his legs over the side of the bed and cautiously stood up.

Oh, yeah. Danny. The kid had gone somewhere. But where? His mind refused to click in. Matt stumbled into the bathroom, took a piss, then ran cold water over his face. He felt marginally better.

He walked into the living room of his beachfront condo and stared at the answering machine with the accusing red light. He pushed the Play button and waited as the tape rewound for an endless amount of time. Finally, it began to play back.

"Matt, Howard Ralston. Call me on Monday. I may have a lead on a job for you."

Yeah, right, Matt thought. Ralston was his former agent, the one who had done diddly squat for him when his career ended six years earlier.

"Matt, this is Merrilee. There's been an accident." Matt felt his gut tighten. "Danny was hit by a car. I'm at Peninsula Hospital. Come as soon as you can."

Hospital? Danny?

Matt leaned against the back of a chair, his legs suddenly weak.

"Matt, where are you?" Merrilee's voice again, more frantic this time. "Jenny is sitting here like a zombie. I don't know what to do."

"Matt? Alan Brady here. We're still at the hospital. We'll probably be here all night. Danny's out of surgery. He's in ICU."

ICU? As in intensive care? Matt closed his eyes and tried desperately to breathe. Oh, God, what was happening?

"Matt, it's Merrilee again. It's after midnight. Where are you? I'm home now. Jenny is staying at the hospital. I don't know much more except that the person who hit Danny didn't stop. Call me as soon as you get home, no matter what time it is."

"Matt, Alan Brady. It's six o'clock in the morning. Jesus, man, where are you? Danny is in a coma. It doesn't look good. I'm going to the station to see if we have any leads on the son of a bitch who did this to him. The kid was almost home, too. Probably some drunk who hit him."

The machine beeped. Then the final message from Merrilee came again, the one he had awoken to. Matt stared at the machine, willing it to say something more, to tell him that Danny was out of danger, that everything was okay, and everyone was home now. It stayed ominously silent.

A thousand questions ran through his mind, but only one answer. He had to get to Jenny and Danny. He ran back to his bedroom, grabbed a pair of jeans off the floor and pulled them over his briefs. He picked up a wrinkled shirt from the chair, kicked on his tennis shoes and ran back to the living room, grabbing his keys off the table on his way to the door.

When he got to the front porch, he stopped abruptly. His Jeep Wrangler was not in the driveway where he usually parked it. He looked at the street. It was empty. His mind grappled with the problem as he tried to remember where he had parked his car when he had gotten home last night.

His mind went blank. He remembered walking into the parking lot at the Acapulco Lounge, trying to get the key into the ignition. But it was foggy, and he had been a little high. Then there was nothing but blankness. Had he gotten in the car? Had he driven it home? He had his keys. How could he have his keys and not his car?

Matt sank down on the step in front of his condo as he tried to make sense of what was happening. His car had to be somewhere. Maybe it was at the next bar they had gone to. At least he thought they had gone somewhere else. He vaguely remembered bouncing along the road, wondering why the fog was so thick, why there weren't any lights.

Shit. Where the hell was his car? And how had he gotten home? He had to get to the hospital, to see Jenny, to find out what had happened to Danny.

What had happened?

Danny had been hit by a car.

A few blocks from home.

The car didn't stop.

Probably some drunk . . .

Fuck. Matt buried his face in his hands as a terrible feeling of disaster filled his body. His mind screamed out a desperate protest. It couldn't have been him. Could it?

8

◄O►

"HUSH LITTLE BABY, DON'T YOU CRY,
Momma's going to sing you a lull-
aby . . ." Jenny's voice dropped to a
whisper, then came to a complete stop. Danny wasn't
crying. He didn't need a song to soothe him. He
needed something loud, something to wake him up.

Jenny clapped her hands in front of his face. Not a
muscle moved. His lids didn't even flicker.

"Wake up, Danny. Wake up."

She grabbed his arm tightly, the way she did when
she was angry with him, when she wanted him to
stay and listen, and he wanted to turn and run. Then
she felt guilty for the pressure of her hand on his arm.
What if she hurt him?

The doctors said he wasn't in pain. God, she hoped
they were right. It was hard enough to look at him
lying there, without worrying that he was hurting inside and unable to cry out for help.

A nurse walked into the room, breaking the silence
with a cheerful hello.

"The doctors will be here shortly to do their

rounds," the nurse said. "They'd appreciate it if you would wait outside for a few minutes."

"Do I have to?" Jenny glanced over at Danny, so still, so fragile. She was afraid to leave, afraid he would disappear into thin air, vanish like a puff of smoke on a cool breeze.

Her fingers twisted around Danny's fingers, as if she could pull him back to life with the strength of her hand. He didn't respond.

"Mrs. St. Claire, please."

The nurse stood at the end of the bed, waiting.

Jenny stood up. "Shouldn't he be awake by now?"

The nurse hesitated. "He was heavily sedated for the surgery."

"It's not just the medicine that's keeping him out, is it?"

"We'll know more after the doctors take a look at him. It will probably be about a half hour."

"So long?"

"They'll want to do a thorough examination. By the way, my name is Leslie, and I'll be one of the nurses taking care of Danny during the day. Someone will be watching him twenty-four hours a day while he's here."

"That's good."

"Why don't you take a break?" Leslie said. "You've had a long night."

Leslie was trying to be helpful, but at that moment Jenny hated the nurse's round, cheery face, hated the fact that for her Danny was just another sick body and not a person. "I'll be in the waiting room. Please let me know the second I can come back."

"I will."

Leslie walked over to Danny's IV to check the fluid level. Her movements were brisk and efficient. She looked up as Jenny remained in the room. "Did you want to ask me something?"

"Do you . . . have you . . . have you seen other patients like this before?"

"Yes."

"Did they . . ." Jenny licked her lips. "Did they recover?"

The nurse smiled at her with compassion. "Some did."

And some didn't. The words hung between them like a thick curtain that Jenny didn't want to look behind.

"I see." Jenny started to turn away.

"Mrs. St. Claire?"

"Yes?"

"I've seen miracles happen right here in this room. I still believe in them."

"Really?" Jenny wanted desperately to believe that a miracle was waiting just around the corner.

Leslie nodded. "Yes. And I have two kids at home. I'll take good care of Danny."

Jenny's eyes filled with tears as Leslie put a gentle hand on Danny's head and pulled at the cowlick that sent three hairs straight up in relief at the back of his head.

"He's always had that," Jenny said. "Every morning I wet it down, and by lunchtime, it's back up again. He hates when I fool with it." She smiled fondly. "And I always fool with it." She walked over to the bed, wet her fingers and pushed the hair back into place. It popped back up. At least a part of Danny was still fighting. She hoped the rest of him would come to life with the same energy.

Jenny walked out of Danny's room, past the nurses' station, down the hall, and through a set of double doors to the waiting room. A television was on. She glanced at the game show—laughter, joking, bells ringing. She felt nauseated at the thought of so much confusion. How could people be happy when her world was falling apart?

There was no one else in the room, so she turned off the television. It was quieter now, but not as quiet as Danny's room. The elevator continued to ring its arrival. Nurses and doctors got on and off. Down the hall, a child squealed in protest at something unjust. Her mother scolded her for being too noisy. Jenny wanted to run down the hall and shake the mother, tell her that at least her child could cry and scream and be bad. At least her child was alive.

Oh God! What was she thinking? Danny was alive, too. He was just sedated from the surgery. He would come around. He would recover.

Hugging her arms around her waist, Jenny walked over to the window and glanced out into the atrium. It was morning, almost ten. The fog was lifting. Sunshine bounced off the branches of the trees, spilling across a table where a doctor and a nurse were having coffee.

Jenny didn't want to see the sun. She wanted it to be dark and cloudy, in keeping with her feelings. Then again, Danny was a child of the sun. He hated the rain, loved summer and everything that went with it, body surfing, watermelon, and the Fourth of July.

She wanted him to have another summer, at least another fifty summers, until he was old and gray. It couldn't end now, not like this.

Danny needed to wake up today. He could have one last beach fling before Thanksgiving, before winter set in for good.

"Jenny."

She turned to face her sister. Merrilee was wearing black slacks, a white blouse, and a gray blazer with a black-and-white necklace. Her pumps were black and shiny. Her watch and rings accessorized the outfit.

Perfection—thy name is Merrilee.

For a moment, Jenny felt calmer at the sight. At least with Merrilee, she knew what to expect. No changes. No unpredictability. No emotion. Merrilee wouldn't give her sympathy, wouldn't make her weep. At the moment, it was almost a relief to see her cool, calm face.

"How's Danny?" Merrilee asked.

"The same."

"And you?"

Jenny shrugged. "I don't know. I don't care."

Merrilee looked at her with troubled eyes. "Well, I do care about you."

"I know you do."

Merrilee opened her arms to her. Jenny hesitated, then saw the apprehension on Merrilee's face and felt guilty at the way she had treated her sister the night before. She walked into Merrilee's embrace and hugged her tightly.

It had been a long time since she had hugged her sister. Merrilee smelled like Chanel perfume. It took her back to the days when their mother had worn the same scent, given the same hug. Her mother had been round, soft, and loving. Merrilee was skin and bones, taut muscles and disapproving looks. Merrilee could never take her mother's place, no matter how hard she tried.

Jenny stepped away and walked over to the couch. She sat down and leaned her head back, closing her eyes.

Merrilee sat down next to her. For a moment she was blessedly quiet. It didn't last long.

"Alan picked up the car you were driving and parked it at your house. He said it wasn't yours."

"No, it was Barry's. I borrowed it. He's probably wondering where it is."

"I'll call him for you."

"He's the bartender at the Acapulco Lounge. You can reach him there." Jenny opened her eyes. "I just remembered I'm supposed to go to work tonight."

"I'll call them, too. Is there anything else I can do?"

"I don't think so."

Merrilee paused for a moment. "Maybe you should go home, change your clothes, get some rest."

Jenny shook her head. "I'm not leaving. Not now."

"Danny might be asleep for a long time," Merrilee said, choosing her words with care.

"He's not asleep. He's in a coma."

Merrilee looked uneasy. "He's still asleep—whatever word you want to use."

"I'm trying not to lie to myself about his condition."

"It's too soon for the doctors to know anything. Keep the faith, Jenny. Danny will come out of this."

Of course Merrilee believed her own words. She was a woman who denied the existence of anything negative in her life. Unfortunately, Jenny didn't have the same control over her emotions. When she felt sad, she cried. When she felt happy, she laughed. When she felt scared, she wanted to run away and hide.

A coward; she had always been a coward at heart. Jenny hated scenes, confrontations. Maybe it was a throwback to her childhood years, when her father had yelled at her mother about stupid things, like socks that didn't match, or a newspaper that had coupons torn out of it. She remembered curling into a small ball in the corner of her bedroom, her stomach twisting into knots as she listened to his anger.

It wasn't just the fights that made her uncomfortable. It was the times they went out to dinner and her father sent his meal back because it wasn't good enough or asked that their seats be changed, because they were too close to the kitchen. So many little scenes. So many upset stomachs.

Jenny felt sick right now, because she knew she had to fight for Danny, and she wasn't sure she could do it. What if she wasn't strong enough? What if she failed? Danny's life might depend on her courage or lack thereof.

"Jenny, I'm talking to you."

Jenny blinked. "What?"

"I asked you if Alan has any information on the driver of the car?"

"I don't know. He left a few hours ago."

"I'm glad he was with you. He's a good man."

"Yes." Jenny stood up and paced restlessly around the waiting room.

"Did you tell him about Luke?"

Merrilee's question made her pause. Slowly, she turned. "You did that for me."

"I only said that Danny was looking for his father," Merrilee said defensively. "I wasn't thinking about his reaction at the time."

"It doesn't matter."

"Did you speak to Luke last night when you went to his house? You never said."

"No. I looked through the window. I did ring the bell, but the housekeeper wouldn't let me in. She told me Danny wasn't there, so I left."

"Don't tell Luke now, Jenny. Keep him out of your life. It's for the best."

"Believe me, I have no intention of contacting Luke."

"You won't have to, because I'm already here."

The voice, so familiar, so haunting, made Jenny whirl around in disbelief. Standing in the doorway was Luke Sheridan, the man who had given her so much joy, so much heartbreak, so much anger.

Jenny couldn't say anything. She simply stared into Luke's face. He was an older, harder version of Danny, but he had the same blond hair, the same bright blue eyes, the same cleft in the chin. She remembered tracing his lips with her fingers, tickling his nose with her hair, kissing his eyelids, the long curve of his aristocratic nose. He had been her soul mate, her playmate, her lover.

Luke's face was grim and stern. He didn't have Danny's pug nose, Danny's dimples, or her son's generous mouth. Those features came from her, reminding her with bittersweet irony that Danny came from her as well as from Luke, that this man was Danny's father.

Why now? Why did he have to come back now? As she studied his face, his eyes grew dark. Worry lines shadowed the corners of his eyes.

Merrilee came up behind Jenny and put a strong arm around her shoulders. "What do you want, Mr. Sheridan?" Merrilee asked.

Luke didn't answer Merrilee. His attention was focused solely on Jenny, as if he could see right through to her soul. Luke had always read her so well. She didn't want him to read her now, didn't want him to know how strongly he affected her. It had been thirteen years since she had been this close to him. She shouldn't be feeling anything, but she was.

He smelled like her youth, like warm summer days and hot sultry nights. His voice took her back to bonfires on the beach, to love songs played on an old guitar. Her gaze traveled down his body to his hands, to the strong, capable hands that had played her like a fine instrument.

Jenny closed her eyes and felt dizzy. Her body swayed. If Merrilee hadn't been holding her up, she probably would have crumpled to the ground. It was too much to take in. Danny's accident. Now Luke.

"Jenny, Jenny," Merrilee said with a shake. "Are you all right?"

Jenny opened her eyes again, hoping he was gone. He wasn't. "I'm fine," she muttered.

"What are you doing here?" Merrilee asked Luke. "Can't you see you're upsetting her? Go away."

"I can't go away. I have to speak to Jenny."

"She's upset. She can't talk to you right now."

"It's important."

Jenny watched the play between them like a tennis match.

"I want to speak to Jenny—alone," Luke said firmly.

"Anything you have to say can be said in front of me. I'm her sister, in case you've forgotten."

"How could I forget? You're quite the protector."

"Someone has to take care of her."

Jenny straightened at her sister's words. They were talking about her as if she were a child. "What do you want, Luke?"

"Jenny, you don't have to talk to him," Merrilee protested.

"It's okay."

"I saw an article in the paper," Luke said. "A boy was hit by a car. Your son?"

Jenny slowly nodded. "Yes. Danny." Her voice caught.

Luke took an impulsive step forward, his hand reaching out to her.

Jenny stiffened, feeling the pull between them as strongly as he did.

Luke stopped abruptly. He lowered his arm and dug his hands into the pockets of his slacks, wrinkling his fine suit coat in the process.

"How—how is he?" Luke asked.

"Not good. He has a head injury."

"Jenny, why don't you sit down?" Merrilee suggested. "You can speak to Mr. Sheridan later—much later."

"Jenny, I need to talk to you alone, just for a moment."

Jenny hesitated, her brain sending out a thousand screaming warnings to say no. But Luke sounded desperate, and it wasn't an emotion she had ever associated with him.

"Merrilee, could you get me some coffee?" she asked.

"What?" her sister replied, completely incensed. "You want me to leave?"

"I can handle this."

"Jenny, no."

ing about him last night. When I saw his picture in this morning's paper, I felt sure it was the same boy."

"Sometimes Danny sells candy for his school."

"So, he was in my neighborhood yesterday?"

"Maybe. He was with a friend. I'm not sure exactly where they went. I was at work."

"You don't know where your son goes after school?"

Anger flared at his insinuation, and she stood up, squaring her shoulders. "I take good care of my son. What he does after school is none of your business."

Jenny walked to the door of the waiting room. She had to get away from Luke.

"Jenny, wait." Luke's voice stopped her.

She paused, one hand on the edge of the doorjamb. "What?" she asked, her back to Luke.

"Where is Danny's father?"

She took in a deep breath and slowly counted to ten. "He's not here."

"Isn't he?" Luke walked up to her and put a hand on her shoulder. He spun her around.

His touch was searing, his eyes demanding, impatient.

Oh God, he knew!

"Is Danny my son?" Luke whispered, gripping her shoulders with hands so tight they bit into her skin.

"No. No." She shook her head. "Why would you think that? You told me to get an abortion."

"And you took my money. But that doesn't mean you got one. Besides, the paper said he's twelve years old."

"So what?"

"I can count."

"I have to go. My son needs me." She struggled to pull out of his arms, but he wouldn't let her go.

"Don't lie to me, Jenny."

"I'm not."

"You are. You're transparently honest, you always

have been. You're not looking at me. You're avoiding me. Why? Because I'm Danny's father? Because you never told me we have a son?" Luke shook her, his eyes flaring with fury. "Danny's my son, isn't he?" He shook her. "Isn't he?"

9

"**M**RS. ST. CLAIRE." THE NURSE CALLED her name from a few steps away.

Luke's hands tightened, then released. Jenny turned around, thankful to be free from Luke's punishing gaze.

"Yes?"

Leslie looked at her a little strangely. "The doctors are done. You can go in now."

"Thank you. I'll be right there."

"This isn't the end, Jenny," Luke said.

"It is the end." Jenny faced him with as much courage as she could muster. "Go away, Luke. Danny isn't your son. You and I have absolutely nothing to talk about."

Jenny abruptly turned and walked away, her back as stiff as a rod, her head held proudly, defiantly.

It was a good exit line, Luke thought cynically, but he didn't believe her for a second. Damn her. She had had his baby twelve years ago and never said a word.

She could deny the truth all she wanted, but his ego refused to entertain the possibility that there had been another man all those years ago. No, impossible.

He had seen her face that day. Seen her tears. She had told him she was pregnant. She had said he was the father.

Luke ran a hand through his hair in complete frustration. For the first time in a long time he didn't know what to do. He was married to another woman for God's sake. The easiest thing to do would be to walk away. Jenny didn't want him to be involved. Denise certainly wouldn't want him to be involved.

But what about the boy? He saw the vision in his mind as clearly as he had the night before. Danny had called him Dad. How could he forget that?

He couldn't. This wasn't over. Not by a long shot.

"Hey, he's leaving. My dad's leaving," Danny protested. "Come back. Come back," he shouted, but Luke stepped through the elevator doors and disappeared. "What's he doing? He's supposed to see me."

Jacob chewed on a wad of tobacco as he considered the situation. "Looks like he's running scared. Too bad."

"Too bad? I think it's terrible. What are you going to do?"

"Me? I was thinking of catching some college football on the tube, maybe taking a snooze."

"Sleep? You're going to sleep now?"

Jacob shrugged. "It's just a thought."

"I want you to stop my dad. Make him come back."

"I think that's up to you, kid."

"Me?" Danny looked at the elevator doors, then back at Jacob, who was walking upside down on the ceiling and whistling a silly tune. Making a sudden decision, Danny walked over to the elevator doors, paused, then tried to go through them. He found himself in midair and falling.

"J-a-c-o-b!" he screamed.

The elevator shaft was one long, dark tunnel. After an incredible free fall, Danny landed on top of the elevator, spread-eagled. He grabbed on to the sides with his fingertips, feeling like Indiana Jones on a wild adventure. The elevator seemed to be moving at an incredible pace. It was as terrifying as it was exciting.

Jacob suddenly appeared next to him, sitting cross-legged and tossing a baseball up and down in one hand. "What's the matter, kid? Afraid you're going to die?"

"Very funny." Danny pulled himself into a sitting position as the elevator stopped on a floor.

"What are you doing, anyway?" Jacob asked. "Just out of curiosity."

"I want to talk to my dad."

"He ain't here." Jacob waved his hand around the shaft as the elevator creaked and groaned and lurched into another floor of descent.

"I know that. He's inside this thing."

"Then, maybe you ought to go inside."

"How do I do that?"

Jacob reached out and pulled open the top of the elevator as if he were popping the top on a can of soda. "Allow me."

Danny jumped down into the elevator. Luke was standing against the back wall, his arms crossed in front of his chest, his expression grim. Next to him was an older woman, plain and square, dressed in a lumpy black dress and clutching an oversized black leather purse to her chest. A little girl, about seven, stood in front of the woman, holding a large red Tootsie Pop in her hand.

Danny sighed. He wanted to talk to his dad alone, but he didn't have a choice. "Hey, Dad." Danny touched Luke's arm with his hand.

Luke didn't look at him, but he did shake his arm, as if he had felt the phantom touch.

"Dad, where are you going? You're supposed to be upstairs. You're supposed to be visiting me." Danny pointed to his chest. "Me, your kid, the one who's lying in a hospital bed."

Luke didn't respond, he just shifted his weight from one foot to the other. Danny looked up at Jacob. "How can I make him hear me?"

"You have to want it bad enough, that's all."

"I do want it." Danny felt a sense of desperation. He didn't understand what was happening to him or to the world for that matter. Everything was crazy. He was invisible, maybe even dead. And Jacob wasn't helping at all.

"What kind of an angel are you anyway?"

Jacob laughed. "You ain't the first to ask that question."

"I don't like this. I want to talk to my dad, and I want to do it, now."

"Easy, kid," Jacob said.

"I don't want to take it easy. I want to be alive again." Danny shouted. "This isn't fair. Why can't you just let me go back?"

"Ain't up to me."

"Then who?"

Jacob grinned in a toothy, knowing way that made Danny even madder. "Why don't you try again? Only this time, start with the elevator switch." Jacob tipped his head toward the panels. "Give yourself some time. Better hurry. They're almost down now."

Danny looked over at the buttons and impulsively jabbed the one that said Stop. The elevator came to a lurching halt.

The older woman screamed as she braced her hand against the wall. The little girl buried her face in the woman's skirt and started to cry. Luke said, "Damn."

"Oh, my. Oh, my," the woman said, panting with fear. "I don't like this. I don't like this at all."

"It's okay," Luke said. "I'm sure they'll get us going again in just a second."

The woman licked her lips and began to take in

quick short breaths. "We're going to die. I just know we're going to die." She gripped the railing that ran along the back of the elevator.

The little girl screamed louder.

"We'll be fine," Luke said reassuringly. He reached out to pat the child on the head, but his gesture made her jump, and she dropped her Tootsie Pop on the floor.

The little girl pointed an accusing finger at Luke, her mouth drooping even lower. "You made me drop my candy," she cried. "I want my candy."

"I'll get it for you." Luke picked up the sticky red blob that was now covered in fine carpet hairs from the floor of the elevator.

"It's dirty," the little girl wailed.

"I'm sorry," Luke said.

"I hate you," she said.

Luke stepped back at the angry look on her ferocious little face.

The older woman started pressing the walls with her hand. "I can't stand this. I have to get out of here. I can't breathe. The walls are closing in on me. I have to get out of here now." She put a hand to heart. "Oh my God, I'm having a heart attack."

"Just calm down," Luke said. "Take deep breaths."

The woman started to gasp for air.

"Are we going die, Grandma?" the little girl asked with a trembling lip.

"We're not going to die," Luke said loudly and firmly. "The elevator is stuck, that's all. Now, calm down, both of you."

Danny looked up at Jacob and rolled his eyes. "Great idea, dude."

Jacob laughed. "You wanted to talk to your dad. Here's your chance."

"Okay. Okay."

"Don't take all day now. The service people in this hospital are pretty quick about stuck elevators."

"I'm thinking."

"That's a good start."

Luke sighed as the little girl's wailing rose to a shrill peak. Any higher, and he'd bust an eardrum. He looked over at the box, hoping for an emergency phone. Sure enough, there was a panel just begging to be opened. He reached out his hand, but he couldn't touch the box. It was the strangest thing. His hand was blocked by something. He couldn't even straighten it out. He pushed harder.

"Stop, you're hurting my shoulder," a voice said.

"What?"

"Ouch. Ooh, that tickles."

Luke heard a giggle, then blinked as the shape in front of him became clear. A boy appeared before him, his mirror image—Danny. Good Lord, he was seeing him again.

"I don't want you to call anyone yet," Danny said. "We have to talk."

"Talk?" Luke murmured as he put his hand on what looked like Danny's arm. But what he could see, he couldn't feel. The boy had no substance. He simply did not exist. "I'm not talking to you. You're not real. You're not here."

"You can see me, can't you?"

"Yes, but who are you? Danny?"

"Who else would I be?"

"Grandma, that man is talking to you," the little girl said, interrupting their conversation.

Danny ignored her. "You're supposed to be upstairs, Dad. You're supposed to be visiting me."

Luke stared at Danny's pleading blue eyes. He looked so damn real, and yet he couldn't be anything but a hallucination. "Your mother wouldn't let me."

"Excuse me?" the woman in the elevator said, drawing Luke's attention back to her.

"I wasn't talking to you."

"Then who were you talking to?"

"Him." Luke pointed at Danny.

"I don't see anyone."

"She can't see me, Dad. Only you can," Danny explained.

"Oh, my God. I'm trapped in this elevator with a lunatic," the woman said, putting both her arms around the little girl.

Luke sighed again, looking back at Danny. "I probably am crazy. Because I'm talking to you, and you don't exist."

"You have to talk to Mom again. It's important."

"Am I really your father?" Luke asked in bewilderment. He couldn't believe in this vision. He was a scientist, a man of logic, grounded in reality. Yet, here he was talking to an imaginary boy in an elevator stuck between the second and third floors.

"Of course, you're my dad."

"I never knew."

"She said you didn't want me."

"Want you? Of course, I want you," Luke said loudly.

The woman next to him gasped. "Well, I don't want you. I'm a happily married woman. My goodness. Whatever are you thinking?"

Luke licked his lips in desperation. He turned back to Danny, but the vision was fading. "Wait, don't go. I want to see you. I want to touch you. I want to feel that you're real."

"Don't you dare lay a hand on me," the woman said. "I'll scream."

"I'm not talking to you," Luke said with complete exasperation.

Danny touched his arm. "Talk to Mom again. Don't wait too long. I'm hurt pretty bad. I might not make it."

"Wait. How do you know that?"

"I just do."

Luke hit the wall as the air in front of him was

suddenly clear. No Danny. No nothing. "Damn it all," he swore.

"Oh, my," the woman said. She started to breathe faster again. The little girl screamed.

Finally the elevator began to move.

When the doors opened on the first floor, the woman and child rushed out. Luke followed more slowly, not sure what to do. He had half a mind to go back and talk to Jenny. But what could he say? That he had seen Danny in his dreams and just now in the elevator? She would think he was crazy, too.

And she would be right. He didn't believe in ghosts or visions. This was ridiculous, probably the result of too little sleep and too much anger over Denise's tubal ligation. He had kids on the brain, and his fatherly hormones were kicking into high gear.

Just because Jenny had a twelve-year-old son didn't mean the boy was his. There could have been other men.

But would she have gotten pregnant again so quickly?

The answer was disturbingly clear. Of course not. Jenny had taken his money to get an abortion, then bailed out. She had had his son and never told him. He supposed he could understand why. He had made his position very clear at the time.

Only now, things were different. He wanted this boy who was made up of everything good that was Jenny and everything good that was him. Because what he had with Jenny had been great, splendid, the best time of his life. Unfortunately, staying with Jenny would have gotten in the way of everything he had wanted and everything his parents had wanted for him, medical school, prestige, money, and power.

Now he had all those things, but he didn't have Jenny. And he didn't have his son. His shoulders stooped under the weight of his thoughts.

Luke tried to walk away from the elevators, but his feet were heavy. When he moved, it felt like someone was hanging on to his neck, two thin arms—a boy hitching a piggyback ride.

Danny. Luke smiled to himself. The kid was persistent.

Making a sudden decision, Luke turned toward the elevator and pushed the Up button. Maybe he couldn't get past Jenny to see Danny, but at the very least he could see Danny's doctors. One way or another he would get some answers.

Jenny looked up as Merrilee walked into Danny's hospital room. "Is Luke gone?"

"Yes." Merrilee stopped a couple of feet from Jenny, looking uncomfortable and out of place. But then Merrilee had never been very good when people were sick. "He's so—pale," Merrilee said. "I didn't realize."

Jenny met Merrilee's eyes and saw fear and uncertainty in them. "He's going to make it," Jenny said fiercely.

"Of course, he is." Merrilee thrust her chin in the air. "No doubt about it."

"Right. No doubt."

Silence fell between them, broken only by the beeps on the monitor and the sound of the ventilator pushing air in and out of her son's chest. So much equipment for one small boy. But it was giving him life, and that's all that mattered.

"Jenny, maybe you should take a break," Merrilee said. "You've been here for hours. You need food and rest."

"I'm not hungry."

"When did you last eat? You spent half the evening looking for Danny and the rest of the night here in his room. You can't let yourself get sick."

"Please, don't fuss." Jenny stroked Danny's hand. "I want to be here when he wakes up."

Merrilee shifted her feet, still keeping a few feet of

distance between herself and the bed. "Richard said he'd come by later. He had to meet with clients this morning." Merrilee fidgeted, running her hand under the collar of her blouse. "They're from out of town."

Jenny sent her a curious glance. "Is everything okay with you two?"

"Of course, why wouldn't it be? Richard's just busy. So am I for that matter."

"You don't have to stay—"

"I didn't mean it that way."

"I know. Still, it could be a while before—before Danny wakes up. William and Constance need you."

"They're both upset about Danny. I told them he'd be fine, and soon. After all, Thanksgiving is next week. We can't have it without Danny."

Jenny's heart caught at the simple words, *without Danny*. She turned to her sister in desperation. "Oh, God, Merrilee, what if he isn't there?"

Merrilee put a hand on her arm. "He'll be there. He knows I never take no for an answer."

Jenny took in a deep breath and let it out. She couldn't let the doubts take hold. She had to keep them at bay, otherwise, she would break down completely. "You're right."

"I usually am," Merrilee said with a bright smile.

Jenny gave her a reluctant grin. "That you are. Did you talk to Matt?"

Merrilee's smile faded. "I left him a dozen messages. Maybe he went away for the weekend."

"I saw him last night. He's probably at Brenda's."

"I wish he'd get his life straightened out."

"So do I."

"Jenny," Merrilee said, "I have to ask. What did you tell Luke?"

Jenny looked at Danny, avoiding Merrilee's probing gaze. "I didn't tell him anything."

"Good. There's nothing to be gained by telling him

that he's Danny's father. He'll only complicate things."

"I know," Jenny said, but deep down she felt a twinge of longing for the man who had fathered her son, the man Danny wanted so desperately to meet. How ironic that Luke should come now, a day late. Their timing had never been good.

Jenny stroked Danny's cheek. "The nurse said I should talk to Danny, that maybe he can hear me. Can you hear me, buddy? I love you, you know." Her voice faltered. "You have to fight to wake up. Push hard, baby. The sandman put an extra dose of sand in your eyes, but you can brush it out. You can do it. You're strong. You're a fighter."

"Jenny—"

Jenny glanced back at her sister. "He's my courage, my strength, Merrilee. One night when we came home late from the movies, the back door was ajar. I was scared to death. I wanted to run next door and call the cops, but Danny, my twelve-year-old kid, gets his baseball bat and goes with me to check things out. And I let him, Merrilee. I actually let him." Her voice rose with anguish. "God, I'm a terrible mother. He could have been hurt that night, too. Just like yesterday, when I should have been home, when I should have guessed what he had in mind."

"Jenny, stop. You're not a terrible mother."

"How can you say that? You're the first one to criticize me."

"Only for the little things. I've certainly never thought you put Danny's life in jeopardy."

"Well, now you know. I've done it—lots of times." Jenny sat down in the chair next to Danny's bed. "I wish I could go back and do everything differently."

"There's no point in crying over spilled milk."

Jenny sighed. "Oh, Merrilee. I know you mean well, but would you mind leaving me alone?"

"You want me to leave?" Merrilee asked in surprise.

"Yes."

Merrilee looked taken aback. "Oh, well, all right. Maybe I'll call Matt again. I won't be far away," Merrilee said as she left.

Jenny turned to her son, relieved to be alone. She didn't want to talk to Merrilee. She didn't want to talk to anyone but her son. "Come on, Danny, time to rise and shine. Surf's up. We can hit the beach. You and me. Me and you. The two of us."

Against the world, Jenny silently added. It had always been that way, since the day she had walked away from Luke, with his five hundred dollars burning a hole in her pocket. She had gone to the beach, the way she always did when she was upset. The wind had carried away her tears. The sea had taken away Luke's money.

It had been an impulsive gesture to throw his money into the ocean when she was dead broke, a pregnant eighteen-year-old with one year of college and a part-time job at the ice cream store. But the gesture had soothed her pride.

She didn't need Luke Sheridan. So what if he had given her the summer of her life? Summer was over. The leaves had turned, and so had Luke.

The pain had been unbearable for weeks, months. Every time Jenny looked in the mirror and saw her blossoming stomach, she remembered the night they had made Danny—the the reckless passion that couldn't be stopped not even when the condom broke, the unbearable need to be together, the hot touch of Luke's hand against her breast, his lips trailing love along every inch of her body.

Danny might not have been born into love, but he was certainly conceived in love.

She believed that now as strongly as she had then. Luke had simply been afraid. A decade of distance had brought that truth to her mind. Years later, eons wiser, Jenny now saw the picture clearly—a young man on the brink of a brilliant future, suddenly faced with his barefoot and pregnant girlfriend, who didn't plan beyond her next peanut-butter-and-banana sandwich.

Of course, Luke could have acted like a hero, the man of her dreams. He could have taken her into his arms, proposed marriage or at least a long engagement. But no, he had turned and fled, as if the fires of hell were licking at his fine Italian shoes.

So much time had passed since then, weeks and months and years that should have made any connection between them completely impossible. Yet, how quickly the memories had come back. One look, one word, and Jenny remembered the smell of his shampoo, the tenor of his voice, the cleft in his chin, the feel of his arms around her.

She didn't want to remember those things. She wanted to remember the pain, the coldness in Luke's voice when he told her it was over, the icy touch of his hand as he passed her the money in payoff.

Jenny focused on the anger. It kept the pain away, at least for the moment. As long as she didn't have to see him again, things would be all right.

10

"DR. SHERIDAN. I'M PLEASED TO MEET you." Dr. Bruce Lowenstein stood up as Luke approached his desk. He shook Luke's hand with a strong, confident shake.

Luke was pleased by the intensity of his grip. Dr. Lowenstein was the neurosurgeon who had operated on Danny. It was nice to know he had a steady hand.

"Please call me Luke."

Dr. Lowenstein smiled. "I understand you've taken over Sheri-Tech. You're stepping into some pretty big shoes. Have a seat." Dr. Lowenstein waved his hand toward the leather chair in front of his desk. "How does it feel to be back home?"

Luke sat down and crossed his legs. "Not bad."

"You were at McAuley Perkins, weren't you?"

"Yes, but that was just training ground. Sheri-Tech has always been my final goal."

Dr. Lowenstein nodded. "I've met your parents on numerous occasions. Quite a family you've got there. Very impressive."

"Thank you."

"I've got four kids, and not one of them wants to

111

come near the hospital." He shook his head. "I can't figure that out. Of course, my wife tells me that I shouldn't get my dreams confused with their dreams."

Luke stared at him, touched by his words. He didn't think his dreams had ever been separate from those of his parents.

Dr. Lowenstein scooted his chair in closer to the desk and rested his elbows on the thick layer of glass. "What brings you to my neck of the woods?"

Before Luke could answer, the buzzer on the phone sounded.

"Sorry. Hang on a sec, will you?" Dr. Lowenstein picked up the phone and began to converse with a colleague.

While the other man was talking on the phone, Luke looked around the office. There was the standard brown leather couch along one side, a credenza behind the desk, an array of diplomas on one wall and a lighted panel for reading X rays and other radiographs.

He could have had this. He could have practiced medicine in a hospital or private office, instead of concentrating on research and development, but he had never felt comfortable with the personal part of medicine. He had never wanted to deal with patients, their problems, their fears and sometimes their tears. He didn't know how to give solace, how to impart tragic news with a smile of hope, how to offer a reassuring touch to someone whose heart was breaking.

He had known early on that any future in medicine for him would have to be in the area of research. He could deal with microscopes and lab work, with clinical trials and statistics far better than he could hold someone's hand as they drifted across the line between life and death.

It wasn't that he didn't care; he just couldn't express his feelings, get close to people. His parents had never been affectionate with him. There had been no loving hugs to soothe away tears, no warm embraces to chase away fear. That's why he had fallen so hard and fast for Jenny.

Her natural affection had been like balm to a sore that never quite healed. She had gotten past his defenses, seen through his hard exterior to the lonely, vulnerable man beneath. She had touched his soul, and even though he hadn't seen her in years, hadn't dared to call her or write to her, he had never forgotten her.

Now, they were drawn together again, in the worst possible circumstances, brought together by the child who had once split them apart. A child who might not live another day.

Dr. Lowenstein hung up the phone and offered Luke an apologetic smile. "Sorry about that. I've been trying to catch up with him for two days."

"No problem."

"Now, what can I do for you?"

"I'm interested in one of your patients, Danny St. Claire."

Dr. Lowenstein's expression turned grim. "Kids. I hate operating on kids. I never get used to it. Danny's in critical condition. I guess you already know that."

"Is he breathing on his own?"

"No, he's on the ventilator. There is very little reflexive action. He doesn't respond to commands or to touch. But it's early yet. Jack Berman will look in on him later today," Dr. Lowenstein said, mentioning one of the top neurologists in the Bay area. "I'll be interested to hear his opinion."

"So will I."

The doctor studied Luke with a thoughtful expression. "Mind if I ask what's your interest?"

"I'm a friend of the family," Luke said, choosing to be discreet. He could hardly tell this man that he was the boy's father when he hadn't even told Denise yet.

"His mother seems like a nice woman. She's got backbone. I'm afraid she'll need it."

Luke nodded as he pulled out a business card. "Would you mind keeping me informed? I want the best for Danny. Whatever it takes."

"Of course." Dr. Lowenstein took the card. "Tell me something. Haven't you ever wanted to practice medicine, the way you were trained—hands-on with real people?"

Luke shook his head. "Not once."

"Interesting. I can't imagine being a doctor and not treating patients. That's the part I enjoy the most."

"Even when those patients are twelve-year-old boys in critical condition?" Luke shook his head. "I don't think I could tell someone their child was critical. I couldn't find the words."

"You rarely need words. They almost always know. Especially mothers."

Luke leaned forward in his chair. "I know you don't have any answers, but what does your gut tell you about Danny's prognosis?"

"Seventy to thirty."

"For or against?"

"Against."

The word struck Luke hard, leaving him breathless. He took a moment to regroup. Finally, he could breathe again. "I hope your gut instinct is wrong."

"So do I."

"Thanks for your time."

Dr. Lowenstein got up and walked Luke to the door. "I hope they catch whoever did this to Danny. That little boy is facing the fight of his life. It's a shame, a damn shame."

It was almost five o'clock Saturday evening when Alan threw himself into the beat-up, half-torn leather chair behind his desk and relished the sound of the disapproving squeal. Familiarity. Comfort. At least something in his world was still right side up.

There were three other desks in the room, but only one was occupied, and that individual was on the phone, saving Alan from having to explain to yet another person exactly what had happened the night before. He had already gone over the details of the accident scene with his supervisor and the other officers on duty. Unfortunately, they still had no leads.

Sue Spencer entered the room with two cups of coffee and set one down in front of Alan. "Thought you might need a shot of caffeine. You look like hell."

Alan rubbed the day's growth of beard on his chin and frowned as he took a sip of coffee. "Jesus, Armando made the coffee again?"

"He likes it strong."

"Remind me to have him make a batch when we want to retar the roof."

Sue perched her lithe, trim body on the corner of his desk and smiled, but her usually friendly eyes were filled with concern. "I thought you were taking the night off."

"I might as well be working. I'm not doing any good anywhere else."

"How's Danny?"

Alan shook his head, feeling his entire body tighten up at the familiar question. The words were beginning to echo like a maddening refrain that wouldn't leave his mind. "Not good."

"Damn."

"You can say that again. I need answers, Spence, and I need them fast. Witnesses, skid marks, anything?"

"Broken glass, probably from a headlight. That's it. The road is narrow, and there is thick foliage on both sides. No businesses or houses within a hundred yards. Nearest store, Ida's Ice Cream. No one heard a thing."

"I know. I drove by there a few minutes ago. Just to see if we missed anything."

"So did I, and we didn't. There was nothing to be missed. Danny was struck by the car, apparently hurled at least twenty feet, judging by the position of his body and placement on the road. From the description of his injuries, it appears that the car hit him around the rib cage. His sweatshirt was torn and there were abrasions, possibly cuts from the glass, on his abdomen. He's lucky there wasn't another car coming in the opposite direction or he could have been hit twice."

"Lucky," he echoed. "What about Christopher?"

"When he turned around, he saw lights fading in the distance. He ran into the middle of the road, tried to rouse Danny, and flagged down the first car that came. Thank God he didn't panic and leave him in the road. It was too dark for anyone to see anything."

Alan drummed his fingers restlessly against his desk. He felt frustrated and angry and wanted desperately to hit something or somebody, preferably the somebody who had driven their car into a little boy and left him for dead on the highway.

"Visibility was terrible last night," Sue reminded him. "I did check with the bus driver. He said he dropped the boys off and warned them to be careful, but he didn't see them cross the road."

"There must have been someone. Maybe a customer who left Ida's Ice Cream and drove recklessly away."

"We can go back, see if we can get names. It's a small community. Everyone knows everybody else. I think it's more likely that whoever did this left one of the bars down the road."

Alan nodded grimly. "I hate those fucking drunks. I'm going to find this bastard and nail his ass to the wall."

"I thought you'd say that. Want to pay a visit to the Acapulco Lounge?"

Alan smiled for the first time in the past twenty-four hours. "I like the way you think, Spence."

"We're partners. I'm with you all the way, buddy."

"Thanks. You know, Jenny . . ." He stopped, not sure what he wanted to say, except that he needed someone to talk to, and Spence was a woman after all.

"What about Jenny?"

"She's—Oh, hell, I don't know what she is. I don't know what she's supposed to be. Her heart is breaking. I want to tell her it will be all right, but she looks at me like she hates me." Alan picked up his pen and rolled it around with his fingers.

Sue put a hand on his shoulder. He shrugged it off, not wanting to show any sign of weakness. He was a tough cop, always had been, always would be.

"She's hurting, Alan. And she's angry. Maybe she had to take some of that anger out on you or she'd explode."

"I don't know," Alan said slowly. "Things haven't been good the last couple of weeks. I don't know what this accident will do to us."

"Maybe it will make your relationship stronger."

"Maybe it will break us up."

"Look on the bright side."

"Is there one?"

Sue shrugged apologetically. "Guess not."

Alan tossed his pen down on the desk. "Oh, hell, I can't do anything to help Danny right now, or Jenny for that matter, but I can find whoever did this and make them pay." He stood up. "First stop, the Acapulco Lounge."

Matt hung up his phone for the third time that day and stared at the family picture on the wall. It had been taken years ago when his mother was alive.

They were sitting in the family living room in front of the Christmas tree.

His mom and dad were on a piano bench. The kids were standing behind them. Everyone was smiling, except his father, who never found much in life to smile about.

Matt's gaze turned toward his mother. Katherine St. Claire—she reminded him of Jenny. The same impulsive smile, the same wild brown hair. Katherine had been the soft touch in the family, the one who kissed "owies" and tried to keep his father off his back.

When Katherine died, the family lost the glue that had held them together. Merrilee, who was twenty-two at the time, became an obsessive control freak, taking over Jenny and Matt as if they were preschoolers instead of teenagers.

He hadn't paid her much attention at the time. He had been eighteen and playing his first year at Stanford on a football scholarship. He'd been cocky, arrogant, full of himself. Without his mother to remind him that humbleness was a virtue, he had become a complete asshole.

Jenny had been fifteen, a sophomore in high school, and the most vulnerable of all of them. He looked at her face in the photo and smiled with genuine tenderness. Jen-Jen looked like a young filly, skinny legs, long arms, and hair blowing loose around her face. In the photo she was only a year or two older than Danny was now, and the similarity between them was striking and heartbreaking.

Danny shared the same joy of life as his mother, the same relentless optimism, which is probably why he had been so determined to find his father, confident there could be a happy ending.

God! Matt closed his eyes in despair. Bile rose in his throat. He was suddenly terribly afraid of the future, of losing the one person in the family who still looked up to him. Danny, his best buddy, his pal.

Matt wanted to go to the hospital. Merrilee had called him every hour on the hour all day long. He hadn't answered the phone, because he didn't know what to say, how to explain. And he couldn't face her complaints or her insults. He didn't have the strength or the right answers.

First, he had to find his car—his goddamned car. Where the hell was it? He had tried Brenda, but all he got was her machine. Kenny was fishing and wouldn't be back till late, and Jody said she had gone straight home after the Acapulco Lounge.

Matt picked up the phone again and dialed the bar. Maybe Barry could reassure him with the news that his car was still safely parked in the lot.

A busy tone buzzed in his ear.

Damn.

Matt didn't want to wait. Not one more second. The Acapulco Lounge was only a mile or so away. He'd take his bike, find his car, throw the bike in the back and go to the hospital with a clean conscience.

Merrilee looked down at her watch as Richard stepped off the hospital elevator. He had been gone all day. No calls. Nothing. Just like always. Why was she surprised? He had been that way for months.

"Merrilee." Richard leaned down to kiss her on the cheek. She turned her head away, giving him her profile.

"It's almost six," she said.

"We had a long lunch." Richard sat down on the couch next to her and tugged at his tie. He looked tired, older than his forty-three years. "Any change?"

Merrilee shrugged. "Danny moved a few fingers. Jenny was practically delirious with joy, but the doctor said it was just a reflex. He's in a coma."

"I can't believe this is happening."

"Jenny won't leave his bedside. Matt hasn't shown up, and my father refuses to come down here." Her voice caught and for the first time in a long time, her iron control slipped away. "I feel so alone. I don't know what to do—what to say. Every word that comes out of my mouth seems to be wrong."

Richard put an arm around her and pulled her against his chest. He hadn't held her so close in ages. Merrilee closed her eyes and breathed in the scent of him. But the flowery smell disturbed her—another woman's perfume.

She pushed the thought out of her mind. He had been with clients; one had probably been a woman.

"It's okay, Merrilee," Richard said. "You're trying to help. That's all you can do."

At least, he had admitted she was trying. God, she didn't think anyone had noticed. Her eyes filled with tears. She never cried, never. Blinking them away, she lifted her head. "Can I borrow your handkerchief?"

Without waiting for him to answer, she reached into the inside pocket of his jacket and pulled out the square piece of white linen. Something fell out along with it, something gold and round with a diamond in the center.

His wedding ring, the ring she had slipped onto his finger seventeen years ago.

It landed on the carpet. Richard reached for it at the same time she did. Her hand closed around it first. She opened her palm in front of his disturbed gaze.

"Why aren't you wearing your ring?" she asked.

"I—I've gained a few pounds. It was getting tight."

"Liar." She said the word out loud, shocking herself as much as him.

"What?"

"You've lost weight if anything."

"What are you accusing me of?" Richard asked. He didn't look scared or embarrassed or caught red-handed. It was almost as if he wanted her to say it out loud, wanted to end the farce between them.

Merrilee couldn't say the words. She couldn't risk losing everything.

"Nothing. I'm not accusing you of anything. Maybe we should have this enlarged." Merrilee handed him back the ring. "I want you to be able to wear it for the rest of your life. You want that, too, don't you?"

"Of course," Richard muttered as he slid the ring back on his finger without any trouble at all.

The parking lot of the Acapulco Lounge was empty. The Saturday night crowd had not yet arrived. Matt parked his ten-speed bike along the side wall. He scanned the parking lot for his car. It wasn't there.

He walked toward the front door, then hesitated. A police car was parked diagonally across two spaces. It had to be a coincidence, probably some drunk stirring up trouble. Nothing more. He certainly didn't have anything to worry about.

Still, Matt had been wary of cops for the past two years. He'd done his share of speeding and driving under the influence. He hadn't been caught yet, but he had come close. When he was sober, he knew he was flirting with disaster, but danger had always been a part of his life.

Football was danger—violence, thrills, excitement. He missed the game as deeply as if someone had cut off his right arm, his golden arm. He had been so damn good. Better than the shit that was playing in the NFL now.

It wasn't fair that five years ago Bernie Steinman, a defensive lineman, had ruined everything with one tackle. Matt's leg had broken in three places. He could still hear the pops, one-two-three.

The pain came back into his leg, and it was so sharp, he stopped. It wasn't really there, of course. His leg had long since healed. But his heart was still broken, and his mind still blurred by the sudden ending of everything he had ever wanted.

He was nothing without football. Except when he drank. Then he felt better. He could forget the pain for a while, pretend he was at a party, pretend the babes were still hot for him. There were a few, of course, wanting to get a vicarious thrill by laying a famous ex-quarterback. Even those had started to fade away, looking for the next hot jock.

The only one who really gave a damn about him was Jen-Jen. Which reminded him of why he was standing in the parking lot, too afraid to go inside.

Deep down, he didn't believe that he could have driven a car into his nephew and fled. Still, he couldn't remember one thing about the night, and his car was nowhere to be found.

Squaring his shoulders, Matt pushed open the door and walked into the lounge.

There were two cops standing at the bar, talking to Joseph, one of the waiters. The first, a woman he didn't recognize. The second was Alan Brady, his sister's boyfriend. Shit.

Matt wanted to turn and run, get the hell out of the bar, but Alan saw him, and he couldn't move.

"Matt," Alan said in surprise, "where the hell have you been? I've left a dozen messages for you."

"I know. I just got them."

"Have you been to the hospital? Have you seen Jenny?"

Matt knew he would look like an ass if he admitted that he hadn't been anywhere except this low-dive bar. But he couldn't think of another thing to say. Not even the lies came easily these days.

"Not yet," he mumbled.

Alan narrowed his gaze. "Why not?"

His voice was deceptively quiet, but Matt stiffened. He and Alan had never gotten to be friends, because Alan thought he was a worthless piece of shit, and Matt didn't feel like hanging out with one of the long arms of the law. "I'm not good at hospitals. I'd just bring her down."

"She couldn't get any lower. She needs you, Matt. Merrilee is driving her crazy."

"That doesn't surprise me."

"Can I get you a drink?" Joseph asked.

"A beer, thanks."

"A beer?" Alan questioned. "You're going to sit in here and get drunk while your nephew is in the hospital?"

"Alan, careful," the female cop admonished.

Alan glared at Matt. "You're a bastard."

Matt shrugged, hiding the pain that Alan's words created. He was a bastard. Only he wasn't sure how much of a bastard he was. If he had driven his car into Danny, how could he ever live with himself?

"How can you be such an asshole?" Alan persisted as he took a step forward.

Alan was bigger than he was, and Matt instinctively backed up, but Alan's hand came around his arm in a steel grip. "I want you to go outside, get in your car, and go to the hospital now."

"I can't."

"You can and you will." Alan strong-armed him, pulling him forcefully across the room and out into the parking lot. "Where's your car?" he demanded.

"I rode my bike," Matt said, avoiding Alan's gaze. Shit, he was in trouble now.

"Your bike? What happened to your car?"

"Nothing. I felt like some exercise."

"Really. Really?" Alan pushed Matt up against the wall of the building.

"Hey, watch it, you're hurting me."

"Not as much as I'd like to. Now, let me ask you another question. Were you drinking in this bar last night?"

"What's it to you?"

"The waiter said there was a pretty good crowd here when he arrived around eight."

"So?"

"Where the hell is your car, Matt? You better tell me right now that it doesn't have a broken headlight or I'm going to beat the living crap out of you."

11

J ENNY LEANED HER HEAD BACK AGAINST THE CHAIR and shut out the sight of Danny's hospital room. She had to rest, if only for a moment. The weariness was too much.

As she let herself drift into sleep, the dream came again. Jenny saw herself and Luke in her bright red Volkswagen convertible driving along the Pacific Coast Highway. The scenery was spectacular—dark jagged cliffs that dropped a few feet off the side of the road into the swirling, white-topped waves of the Pacific Ocean. The radio was playing Elton John's "Crocodile Rock," and she was singing off-key with the chorus.

Luke had his hand along the back of her seat. His fingers rubbed against her shoulder, bare in the warm, midday sun. She felt alive, young, and in love, strong enough to conquer the world. Her foot came down heavy on the gas pedal. The car sped forward. Her brown hair fell loose from a ponytail ribbon that flew into the wind. She laughed. So did Luke.

He looked at her and smiled, white teeth against a tanned face. Luke lifted his sunglasses, and the blue of his eyes took her breath away. Her hand clenched on the wheel and the

car swung to the right. Luke grabbed the side of the door
and she straightened the car in apology.

"Slow down," he said. "You're going too fast."

"If we go fast enough, we might be able to fly." She
laughed at his horrified expression. "Don't worry, I'm not
that crazy." Jenny slowed the car down and pulled off to
the side at a vista point. She got out of the car and walked
over to the railing so she could look at the sea.

Luke followed her. He put his arms around her waist and
pulled her back against his body.

"Isn't this wonderful?" Jenny asked, twisting in his
arms to face him. "You, me, this fabulous day, this glorious
summer. We don't need anything else. We've got it all."

Luke looked down at her. "You make me want to believe
that."

"Then believe it."

Jenny kissed him on the cheek, drawing her lips along
his jawline until she caught the corner of his mouth. He
sucked in his breath. She loved the sound of his breathing.
It was often the only sign she had that he was vulnerable
to her, not in control as he pretended to be.

Luke turned his mouth fully into hers. He deepened the
kiss, pushing past her lips, into the warmth of her mouth.
His tongue danced with hers. His hands slipped under her
sweater, caressing her curves as if she were a delicate piece
of china.

Luke was so much more sophisticated than the boys she
had dated. In fact, he wasn't a boy. He was a man. And he
made her feel like a woman.

Despite their outward differences, they were completely
in tune with each other. She covered her loneliness with
boisterous laughter. Luke covered his loneliness with arrogant silence. Together, they chased the loneliness away,
found love and joy in each other's arms.

When Luke lifted his head, his breathing was ragged. His
pulse beat rapidly in the corner of his throat. But that was
Luke, always in a hurry, with places to go, people to see,
things to accomplish. Jenny liked speed, but only for the

joy of going fast, not the purpose of getting to the next step in her life.

"I'd like to make love to you right here," Luke whispered.

She ran her hand along the back of his neck, sliding her fingers into his hair. "Why don't we?"

"Are you nuts? We're on the side of a highway."

"Once you start kissing me, I don't think I'll notice."

He grinned. "You're probably right about that." His smile faded. "We're all wrong for each other, Jenny."

"Not in the ways that count the most."

"I'm leaving at the end of the summer."

"We have another month."

"I'll be busy with medical school."

"You'll still have time to think about me, to write a letter once in a while, to pick up the phone."

"I'm not sure I will."

Her heart grew heavy at his words. "Don't be silly, Luke, you'll make time. I love you. You love me."

She waited, wanting him to assure her that he did love her, but he never said the words, he just nodded. Someday, he would say them. She would make sure of that.

"We have to go. My parents are taking me out to dinner tonight," Luke said.

"I wish I could meet them."

Luke stiffened and looked past her. "I'm sure you will. Someday."

"Why not tonight?"

"We're dining with old friends—boring old friends. You'd have a terrible time."

"I could never have a terrible time with you."

She lowered her arms to his waist and rested her head on his chest, reveling in the sound of his heartbeat. She loved his body, the power of his muscles, the gentleness of his hands, the way he moved against her, inside her. He was her first and only lover. She couldn't imagine being with anyone else.

"I've never met anyone like you," Luke said quietly. "I don't think I ever will again."

"Good."

"You make me think I can do anything."

"You can do anything." She looked into his eyes. *"I believe in you."*

He looked at her searchingly. *"Why?"*

"Because you're smart, and because you care. Sometimes you try to hide it, but I know that deep down you aren't as closed off as you'd like to be."

"Not with you. But you're the only one. I've never had close friends, Jen. Never. Something about you makes me want to spill my guts."

"Then spill 'em. Don't you get it, Sheridan?" She punched him playfully.

"Get what?"

"I'll love you no matter what. You don't have to be rich or important or anything else. In fact, I almost wish you weren't any of those things."

"I am, Jenny. I can't stop being me."

"I don't think you've started being you—at least not yet. It's almost as if you're afraid to let the real Luke out. I don't understand why."

Luke cut her off with a kiss, and she let him get away with it, because it was tender and passionate, as warm and lovely as the day surrounding them. She skipped out of his embrace and threw her arms out to the sea. *"I will never ever forget this day—or last night,"* she said, turning back to him.

His eyes reflected the memory of their night together, the passion, the love. *"Neither will I."*

"Take off your shirt," she said.

Luke's mouth dropped open. *"What?"*

"We have to throw something into the sea, to seal our promise not to forget."

"My shirt? You want to throw my shirt into the water? This is a Polo shirt, Jenny. It cost a fair amount of money."

"Oh, pooh." She pulled at the edges of his shirt as Luke reluctantly took it off.

"Okay, I've done it. Now you take off your shirt," he said with a wicked grin.

Jenny laughed. "Not on your life."

"Why not? You're the one who likes to live dangerously."

Jenny looked at the road. It was empty for an early morning weekday. "Oh, what the hell." She pulled her shirt over her head and stood there in her black lace bra.

Luke immediately stepped behind her. "I can't believe you actually did that."

"You told me to."

"I was kidding."

"Too late. Come on." She took his hand and walked to the edge. "Let's do it together."

She held her shirt in one hand and Luke's in the other. They looked out at the sea for a long moment.

"Hurry up. I'm freezing," he said.

"Okay. To us, Luke and Jenny, now and forever."

They tossed their shirts over the cliff, watching as the pink and white floated together, entwined as they themselves were. The clothing drifted into the sea, like a ghostly vision, swallowed by the waves.

Luke pulled Jenny into his arms, and wound his hands through her hair, passionately, desperately, as if he were afraid to let her go. He said her name over and over again.

His voice got louder and louder. Jenny blinked her eyes open and lifted her head. The ocean was gone. The convertible was gone. The cliffs in front of her were replaced by the white sheet of a hospital bed, and she was no longer eighteen and in love.

The voice came again. She straightened in the chair next to Danny's bed and turned her head toward the door.

Luke. He was standing at the end of the bed. He wasn't looking at her, but at Danny—his son.

She had imagined the moment a thousand times, but never like this—never like this.

His blue eyes filled with pain. His face tightened until his jaw stood out in stark relief.

"My God, he's real. He's real," Luke said in wonder.

She stood up. "Luke—"

He held up a hand. "Let me look at him, please. I just want to look at him."

Jenny swallowed hard, taking a step back so Luke could move closer to the bed.

It was disturbing to see Luke now, and difficult to deny him anything. The vivid dream had taken her back to a time when she had loved this man more than life itself. Now and forever, she had promised.

The now, of course, had vanished. Forever had been a pipe dream. Which left only the present to contend with.

"He's so still," Luke muttered.

"He's in a coma. I'm sure you already know that. You're a doctor after all."

Luke wasn't looking at Danny like a doctor. He was looking at him like a father.

When Luke touched Danny's shoulder with gentle tenderness, Jenny wanted to burst into tears. For years, she had dreamed of telling Luke he had a son, of seeing them together. But she had always been afraid.

In the beginning she had been hurt and angry. Then Luke had married Denise, and she had known it was too late. He had his life, and she had hers. Luke didn't want children, or at least not her child. He had made that abundantly clear.

But Jenny had never completely let go of the thought of Luke and Danny having a relationship— being father and son. Maybe that's why she had wavered when Danny started pressing her to see Luke. Part of her was afraid that Luke would try to take Danny away, and part of her was afraid he wouldn't care at all.

Now, Luke was here. Danny would be so happy— if only he knew. A tear escaped her eye and drifted down her cheek. Danny had wanted to see his father so badly. And now it was too late. He couldn't open his eyes. He couldn't ask Luke the questions that were burning a hole in his heart.

"Oh, Danny," she whispered. "Wake up, baby. He's here."

She looked over at Luke, not sure what to say or do next. The air between them came alive. Every sound in the room got louder, including the beat of her heart.

Luke slowly and illogically opened his arms. Slowly and irrationally, she walked into his embrace.

Jenny leaned her head against his chest and closed her eyes. She had come home.

Luke rested his chin on the top of her head. His arms locked around her waist. She didn't speak. Neither did he.

The minutes passed. There was so much to be said, yet neither one was inclined to speak. Finally, Jenny stepped back. Luke shoved his hands into his pockets. Jenny crossed her arms in front of her chest. She reminded herself that this man was not the same man to whom she had pledged her undying love. He had changed, gone on to medical school, a career, and another woman. She was different, too, older, not as carefree, not as trusting or naive.

"How long are you going to pretend I'm not Danny's father?" Luke asked.

She glanced over at Danny to see if he showed any sign of recognition. He didn't move, not even at the sound of his father's voice. Still, she didn't want to take the chance that Danny could hear their conversation. "I won't talk to you about this in here, Luke."

"Then come with me."

"I want to be here when Danny wakes up."

"Five minutes in the hallway. The nurse can call you if he opens his eyes."

"I don't have anything to say to you."

"Don't you? Come on, Jenny. Talk to me. I'm not going away no matter how much you want me to."

Jenny debated her options. Luke was as stubborn as a bulldog. When he wanted something, he went after it until he got it. "Fine. Five minutes." She spoke to the nurse. "I'll be back."

The hallway outside of ICU was empty. Jenny glanced down at her watch. It was ten o'clock at night. Visiting hours were over except for those with relatives who were critically ill. She walked down the corridor, avoiding the waiting room. At the end of the hall was a window seat that overlooked the hospital parking lot. It wasn't much of a view, but it reminded her that there was another world outside the hospital.

Luke leaned against the wall. Now that he had her alone, he seemed in no hurry to speak.

"Can we get this over with?" Jenny asked. She didn't want to deal with Luke right now. She wanted to stay focused on Danny.

"What's he like?" Luke asked unexpectedly.

"Danny?"

"Yes."

"Why do you want to know?"

"Just tell me."

"Well, he's a great kid. Wild sense of humor, mischievous, reckless sometimes." Jenny smiled fondly. "He's smart as a whip, gets good grades even though it is definitely not cool to do so. So far his greatest passion is baseball, but I don't think girls are too far behind."

"You're close—the two of you?"

"Very. More than just mother and son. In some ways, we've grown up together."

"You were awfully young to have a child, weren't you?"

"When God hands you a gift, you don't send it back."

Luke looked directly into her eyes. "You didn't get an abortion."

"No," she whispered, unable to turn away from him. His reaction was a mixed bag, confusion, anger, frustration, and what looked like joy. But it didn't last long.

When he spoke his voice was filled with anger. "You should have told me," he said. "Dammit, you should have told me. All these years, I never knew I had a son. You had no right to keep that from me."

Jenny stared at him in amazement, furious that he could be angry with her.

"Where the hell do you get off? You didn't want a kid. You wanted to be a rich and famous doctor like your parents."

"I was twenty-two years old. I was a kid myself."

"And that excuses your behavior?"

"Didn't it ever occur to you in the last thirteen years that I might have changed, that I might want to know that I have a son?"

"Don't you dare try to turn this around. You threw me away like yesterday's newspaper. You abandoned me. I didn't fit into your life, and how damned in-convenient of me—of *me*," she emphasized, "to get pregnant, as if you barely participated in the act."

"Jen—"

"Now, *now* you're saying that I should care that you might have had second thoughts? Go to hell."

"I did have second thoughts," he shouted back, dropping his voice as a nurse walked down the hall-way and put a finger to her lips.

Jenny hardened her heart. "Tough."

"That's it? That's all you can say to me?"

"What do you want me to say? That I'm thrilled you've come back into Danny's life? Well, I'm not. You don't belong here. You don't belong with me. You told me that years ago, and you were right. I don't fit into your world and you don't fit into mine."

"We have a child together, Jenny. Now that I know about Danny, I want to be a part of his life."

"That's too bad. Because you're not going to be a part of his life."

"Danny came to see me yesterday. He obviously doesn't feel the same way you do. I'm not leaving. I want to be here when Danny wakes up. I think that's the way he wants it, too."

Jenny shook her head in frustration. "How would you know what he wants?"

"Think what you will, Jenny, but I'm staying with you."

"You're going to stay here twenty-four hours a day—with me?" She got up and walked over to him, poking her finger into the middle of his chest to emphasize each word. "You're going to take time out of your business, your life, to wait for a little boy whom you've never met to wake up?"

"That's right."

"Funny. I thought I was the illogical one."

"You are."

"Oh yeah? Then tell me, Luke, just what the hell are you going to say to your arrogant, overachieving parents and your fancy wife when they want you to lunch at the country club? That you have to stay at the hospital, because you just discovered that you and your impossibly unsuitable girlfriend—I believe those were your mother's words—made a child together, and that that child is now in critical condition? They'll be thrilled."

"They'll understand," Luke said slowly.

"Will they? Will they really, Luke? Now who's living in a dreamworld?"

12

S UNDAY MORNING CAME TOO QUICKLY AS FAR AS
Luke was concerned. He had spent a long night
debating how to tell Denise about his son. It
was now almost eleven o'clock in the morning, and
he was still stalling. He didn't usually avoid chal-
lenges, but this situation went beyond anything he
had ever dealt with. He had the feeling that telling
Denise about Danny would change his marriage forever.

Putting down his sixth cup of coffee, Luke walked
through the kitchen, the family room, and out onto
the backyard deck that overlooked the pool. It was a
gloriously green backyard, colorful with landscaping.
It was a grown-up backyard.

Luke couldn't imagine Danny in this yard, at least
not the kid that he saw in his mind, the one in the
backward baseball cap, baggy jeans, and sweatshirt.
That kid probably needed a basketball hoop at the
very least.

Maybe he would put one up today, in the driveway
over the garage. Luke smiled at the thought. He had
wanted a basketball hoop when he was a kid, had in

fact asked for one every Christmas for three straight years, until he had finally realized that his father didn't think much of sports or his desire to be an athlete. Books, college, and medicine had been his father's focus and in turn *his* focus.

He'd forgotten about basketball until now—until Danny. The thought of having a son filled Luke with intense pleasure. He wanted Danny to know him, and he, in turn, wanted to know Danny. For that they would need time.

Danny simply had to get better. Then they would have a chance to be father and son—if Jenny allowed it.

The rational part of Luke understood that he had hurt her, that she had retaliated by keeping Danny to herself. The irrational part of him was furious that she had never given him a chance to know his son, that now it might be too late to have the kind of relationship that both he and Danny deserved to have.

Jenny should have told him. Maybe not right away, but sometime during the past twelve years she should have come forward. They could have worked things out. They could have shared custody.

"Luke, L-u-k-e."

Luke turned toward the house as his wife walked out on the deck. She wore beige slacks, a forest green blouse, and a dark brown belt that emphasized her tiny waist and large breasts. She didn't look like a woman he could ask to hold a ladder while he put a basketball hoop up over the garage.

Denise kissed him on the mouth. Her lips lingered. Her fingernails grazed the back of his neck. She made it clear she wanted to prolong the kiss. He thought it might be a good idea. Maybe then, he could put Jenny out of his mind, remind himself that he was married.

But Denise's mouth didn't feel right. It didn't taste like honey and saltwater. Good Lord! How could he be remembering a kiss that happened thirteen years earlier when he had made love to Denise hundreds of times in their marriage? It was *her* scent that should be clinging to his mind, not Jenny's.

Luke lifted his head and took a deep breath. Denise gave him a quizzical look. "You're still angry?"

He shook his head.

"You got out of bed so early this morning. Maybe you should think about taking a nap—with me."

Luke stepped back and leaned against the rail. "Why do I get the feeling that sleep is not what you have in mind?"

"We haven't been together in a while. You've been so busy."

She moved closer to him, playing with the collar of his shirt. Her fingernails were stark red, flamboyant, arrogant. Jenny's nails had been clear. Damn her. Why did she have to stick in his head?

"We have to talk, Denise."

Her lips turned into a pout. "I don't want to talk. And I don't want to argue." She stood on tiptoe and ran her tongue around the edge of his earlobe.

His body tightened at the motion. With a sudden decision, he put his arms around her and turned her face into his. He plunged his tongue into her mouth, frantic to find the passion that they had once had. He ran his hands down her arms, across her full breasts.

When he tugged at her belt buckle, Denise drew back. "Not here. In the bedroom," she murmured.

"Here, now." He kissed her again.

"Luke, please."

"We're alone for God's sake. Not even the housekeeper is here."

"We're outside. I don't like it outside."

Luke sighed, feeling the air go out of his body along with the tiny bit of desire he had drummed up.

Denise took his hand and tried to pull him into the house. He resisted. The impulse to make love to her had completely vanished.

Denise put her hands on her hips and looked at him with annoyance. "What on earth is wrong?"

"Nothing."

"Then why are you acting so crazy?"

"Me?" he asked in amazement. "You just ruined a perfectly beautiful moment."

"You think I'm going to roll around on this deck with you? For heaven's sake. Aren't we a little more civilized than that?"

"You're right, we are too civilized for that. At least you are."

Denise threw up her hands. "I don't understand you anymore, Luke. Every day you draw further away from me. Tell me why. What have I done?"

His eyes narrowed in response.

"Besides that." She changed the subject. "Where did you go yesterday? You were gone for hours."

Luke hesitated. Here was his chance to tell her. What could he say? That his long, lost son had come home? Well, not exactly home, and not exactly to him. But that didn't matter. Denise wouldn't welcome the thought of him having a child. She would be horrified.

"Luke, talk to me," she said. "Don't shut me out. I deserve better than that."

"I don't know how to tell you this."

Her face whitened, and she tried to joke away her anxiety. "You sound so solemn. You're scaring me."

"I don't mean to, but this is difficult."

"Just say the words."

Luke took a deep breath. "A long time ago, before I went to medical school, before I met you, I was involved with a woman."

Denise put her hands over her ears.

"Denise, please. You asked."

"I know what you're going to say. It was that kid who came to our door."

"I think he may be my son."

"No," she cried. "No."

Luke grabbed her hands and pulled them away from her ears. "You have to listen to this."

"I don't want to."

"Danny, that's his name, was hurt in an automobile accident, Friday night. He's in critical condition. Yesterday, I went to the hospital to see him."

"Oh God." Denise sat down on a deck chair, visibly trembling. "Is he going to live?"

"They don't know. He's still unconscious."

"I see." She looked up at him. "And his mother—the woman you were involved with—did you see her, too?"

Luke nodded, his throat tight. "Yes. At first she told me that I wasn't the father, but as soon as I saw him, I knew the truth."

"Yes." She let out a breath. "I knew that, too, even before he said anything."

"Before?" Luke sat down across from her. "What did he say to you?"

"Just that he was your kid, and he wanted to see you."

"Why did you shut the door in his face?"

"Because, dammit, we were having a party."

His jaw dropped. "What the hell does that have to do with it?"

"We'd just had a fight about children. I didn't want to believe your son was standing on the doorstep. I wanted him to go away, and he did."

"Yes, he did. And on the way home he got hit by a car. If you'd only let him in . . ." Luke ran a hand through his hair. "Why did you lie to me?" He laughed bitterly. "Because you always lie to me," he said, answering his own question.

"You're not blaming me for his accident?" Denise asked, straightening with anger. "I didn't do anything. He took me by surprise. How was I supposed to react?"

"Maybe with a little humanity, kindness."

"Is that what *she's* like, humane, kind, everything I'm not?" Her voice turned brittle. "Goodness, why on earth did you ever leave her?"

"Because I was going to medical school. My parents couldn't stand her. She didn't fit in."

A gleam of relief entered Denise's eyes. "Your parents didn't like her?"

"No. No woman measured up until you came along."

"For you, too, I hope?"

"I married you, didn't I?"

"Yes, you did do that." A silence fell between them. "What are you going to do?" Denise asked. "Did you tell Charles and Beverly before they left?"

"No. I wanted to tell you first."

"I see."

"Would you stop saying that?"

"I don't know what to say."

Luke stood up. "I'm going to the hospital."

"Can I come with you?"

"No." The word burst out of him before he could even think of accounting for Denise's feelings.

"Why not?" she asked, obviously wounded by his harshness.

"Danny is in intensive care. He's critical. Jenny and her family are distraught. They're already upset that I'm there."

"They didn't welcome you with open arms?"

"Why would they? I told Jenny to get an abortion."

Her eyes widened. "So I was right. You didn't want children."

"Not when I was twenty-two."

"Not when you were twenty-six either."

"I'm thirty-five now, Denise. People change. I've changed, can't you see that?"

She put her arms around his neck. "What I see is the man I married, the man I love and adore. I won't lose you, Luke. We'll get through this. We'll work it out. Maybe Danny can—uh, visit us once in a while. You can get your fatherly fix."

Luke's temper flared at her choice of words. "I don't want to be a part-time father. I want to be full-time. I want to know this kid. I want him to be a part of my life."

"Don't you mean *our* life?"

"Can you accept him, Denise?"

"Another woman's child as your son?" She shook her head in bewilderment. "It won't be easy, but I would try—for your sake."

He softened at her tone. Maybe he was being too hard on her. "I'm sorry."

"I'm sorry, too. Are you sure I can't talk you into coming in the bedroom with me? Making up is the best part of a fight." Her eyes promised him everything he could possibly want. The only problem was, he didn't want anything from her.

"I have to see Danny again."

"Just as long as it's him, and not *her*, that you want to see."

Luke walked into the kitchen, pretending he hadn't heard her final shot. Because he sure as hell couldn't deny the fact that he wanted to see Jenny again. God help him. God help them all.

"Hey, Dad, psst."

Luke looked over at the door that opened onto the driveway. It was halfway open, a pair of grimy fingers curled around the side. A tennis shoe stuck out between the door and the wall. Anticipation took Luke to the door. The hand and shoe disappeared.

Luke walked out to the driveway and stopped in amazement. Danny was shooting baskets through a hoop that appeared to be attached over the garage.

"Two points," Danny said as the ball bounced off

the backboard and through the hoop. "Your turn, Dad." He tossed Luke the ball.

Luke didn't expect to feel anything, certainly not a full-sized basketball hitting him in the stomach. Danny couldn't be real. The basket couldn't be real, and the ball definitely did not exist. So why did his gut sting? Why did the ball bounce off his foot and into the bushes?

Danny ran over to get it. "Try again, Dad. Let me see your stuff."

"You're not real, Danny."

"I know that. Come on, shoot."

Luke took the basketball from Danny and rolled it between his hands, trying to get the right feel for the ball. "I haven't done this in a long time," he said.

"Give it your best shot."

Luke tossed the ball toward the basket. It fell short. He was almost afraid to look at Danny, to see his failure reflected in his son's eyes. How many times had he looked into his own father's eyes and seen condemnation, disgust? So many times.

"Not bad. You're probably a little rusty, that's all." Danny took the rebound and stuffed it. "Let's play some ball."

There was no disgust in Danny's eyes, just curiosity, openness. At that moment, he looked a lot like Jenny. "I'm not much of an athlete, Danny. I never had a chance to play. My parents . . ." Luke shook his head. "They didn't care much for sports. In fact, I always wanted a hoop out here."

Luke walked over to the garage and stood under the net, trying to figure out how it was attached to the wall. There didn't appear to be any screws, no obvious sign of attachment.

"One on one," Danny said. "First to ten wins. I'll go first."

Luke smiled, enjoying the encounter for whatever it was. "How come you get to go first?"

"Because I'm a kid." Danny's mouth curved into a grin.

"I should go first, because I'm the oldest."

"You are old," Danny said thoughtfully.

"Hey, I didn't say old, I said oldest."

Danny dribbled the ball around Luke and took his first shot. A swish. "Yes." He pumped his fist. "One to nothing." He passed the ball to Luke.

Luke sank a shot from the corner, feeling a rush of adrenaline. "One-one."

"Not bad, Dad. But I'm pretty good."

"Cocky, too. You must get that from me."

Danny charged. Luke tried to block. The boy hit another basket. The game began in earnest, two competitors sizing each other up, building respect for each other, understanding, friendship. They did it without words, but they both understood there was more at stake than just a game.

Thirty minutes later, Luke put his hands on his knees and tried to catch his breath. He could feel sweat running down the backs of his legs, underneath his cotton twill slacks.

"I win," Danny said. He put the ball on the ground and sat on it, studying Luke for a long, disturbing moment. "That was cool. I wasn't sure you'd play with me."

"Why not?"

"Mom always said you were a busy man, probably too busy to have a kid."

"I'll always have time for you, Danny. I want to make it up to you, everything we've missed doing together."

"You're all right, Dad."

"So are you. Danny—"

"Dad—"

They both spoke at the same time. Luke waved his hand. "You first."

"I'm glad I met you—no matter what happens."

Luke felt a sudden tingle of fear creep along his spine as Danny's image began to fade. "Don't go."

"Jacob's back," Danny said.

"Who's Jacob?"

"My guardian angel."

Guardian angel? Luke shook his head. He was losing his mind, talking to a kid who didn't exist about angels, who also didn't exist.

"You've got to believe in me, Dad," Danny said, his words mirroring Luke's thoughts. "I think it's important. Really important."

"What do you mean?"

"I can't explain. It's just something you gotta do."

"Don't go. We have so much to talk about."

"Jacob's pulling my ear again. Ow, stop that," Danny growled.

"Come back. Okay, Danny?" Luke pleaded.

"I'll try. Jacob says you need work on your hook shot. Here, keep this." Danny tossed him the ball.

Luke stared at the ball, completely bemused. When he looked up, Danny was gone.

Denise came out of the house and stopped when she saw him. "What are you doing? My God, you're sweating." She wrinkled her nose in distaste. "What did you do—go for a run in your dress shoes?"

"I was playing basketball."

Denise looked at him in amazement. "Basketball? Where?"

"Here." But as Luke looked up, the net over the garage disappeared, and he was left holding the ball, literally. "I'm thinking about putting a hoop over the garage."

"Why?"

"So Danny and I can play when he gets better."

Her lips tightened at the sound of Danny's name. "I don't want a hoop over the garage. It's unsightly. What has gotten into you? You're not the man I married. I don't know who you are. But I'd like to know what you've done with my husband."

Luke smiled and tossed her the ball. "I've sent him out to play. Your shot."

Denise threw the basketball over the fence. "Game's over, Luke. I win."

Matt rode his bike along the walkway to Jenny's small house and leaned it against the porch railing. He walked up the steps to the front door. Jenny's car was in the driveway, but that didn't mean anything. Her car was broken down more often than it was working.

He rang the doorbell three times. She didn't answer. The house was quiet, absolutely and utterly quiet. Matt sighed and walked to the edge of the porch, looking down the street.

One of Jenny's neighbors was mowing his lawn three doors down. A couple of kids were riding skateboards off the curb, and a dog was barking at something or somebody—a perfectly normal Sunday afternoon. Matt sat down on the steps and rested his head in his hands.

He felt sober, depressingly sober. Everything was clear, and the clarity was blinding. He was a drunk, a goddamned drunk, who couldn't remember what had happened during twenty-four hours in his life, the same twenty-four hours in which some "drunk" had run over his nephew.

The thought that he could have done such a thing to Danny was destroying him, slowly, tortuously. Every time he closed his eyes, he saw Danny's freckled face. Every time he wanted to smile, he remembered Danny's crooked grin, his laugh that was always a little too loud and a little too long. Danny, his adoring nephew, the one who still watched videotapes of Matt playing in the NFL, the one who still thought he was pretty cool.

"I'm sorry, pal," Matt whispered. "I'm sorry you're hurt. God, I'd do anything if I could stop you from being hurt."

But there was nothing he could do. Nothing except find his goddamn car and reassure himself that someone else had hit Danny, not him. That wouldn't change things for Danny, but at least he could go to the hospital with a clear conscience.

His buddy Kenny had been unable to provide any answers, saying he had seen Matt heading for his car, but had gone on home and didn't see him again that night. Kenny suggested he call Brenda. Unfortunately, Brenda wasn't home. Matt had gone by her house, but his car was not parked in front. He had come up empty again.

"Yoo hoo. Yoo hoo." Gracie Patterson, the elderly woman from next door, called out to him.

Matt looked up and smiled. Gracie had a soft spot in her heart for him. She was one of the few people, besides Danny, who thought he had something to offer the world. Matt got to his feet and walked over to the chain-link fence that separated the two properties.

"Hi, Gracie. How are you today?"

"Just terrible, Matthew. I heard about poor Jenny and poor, poor Danny. My heart is breaking."

Matt felt the lump in his throat return. "Yeah. I know." He dug the toe of his tennis shoe into the dirt at his feet.

"I keep seeing Danny in my head. He was just a year old when Jenny moved into that house. I've spent so much time with him, babysitting and all. I feel like he's one of my own. Just the other day he came by to show me one of those cars that races all over the place. He was so happy, so silly, you know, just like a boy should be." Gracie cleared her throat as she tried not to cry and held out a casserole dish in her hands. "Anyway, I made some lasagne for

Jenny. She won't be feeling like cooking any time soon."

Matt took the dish out of her hands. "Thanks, I know she'll appreciate this."

"And how are you? You don't look too good," she said with a gentle but sharp voice.

"I'm not doing too good."

"Can I help?"

"Do you know where my car is?"

"Goodness me, no." Gracie put a hand to her head as if confused by his question. "Have you lost it?"

"It looks that way. I better go look for it. Thanks for the chow, Gracie."

"Tell Jenny and David that I'm thinking about them."

"You mean Danny?"

"Oh, goodness me, yes. Danny, of course. Now, I must go. My sister is coming for dinner, and I have dozens of things to do. She was supposed to come Friday night. In fact, I bought all that food for her, and she didn't come. I just don't understand how people can be so rude—especially family folk. Now you tell Jenny that I'll come and see her as soon as I can." She waved a thin, dark-veined hand in Matt's direction and bustled back toward the house.

Family folk, Matt thought with irony. He was one hell of a lousy family member. But then, his family hadn't been much of a family since his mom died. Maybe that was his fault.

It was time. Time to go to the hospital. Time to see Jenny. Time to face his fate.

13

"I 'M BEGINNING TO THINK YOU LOOK WORSE than Danny," Alan said as he walked into intensive care and took Jenny into his arms. As he held her small frame, Alan felt an overwhelming sense of protectiveness toward her. He wanted to wipe away her worries. He wanted to make things right for her. But along with the desire to help came the sense of inevitable futility. There was nothing he could do to get Danny well, and that's all Jenny wanted.

Jenny leaned against him for the briefest of moments, then pulled away. He noticed how stiff her posture was, as if she were afraid to let herself relax for even a second. The teary-eyed woman from the night before had been replaced by a proud warrior, a mother determined to fight for her son.

"Danny moved his foot—just a teeny bit, when they poked him," Jenny said. "The nurse said it could be just a reflex action. I think it's something more. I think he's waking up."

"I hope so, Jenny." Alan squeezed her shoulder. "How about taking a break? I'll give you a ride home.

You can shower, change your clothes, take a nap, get some food."

She looked up at him in horror. "No, I'm not leaving, not until he wakes up. It might be any minute now."

Alan turned her to face him, his hands on her shoulders. "Jenny, I spoke to the nurse. She told me Danny could be like this for—for a long time, days, maybe a week."

"He moved his foot. Dammit, he moved his foot. Don't you understand?"

"I do understand. It's a good sign. But it may still be a while." His voice softened. "I'm worried about you. When Danny wakes up, he will need you to be strong and healthy. You can't go without sleep and food indefinitely. You've been here for hours."

Jenny suddenly felt too weak to argue. In truth, she was exhausted. Her body was beyond hungry, beyond craving food. It just wanted peace, oblivion. She moved into Alan's arms and rested her head against his chest. "You're right. I need to lie down. I can't go all the way home, though. It's too far. It would take me twenty minutes or more to get back."

"I'll take you to Merrilee's. It's ten minutes away."

"Merrilee? That doesn't sound very restful."

"It's close."

"I guess so." Jenny lifted her head. "Have you spoken to Matt? I really want to talk to him."

Alan's face turned grim at her question, and Jenny looked at him inquiringly. "You spoke to him?"

"I saw him."

"Where? Is he in the waiting room? Downstairs?"

"No. He's at the Acapulco Lounge."

Jenny looked at him in confusion. "He didn't know?"

"He knew." Alan shrugged. "I think he's afraid to come down here."

"Why?"

"Because he's a bastard."

"Don't say that. Matt is my brother. He's been there for me in the past. If he's not here, he must have a good reason."

"You make excuses for everybody."

"No, just Danny and Matt. I love them."

"Sometimes love is blind."

"What does that mean?"

"Nothing. I don't want to fight with you. I care about Danny, too." Alan tipped his head to one side. "Your brother, he's a different story. Right now, the person I'm most concerned about is you."

"I appreciate that, Alan. I just wish you could see that Matt has a good side. The last five years have been difficult for him. Can't you cut him some slack?"

Alan ignored her comment. "Are you ready to go?"

Jenny sighed. "In a minute." She turned toward the bed and picked up Danny's hand. She wished his fingers would curl around hers, but they remained limp. During the past forty-eight hours, Jenny had been struck by the feeling that Danny was already gone, that he wasn't in this body that rested so still on the hospital bed. Yet, his heart was still beating.

"I'm going away for a little while," she said to Danny. "I'll be back before you know it. Rest and get better. Dream happy thoughts. I love you so much, honey. I can't lose you. I can't let you go, not even to God or to heaven or to all the angels in the world. You're my baby. You tell them you're not ready, that you have to stay here—with your mom."

Jenny squeezed Danny's hand and closed her eyes. After a moment, she felt an answering twitch. She opened her eyes and looked down at their entwined hands. It happened again, small, insignificant, barely a whisper of a touch as his first finger tapped against hers.

"Oh, God. Did you see that, Alan? Did you see that? He squeezed my hand."

Alan stared at her without saying a word.

"I felt it. He heard me. I know he heard me."

"I'm sure he did."

"Don't patronize me. You don't believe me, do you?"

"I was watching you, Jenny, watching your hands. I didn't see anything."

"I felt it," she protested. "It happened. How can I leave now?"

"Jenny, don't do this to yourself. You have to leave sometime."

"Why? Why?"

"Because you can't go on living without sleep and food and water. Besides, you told Danny you were leaving. Maybe what you felt was him saying it was okay—to go."

"You don't even believe his fingers moved."

"Jenny, please."

She cast one last, lingering look at her son. There was no further sign of movement. "All right." She leaned over and kissed Danny on the cheek. "I'll be back soon, buddy. You get better for Mom. Hear me?"

Danny wiped his eyes with the sleeve of his sweatshirt as he watched his mother leave his hospital room. He didn't want to look at the boy in the bed. It scared him. The boy didn't seem real, even though he knew it was him.

He turned to Jacob with fierce anger. "I want to go back."

"You can't."

"So I *am* dead?"

"No."

"Then what are you saying?"

"I'm saying that you and your mother and father still have things to learn from all this."

"Like what?"

"You'll know when you learn it," Jacob said stubbornly. "And so will they."

"I've already learned the most important thing," Danny replied. "That I want to live, that I want to be with my mom and my dad."

"They're not together—Danny. Your mother is thinking about marrying Alan. And your father is already married."

"But they belong together. They still love each other, I know they do. My mom saved everything from when they were together—photographs, a love letter, even a stupid curl of his hair."

"We know she used to love him; that's why she saved those things. But I'm not sure about now."

"Why don't we ask her?" Danny put his hand on Jacob's arm. "Can I talk to her, the way I talk to my dad? There are so many things I want to tell her. I was mean to her on Friday, and I feel so bad. Please, please, let me talk to her. I think she'd feel so much better if she could see me."

Jacob shook his head. "I told you. It ain't allowed. Your parents need to learn different things. Your father must learn to have faith in things that he can't touch or feel, and your mother has to develop strength and courage to fight for what she wants."

Danny put his hands on his hips and shook his head. "I want to talk to someone else."

Jacob laughed. "You want to go over my head, kid? Nobody goes over my head."

"Oh, yeah. Well, I want a different angel then, someone younger, prettier, nicer."

"Lesson number one, Danny boy. You can't have everything you want."

"Now you sound like my mother."

"Who do you think taught her? Patience, kid. Everything in good time." Jacob unfolded his legs from a strange yoga position he had put himself into at the end of Danny's bed. "Let's go into the hallway.

I have a feeling the show's about to start."

"Why?"

"Because Alan and Jenny are about to come face-to-face with your father."

Luke tapped his foot impatiently as the elevator stopped on yet another floor. At this rate, it would be evening before he saw Jenny again. The elevator began its ascent and thankfully bypassed the next floor to stop at his destination. Finally.

He got off and turned toward ICU, only to come face-to-face with Jenny and a man, a big, strong man who had a possessive arm around Jenny's shoulders.

Luke felt an incredible surge of anger at the simple gesture, at the sight of his woman in another man's arms. Good grief. Was he crazy? Jenny wasn't his woman, hadn't been in over a decade. Still, it bothered him, more than he cared to admit, even to himself.

Jenny stopped when she saw him. The guy looked at him suspiciously. Luke felt as if they were two gunslingers facing off on Main Street at high noon.

"Luke," she murmured.

The man's grip tightened on Jenny's shoulders.

"I want to see Danny," Luke said.

"Who the hell are you?" the man demanded, stepping in front of Jenny.

"Who's asking?" Luke countered.

"I'm Jenny's fiancé, Alan Brady."

"I'm Luke Sheridan, Danny's father."

The world stopped. At least that's the way it felt to Jenny. The two men went as still as statues. Animosity electrified the air.

"You bastard," Alan said with deceptive quiet. "You're responsible for this."

"I'm going to see Danny."

Luke turned to Jenny.

Alan turned to Jenny.

Jenny wanted to run and hide. Better yet, she wanted to wake up from this horrible nightmare that was becoming her reality. She could tell Luke no, but he wouldn't listen. She could say yes, and Alan would be furious. Either way she would lose, and she was just too damn weary to think of another alternative. She swayed on her feet.

Alan, who was standing barely a foot from her, didn't register the movement, but Luke did. He was at her side, his hands strong on her waist as she started to crumple.

What a coward I am, she thought as she was going down. Fainting like some spoiled, pampered woman instead of acting like the tough, single mother she was.

Luke pulled her over to one of the chairs in the corridor. Alan pushed Luke's hands away and put his arm around her. Jenny suddenly felt like a wishbone.

"I can't do this," she muttered. "I'm too tired."

"Come on, Jenny. Let me take you to Merrilee's house where you can rest," Alan said.

Jenny looked up at Luke. "I don't want you to go in there without me."

"Why not?"

"If Danny should wake up—when he wakes up, I don't want him to be confronted by you, unless we're both there together. It would be confusing."

"He doesn't need to be in there at all," Alan declared, facing Luke. "You gave up your rights before this kid was born. Jenny told me what happened. What in the hell right do you have to come here now and intrude into this family?"

"I'm Danny's father. I'd say that gives me more rights than you."

Alan stood up. Luke stood up. Jenny sighed. Her moment as damsel in distress was over. She got to her feet. "I'm going to my sister's house to rest for a few hours. I will be back here by five, Luke. I'd appreciate it if you would wait until then before you see Danny."

Luke stared at her for a long moment. Finally, he nodded. "All right. I'll do as you wish."

"Thank you." She slipped her arm through Alan's. "Let's go."

Danny looked over at Jacob. "My dad doesn't like Alan either."

"The cop's a good dude."

"He's a dweeb. I drive him crazy."

Jacob laughed. "On purpose, kid."

Danny grinned. "Yeah, maybe. He's no good for my mom. She doesn't smile when she's with him. And Alan hates the beach. Can you imagine living in Half Moon Bay and hating the beach? I bet my dad likes the beach."

"Your dad spends all his time at work making money."

"And making drugs to help people," Danny said defensively.

"You like him, don't you?"

"I—I want to," Danny said slowly. "I'm not sure yet. I mean I can't forget that he lives in that huge house that's five times the size of my mom's house. She's had to do everything all these years, because he didn't want me."

"But you still think you might want him as a dad?"

"He is my dad. And he did come to the hospital. Now that he knows about me, he wants to be with me. That should count for something."

"Okay, we'll give him a chance then."

"What does that mean?"

"It means I'm tired of this hospital. Let's have some fun."

Danny's eyes widened. "Fun? Like what?"

"Ever wondered what it feels like to fly like a bird?"

"No."

"Then it's about time you did."

Danny felt himself being lifted. Jacob pulled back the ceiling like it was a skylight, and suddenly they were surrounded by nothing but blue. Danny held on to Jacob's arms as they started to fly.

"This is actually cool," he shouted with some amazement. "Can I do it by myself?"

"Give it a try."

Danny let go of Jacob's arms and started to free-fall. He flapped his arms in wild abandon, feeling like a cross between a bird and a very heavy elephant. "I can't do it," he said in panic.

"Just believe in yourself, Danny boy."

"Okay," Danny said doubtfully. "I'll try. I can do it. I can do it."

He flapped his arms, kicked his feet, and repeated the words over and over again, feeling more like the "little engine that could" than an angel.

Finally, Danny started to take control of his actions. In fact, when he slowed the movement of his arms, he could actually feel the air around him. As his anxiety eased, everything became clearer. He felt like a bird, wild and free.

After a few moments, he began to try out new things, flying low and kicking at the branches on the tallest tips of the trees, disturbing a bird's nest, scattering a group of sparrows with a shrill whistle.

Jacob vanished from view, and Danny felt suddenly alone and afraid—again. What was he doing? Would this be his world forever—caught in a place between life and death with only Jacob to talk to?

Danny missed his mother, missed Christopher, missed Uncle Matt, and even his nerdy cousins, William and Constance, although Constance was a definite pain, and Aunt Merrilee was right up there with the Wicked Witch of the East. Uncle Richard wasn't bad, not around much though. Danny barely knew his grandfather. John St. Claire didn't have time for them, and when he did speak, it was usually to criticize.

Still and all, they were his family, and it was sad to think that he might never see them again, might never feel his mother's arms around his body, smell her perfume, laugh at her stupid lullabyes.

Actually, he didn't mind hearing her sing. He just couldn't tell her that, because it was definitely not cool.

Danny's heart felt heavy. It might be too late to tell his mother anything ever again. Had he told her he loved her before he left for school on Friday? No, he had been mad because she didn't want him to see Luke. He had just walked out on her. If only he could go back and tell her he loved her. If only he could turn back time and do Friday completely differently.

Suddenly, Danny looked up and the ground was inches away. He landed with a thump in a rosebush, his legs tangled in the vines. Even though his skin didn't show a scratch, he felt a tingling of pain where the thorns touched his flesh. He looked up and saw Jacob sitting in a swing that was attached to nothing, going up and down and all the way around, laughing like a boy instead of the old, ornery man that he was.

"You started thinking about your mom, didn't you?" Jacob slid off the swing and walked over to Danny.

"I can't help it. I miss her."

"I know, kid."

"Don't you miss your mother?"

"She's dead, too."

Danny looked at him with curiosity. "Can you be with her—up here or wherever it is that we are? Since you're both dead?"

"Not yet. But someday, I think. There are a few things I have to do first."

"Like what?"

Jacob tugged Danny's cap down tighter on his head. "Like set you on the right path."

"What does that mean?"

"That means, kid, that I have to help you learn a few things during the time we have together. I have to sort of prove myself to the Big Guy upstairs. See, I haven't always been the perfect angel . . ."

Danny snorted. "I can believe that."

"Hey, I taught you how to fly, didn't I?"

"Yeah. But next time you better teach me how to land." Danny untangled himself from the bush. For the first time he looked around him. "Look, we're at my Aunt Merrilee's house."

Jacob grinned at him over his shoulder. "Imagine that."

"And there's my mom and Alan," Danny said, pointing to the Ford truck pulling up in the driveway.

The truck stopped and Jenny got out. She stood for a moment, shielding her eyes against the midday sun. Alan came around to her side and took her hand. Then, the front door flew open, and Merrilee rushed out.

"Oh, thank goodness," Merrilee said.

"Why? Has something happened? Did the hospital call?" Jenny asked in panic.

"No, no, I'm just relieved that you decided to finally get some rest."

"Oh." Jenny let out her breath.

"Are you hungry? I made some fresh pasta and a salad."

"Oh, Merrilee, I wish you hadn't gone to the trouble."

"No trouble at all," Merrilee said firmly. "Good nourishment will get you through this."

As they walked up the path to the house, Merrilee stopped abruptly. She looked at the rosebush in front of her living room window. "What on earth happened to my roses? They're—" She took a step closer. "Why, they're completely smashed, as if someone sat in them."

"Oops," Danny muttered, looking over at Jacob. "Guess I did that."

"I may have to replant," Merrilee added.

Alan cleared his throat. "Merrilee, uh, do you think you could worry about your roses later?"

"I'm sorry. Let's go in the house."

Jenny didn't move. She stared at the rosebush for a long moment. "It's odd," she murmured, putting a hand over her heart. "I feel strange."

"Do you think she can see me?" Danny asked.

Jacob shook his head. "No, but she might sense that you're here, if you're as close as you say you are."

"We've always been close. Two peas in a pod, my mom always said."

"Danny," Jenny said.

"What's wrong?" Alan asked in concern.

She pointed at the bush. "That looks like something Danny would do. I almost feel like he's here—right now."

"Of course, you do," Merrilee said, patting her arm reassuringly. "He's on your mind."

"Remember last Easter, when Danny kicked the soccer ball through your window?"

"How could I forget?" Merrilee muttered. "I love your kid, but he's accident-prone."

"I am not accident-prone," Danny said, making a face at Merrilee.

"Ooh, watch out, here comes your mom."

Jacob pulled Danny off to one side as Jenny walked over to the bush and picked off a perfect red rose. Lifting it to her nose, she inhaled the scent then looked around the yard. "I feel as if Danny's going to pop out from behind a bush any minute."

"Can I?" Danny asked.

Jacob shook his head. "Not on your life."

"Jenny, let's go in the house," Merrilee urged.

Alan sent her a strange look. "Are you all right? You look funny."

Jenny smiled. "Actually, I feel better now. In fact, I think I could even eat something."

Jacob turned to Danny. "Do you want to go inside?"

Danny didn't answer. He was already disappearing through the wall into the living room. Being invisible was beginning to have its moments.

14

MERRILEE'S LIVING ROOM WAS COMPLETELY white—carpet, sofa, drapes, and paint. The only color was the stark black grand piano in the corner. It was a stupid room, Danny thought, looking around in disgust. Certainly not a place where a kid could hang out and play video games. He wondered how his cousins could stand living in a house that was always clean.

Jacob picked up an antique vase on the coffee table and twirled it around.

"Hey, be careful," Danny said. "That's probably a hundred years old and worth a million bucks."

"It's a vase," Jacob said, tossing it in the air and deftly catching it with one hand. "You stick flowers in it."

Danny ran over and grabbed it out of his hand. Jacob laughingly pulled it away. It slipped between both their hands and crashed to the floor.

"Oops," Jacob said.

"Oh, no!" Danny cried, looking at the broken vase on the floor. He knelt down in dismay, then glanced up at Jacob. "How could you do that?"

"You grabbed it out of my hand."

"Are you sure you're an angel?" Danny demanded. "You don't act like an angel."

Jacob drew himself up in height, stretching his body into such thinness that his head touched the ceiling. "And just what do I act like?"

"A jerk."

"You could get into trouble for that, kid."

"Yeah, right. What are you going to do? Kill me?"

Jacob laughed in a long guffaw. "Good one, Danny boy."

"Come on, help me clean this up," Danny said.

"I can put it back together. I do have some power."

Danny raised an eyebrow. "Really? Cool. Let's see it."

Before Jacob could move, Merrilee rushed into the living room with Jenny close behind her.

"I thought I heard a crash," Merrilee said. "Oh, my." Her hands flew to her cheeks. "My vase, it's broken."

"How did that happen? No one was in here," Alan said.

Jenny stared at the broken vase. "Danny," she murmured. "This is too weird."

"Constance, William," Merrilee yelled. "Come down here this instant.

Danny watched as his cousins came into the room, Constance moved slowly, with definite annoyance on her face. William bounded in with bright eyes and a cheerful smile.

"Yes, Mother," he said.

Danny rolled his eyes. "Geek."

"Did you break my vase?"

"No, Mother. I'm not allowed to play in the living room."

"I know the rule," Merrilee said crossly, turning to her daughter. "Constance?"

"I was on the phone. Can I go to the mall?"

"What? No." Merrilee shook her head. "I want you here."

"Mother. You wouldn't let me go out last night, and you won't let me go out today. Why are you holding me prisoner?"

"I want you to be here in case we all need to go to the hospital or something," Merrilee said.

Constance sighed. "Can I go now?"

"No, you can't. Someone in this house broke my vase."

"Maybe it was sitting close to the edge and just tipped off," Alan suggested.

Merrilee immediately shook her head, disregarding his comment completely. "I want the culprit to confess right this instant."

No one answered. Finally Jenny spoke. "Danny did it."

All eyes turned to her in surprise.

"I don't know how, but he did it. I can feel it. I can feel him in this room, right now."

"You mean like Danny's a ghost or something?" Constance asked, with new life in her voice. "Awesome."

"Jenny, you're not thinking clearly. You're distraught," Merrilee said. "Danny is in the hospital. He's not here."

"Look, this isn't getting us anywhere. I brought Jenny here to rest. Maybe I should take her to a hotel," Alan said.

"Don't be ridiculous. Let's go back to the kitchen. Jenny can eat, then lie down in the guest room."

Merrilee led the way out of the living room, followed by her children and Alan. Jenny was the last to move. She paused in the doorway between the living room and dining room, glancing back one last time.

"Danny," she murmured.

"Can I let her see me, please?" Danny asked.

Jacob shook his head, his expression suddenly serious. "I'm sorry, kid. Not yet."

"I love you, Danny," Jenny whispered. "Wherever you are." She walked back to the kitchen.

"I want to talk to her, Jacob. Tell me when I can."

"Maybe soon."

"Maybe soon or maybe never?" Danny's voice trembled. "I'm going to die, aren't I? Aren't I? When is it going to happen? Today, tomorrow? Next week?"

"You haven't learned anything yet, have you?"

"What am I supposed to learn?" Danny shouted in frustration. "Tell me, and I'll learn it."

"That's the problem. I can't tell you."

"Then tell me this—who gets to decide if I live or if I die? Do you?"

"No, not me."

"Then God. I want to see Him."

"This isn't Mars, Danny. You can't demand that I take you to my leader. You know, you've had things pretty much your own way all your life. Your mom didn't have much money, but she scraped to get by, to give you those shoes you wanted that were what— ninety dollars?"

"Seventy-two," Danny said grumpily.

"And what about that trip to the mountains with Christopher's family over—Thanksgiving, no less? Do you know what your mom did that holiday?"

"Yeah, she spent it with my Aunt Merrilee."

"No, she served drinks at the Acapulco Lounge every night till two A.M. to prevent the check she wrote for your skis from bouncing. She didn't get one bite of turkey. And what about that window you broke last Halloween and blamed on Christopher?"

"All right, I get the picture." Danny frowned at Jacob. "So I'm being punished?"

"No. But you have to admit you've been pretty selfish."

"If I promise to be a better kid, do I get to live?"

"If it were that easy, there'd be very few of us in heaven. You can't bargain for your life, Danny."

"You know something, I don't like you very much," Danny said, crossing his arms in front of him. "And I'm not sure I even believe there is a God. No one answers my questions."

"But sometimes your prayers are answered. Do you remember the prayer you said on the bus trip to your father's house?"

Danny thought back. "I don't know. I probably said I wanted to meet my dad."

"Have you met him?"

"Sort of."

"Do you think you would have met him if you hadn't had this accident?"

"You mean I brought it on myself?"

Jacob didn't answer him. "What do you want more than anything else in this world, Danny?"

"I want to live."

"And?"

"I want my parents to get back together."

"What if you had to choose, Danny, between living and your parents getting back together? What would you choose?"

"I can't choose. I want them both. Are you saying I have to make a choice?"

Choices. Stay here or go home to his wife. Not much of a choice. Richard set his glass of Chardonnay down on the kitchen counter and picked up a piece of cold, soggy pizza. The spicy pepperoni was the only good thing about it. But he was hungry, and it was food, nothing like the dinner Merrilee probably had waiting at home for him. Thank God! He'd come to associate her dinners with migraine headaches.

Everything was too perfect—the china, the glassware, the presentation of food, even the conversation. The kids suffered in silence while Merrilee pretended they were as happy as a sitcom family on television.

Come to think of it, not even a sitcom family was as "happy" as they were.

Enough was enough. For seventeen years, he had tried to make it work. Merrilee didn't help. She refused to admit they had problems, so how the hell could they solve them? Now, he just wanted out. Out of the marriage, out of the pressure of being the perfect husband to go with his perfect wife.

He was forty-three years old, for God's sake, and he had been in marriage hell for most of that time. The first year, before Merrilee's mother died, had been good. She had been a sweet young girl who adored him. Then she had taken over raising her brother and sister, not to mention her own kids. The sweet girl had vanished. Merrilee had become a demanding control freak.

Everything was a responsibility to her, even making love. No spontaneity. No humor. It had gotten so bad, Richard was afraid to make a move for fear he was going out of order. First he had to touch her breasts, five minutes or more, then use his mouth, then work his hands between her thighs. It had become a fucking bore—literally.

Richard smiled, not only at his thoughts, but at the pair of hands sliding under his shirt from behind, wrapping around his waist, teasingly threatening to open the snap on his pants. He grew hard at the motion.

Richard closed his eyes, and for a moment, he pretended the woman was Merrilee, that she was his fantasy lover, not his rigid, demanding wife. His pants slid down over his hips. He could feel her body moving around his, her breath against his bare stomach, her tongue against his navel, sliding lower and lower.

He groaned as she moved her mouth over him. It was exquisite, excruciating pleasure. He began to move restlessly, pumping his hips, letting himself come, screaming out her name—Merrilee.

The silence afterward was deafening. He looked down. She looked up.

"I'm sorry."

"So am I."

Merrilee opened the door Sunday evening to find her father on the step. John St. Claire looked every bit of his sixty-seven years. His hair was a coarse gray, his skin pale, his eyes wrinkled, not from laughing, but from frowning at a world that never quite measured up to his standards.

John had spent twenty-seven years driving a truck for the Peninsula Newspaper Agency. He was a Teamster, a union man, and a hard man. Never missed work, never let himself be sick, and never forgave anybody for anything. He had been forced to retire two years earlier, and since then his mood had gotten worse. He didn't seem to know how to talk to any of them anymore.

"Dad," she said faintly, "what a pleasant surprise."

"Where's that foolish sister of yours?"

Jenny. It always came down to Jenny. Merrilee couldn't remember a time when she had come first in her father's thoughts. And she had tried so hard, especially after her mother died.

Her father brushed past her without waiting for an answer. He bypassed the living room and headed for the kitchen, helping himself to a beer in the refrigerator. John knew the beer was there, because Merrilee kept a supply just for him. Not even Richard was allowed to touch her father's beer.

"Would you like a mug?" she asked.

He shook his head and popped the top. "She still at the hospital?"

"Yes. She practically lives there."

"And the boy?"

"Danny is the same, critical," Merrilee replied, deliberately using his name.

"What the hell was Jenny thinking—letting her son take a bus over the hill?"

"Danny went without her permission."

"Of course, because she's too damn lenient."

"Yes, she is," Merrilee agreed. "Are you going to see her?"

"Hate hospitals. Always have." John took a long draft of his beer. "Haven't been in one since ... well, since you know."

Since Mom died. "I know," Merrilee replied. "But I think Jenny would like to see you." Actually Jenny would probably rather have a root canal than see her father, but it was the right thing to say at this moment, and Merrilee prided herself on saying the right thing.

Her father tipped his head, considering. "Maybe tomorrow."

"Dad." Merrilee wanted to tell him he had to reconsider, that he owed it to Jenny to support her. She was his daughter, dammit. But when John looked at her through hard, unforgiving eyes she knew her pleas would only alienate him, not bring about a change. "Would you like to stay for dinner?" she asked.

"What are you having?"

Merrilee silently counted to ten. "Ham, green beans, and au gratin potatoes."

"I suppose. Where's your husband?"

"He had to go into the office for a while."

John looked at the clock over her head. "It's seven o'clock on a Sunday night."

"He's very dedicated."

"You're lucky you found such a good man," John said. "Richard will always take care of you. You'll never end up like your sister, all alone and trying to raise a kid without a father."

"You're right about that," Merrilee said tightly. "Speaking of children, William is upstairs working on the computer. Why don't you go up and say hello?"

John nodded and shuffled off. John liked William, thought he was a good kid, mainly because William was too scared of his grandfather to argue with him. Constance and Danny were another story.

Danny. Merrilee sighed as she wiped off the kitchen counter. She supposed she should go to the hospital after dinner, at least try and talk Jenny into spending the night at her house. It was her duty as the older sister to take care of things.

The front door opened and closed. Her emotions went from relieved to angry in thirty seconds, the time it took Richard to walk to the kitchen.

When he arrived, she had her head in the refrigerator. She heard him reach for a glass and run water out of the tap. He didn't say anything. Neither did she.

Finally, she straightened up and shut the door. "Are you hungry?" she asked.

Richard shook his head. "No, I ate earlier."

"I see. My father's upstairs."

"Oh, great." Richard sat down at the kitchen table and picked up the newspaper.

"He's worried about Danny."

"I think you're giving him too much credit." Richard looked at her. "Why do you expect so much from people? Why can't you just let them be who they are—whether it's good or bad?"

Merrilee stared into his eyes, knowing that he was asking her something far more serious than his words implied. But she didn't want to read into his statement, get into a discussion of anything remotely connected to their marriage. Whatever was going on with Richard would pass—if she left it alone, if she stuck by him, the way a wife should.

"I'll get dinner on the table. The kids are probably

starving," she muttered, setting to work.

"How's Danny, any change?"

"The same. I thought you might have gone to the hospital."

"I ran out of time. I'll go by tomorrow before work."

"I'm sure Jenny would appreciate that."

Richard leafed through the newspaper while Merrilee set dinner on the table. It should have been a cozy, companionable time. They should have been talking to each other, but there were so many subjects Merrilee didn't want to discuss that it was difficult to think of anything to say. Finally, Constance danced into the room, headphones on her head and the sound of rap music spilling out of her Walkman.

"Who's the man ... I say who's the man ..." she rapped out. Her eyes lit up as she saw her father at the table. "Daddy." She ran over and gave him a big hug.

Merrilee felt a sharp pain cut across her stomach. It hurt to see Constance so enthralled with her father when the man barely made an appearance in his daughter's life. She, on the other hand, did everything for Constance and got nothing but negative comments and nasty looks in return.

"Hi, doll face," Richard said, affectionately running a hand through her hair. "How are you?"

"Fine. Can I go to Cindy's? We need to finish a project for school tomorrow."

"It's okay by me."

Merrilee stiffened. "Absolutely not, Constance. You haven't had dinner and tomorrow is a schoolday. You still need a shower and—"

"Mother, I am not seven years old. I can figure out when I need to take a shower."

"You're still not going. I would think you'd feel guilty having a good time when your cousin is fighting for his life. You should have more respect."

"How can my staying home help Danny? Ever since he got hit by the car, you've been watching me like a hawk." Constance argued. "I need to finish my project. Daddy, please say I can go."

"Mm-mm," Richard muttered as he read the paper.

"Thanks." Constance tossed her mother a triumphant look and ran from the room.

"You better be going to Cindy's and not out with that boy," Merrilee shouted after her, but the only reply was the slamming of the front door. Merrilee turned to her husband in frustration. "Richard, what are you doing? You knew I didn't want Constance to go to Cindy's and you overruled me."

Richard looked up. "What's the big deal?"

"You're impossible. You're never here, and when you are here, you . . ." She searched for the appropriate word but was afraid to use it.

"I'm what?" Richard asked quietly. "Am I failing again in some new area that you've just discovered?"

"Forget it. I don't want to argue with you."

Richard slammed his fist down on the table. "Well, I want to argue with you, dammit."

"Richard, please, my father is upstairs. I don't want him to hear us fighting."

"Why not? Afraid he'll think you don't have a successful marriage?"

"I do have a good marriage. And a wonderful husband," she said, hoping to soothe his ego and protect herself from getting into an argument in front of her father.

Richard stood up and walked over to her. "I'm not perfect, Merrilee. Don't you think it's about time you admitted it—if not to me, then at least to yourself?"

"Richard, I love you," Merrilee said, reaching into her arsenal for some weapon of defense.

Richard hesitated. Merrilee stood on tiptoes and kissed him on the lips, the first time she had taken the initiative to touch him in a long time. She prolonged the kiss, running her hands up his chest and around his neck.

When she broke away, Richard looked at her with a glitter of desire in his eyes, so intense she dropped her gaze. It landed on a smear of red by Richard's collar. She pulled his coat away from the edge of his shirt. Lipstick. And not her color.

"Aren't you going to ask me how it got there, Merrilee? Don't you want to know?"

Every nerve ending in her body screamed no. She didn't want to know. She never wanted to know.

"It's time for dinner." She walked into the hall, hoping he wouldn't follow. He didn't. When she returned to the kitchen with her father and William, Richard was gone. She looked out the window just in time to see the taillights on his car disappear down the driveway.

15

"I 'M SORRY, JENNY," RICHARD SAID, TWENTY
minutes later as he enfolded his sister-in-
law in his arms. It was the third time that
day he'd held a woman close, and the first time it
actually felt good, not because he had any desire for
Jenny, but because he genuinely liked her. She was
one of the few people with whom he felt he could be
himself.

"Thanks for coming. You didn't bring Merrilee with
you?"

"I thought you could use a break from her."

"She tries."

Richard moved closer to the bed so he could see
Danny. The boy was lying on his back, the head of
the bed slightly raised. There were tubes coming out
of his nose and arm.

"He's not breathing on his own, is he?" he asked.

Jenny shook her head. "Not yet."

"Any word on who did this to him?"

"Alan is looking into it. Part of me doesn't care,
because it won't change anything. Another part of me
is filled with rage that someone could do this to a

child and walk away." She leaned over and ran her hand along Danny's cheek. "Hi, baby. Uncle Richard is here to see you."

"Yeah," Richard said gruffly, clearing his throat. "And Connie and William send you their love. They want you to get better soon—real soon." Richard looked over at Jenny. "Can he hear me?"

"I'd like to think he can. The doctor said I should talk to him as much as possible, try to stimulate him in some way to bring him out of this coma."

Richard nodded. "Are you okay? Do you need anything?"

"Just Danny."

"He'll make it. He's tough, a lot like his mother."

"Me?" Jenny uttered a shaky laugh. "Hardly."

"You just don't see yourself the way you really are."

"That's because I don't like to look too closely."

"I've been having that problem myself."

Jenny put a hand on his arm. "Let me walk you to the elevator."

The corridor was nearly empty. Visiting hours were ending. They paused by the elevator, but neither one pushed the button.

"Is everything okay with you and Merrilee?" Jenny asked.

Richard shook his head. "No."

"Does Merrilee know that?"

"She won't admit it."

"She loves you, Richard."

"I can think of a dozen reasons why she shouldn't." He punched the button for the elevator.

"Do you want her to catch you, Richard? Is that why you're making it so obvious?" Jenny asked.

He stiffened at her comment, caught off guard by the honesty of it. But then, Jenny had always been absolutely and utterly truthful. "Merrilee doesn't care enough to want to catch me."

"That isn't true. She does care. She just doesn't know how to show it."

"I hope she learns—before it's too late."

The elevator opened, and Richard stepped inside. Jenny held the door open with her hand. "Don't give up on her, Richard. Especially now, when we can see how fleeting life can be. Don't waste a second of it. Make it work."

"You can't make love work, Jenny. You can't fit a round screw into a square peg. I would think you, of all people, would know that."

She looked away. "If you're talking about Alan and me, I know we're different, but he's a good man, and Danny needs a father. Besides, I know that Alan will never hurt me."

Richard shook his head, hating to see her settle for less than she deserved. "He can't hurt you, because you don't love him enough."

"That's not true."

"I remember you and Luke. I remember that summer you were together. There was so much electricity between the two of you, I thought you'd set our house on fire. I've never seen you look at Alan the way you looked at Luke. Have you even slept with him yet?"

"Richard!" Jenny looked over her shoulder to make sure no one was listening to their conversation.

"We're both adults, Jenny. You used to have so much passion."

"Yes, and look where that got me. I'm not eighteen years old anymore. I don't look at any man the way I looked at Luke. But Luke is only around now because he found out about Danny. There's nothing between us, and there won't be ever again."

The elevator beeped in protest at being stalled too long.

"I never realized that you are just like Merrilee, not until this very moment," Richard said.

"What do you mean by that?"

"She only sees what she wants to see—and so do you."

The elevator doors closed, and Jenny was left staring at her own reflection. Richard's words ran through her mind, taunting her, tormenting her. Not that he was right. He was absolutely wrong. She would never be with Luke again. She would never open herself up to that kind of pain.

But what about Alan? Was she being fair to him?

They hadn't made love yet. They had come close a few times, but something had always held her back—a late night, an early morning work schedule, Danny . . .

It wasn't that she didn't desire Alan. She just didn't feel that desperate, reckless passion of her youth that had made her put sex above the mundane chores of life. Since Danny's birth, she could count on one hand the number of men she had made love with. She could barely remember their faces.

The elevator opened in front of her, empty and waiting. Subconsciously, she had pushed the button. Jenny looked back over her shoulder, down the hall toward Danny's room, then back at the elevator. She needed to take a break, and after a moment's thought she knew just where to go.

The babies were settling down for the night, tucked into their blankets so tightly they could barely move. Jenny leaned against the nursery window and looked at each and every one. The Jefferson baby was big and bald. The Lucchesi baby was skinny with a pink rash on his face. The Peschi baby sucked avidly on a pacifier, and the Sterling baby screamed continuously.

A nurse picked up the crying baby and pushed a bottle of sugar water into his mouth. The baby looked startled, then began to suck, his tiny hands flailing against the bottle, as if he wanted to pour it down his throat.

"Which one looks like Danny?"

Jenny didn't have to turn around to know that Luke was behind her. "None of them. That one eats like him though."

"I wish I could have seen him when he was a baby."

Jenny tensed. "You made your choice."

"How big was he?"

"Eight pounds, two ounces."

"Any hair?"

"Not a strand."

"I was bald, too."

"Danny looks like you. He always has." Jenny glanced at Luke. "It used to make me mad. I was the one who had him, who got up in the middle of the night and changed his diapers—but he had to look like you."

"What did you tell him about me?"

"The truth."

Luke nodded. "I should have figured. I don't think you ever lied to me. Although when you left, I really did think you'd get an abortion."

"I couldn't get rid of our baby." Jenny pressed her fingertips against the glass in front of her, feeling the same pain she had felt thirteen years earlier when she had first considered that option. "Whatever you felt for me—at that moment in time I loved you, and Danny was a part of that love—the best part." She changed the subject. "How did you know I was here?"

"When I was in medical school, I used to go to the nursery when things got intense. It helps to remember that good things can happen in hospitals as well as bad."

Luke leaned against the wall, his hands in the pockets of his casual slacks, the sleeves on his navy blue sweater pushed up to the elbows. He looked tired, as if he hadn't had a good night's sleep in two days. That thought made Jenny smile. He deserved a few lost nights of sleep. She had had too many to count.

"The last time I was here was when I had Danny," Jenny said. "I remember the long night when I tried desperately to breastfeed—the loneliness, the fear of not getting it right. Yet, it was a happy time. I was surrounded by joy. I wasn't even aware there was anything else going on in this hospital but babies being born." She paused. "I guess being in a hospital is like a second home to you."

"Actually, I haven't spent much time in hospitals since I got out of medical school. I've spent the last few years in a lab behind a microscope. Now, I find myself sitting in an executive office with a view of the bay."

"Just what you always wanted, and your parents, too. They must be proud of you." She paused, reminded again of how he had chosen his parents' dreams over hers. "I need to get back to Danny."

Jenny walked down the hall toward the elevator. Luke kept pace alongside her. Jenny was torn between wanting him to go and wanting him to stay. To have him back in her life after so many years took a little getting used to.

"We need to talk, Jenny," Luke said as they waited for the elevator.

"About what?"

"I spent a few hours on the phone today, speaking to other physicians about Danny. I'd like to fly in Dr. Paul Buckley from the Mayo Clinic. He's the top neurosurgeon in the country."

Jenny looked at him in surprise. "Why?"

"To get a second opinion."

"Do you know something I don't know, Luke?" She grabbed his arm. "That's it, isn't it? You're a doctor, and they told you that Danny is not—is not going to—" She stopped as Luke put a finger against her lips.

"Sh-sh," he whispered. "Don't say it."

"You have to tell me the truth."

"Danny's in a coma. That's the truth."

"People come out of comas."

"Of course they do. I just want to make sure Danny has the best care available."

"I want that, too."

"Then I'll call Buckley in the morning."

"That's going to cost money, Luke. I don't know what my insurance will cover."

"I'll pay."

"I don't want you to pay." She looked away from him. "I'll find a way to pay for it."

"Don't be stupid, Jenny."

She bristled with anger as she glared at him. "I'm not stupid. Danny is my son. My responsibility."

"Mine, too."

Jenny searched his face for answers to the sudden change in his personality. "Why now, Luke? Why do you care now? You don't know Danny at all."

"I want to know him. I'm older, Jenny. I'd like to think I'm a little wiser. I made a mistake. A big one. I shouldn't have told you to get an abortion. I was—"

"Scared," she finished. "I was scared, too. When I told my father, he kicked me out of the house. I had to live with Merrilee and Richard."

"I'm sorry."

"I was eighteen years old. I had a high school education, no job and no money."

"You had five hundred dollars."

She smiled bitterly. "I threw it in the ocean on my way home from your house. It was stupid and impractical, but it gave me enormous pleasure."

Luke sighed. "I can accept the fact that you hate me. Logically, I know I've given you good reason to feel the way you do."

"And you're always logical. That's what broke us up in the first place."

"You knew from the beginning I was leaving."

"I didn't know how much it would hurt."

"Neither did I."

She sniffed in disgust. "Oh, come on. You didn't look sad the day you left. You looked exuberant. You were starting an exciting adventure in your life, and you didn't want or need me in it. As it turns out, I had my own adventure. I had a child. I had Danny, and he means more to me than anything in this world."

They got on the elevator with two other people and were silent until they reached the next floor. As they stepped out, Luke turned to Jenny. "I'm going to get Buckley here tomorrow if I can. We'll bring in other specialists and run as many tests as necessary. Tomorrow I'll assign two of my researchers to go over the medical data available on head injuries and comas. I won't leave anything to chance. Lowenstein is a good doctor, one of the best, but he's not infallible."

Jenny stared at him as he continued to outline his plan of attack. He was taking control, steamrolling over her, the way he had always done. She wanted to fight back, but she couldn't do that. She had to swallow her pride—for Danny's sake.

"Lastly, I want to be able to visit Danny whenever I can," Luke finished.

Jenny shook her head. "No. You're going too fast for me." She started to walk away.

"Too fast?" Luke grabbed her by the shoulders and spun her around. "Too fast? The woman who drove eighty miles an hour down the hairpin curves of Highway 1 thinks I'm going too fast?"

"That was a lifetime ago. I'm a grown-up now, with responsibilities. This isn't just me we're talking about. It's Danny. My son."

"Our son." He paused. "You've had him all to yourself for twelve years. Okay, that's the way you thought I wanted it. That's over and done with. But today, right now, is what I'm concerned about. Please, give me this time to be with Danny. I need to be with my son.''

Jenny looked at Luke for a long moment, studying the sincerity in his eyes, the desperation in his voice, the longing. It was the last that did it for her. The fact that Luke didn't just want to see Danny, but that he needed to see him, reminded her of how much her son had needed to know his father.

"What about your wife?" she asked, trying to find a good reason why she should deny him access to Danny. "Your parents never liked me. They won't want Danny to be your son. They won't want him to be their grandson. Have you told them yet?"

"Not yet, but I will. Your family never liked me either, Jenny. This isn't about them. It's about us.''

"Us?" The word cut her so deeply, Jenny gasped from the pain. "Us? There is no us."

"There was and always will be an us, because we're tied together by our son. We made him together.''

"But I had him alone, Luke. And I've raised him alone. You gave up your rights a long time ago.''

"I could sue you for custody," Luke said abruptly. "I could force you to let me in there. I don't want to do that.''

"Why the hell not?" she asked, furious at his power play. "You've always taken what you wanted and left what you didn't. Not anymore. This time, I'm in charge. I decide. I make the plans.''

"You? Plan? You never planned beyond your next meal.''

"I was never sure I'd have enough money to pay for my next meal," she said, her voice rising with agitation.

"That's bullshit, Jenny. You always lived for the moment. It was who you were.''

"It's not who I am now. I'm not a foolish young girl, Luke. I'm a mother, and I'm in charge of Danny's care. I will take your advice because you're a doctor. I will listen to your suggestions, and dammit to hell, I will even take your money, because Danny means more to me than pride."

"And I can see him?" Luke persisted.

"Yes. Because Danny wanted to know you. That's why he went to see you. That's why he got hurt. He doesn't respond to my voice." Her tone trembled as the sadness ripped through her. "Maybe he'll respond to yours. Maybe the desire to talk to you will be so strong that it will pull him out of this place that he's gone to. But I call the shots, you got that?"

Luke nodded, feeling a sudden admiration for the woman before him. He had always been drawn to her laughter, her imagination, her joy, but he didn't remember her courage or her strength. Perhaps those qualities had developed later, born of maturity, born of Danny.

Jenny stopped at the double doors leading to ICU. "Are you coming?"

It was the same question she had asked him years ago. Then she had offered a simple swim in the moonlight, the beginning of their relationship. Tonight it was quite possibly the beginning of a relationship with his son.

"I'm coming," he said.

Alan pushed the button on the remote control, speeding through the Sunday night movies, the sports channel, and CNN. Nothing caught his attention. He kept thinking about Jenny. He had spent the afternoon with her and part of the evening, but to be honest he had gotten tired of the hospital, of her total absorption in her son, and her withdrawal from him.

The accident was driving them apart instead of bringing them together. He always seemed to say the wrong thing at the wrong time. But then, he hadn't had much experience with women. As the oldest of four boys, he had been surrounded by males, and his mother had been a tough, no-nonsense woman who didn't put much effort into nurturing. As far as she was concerned, just giving her boys life was enough.

He had been slow to start dating and his first sexual experiences had been a tangle of arms and legs, and girls who never wanted to see him again. Over the years, he had developed more finesse and confidence in himself, but he had never found the right woman, the perfect woman. Until Jenny.

Jenny was soft and loving, generous to a fault. With her he saw a future where there had been nothing before. The only problem was that Jenny's passion for life didn't seem to extend to him.

Six months, and they still hadn't made love. Jenny had told him from the beginning that she was cautious about relationships, that she had been hurt in the past, and with a child to worry about, she couldn't afford to jump into bed with the first man who came along. He had accepted her reasoning, had even been impressed by her restraint. After all, he was looking for a partner, not just a lay. But even his patience had a limit.

In the last few weeks, their evenings had had more silences than conversation, maybe because they were both feeling tense about the future of their relationship. Jenny had told him just last week that she wanted to make love with him, that she wanted things to work out, that he was a good man and that she cared for him—*but* . . . and that was the problem, there always seemed to be a reason why she wasn't ready.

He knew Danny wasn't helping. Despite Alan's efforts to be a substitute dad, he had never hit it off with Danny, which drove another wedge between him and Jenny.

Alan flipped through two more channels and mindlessly perused a soccer match, not realizing for a good five minutes that the announcer was speaking Spanish.

In disgust, he turned off the television and swung his legs off the couch. His apartment was small and cluttered. His dirty gym clothes lay in a heap by the front door. His gun lay on the dining room table along with three half-finished cartons of Chinese food.

What a dump, he thought. He had been living in northern California for three years and still hadn't hung a picture on the wall. In fact, he spent as little time as possible in his apartment. Most of his time was spent in his patrol car, at the station, or at Jenny's house.

Alan remembered the first time he had met Jenny. She had been working the cash register at McDougal's Market. Her smile had caught his eye. For six weeks, he had gone to her line, even though the others were shorter, because Jenny had a tendency to chat with anyone who came by.

Finally, he had asked her out for dinner. They had gone to dinner at Chuck's Steakhouse. He had blown a week's salary on a bottle of champagne, hoping to impress her. Of course, it hadn't taken him long to realize that Jenny didn't give a damn about expensive gestures.

Reaching over, he picked up the photograph on the coffee table—Jenny at the Pumpkin Festival. Danny had taken the picture, so he wasn't in it, but Alan remembered the day, wishing it could have been as nice as the picture. Danny had spoiled it, wanting Jenny's complete attention, refusing to pick out any pumpkin that Alan liked, and generally being obnoxious. Jenny had scolded him quietly, gently, but her words had had no effect.

The same softness that appealed to Alan also allowed Danny to manipulate his mother. If—when he and Jenny got married, he would lay down rules, restrictions. That is, if Danny pulled through. And if—

his gut tightened—if Luke Sheridan stayed the hell out of their lives.

Alan knew that Luke was the biggest threat to their relationship. Whatever problems he and Jenny had could be worked out. Danny would eventually see that Alan cared about him even if he was strict.

But none of that would happen if Jenny let her first love back into her life. Alan had seen the way she looked at Luke, the way Luke had looked at her. It was an image that haunted him, terrified him, because Jenny had never looked at him like that, with longing, desire.

He had tried to rationalize that her lack of interest in sex probably meant that she just wasn't a woman who really enjoyed sex. But one look between Luke and Jenny had sent that thought right out of his mind.

He knew she had been with Luke. After all, he was apparently Danny's father. The fact that Luke had slept with Jenny and Alan hadn't made him illogically angry. He wished he could make her his now, tonight, drive all thoughts of Luke Sheridan from her mind.

But Jenny was at the hospital, and he was alone.

Damn it all.

He was getting old, almost forty. He was going to be alone for the rest of his life if he didn't find the right mate soon. He had invested six months in dating Jenny, going slow at her request. He'd be damned if Luke Sheridan could waltz back into her life and steal her away. Alan Brady protected what was his, and Jenny was his.

A knock came at the door, and Alan instinctively tensed. It was almost ten. Maybe it was Jenny. When he opened the door, Sue was standing on the doorstep, her expression grim.

"What's wrong?" he asked.

"I went down to the Acapulco Lounge again. I wanted to talk to the bartender who was working Friday night."

Alan pulled her into the apartment and shut the door behind her. "And?"

"He said Matt St. Claire was drinking heavily that night. He left a few minutes before the accident with a group of people. They were heading down Tully Road, the same road on which Danny was hit."

"Go on."

"The bartender also said that Matt can't find his car and has no recollection of where he went Friday night."

Alan stared at her, knowing that she was saying aloud exactly what he had been thinking, that Jenny's beloved brother was driving the car that hit her beloved son.

"Good God in heaven. Jenny will die," he said.

"Jenny won't die. But Danny might. Like it or not, we have our first suspect."

16

MONDAY DAWNED WITH CRISP, CLEAR SUN-
shine, making the fogginess of Friday seem
like a lifetime ago. Jenny parked Merrilee's
navy blue Lexus in the hospital parking lot and got
out of the car.

Today was a new day, a beginning, and even with
only four hours of sleep behind her, Jenny felt more
optimistic than she had the day before. Maybe it had
something to do with talking to Luke, making her position clear, taking charge, instead of wondering when
and where he would show up next. Whatever the reason, Jenny felt confident that the day would bring
new hope, new possibilities.

As she walked toward the hospital, she noticed a
lone man sitting on a bench just to the side of the front
door. The man was dressed in faded blue jeans and a
dark-hooded sweatshirt. Next to him was an old ten-
speed bicycle. It looked familiar. He looked familiar.

The man raised his head as she approached. His
eyes met hers. They were filled with anguish.

"Matt," she said quietly.

"I'm sorry. I'm so sorry."

Jenny studied his unshaven face, his bloodshot eyes. Matt looked terrible, hung over, and much older than his thirty-four years. She felt a twinge of pity at the sight and put a hand on his knee, once again feeling like the big sister instead of the little sister. "Are you all right?"

"Jesus, how can you ask me that? I should be asking you. Asking about Danny. Tell me—how is he?"

"He's not good, Matt. He has a head injury and he's been unconscious since the accident. The doctors say he's in a coma. It could go on indefinitely."

"Shit." Matt shook his head. "God, why did it have to happen to him? He's just a stupid kid."

"I don't know. I don't think there's an answer."

"You sound like you've given up."

"Not on your life," Jenny said fiercely. "I won't give up, not ever. But I'm trying to get beyond anger and blame. Those emotions won't help Danny. I need a plan of attack, things I can do to encourage him to wake up."

"Like what? What can you do? What can anyone do?"

"Talk to him, sing to him, visit him." Jenny opened her purse and pulled out a sheet of paper. "I wrote down a list of his favorite songs and his favorite movies, books, T.V. shows, everything I could think of. I spoke to the nurses. They said I can bring in some of Danny's friends one at a time for a short while to see if anyone can get through to him."

Matt looked at her in amazement. "Wow, you're really together, Jen-Jen. I don't know what I expected, but it wasn't this."

"I have to be together, Matt. I can't cry every day—all day. I can't wish this away, because I've tried, and nothing happened. And unlike my sister, I can't pretend everything will be all right, when I know"—she took a deep breath—"that there's a good chance it won't be all right."

"Don't say that."

"I have to say it. I have to face it. I don't want to lose my son. Not now, not to this horrible freak accident. I've had time to think during the past few days, Matt. You know why I didn't tell Danny about Luke? Because I was afraid of losing him to his father, and now I may have lost him forever."

"I thought you were through with blame," Matt said.

"I'm trying to be honest."

"You're always honest. I don't know where you get that from. Everyone else in the family lies through their teeth."

Jenny stood up. "Let's go see Danny."

Matt hesitated. "I'm not good in hospitals, not since my leg got busted up. I still remember that goddamned doctor telling me my career was over."

Jenny fumed at yet another display of his selfishness. "Oh, for God's sake, this isn't about you. I'm not afraid Danny won't be able to play a sport, I'm afraid he won't wake up. Don't you get it?"

Matt stared at her in shock.

"Where have you been, Matt?" she demanded "Where the hell have you been? Getting drunk? I needed you this weekend, and you let me down."

"I'm sorry. I wasn't in any condition to come over here. I thought I'd make things worse."

"Maybe you're right. Maybe you shouldn't be here. Maybe you should be drowning yourself in a bottle of beer. That's your answer to everything, isn't it?"

"I've had a rough couple of years."

"Tough. Grow up, Matt. I need a big brother I can depend on."

Matt stood up. "I'll get out of your way."

"No, you won't get out of my way!" she shouted. "You won't run away from this. You can't. I need you. Danny needs you."

"I'll come back later," Matt said desperately.

"Later? After you've had a couple more drinks? For once in your life, think about someone besides yourself, Matt. Think about your family." She walked away.

I am. Matt wanted to scream the words. He wanted to tell her he was worried about Danny and terrified about what he might have done. He wanted to hold her, comfort her, but she was gone. And he didn't know how to get her back—how to get anything in his life back.

"Have you thought about what this will do to your parents?" Denise asked.

Luke gripped the steering wheel, using the traffic as an excuse not to answer her question. Of course he had thought about his parents. They had been on his mind since the accident. That's why he had decided to take off work for the day and drive down the coast to Carmel. He wanted to tell them in person, not over the telephone.

Charles and Beverly Sheridan would not be happy that he had fathered a child, especially not with Jenny as the mother. They had disliked Jenny on sight. She had been too carefree for them, too unspoiled, too honest.

His father had picked apart Jenny's lack of education, her lack of goals. His mother had derided Jenny's clothes, her table manners, her näiveté. They had made it clear that they wanted someone entirely different for him, and like everything else in his life, Luke had gone along with their plans.

As an only child, he had been their sole focus outside of medicine. Every minute of his day had been monitored. He was tutored in math and science from the time he was six years old until he graduated from high school, class valedictorian. He never needed the tutor to keep up, but to get ahead and to stay ahead.

Being first, the best, the most important, was all that

mattered to his parents. They had both been over-achievers, both valedictorian of their classes. Living up to their standard had sometimes seemed impossible. He had tried. Lord, he had tried, in so many different ways.

For a long time he had wanted what they wanted. Their teachings had completely filled his head, and because they isolated him from outside distractions, he never had the time or the inclination to question their values. Until that summer so many years ago, until a slender, wild-eyed girl had taught him there was so much more to life.

Luke wearily rubbed the back of his neck. He cast a side glance at Denise. After having received no response to her question, she was looking idly out the window.

Luke drummed his fingers on the steering wheel as the traffic slowed yet again. Why had he surrounded himself with so many ambitious people? Denise was just another example. Although she wasn't a doctor, she did have a college degree in communications from UCLA, and had been working as an account executive at a public relations firm when they had met. And while Denise's parents weren't rich, they were both business people, white collar.

His parents had admired Denise's savvy, her public relations expertise and total dedication to advancing Luke's career, at the expense of her own. They had fallen in love with Denise before he had. Sometimes, he thought he had married her just to please them.

What a bastard he was. He had to change. He had to put things right for all of them, especially Danny.

His son. The thought filled his heart with joy. They could do so much together. He would be a real father to Danny. They would go to ball games and go fishing—of course he would have to learn how to fish first, but he could study it, research it—maybe he would even learn how to play video games. He would be nothing like his father. He would listen, care, not try to change Danny but simply accept him.

"Did you talk to *her* last night?" Denise pulled out a nail file and began to work on her pinky finger.

"Yes."

"Is she happy to have you back in her life?"

Luke smiled grimly. "I wouldn't say she's happy about much of anything right now—especially not me."

"I don't know. You're rich. She's not. Sounds like she'd be very interested in you."

"Jenny was never interested in my money."

"Maybe not at eighteen. Things are different now."

"Not for Jenny. She has too much pride."

Luke sighed with relief as they made their way out of the Santa Cruz mountains. The ocean came into view over the horizon. The ocean had always brought him peace. Thirteen summers ago it had also brought him love and passion, the first he had ever known, the deepest he had ever felt.

Maybe he could recapture it with Denise. Show her another side of himself. Bring them closer together. He signaled to pull off the highway.

Denise looked at him in surprise. "What are you doing? This isn't the exit."

"The ocean is right there." He pointed out the window.

Her expression told him she had thought he had lost his mind. "So?"

"Let's walk along the beach, feel the sand between our toes."

"Are you crazy? I'm wearing hose."

"Take them off. Go barefoot."

"It's November, Luke. It's cold. No one goes to the beach in November." She sat back in her seat and crossed her arms in front of her chest.

Luke pulled up at the stoplight, grinning as he watched a carload of teenagers pull through the

McDonald's drive-thru on the corner. To be that young again. To be that free . . .

The beach was just ahead. He pulled into a parking space and got out. Every breath he took reminded him of the past. It was glorious. The air was cold and salty. The wind blew the cobwebs from his mind.

He looked over his shoulder. Denise was still sitting in the car—annoyed.

Luke walked over to the passenger door and pulled it open. "Come on, it's gorgeous out."

"It's windy. I'll mess up my hair. I want to look nice for your parents. And if we don't leave right this second, we'll be late. You know Charles hates it when you're late." She tapped her fingernail against the solid gold Rolex watch on her wrist.

"You should have been their child, not me," Luke replied. "I'm taking a walk. Are you coming?"

"What is this, Luke? Are you regressing or something?"

"Or something," he replied. "Suit yourself, Denise."

He kicked off his leather dress shoes and his black socks. The sand and gravel grated against skin that rarely saw the bare floor much less a sandy beach. Luke started to walk, then run. His heart began to pound. His mind took flight and suddenly Jenny was right beside him, and they were young again.

"I'll race you, Luke," Jenny said with a laughing smile. "On your mark, get set . . . oh, look, a hang glider."

Luke turned his head. Jenny took off like a bird in flight. She was fast on her feet, poetry in motion. He could have watched her run for the rest of his life and counted himself happy. But the challenging look she flung over her shoulder forced him to run faster. He caught her, tackled her. They landed hard in the sand.

Jenny's body was under him. Her heart beat against his chest. Her breath came in short, rapid gasps. Her brown eyes danced with excitement.

"Kiss me," she said.

It was what he wanted to do, but a little devil inside made him tease her. *"Good girls wait to be asked."*

"I'm a good girl. Kiss me and see."

"Why should I?"

"Because you're crazy about me."

He brushed the hair away from her forehead and cupped her face between his hands, loving everything about her. *"I am crazy."*

"For me."

"For you," he admitted. *"We're wrong for each other, you know."*

"I know. Your parents hate me. I'm not smart enough or pretty enough. I'm middle-class and going nowhere fast."

"That's not true."

"It is to them."

"Well, your sister hates me. Thinks I'm a snob, arrogant, and looking for a summer fling."

"We're like Romeo and Juliet." Jenny traced his lips with her finger. *"Would you die for me?"*

"I don't think so."

She punched him in the arm. *"Wrong answer."*

He grinned, but his words were serious. *"I'm not hero material, Jenny. I can't carry you off on my white horse and promise we'll live happily ever after."*

"Who asked you to?"

"No one, but when I'm with you, that's what I want to do. You make me want to change everything."

"You think too much."

"You don't think enough."

"Kiss me, and neither one of us will have to think."

He lowered his head and touched her lips with his mouth. She was delicious, like a cold beer on a hot day, like a burst of watermelon in the middle of summer, like every sweet candy he had ever denied himself.

The memories mixed together. The past became the present, and Luke fell in a breathless heap on the sand. Thirteen years later, and he could almost taste her again. Why couldn't he get her out of his head?

For years he had kept her image, her voice, her scent away from conscious thought. Once in a while she had entered his dreams, but he had worked so many long hours that eventually he stopped dreaming altogether.

Now, Jenny was back, as potent as she had been the first time he met her.

It had been the wrong time then. It was the wrong time now. His eyes filled with tears. Luke couldn't believe it. He blinked them away. They came again. He didn't cry. Never, not even as a child.

Luke stood up and ran back toward the car, hoping the sea breeze would explain the moisture on his face.

An hour later, Luke pulled into the private driveway that led to his parents' home in Carmel. It was their retirement dream house, a stately looking home with four bedrooms, a formal dining room, den, and a patio/garden/deck that overlooked the Pacific Ocean.

Charles and Beverly were waiting on the deck when they arrived. His father was reading the *Wall Street Journal*, and his mother was leafing through a scientific journal. It was the way Luke often found them, wrapped up in their pursuit of knowledge, of success.

Charles turned the page without acknowledging his presence. "You're late," he said.

"We hit some traffic."

Luke looked at Denise, wondering if she would deny his excuse, but she simply leaned over to kiss his mother hello. Denise had been furious when he had arrived back at the car. He had been too emotionally drained to give her more than lip service, and eventually she had fallen silent. He had a feeling that was about to end.

Beverly put down her magazine and reached for a bottle of Chardonnay cooling in an ice bucket. "Wine?"

"None for me," Luke said.

"I'd love a glass," Denise replied, sitting down in the chair next to his mother.

Beverly poured three glasses of wine. "Why don't you put down your paper, Charles? Luke obviously wants to speak to us about something important. After all, we just saw you yesterday."

"If he'd gotten here on time, we wouldn't be rushed. Your mother and I have plans for this evening," Charles said. Reluctantly he put his paper down on the table and tapped his fingers together in front of his face.

Luke pulled out a chair and sat down. They were certainly off to a great start. "Maybe I'll have a glass of wine after all."

His mother poured him a glass without comment.

"Well, speak your mind," Charles said.

Luke cleared his throat. "I don't know if you remember, but right before I went to medical school, I was involved with a young woman. Her name was Jenny St. Claire." Luke watched as his parents exchanged a long look. "I see that you do remember."

"Of course. We're not senile," Charles replied. "What does she have to do with anything?"

Luke took a breath and plowed ahead. "She had a baby, my baby, twelve years ago. His name is Danny."

"Oh, my." Beverly put a hand to her heart.

Charles froze.

Denise looked out at the ocean.

"I suppose she's come after you for money," Charles said finally. "You'll have to pay her off. We can't have that kind of information going out to the press."

"This isn't about money," Luke said, knowing that

his protest was futile because to Charles everything was about money, even medicine. His father, the doctor, had coldheartedly gone into the profession to be rich and respected. He had achieved both.

"Of course, it's about money," Charles replied, echoing Luke's thoughts. "How much does she want? A million?"

"She doesn't want money. She doesn't want anything. Her son—*my* son," he corrected, "was hit by a car on Friday night. He's in intensive care."

"What are his injuries?" Beverly asked. She wasn't as coldhearted as his father, but sometimes she could be just as clinical.

"Subdural hematoma. They removed the clot, but he hasn't regained consciousness."

"And it's been how long? Three days?"

"Yes."

"Not a good sign." Beverly looked over at Denise. "Are you all right, Denise?"

Denise nodded, donning a bright, false smile. "I'm fine. The news was a bit of a shock, but it happened a long time ago, before Luke and I met. It doesn't mean anything."

Of course it meant something, Luke wanted to shout. It meant everything. He had a son—a son. He opened his mouth, then closed it, waiting.

"So, what does she want?" Charles asked again.

"She doesn't want anything. I do. I want to get to know my son."

"If he's unconscious, you won't have much chance of that," Charles said.

"I'm hoping he'll recover." Luke tried desperately to hang on to his temper. He wondered when his father's logic had become so irritating. "He's your grandson. I thought you'd want to know."

"Of course we want to know," Beverly interjected, putting a hand on Charles' arm. "You were right to tell us. After all, if he's your child, that's important.

But are you sure, Luke? Are you absolutely sure he is your child?"

"Yes, I am."

"Have you run a DNA test?"

Luke sighed. "No, but Jenny told me I was the father, and I believe her."

"For Christ's sake, Luke. Did I raise you to be a fool?" Charles demanded. "You're a wealthy man. Of course, you're the father. There are probably a dozen other women waiting to make that claim."

"I certainly hope not," Denise said flatly.

Beverly gave Charles an irritated look, then patted Denise's hand. "He didn't mean that the way it sounded. Why don't we have lunch?"

"That's it? That's all you can say?" Luke asked in amazement. "You have a grandson. Aren't you the slightest bit curious about him? Don't you want to know what he looks like?"

"I—I—" Beverly looked desperately at Charles. "I don't think this is the best time, Luke."

Charles pushed back his chair and stood up. "Pay her off, Luke. Set up a trust fund for the child, and keep your distance. You don't want to get dragged into this woman's problems. The boy could rack up all kinds of medical bills that she can't pay, and you'll be left holding the bag."

"Danny looks just like me," Luke said. "Blue eyes, sandy blond hair, freckles. He's a Sheridan. He deserves our name, our love."

"Stop, please." Denise held up her hand. There was pain in her eyes. "I can't listen to this right now, and I don't think your parents can either."

"She's right, Luke. We need time," Beverly said.

Luke got to his feet. "You don't have time, Mother. Danny may be dying. If you want to see your grandson, you'll have to go back with us today."

"I don't know. Charles?"

His father shook his head, his mouth set in a grim line.

"Danny might be your only grandchild. Are you really willing to look the other way?" Luke asked.

"Don't be silly. You and Denise will have children," Beverly said. "Isn't that right, dear?"

Denise took another sip of wine. "I don't know."

Luke shook his head in disgust at Denise's evasive answer. Of course, she didn't want to tell his parents about her deceit.

Charles walked toward the house, pausing by the door. "If you think we're going to drive two hours to see some kid we've never met just because you were stupid enough to impregnate that woman, you're a damn fool. And this sure as hell better not interfere with Sheri-Tech. I gave you my company. I gave you my home. Don't you dare bring shame to this family."

Luke glared at his father, feeling so much anger that he thought he might explode.

"That kid is my son. If you don't want to acknowledge that fact, fine. He doesn't need you. He needs me. And I will not walk away from him."

Charles stormed into the house.

"Oh, Luke. This isn't good for his heart, you know." Beverly went into the house, leaving Luke and Denise alone.

Denise set down her glass of wine. "Gee, that went well."

"How can they be so unfeeling? How can they not care?"

"How can you care so much?" Denise countered. "You don't even know this child. He might be a spoiled brat. It's not like he's a tiny, cuddly baby and you can tickle his toes. He's an adolescent teenager with hormones raging and probably a smart-ass attitude."

"He's not."

"How do you know? You've never spoken to him."

"I have," Luke said, before he could catch himself.

Denise raised an eyebrow. "I thought you said he was unconscious."

"You wouldn't understand." He stalked over to the steps leading into the garden. He had to get away from her, from all of them.

"You're right, I wouldn't understand," she cried after him. "In the last few months, since we moved up from L.A., you've changed. I want you to change back. I want things to be the way they were before."

"So do I," Luke said, but he wasn't talking about days before. He was talking about years before—about Jenny.

17

THREE HOURS LATER, LUKE PULLED UP IN FRONT of their Hillsborough home. He hit the remote control for the garage and pulled the car inside. The light went on as the door closed behind them, and for a moment he and Denise were caught in the quiet intimacy of the garage.

As he reached for the door handle, her hand caught his arm. He turned his head. She was crying—silent tears that dripped down her face in almost perfect symmetry.

"Don't go back to her," she said. "I need you."

Luke felt a sudden, constricting pain in his chest. Guilt rushed over him like a wave, threatening to pull him under, rendering him helpless. He hated being out of control and right now he was so far out of control, it was laughable.

"I have to see if there's been any change."

"You called thirty minutes ago." Her hand dropped to the phone in the car. "You know there hasn't been any change."

"His condition is minute-by-minute."

"Luke, be honest." Denise licked her lips, as if uncertain whether or not she wanted to pursue the conversation.

"I'm trying to be honest. For the first time in a long time, I'm telling you how I feel. If it's not what you want to hear, I'm sorry. This isn't about us. It's about me and my son, a bond that you obviously don't understand."

"I want you to stay home tonight. I want you to go upstairs with me, right now, and make love."

Luke rested his arm on the steering wheel. He looked out the front window of the car at the rows of meticulously placed tools on the wall, reminded that this was his father's house, the house he had grown up in, the house where his life had been planned out to the last detail. He had followed the plan exactly, with only one minor detour, a two-month summer-long fantasy with Jenny. Aside from that, he had done everything he was expected to do, including making love to his wife whenever she requested it.

But this—this demand hit him the wrong way. How the hell could he make love when his son was lying in a coma? He wasn't a robot. He had feelings, even if they had been buried for most of his life.

"Don't you want me anymore?" Denise asked. "Have I gained weight? Is there gray in my hair, wrinkles around my eyes. Tell me, I'll fix it."

Luke sighed. With Denise, everything revolved around her. Even now, she was surreptitiously looking in the mirror, checking to see if her hair was mussed, or her lipstick smudged.

"It's not a question of that," Luke said. "You're a beautiful woman."

"Then why is it so hard for my husband to come upstairs and make love to me?"

She leaned over and kissed him on the mouth—practiced, seductive lips that could please when they wanted to. And right now Denise wanted to, because she was afraid. Luke was smart enough to know that

Denise wanted to solidify her position more than she wanted an orgasm. She would do whatever it took. He had always admired her killer instincts. Only now they were turned on him, and that he didn't like.

He pushed her away. "Not now."

Her eyes lit with anger. "When you're finally ready, I may not be."

"I'll take that chance."

Silence fell between them.

"You've changed," she said.

"You've finally noticed."

"Finally? It's only been three days since—you know."

"Danny's accident was a catalyst. We both know our marriage has been faltering for a long time. You had an affair last year, Denise." The words came out before he had a chance to consider them. Once said, Luke was relieved to have it out in the open. He should have confronted her months ago.

"I didn't."

Her denial came fast and swift. She looked shocked and wounded by his statement. Luke didn't buy it for a second. She hadn't looked this innocent the first night they had made love. "Hank Stanford, the tennis pro at the club," he said.

"How could you accuse me of such a thing?"

"He told me."

"He lied."

Luke searched her face for the truth, but she was a skillful liar. He wondered how many other things she had put over him in the past. "Fine. Let's drop the matter of your affair for the moment. You can't deny that you had your tubes tied without telling me."

Denise sat back in her seat and clasped her hands in her lap. "I don't want to talk about that anymore. It's over and done with."

"Well, it looks like we have nothing to talk about. Get out, Denise. I have to go to the hospital."

Her breath came out like the hiss of a snake. "You're cruel, Luke."

"I don't have time for this."

"If you want my support, then let me come with you."

Luke thought about her request. Was he being unfair, asking Denise to support him, to handle a situation that she had yet to see? Maybe she would be able to understand his plight if she could visit Danny. But what about Jenny? And her sister and brother? Did he have the right to bring more tension into a situation that was already tense? Still, he owed Denise something—at least a chance to be kind.

"All right. Come with me," he said.

Denise fidgeted with the strap on her purse. "You mean now?"

"Of course, now."

"You've taken me by surprise. I didn't expect you to say yes. Let me think."

"You don't really want to go, do you?" He saw the answer in her evasive eyes, in her nervous movements. Of course, she didn't want to go to the hospital. She just wanted to make a point.

"I do want to go, but I have a meeting tonight with the Junior League to plan the Christmas fashion show. Tomorrow would be better for me."

"We're not planning a lunch date, Denise. Tomorrow might be too late."

Denise got out of the car in a huff. "Well, I can't do it tonight. There is another life going on outside of that hospital, Luke—our life. And it used to be a life that you loved, that you wanted as much as I did."

Denise was right. The only problem was he didn't want it anymore.

Jenny sat back in the chair next to Danny's bed and closed her eyes. She had been at the hospital for hours, talking, singing, telling stories until her voice grew hoarse. The nurses changed shifts, the IV pumped new fluid into Danny's veins, the ventilator gave him oxygen, and Danny remained hopelessly quiet.

The room felt empty, as if she were the only one in it. It was odd that she had felt Danny's presence so strongly at Merrilee's house and not here. Here was Danny's body, his heart, his legs, his arms, his head, his freckles—her eyes blurred with tears—his adorable freckles that reminded her of how young he really was.

Why did this have to happen to him? Why couldn't it have been her? She had lived thirty years. She had had love and grief and everything in between. But Danny, he was just beginning to live, to grow into his big feet, to be a man.

"Why? Why?" she said out loud. She opened her eyes and looked at the ceiling as if it would allow her a peek into heaven. It didn't. She wondered if there really was a heaven or a God. She wished she had more religion in her life, more faith to fall back on, but she had been an absentee Christian for most of her life.

Maybe that's why God was punishing her. Because she had skipped church and taken Danny out of Sunday school when he complained of boredom. She should have made him stick it out. She should have done everything—different.

"Jenny?"

Something else she should have done differently. Luke.

"You're back," she said.

"I said I would be." Luke walked over to the bed and stared down at his son. "Hi, kid. I came. I'm here. Isn't it about time we actually spoke to each other?"

Jenny watched him in amazement, her anger at his presence vanishing in front of his unexpected tenderness.

"I never knew how much I wanted a son until I

found out about you." Luke touched Danny's forehead and pushed one of his stray curls back behind his ear. "I wish I'd been there when you were born, when you took your first step, when you threw your first spoonful of mashed potatoes at your mother." He looked at Jenny and smiled. "Knowing your mom, she probably threw a spoonful back at you."

"I did," Jenny murmured. "We had an old-fashioned food fight. It was great fun."

"I'm sorry I missed it. I missed everything. I should have been there for you. I should have supported you and Danny. I blew it."

"Danny wasn't part of your plan. Neither was I."

"I'm beginning to think that plan was flawed. Come on, Danny, wake up. Talk to me. Yell at me. Tell me I'm the worst father in the world, but dammit—don't die. Don't you dare die on me."

Luke's hands clenched the bedrail until his knuckles turned white. Without conscious thought, Jenny put her arm around his waist. He did the same. Suddenly they weren't strangers but parents sharing their sorrow.

Luke turned to her. She slid into his embrace, and a warm feeling of peace came over her, along with a twinge of guilt. It was wrong to be with Luke. Alan should be giving her comfort, not this man—this man she had loved and hated with so much passion, so much anger.

But Jenny didn't pull away. She couldn't. The connection between them was too strong. They were bound together by their son—at least for this moment.

"I want to see Danny's room, his things," Luke said. "I want to know where he sleeps, what he wears to school. Would you let me take you home? Please."

Jenny considered the question. It was the *please* at the end that convinced her. If Luke had demanded, she would have said no. Even now, she hesitated. She hadn't been home since the accident. She didn't want to leave, and yet, she didn't seem to be doing much good here. Maybe if she went home, she would feel in touch with Danny again, the way she had felt at Merrilee's house.

"All right," she said. "If you'll drive. My car broke down last week, and with the accident, I haven't had a chance to do anything about it. I have Merrilee's car, but I don't want to take it out to the coast. She thinks the salt air does things to her paint."

Jenny turned to Danny. "I'll see you in the morning, honey. Sleep tight—don't let the bed bugs bite. I love you." She waited, wanting to hear his answering refrain, *I love you, too, Mom.* But nothing came.

"It's so hard." She touched his cowlick with her fingers. "Please, Danny. Tell me you love me back. I want so badly to hear you say the words."

Silence. God, how she hated the silence.

Twenty minutes later, Luke turned on to Highway 1 and asked Jenny for directions to her house. They had made the drive in companionable silence, listening to music on the radio, the occasional sports and traffic update, and the lively banter of a deejay determined to entertain.

"Is that it?" Luke asked. "One-twenty-five, you said?"

"The yellow house with the green shutters." She smiled suddenly as Luke grinned at her. "Okay, I lived out one fantasy. Sue me."

"Did you paint it or did you buy it that color?"

"I painted it. I hate white houses," she said.

"I remember. You always wanted a house on the beach."

"It's hardly a house on the beach. More like a broken-down cottage a block from the beach, with bad plumbing, floors that slope, and absolutely no view," she corrected. "But it's home."

Luke parked the car in front of her house, and they got out.

"Say, you don't know anything about cars, do you?" Jenny asked.

Luke eyed her warily. "I know if you push down the gas pedal, the car goes forward."

"Thanks, Einstein." Jenny pointed to her ten-year-old white Honda, which looked like a poor relative next to Luke's sleek black Mercedes. "My car stopped running a couple of days ago, and I have no idea what the problem is."

"Why don't you take it to a mechanic?"

"I don't have an extra hundred bucks at the moment. I don't really need the car much around here. I can bike to work. And Danny walks to school."

"Let me take care of it for you," Luke said urgently. "I'll have it towed to a garage first thing in the morning. I'll pay for everything."

"No." Jenny shook her head and turned away. Luke caught her by the arm.

"Why not?" he demanded. "You'll need a car to get back to the hospital."

"One of the neighbors will give me a ride. And I'll fix my own car in my own time with my own money. I'm sorry I brought it up."

"You are so stubborn, Jenny. Why won't you let me help you?"

"Because."

"Because why?" he persisted, sounding a lot like her son.

Jenny searched for a logical, calm explanation, but instead her words came out in a torrent. "Because you're rushing me. As of a week ago, I hadn't seen or heard from you in over a decade. Now, you want to claim my son as your own, see my house, take care of my car, and pay my bills. I can't handle it. Back off."

The air crackled between them, and Jenny felt almost breathless by the exchange.

Luke put a hand up in apology. "Okay. You're right. It was just an offer. I'm not trying to take over your life."

"Good, because it's my life, Luke. I had to stand on my own two feet a long time ago. The girl you once knew is gone forever. Don't get me and her confused."

Luke sent her a curious look, and something that seemed like admiration passed through his eyes. Luke had never looked at her with respect before, not even all those years ago. He had looked at her with desire and passion and often complete bewilderment at some outrageous plan she had concocted, but never with respect. She stood a little straighter.

"You've changed, Jenny."

"We both have."

Jenny turned toward the house, then paused as she spotted a flash of white on the other side of the fence. "Gracie?"

The older woman came into view. She was holding a spade and wearing a pair of white overalls. On her head was the straw hat she wore to protect herself from the sun. Only, it was almost seven o'clock at night, and the sun had long since gone down.

"Jenny. I heard about Danny. How is he?"

Jenny walked over to the fence. "He's badly hurt, but we're hoping for the best."

Gracie looked at her through worried eyes. "I say prayers for him every night."

"Thank you." Jenny pointed to the spade in her hand. "What are you doing?"

"Why, some gardening, dear, isn't it obvious?"

"It's late, Gracie. It's dark."

"Oh?" Gracie looked around somewhat distractedly. "So it is. I just didn't take notice, I guess."

"You'll have to finish tomorrow."

"Yes. Yes, I'll do that." Gracie brushed some dirt off her sleeve with a noticeably trembling hand.

"Are you all right?" Jenny asked with concern. Gracie was more than just a neighbor. She was Jenny's second mother, and it had become apparent in recent weeks that the woman's health was beginning to fail.

"I'm fine, fine," Gracie said with a dismissive wave of her hand. "I gave your brother some lasagne. I hope he put it in the refrigerator for you."

"Matt was here?"

"Yes. Yes, he was. Yesterday, or was it the day before? No, I think it was yesterday because Doris had just gotten back from her trip. She was so upset to hear about Danny. She said she would drive me to the hospital to see you both. She just hasn't had a chance yet."

"I know she's busy looking for a job," Jenny said. Doris was Gracie's niece and had come to live with Gracie so the older woman wouldn't be alone. "Danny's unconscious," Jenny added. "He may not know you're there."

"But you will, won't you, dear?" Gracie reached over the fence and squeezed Jenny's hand. "You're family to me. I love you both as if you were my own. If there is anything I can do to help, please tell me."

"Thanks. I know Danny would love to hear your voice. The two of you have been so close over the years."

"I love that boy. Now, who is that young man you're hiding behind you?" Gracie asked.

"Oh, I'm sorry. This is Luke Sheridan." Jenny stepped aside. "This is Gracie, my longtime neighbor and dear friend."

"Nice to meet you, Mrs. . . . "

"Oh, just call me Gracie. Everybody does." She smiled at Jenny. "He's handsome, your new boyfriend."

"He's not my boyfriend."

"Oh, too bad."

"Gracie."

"Well, I'm sorry, but I like him better than that other boy."

Jenny rolled her eyes as Luke smiled at her with amusement. "Good night, Gracie," she said pointedly.

"Good night." Gracie waved and headed toward her house.

"She's a nice lady," Luke commented as Jenny led him up the walkway to her front door. "And she has excellent taste in men."

"She doesn't know you like I do."

"Ouch."

Jenny pulled a key chain out of her purse and slipped her key into the front door. "Gracie used to watch Danny for me when he was a toddler. She still keeps an eye out for him after school."

"Jenny?"

"What?"

"You're stalling."

Jenny looked at the door in front of her and realized she had yet to turn the knob. "I want to go in and call Danny's name and have him come running. That isn't going to happen, is it?"

Luke shook his head.

"Right." She opened the door.

The house smelled stale. Jenny flipped on the light switch, still half expecting Danny to pop out and yell surprise. He didn't.

They walked through the living room/dining room, into the kitchen. A slab of melted butter was sitting out on the counter. Danny's cereal bowl from Friday morning was still on the table, Fruit Loops soaked in milk.

Jenny stared at the cereal and burst into tears. "Oh, God. He's gone, Luke. He's really gone."

Luke pulled her into his arms. "He's not gone, Jenny. He's going to make it. You have to have faith."

"How can I? It's been three days. How can I go on without him? He's just a little boy, but he's my life."

Luke shut his eyes as he closed his arms around her waist. He wanted to cry with her, but she needed him to be strong, and this much he could give her.

"Everyone I've ever loved has gone away," Jenny said. "My mother, then you, now Danny. What did I do wrong, Luke?" She lifted her head. "Why am I being punished?"

"You didn't do anything wrong."

"I must have. Merrilee says I screw up everything."

"Merrilee doesn't know what she's talking about."

"My father thinks I'm a slut."

"Jenny, stop."

"And your parents. What was it your mother called me—a silly, foolish girl? Everyone can't be wrong."

"I never thought you were any of those things."

"Then why did you leave me? Why did you break us up? We were so damn good together." It was a question she had wanted to ask him for years. Now, it burst out of her before she could stop it.

"I was afraid. My parents had such high expectations. I didn't want to disappoint them. We were young, Jenny, kids. We didn't know what love was."

"I did. I loved you more than anyone else on this earth." The confession came from her soul, and it felt good. She needed to get it out in the open, so the wound could heal. "I gave my heart, my soul, and my body to you. Maybe you thought I gave it lightly, but I didn't."

"I know you didn't."

"You just couldn't love me back the way I loved you."

"No, because I wasn't as generous or as courageous. You were the only rebellion of my life. The only time I was my own person were those two months with you."

Jenny stared at him in amazement. "I can't believe that."

"Why not?"

"Because you made your own decisions. You chose to get married to someone else."

"She was part of the plan, Jenny." Luke ran a hand through his hair. "Denise is not a bad person. It's not her fault that—"

"That what?"

"That she's not you."

Jenny felt herself being sucked into a whirlpool of feeling. Logically, she knew she couldn't let it happen. Emotions were high because of Danny. Everything was more intense because of the danger of losing him.

Luke lowered his head. His eyes narrowed. He was going to kiss her. And she wanted him to.

No!

She had to remember who she was, and who Luke was, and how much he had hurt her the first time around.

Slowly, she disengaged herself from his arms.

"Jenny."

She held up a hand. "Don't say anything. Just go." Her voice shook. "I can't do this with you."

"What about Danny's room?"

"Tomorrow or next week or next month, when it's light out, when I can remember that you're married, and we mean nothing to each other."

"Nothing, Jenny?" Luke tilted up her chin and looked deep into her eyes. "You never used to lie to me."

18

"DON'T LIE TO ME, MATT. I WANT TO KNOW where you were Friday night." Alan sat down on the edge of the sofa while Matt tossed back another beer.

"I went to the Acapulco Lounge and had a few brews. What's it to you?"

"The bartender says you were drunk when you left."

Matt swore under his breath and set his bottle of Bud down on the coffee table, next to last month's issue of *Sports Illustrated.* There was a photograph of the new 49er quarterback on the cover of the magazine, with a headline proclaiming him football's newest rising star.

Matt had a similar cover buried away in his desk drawer, a painful reminder of everything he had lost. He wished he could go back to the days when everyone had believed he was a winner, including himself. But they were gone forever.

"Well," Alan persisted.

Matt sat back in his chair. "Why don't you just tell me where you think I was?"

Alan's eyes narrowed. "Don't make me say it, Matt."

"Why the fuck not?" he demanded, tired of the cat-and-mouse game. "Who do you think you are anyway?"

"I'm your sister's boyfriend, the man she's going to marry, and the man who's going to find the bastard who ran over Danny."

Matt jerked to his feet. "You think I would hit my own nephew?"

Alan stood up. Face to face, they were almost of equal height, but Alan was broader in the shoulders, stockier through the thighs. His face was square and rugged, the look in his eyes determined.

Matt dropped back, his quarterback instincts coming to the fore. Alan pressed forward like a defensive lineman smelling an easy sack. There was no one to block, no one to protect him, and not one damn thing he could say in his defense—well, maybe one.

"I was with Brenda," Matt said. "Brenda Channing. She's a flight attendant. We spent the night together."

Alan looked somewhat disappointed at this piece of news. "Channing, huh. Where do I find this Brenda Channing?"

"I don't know. She said something about Tokyo."

"Really. Interesting."

"Is that it?" Matt asked, eager to get Alan out of his house. He had never particularly liked the man. He thought Alan was an awfully cold fish for his warmhearted sister, but if Jenny liked him, that was all that mattered. He had wanted her to be happy for a long time.

Matt just wished she had chosen someone different, someone who didn't look at him like he was a piece of dog shit on the bottom of a shoe. Hell, didn't Alan know he had once taken the 49ers to a division championship? He was important. He deserved to be treated with respect.

"I'd like to see your car," Alan said.

Matt's puff of confidence vanished as quickly as it had appeared. "Uh—my car's not here. It's at a friend's house."

"Fine. Let's go to your friend's house."

"He's not home."

"What's his name?"

"Why do you want to know?"

"Why don't you want to tell me?" Alan wrinkled his nose as if smelling the scent of guilt.

Matt tried to look unconcerned. "I just don't see the point of this conversation. Does Jenny know you're here?"

"Where's your car, Matt?" Alan grabbed him by the collar. "Tell me where your car is."

"I don't know. Okay? I don't know!" Matt yelled, knocking Alan's hands away from him.

"What are you saying?"

"I'm saying, asshole, that I don't know where my car is, and that I can't remember what the hell I did on Friday night after I left the Acapulco Lounge."

"Jesus, Matt. What are you using for brains these days?"

Matt picked up his beer, and took a defiant sip. "What do you think?"

Alan grabbed the bottle out of his hand and threw it against the fireplace, shattering it into a hundred pieces of glass. "I think you better get a lawyer."

Tuesday, four days since the accident—two days before Thanksgiving. Merrilee stared at the calendar in dismay. So much to do. So little time. So little desire. She'd always loved decorating the house, baking pies, stuffing turkey. It was something she had shared with her mother, a tradition that she carried on for her family.

Her family—what a mess they were in.

Merrilee turned her attention to the task at hand.

She rolled out the pie dough, picked it up and flipped it onto the other side, pushing it around in the flour so it wouldn't stick to the board.

"Mother, I'm going to the library to work on my book report," Constance said.

Merrilee looked up in surprise. "It's almost dinnertime. I thought you wanted to help me with the pies."

"You don't need my help. You don't need anyone's help." Constance stared at her defiantly. "Don't say I can't go."

"You can't go."

"Mother."

"It's raining out. It's cold."

"Thanks for the weather report. So what?"

"Don't speak to me like that. I'm your mother. I deserve better. And besides, I don't believe you're going to the library at all. It's that boy, isn't it? The one who calls after midnight when you think I'm asleep."

Constance stared at her in shock. "How do you know ... are you listening in on my calls?"

"No. But I probably should be." Merrilee looked at her daughter and felt the anger drain out of her. She loved this willful, often disrepectful child, because she still remembered the sweet little girl who had read with her and laughed with her and sung silly songs while she cooked dinner every night. Where had that little girl gone? Teenage hell. Now, everything was a fight, a battle for territory, for respect, for independence.

Merrilee didn't know how to let go, and since Danny's accident her sense of protectiveness had increased. "I don't want anything to happen to you," she said. "Don't you understand that?"

"Nothing's going to happen to me," Constance replied with the confidence of youth.

Merrilee wiped her hands on a dish towel. "Sit down, Constance."

Constance sighed and slumped into a chair at the kitchen table.

"We need to talk," Merrilee said. "Tell me about this boy. What's his name? Where does he live?"

"He's just a guy at school. You wouldn't know him."

"Why don't you invite him over for dinner one night?"

Constance snorted her disgust. "Yeah, right. Like he'd want to come here and be totally depressed."

"I know things have been tense lately," Merrilee said, "but aren't you worried about Danny, too? Maybe—" Merrilee stopped talking as the phone rang. "I better get that. It might be Jenny. Don't go anywhere. We're not done."

Merrilee walked over to the phone and picked it up. "Hello? Matt, what's wrong?" She paused, shock rippling through her body at his words. "Alan wants to arrest you? For what? Oh, my God. I'll be right there."

"I thought we were going to talk," Constance said as Merrilee grabbed her purse.

"I can't. I have to help Matt. You stay here with William. I'll be back as soon as I can."

"What about the library? What about my life?"

Merrilee didn't answer. She couldn't think about Constance's social life right now, not with this latest piece of bad news. What on earth would go wrong next?

"Danny isn't responding to commands," Jenny said as Luke joined her outside Danny's hospital room. Through the glass she could see Dr. Lowenstein moving Danny's arms and legs.

"Maybe he just doesn't like to take orders," Luke said lightly. "I know you never did."

She tried to smile. "Nice try." She stepped toward the door as Dr. Lowenstein left Danny's room.

"Well?" Jenny said.

"He's holding his own," Dr. Lowenstein replied, obviously trying to put a positive spin on Danny's lack of progress.

Dr. Lowenstein turned to Luke, a curious look on his face. He didn't say a word, just shook his head as if struck by a strange thought.

"Something wrong?" Luke asked.

"It's none of my business." Dr. Lowenstein handed Danny's chart to the nurse, who was also watching them with unabashed curiosity.

Suddenly Jenny knew what was going on. It was Luke and Danny. They had seen the resemblance. Her first thought was to warn Luke, to protect him. Her second thought was to let him hang. If he really wanted to be Danny's father, he would have to take the good with the bad.

"Jenny?"

She looked into Luke's eyes and saw the awareness, the unspoken question. "It's up to you," she said.

"I have to go," Dr. Lowenstein said. "I'll catch up with you later."

"Wait. There's something you should know." Luke paused. "I'm more than just a friend of the family. I'm Danny's father."

The nurse gasped. Dr. Lowenstein looked surprised but not completely shocked. Luke looked downright proud.

Jenny smiled at him. "Nice bombshell."

"It's none of my business," Dr. Lowenstein said, "but I must say the resemblance is very strong. If you'll excuse me." He conferred with the nurse in a quiet voice, then left.

Jenny pulled Luke into Danny's room. "Are you sure you wanted to do that?"

"Danny's my son. I don't care if the whole world knows."

"I have a feeling they're going to," Jenny replied.

"This could hurt you, Luke—your reputation, your family, your company. The press loves a scandal. And an illegitimate child is certainly the makings of one."

Luke shrugged. "To hell with my reputation. I've spent thirty-five years worrying about what people will think. Right now the only opinions I care about are Danny's and yours."

"What about your wife? Your parents?"

"What about 'em?" Luke snapped his fingers. "Say, is that hamburger joint still out on the coast? What was the name?"

"Bill's Burger Shack?"

"That's the one—with chili so hot it could burn the roof off your mouth."

"It's still there. Old Bill's nearing seventy, but he says he'll never retire."

"Let's go there. Let's get a burger and sit on the beach and take a break from all this." Luke waved his hand around the room.

Jenny hesitated. "I don't know. Maybe I should stay."

"I've got a beeper, Jenny. If Danny's condition changes, they can page us."

"We'll be twenty minutes away."

"It's only dinner. You need to get out of here. And we need to talk."

"All right. I do have to eat."

"Yes, you do." Luke wrote down the beeper number for the nurse, and they walked out of ICU.

As they passed the pay phone, Jenny paused. "Maybe I should call and let someone know where I am."

"Someone? You mean your fiancé?"

"Alan is not really my fiancé. He said that to—"

"To stake his claim."

"No."

"Yes."

Jenny sighed. "This is a guy thing, right?"

Luke smiled. "Maybe."

"Well, whatever. Alan and I are not engaged. We've been dating each other, seriously, but we haven't made any plans for the future. Anyway, he's at work, so I don't need to call him."

Luke pushed the button for the elevator. "Alan— he's a cop, right?"

"Yes, he's trying to find out who hit Danny."

"Any leads?"

Jenny shook her head. "I don't think so."

"I hope they catch the bastard."

"So do I."

"My mother first brought me here when I was about ten," Jenny said to Luke as she popped the last of her chili burger into her mouth. They were sitting in a small patio at the back of Bill's Burger Shack. The splintered wooden table in front of them was covered with hundreds of initials carved into the weather-beaten wood.

Jenny had so many memories of this place, times with her mother, with Luke, and with Danny. She crinkled the hamburger wrapper between her fingers until it was a tight ball, then pitched it toward the trash can. It fell short.

"Story of my life," she said, attempting a smile. "A day late and a dollar short. Anyway, my mom loved these burgers because they were hot and spicy. My dad wouldn't come near this place. He's a vanilla kind of guy."

"There's nothing wrong with vanilla," Luke protested. "It's my favorite flavor."

"I thought raspberry swirl was your favorite flavor."

He smiled at her. "I only said that to impress you. I knew you'd think I was boring if I ordered vanilla."

"And I thought I knew you so well."

"You did know me, better than anyone."

Jenny looked down at the table, his intimate words making her tense. "I wonder if our initials are still here. I remember the night we carved them. You, of course, just happened to have a pen knife on your key chain along with a survival kit that would put any true Boy Scout to shame."

"I liked to be prepared. Of course, once in a while I slipped up."

He met her eyes, and she knew he was remembering the night they had made love without any protection, because the condom had broken, and neither one of them had wanted to stop. It had been irresponsible, reckless, the way Jenny had lived most of her life. For Luke it had been an aberration, an exception to the rule.

Her heartbeat increased with the memory of their passion. It had been hotter than the chili she had eaten tonight, fiery, intense. The only thing in her life that had ever been perfect.

"It's right there," Luke said, pointing to her end of the table.

"Where?"

"By your hand."

Jenny looked down, but didn't see it, maybe because her eyes were blurred with memories. Luke touched her hand. His fingers covered hers as he pressed their palms against a tiny heart.

JS AND LS FOREVER.

Jenny gulped back a rush of emotion. Forever had only meant two months, two short months. "It was a silly thing to write, wasn't it?" She walked over to the trash can and picked up her wrapper.

Luke followed her. "Not silly, innocent. I'm glad we had that time together. I wouldn't have missed it for the world."

She had always wondered what he thought—if he remembered them at all—and if he did remember, if it was with fondness or regret.

Luke took her arm. "Let's walk, Jenny. It looks like the path to the beach is still there, even if it is overgrown."

"I don't know. Maybe we should go back."

"You? Turning down a walk on the beach? Is nothing sacred?"

She smiled. "I admit, I love the ocean. It brings me peace."

"Then let it bring you peace tonight. Walk with me."

This time, Luke led the way down the path, and Jenny followed, reluctantly accepting his hand over the rocky terrain. When they reached the end of the path, Jenny slipped off her shoes and carried them in one hand.

They walked silently for a time. Jenny listened to the sound of the waves and began to relax. There was a certain rhythm to the ocean, a monotony of sound that comforted her, because it never ended.

"That's where we had the bonfire." Jenny pointed to an empty spot of sand. Tonight there was a beer bottle lying on the ground. She picked it up. "Kids," she said. She carried the bottle until they reached a trash can, then tossed it in.

They walked on, by silent accord, going to the place where it had all begun. When they got there, the magical pool was gone, covered by the sea.

"It's not there," Luke said with disappointment.

"Nothing stays the same."

"I wish we could go back."

"Why? Would you have done things differently? I don't think so. Besides, we can't go back." Jenny sat down on the sand and stared at the water.

Luke sat down beside her. "Would you have done anything differently?"

"Me? I wouldn't have worked at that ice cream shop. I gained ten pounds that summer."

Luke grinned as he played with the sand, letting it

drift through his fingers. "You always made me laugh."

"You're a pretty good straight guy, I must admit."

Luke sent her a curious look. "Why me, Jenny? You could have had any boy you wanted that summer. Your friends thought you were crazy. I was a bookworm. I didn't know how to flirt or make time with the girls. My life was a mathematical equation and the only chemistry I knew about was the kind done in a laboratory."

"I liked your quiet strength," she said, remembering him as a young man. "I liked the way you watched people, as if you knew more than all the rest of us. Of course, you did. Your IQ was beyond compare. And you listened to me. Really listened." She looked him in the eye. "God, Luke. Nobody at my house ever listened to me. My mother was the only one, and she died. After that, I had Merrilee running my life, Matt playing the superstar sports hero, and my father refusing to look at me because I always did everything wrong. When I met you, I felt like a real person."

"You were real to me from the first second. Open, honest, loving. Everything right out there for the world to see."

"That's not such a good thing."

"We were different though, in a lot of ways," Luke said. "I was a conservative Republican, you, a liberal Democrat."

"I liked to go barefoot. You never took your shoes off."

"I drove everywhere. You always wanted to walk," Luke continued.

"I ate dessert first. You hated to even let your meat touch your potatoes."

"And your sand castles." Luke shook his head. "Haven't you ever heard of a blueprint? Your engineering skills were sadly lacking."

"My vision was huge, bigger than life. What a pair, huh?" She smiled at him, and he smiled back, as caught up in the memories as she was.

"You can say that again. Why did we get together?"

She tilted her head in thought. "Because alone we were each a little odd. But together—we made sense. At least for a while." She dug her toes into the sand, enjoying the feel of the cool, wet beach.

Luke leaned all the way back, resting his head on his arms as he looked up at the sky.

Jenny followed his gaze. It was a starry night. No fog. No clouds. Just an endless array of bright, shiny lights.

"Do you believe in heaven?" she asked, then laughed at her own question. "Of course you don't. You're a man of science. You can probably tell me exactly how the universe developed."

"I can." Luke pointed at the stars. "I can also tell you which of those are stars and which are planets. I can even point out the Milky Way. See that shadow?"

Jenny strained her eyes. "Yes. It's almost like a rainbow, only white."

"There's a scientific explanation for the colors," Luke said. "But my grandmother once told me that the Milky Way is the path that souls take to heaven, and it's their spirits that make the shadow white."

"I like that. It's comforting, especially now, when I have so many questions and so few answers." She paused. "I've never heard you speak of your grandmother before."

"She died when I was ten. She was my father's mother. Used to say that God gave everyone else in the family brains, and gave her all the heart. Nana would have liked you."

"I think I would have liked her. Sounds a bit like my mother. Do you think they were really so saintly or do we just remember them that way, now that they're gone?"

"Saintly?" Luke turned to her. "When my grandmother was sixty-two, she married a man who was fifteen years younger than her, a man who wore an earring in his left ear. My father almost had a heart attack. Wouldn't speak to her for three years. No, she wasn't a saint. She was human. We're all human. We all make mistakes."

Jenny sighed. "We were a big mistake, although we did have some good times."

"The best time I ever had was the day we got lost driving to Lake Tahoe."

"You were furious, because I forgot the map."

"And the compass and the water and the directions. But I can still remember that hawk. It was so damned arrogant, so above us."

"Like you." She paused. "And the mountains. They were spectacular."

"That deer came right up to you, practically ate out of your hand."

"We slept in the back of the car. You hogged the blanket."

"You snored."

"You made love to me."

"We made Danny."

Jenny looked at Luke and saw the exact same emotions she was feeling. "You're right. It was the best time we ever had."

19

J ENNY WALKED INTO MCDOUGAL'S MARKET JUST before eight o'clock Wednesday morning. It seemed like a lifetime since she had been to work. Not counting the weekend, she had only missed two days. It hardly seemed possible. So much had changed.

George Hanling, a portly man with a face that looked liked Santa Claus and a belly to match, was the first person to see her arrive. George was the butcher, and a nicer man to yield a cleaver she had yet to meet. He was standing by the bakery counter, jelly dripping down one finger as he bit into the center of a donut.

"Oh, Jesus," he muttered, swallowing as he reached for a napkin.

"Your wife said no more donuts, George."

George cleaned the jelly off his fingers, then took her hand. "I am so sorry, I can't believe what's happened. We've been worried about you. If there's anything I can do . . ."

Jenny nodded and kissed him on the cheek. "Thanks. You're a sweetie."

George turned a dark shade of red as he headed back to work.

Jenny looked up as Prudence Meyers called her name. Pru was a sexy, twenty-seven-year-old blonde with earrings that dangled down to her shoulders, a skirt that crept up her thighs, and a heart as big as the Pacific Ocean. Pru, also a single mother, had been a checker at McDougal's for almost five years, and she and Jenny had become close friends.

Although working as a checker in a grocery store was not Jenny's dream job, it did pay the bills. It also allowed her the opportunity to take classes at night and develop her jewelry business. Someday she would be her own boss and have a chance to express her creative nature full-time, something she could not do while scanning produce and dairy products.

Still, over the past seven years Jenny had made some good friends in the store. She was a social animal by nature, and McDougal's had become a second home to her. Unfortunately, with the retirement of T. W. McDougal six months earlier, and the takeover by his nephew Chuck, McDougal's was now taking on the personality of a supermarket instead of a neighborhood store.

As if on cue, Chuck stuck his head out of the manager's window. Jenny thought, not for the first time, that the man had bugged the counters and planted hidden videos under the bananas. He always seemed to pop up at the worst possible time. He waved for her to come to the office. She waved back but paused by Pru's counter.

"Hi ya, hon, how ya doin?" Pru asked as she finished a checkout and handed the lady her receipt.

"Hanging in there," Jenny said, her voice catching in the face of Pru's sympathetic smile. "This is harder than I thought."

Pru came around the counter and gave Jenny a hug, never minding the fact that a customer looked at both of them, sighed, and moved on to the next aisle.

Jenny smiled at her with watery eyes. "You're going to get in trouble."

"I am so sorry, Jenny."

"I know. Did Merrilee call you? I gave her a list of my friends the other day."

"She did. Your sister is very efficient."

"She is that."

"So, how is our boy?"

"Quiet. Incredibly quiet. He doesn't move, Pru. He doesn't open his eyes, he doesn't talk. I can't stand seeing him like that."

"Oh, God, honey." Pru wiped the corner of her eye. "What do the doctors say?"

"As little as possible. We have to wait. I hate waiting."

"Jennifer," Chuck called her name as he stepped out of his office. "I'd like to see you."

"Give her a break. Her kid is in the hospital," Pru snapped.

"I just want to talk to her," Chuck said defensively. "And you've got a line to take care of."

"Yeah, yeah, yeah." She turned back to Jenny. "Do you want me to go with you?"

Jenny shook her head. "I think I can handle it. After Danny, everything else is a piece of cake."

Pru gave her the thumbs-up sign as Jenny headed toward the manager's office. She knew she had to deal with Chuck sooner or later. It might as well be now.

"I'm sorry about your kid," Chuck said, avoiding direct eye contact as he took a seat behind his desk.

"I appreciate the flowers the store sent," Jenny replied, knowing that Chuck probably had nothing to do with their delivery. She shifted her feet, wishing she could sit down, but Chuck had removed all other chairs from the office. He liked the fact that everyone had to stand in front of him like a child in the principal's office.

"You're one of us, the McDougal family," Chuck said smoothly.

"I'm glad you consider me family, because I know I've left you in the lurch."

"It's understandable." Chuck cleared his throat. "When do you think you'll be back?"

"I'm not sure. My son is in a coma. I don't know how long he'll be unconscious. I need to be with him, to talk to him, work his legs and arms, try to bring him back to life. He needs round-the-clock stimulation."

"I see." Chuck sat back in his chair and pressed his fingertips together in front of his face.

Jenny licked her lips. "I know I don't have any vacation time left, and probably no sick days either, but I will need time off, Mr. McClintock."

Chuck pulled at his tie. "Yes, well, you're entitled to twelve weeks of family leave, unpaid, of course, but we'll hold your job."

Unpaid. Jenny's heart sank at the thought. How could she take three months off without a paycheck? She wouldn't be able to pay her rent, much less buy food. And Danny might need extra treatment, more than her insurance would pay for. What would she do then?

Luke. He would probably be more than willing to help. But dammit, she didn't want his money.

"As a courtesy to you, my uncle would like to compensate you for this week," Chuck added reluctantly. "You can pick up a check on Friday. Your leave will officially start next Monday."

A week's pay. Not nearly enough. But she'd take it. "Thank you."

"I am sympathetic, Jennifer." Chuck shook his head, a regretful expression on his face. "But I have a business to run."

"I understand." Jenny walked out of the office and stopped by Pru's counter, relieved when Pru finished with a customer and had a moment to talk.

"What did Mr. M. say?" Pru asked.

"I can take up to twelve weeks of unpaid leave and they'll hold my job. And T.W. is apparently tossing in a week's pay just to help me out."

"That's good, but Jenny, what will you do for money? Can I lend you something?"

"As if you have anything."

"I could scrape something up."

"It's okay. I have some savings, and I'm sure Matt or Merrilee will help if I get desperate. I just hate to ask them, especially Merrilee. Her money usually comes with strings attached."

"Excuse me, are you open?" a woman demanded.

Pru shook her head. "No, I'm on a break."

"I don't see a sign."

"Trust me. He'll take you over there." Pru pointed to the next aisle.

"Last time I come to this store."

"I hope it is," Pru muttered under her breath. She looked at Jenny. "I almost forgot. My friend Karen wants to buy those darling seashell earrings you made, the ones that look like teardrops. I know it's only ten dollars, but it'll buy you a sandwich and a Coke."

Jenny smiled. "Believe me, I never turn down money, no matter how little it is. I still pick up pennies off the sidewalk. Danny laughs at me . . ." Her voice caught, and she couldn't finish the thought.

Pru bit down on her lip as if she were about to cry. "Ah, jeez. I wish there was something I could do. I've been feeling so bad for you, hon."

"Me, too." Jenny looked her friend in the eye. "By the way, Danny's father has come back."

Pru opened her eyes wide. She was the only person besides Alan who knew about Danny's obsessive longing to find his father.

"How did that happen?" Pru asked. "Did Danny talk to him?"

"No. He tried, but didn't get in to see him. Danny was on his way home when he got hit by the car."

"Oh, Lordy. So what does this guy have to say about things?" Pru stuck a CLOSED sign on the end of her counter, sending yet another customer away.

"Pru, you can't do that."

She waved her hand. "Sure I can. It's time for my break anyway." Pru pulled Jenny over to a quiet corner by the magazine rack. "So, tell me everything."

Jenny shrugged. "Luke says I should have told him about Danny, that he wants to know his son."

"You did tell him, remember?"

"Yeah, but he thinks I should have said something after I had Danny. Maybe he's right. I don't know anymore." She dropped her voice so she wouldn't be overheard. "Seeing him has brought back all the old feelings. I loved him so much, and he hurt me so bad. Part of me wants to keep him away from us, but Luke is Danny's father, and Danny wanted desperately to know him. How can I shut him out? If there's a chance that Luke can get through to Danny, I have to take it."

Pru's eyes narrowed. "What about Alan?"

"He's not happy," Jenny replied, knowing that was an understatement. Alan's attitude toward Luke bordered on homicidal, a mix of jealousy and impatience. At the moment she had neither the time nor the energy to deal with either emotion.

"Alan's probably afraid you have feelings for Luke. It sounds like you do."

"Not feelings—memories. I keep seeing him in my mind, Pru, the way we were. I know we can't go back. He's married. And there is still Alan."

"Alan's not the right guy for you," Pru said. "Now, I don't know this Luke, and he's probably a total jerk because I know he left you and Danny alone, but you have to stop pretending that Alan is ever going to be the love of your life. It ain't going to happen. Wake up and smell the coffee."

"Look who's talking," Jenny said, referring to Pru's endless parade of no-good love affairs.

"So, I give advice better than I take it. Sue me." Pru popped a bubble of gum in front of Jenny's face.

"I'll think about what you said. Say one of your prayers for me, okay?"

"You know I will. And Jenny—oh, forget it."

"What?"

"I believe things happen for a reason."

"What reason could there be?"

"Danny's father was meant to come back into your life."

"I don't want Luke in my life, I want Danny."

"Maybe you can have both."

Later that morning, Luke entered Sheri-Tech with barely a glance at the receptionist or the other employees who wanted to score points by saying hello to the boss. The only thing he had on his mind was Danny. He wanted answers, and he wanted them fast. Danny had been in a coma for five days. It was not a good sign. The longer it took for him to come out of it, the worse his prognosis would be.

As he walked down the hall to his office, Luke felt a rush of frustration. He had spent his entire life pursuing a career in medicine. He'd be damned if he would sit by and let his son die without the fight of his life.

He had resources and money, the best medical minds in the country. Danny would live. He would see to it.

Luke brushed by his secretary, Lorraine Parker, without a word, ignoring her muttered hello and the stack of pink slips in her hand. He had been in the office no more than two hours the day before and not at all on Monday. Such absenteeism was akin to the Pope missing Mass. His father had set a precedence of working hard every day. Luke had always followed that ethic, until now, until his mind refused to let go of Danny and focus on anything else.

"Dr. Sheridan?" His secretary hesitated in the doorway. "Shall I put these on your desk?"

"Fine. Fine."

"Your father called three times. Shall I dial him for you?"

"Not right now, thanks."

Lorraine looked at him in horror. She had worked for his father for ten years and whatever Charles wanted, Charles got.

"It's no trouble. He seemed impatient," she persisted.

Luke frowned at her. "My father is retired, Mrs. Parker. It's about time he learned some patience."

She left the room with an irritated, "Hmph."

Luke set his briefcase down on the floor, picked up the phone and punched out the extension for Keith Avery, Sheri-Tech's top scientist. Keith was smart, thorough, and had a background in neurology. If anyone could help him find a way to bring Danny out of a coma, it would be Keith.

"Avery," the man said.

"Keith, Luke. Have you found anything?"

"No. I'll need more information on the exact injury."

Luke nodded, flipping through his Rolodex as he spoke. "Call Lowenstein. That's Danny's doctor. Tell him you work for me. He'll be happy to cooperate."

"I'm on it."

Luke set down the phone and looked up, not surprised to see Malcolm walking through the door.

"I heard you were back." Malcolm settled into the chair in front of Luke's desk. "Want to tell me why

I've had three calls from the press this morning, claiming you're someone's father?"

Luke sat down in his chair. "You heard."

"Along with the rest of San Mateo County. Don't you know better than to make announcements in a hospital? The news got out the door faster than you did."

"I'd forgotten about the workings of the hospital grapevine."

"So, it is true?"

Luke nodded. "Yes, it's true. Years ago, before Denise, I was involved with someone. She got pregnant. I thought she had an abortion."

"But she didn't." Malcolm let out a long, shrill whistle. "This is not good. How much does she want?"

Luke sighed as he sat back in his chair. Why was he surrounded by people who thought only in terms of dollars and cents? Didn't they realize there was a boy's life at stake?

"She doesn't want anything, Malcolm. Nothing. The child is in a coma." Luke picked up a glass paperweight and rolled it around in the palm of his hand. His initials were engraved on the glass. It had been a present from his parents, celebrating his long-awaited arrival at Sheri-Tech. He had finally come home.

But come home to what? A life that barely needed him in it. Sheri-Tech was so well organized it practically ran itself. Any changes he attempted to make, even small ones, were met with resistance. His father's philosophies and goals were written in stone.

And his home—it was the same. Every time he closed his eyes, he could see his parents' image, feel their smothering love. Their voices rang around in his head. "You'll study hard. You'll be a doctor. You'll take over Sheri-Tech."

He'd done it, all of it. And now he was left with what? What? The answer refused to come.

"Luke." Malcolm snapped his fingers in front of Luke's face. "I'm talking to you."

Luke straightened. "What did you say?"

"I asked how you want to handle this. With clinical trials starting after the first of the year and the possible acquisition of Genesys, we need to present a solid, unified front."

"I'm aware of our plans, Malcolm."

"Then why did you miss the meeting last night?"

Luke sent him a blank look.

"Cappellini's restaurant at seven, remember?"

Luke cleared his throat. He did remember, now. Yesterday he had been thinking only of Jenny. "I forgot. I'll call and apologize."

"Good. If there is any suspicion that your mind is occupied elsewhere or that you'll be entangled in a long, legal battle, Genesys may go elsewhere. They do have other suitors."

Luke looked at Malcolm and shrugged. "If they do, they do. Frankly, I don't give a damn about Genesys or Sheri-Tech right now."

"What?" Malcolm stared at him in disbelief.

Luke leaned forward in his chair. "You heard me. I have a son, Malcolm. You should understand what that means. *You have children.*"

"I—yeah, I guess. But, Luke, this is your business."

"My whole life has been about business. Danny is family. He comes first."

"But Sheri-Tech is also your family, Luke. It's your father's legacy to you."

"My father . . ." Luke suddenly felt an intense rage spread through his body. On impulse, he threw the glass paperweight against the wall. It landed on the marble tile and shattered. The family ties were finally broken.

Malcolm jumped to his feet. "Calm down. Jesus, Luke, I've never seen you lose your cool before. I'll take care of this. Relax, okay?"

"I can't relax. I'm assigning three people to review Danny's case. I'm not leaving anything to chance."

"What can you do that his doctors can't?"

"Dammit, I don't know. I've spent my entire life believing that science has the answer to every human problem. Only things don't add up anymore, and I don't know how to fix them."

"Maybe you can't."

"I have to."

"You're not God." Malcolm walked to the door. "I'll handle Genesys. We'll reschedule the meeting for next week, give you a chance to catch your breath. And I'll write up a press release, short and sweet, just the facts."

"Fine, just don't put anything in there that reflects negatively on the St. Claires. Jenny and Danny have been through enough." Luke paused. "And, Malcolm, tell Lorraine to call maintenance. Have them turn up the heat. It's cold in here."

"Turn it up? Charles thought his staff would fall asleep if they were too warm."

"I'm not my father, Malcolm. It's about time everyone realized that." Luke turned his chair around so he could look out the window. The horizon soothed his jangled nerves. But only for a moment. Then he thought about Danny and the tension came back.

"Where are we going?" Danny asked Jacob as they soared through the sky.

"To meet a friend of mine," Jacob replied, leading him through a white, puffy cloud. "There he is."

Jacob and Danny landed in the middle of a baseball field. There was a game going on, and Danny jumped as the ball suddenly came at him.

Jacob laughed. "You're supposed to catch it, not duck."

"I don't have a mitt." Then Danny looked down at his left hand and saw the leather glove. Before he could ask how it had gotten there, another ball came his way. It was going over his head. He ran backward, then gave a last, hopeless jump. To his amazement, the ball landed right smack in the middle of his mitt.

"Throw it home," Jacob said. "Home," he cried.

Danny hurled the ball to home plate. The catcher made a sweeping tag. The runner was out.

Danny jumped up and down in excitement. "I can't believe I did that."

Another boy came running up to him. "Nice play," he said. "I'm Michael."

"Hi." Danny shifted his feet, not sure what to say, how to act. The game appeared to be over now. The other kids were huddled in the dugout, listening to their coaches. Danny watched as Jacob walked over to the pitcher's mound. He did an exaggerated wind-up, then threw the ball right over the plate.

"S-t-r-i-k-e," Jacob yelled.

Danny rolled his eyes and looked back at Michael. "Do you know him?" he asked.

"Everybody knows Jacob. He comes here all the time. Never brought anyone before though."

Danny looked around at the field. It appeared to be in the middle of nowhere. Could have been any state in the U.S. Or maybe he wasn't in the real world at all. "Is everyone here dead?" he asked.

Michael nodded. "Yep."

There was a wealth of meaning in Michael's simple reply, a meaning that scared Danny, but for the moment he didn't want to face up to the future.

"How did you die?" Danny asked

"I was born with cystic fibrosis," Michael said. "I could hardly breathe. I couldn't play sports. My chest hurt all the time. The worst part was my parents. They cried because they couldn't help me. I wanted to die for a long time. I used to pray to God that he'd take me back. After all, I figured he sent my parents a lemon, and it was time to recall the product."

Danny was shocked by his matter-of-fact attitude. Maybe here in heaven, people just got used to being dead. "I guess he heard you."

"After I died, my father went out and raised money for cystic fibrosis patients," Michael added. "He's done a lot of good for other kids. My mom isn't stressed out anymore. She started painting again— only this time her pictures have more depth. See, Danny, I was only meant to be with them for a short while."

"Don't you miss them now?"

"I can see them," Michael said. "I can't touch them. They can't touch me. But someday we'll be together again. They'll be happy to see me this way." Michael puffed up his chest. "I can breathe great now."

"It's different for me, though. I wasn't sick before."

"You are now. You have a head injury. The doctors don't know what functions you'll have when and if you come out of that coma. They don't know if you'll be able to walk or run or hit a baseball. You might even be retarded."

Danny stared at Michael, suddenly terribly afraid. He didn't want to be sick. He wanted things to be the way they were. "I still want to go back," he said.

"Even if there's pain, Danny? Even if you're a cripple? You had things pretty easy before," Michael pointed out. "Never sick. Great mom. Plenty of food. You don't know what it's like to suffer."

"I don't want to know what it's like." Danny looked around him, wondering if he'd be struck down for such a selfish statement. But no one seemed to notice. "Weren't you scared to die?" he asked Michael, still amazed at the other boy's courage.

Michael nodded. "Yeah. At first. But when my angel came, when I saw the light, I knew it would be all right."

"Was Jacob your angel?"

Michael started to laugh. "No way."

"Why do you say it like that?" Danny asked suspiciously.

"Never mind."

Jacob walked over to them. "Did you see that pitch, kid? Man, I'm good."

Danny frowned. "I want to go back, Jacob. I want to see what's happening—talk to my dad again. What do I have to do to go home?"

Michael and Jacob exchanged a long look.

"Someone tell me," Danny cried.

"Relax, kid. It's a long game. Anything can happen, even with two outs in the bottom of the ninth."

Danny looked at him in confusion, not sure if Jacob was telling him to keep the faith or just saying something stupid. "Can I at least see my dad again?"

"I think that can be arranged. I do have some interesting news. Your dad came right out and told everyone you're his kid."

Danny's eyes widened in amazement. "He did?"

"Yes sirree."

"Are my parents getting back together?"

"Your father is married."

"He could get a divorce. My mother still loves him. I know she does."

"Your accident brought them back together."

Danny nodded, beginning to understand what was happening. "That's why it happened, isn't it? You didn't just make a mistake. It was meant to be."

Jacob smiled and stroked his chin in an annoyingly knowing way. "When the Big Guy closes a door, he usually opens a window."

20

"IBETTER OPEN A WINDOW. IT STINKS IN HERE," Jenny said as she entered Danny's bedroom.

Luke wrinkled his nose in distaste."Where on earth is that smell coming from?"

"Something's rotting. We have to find it."

"Excuse me?"

Jenny ignored him, intent on finding the offending item. She turned down the covers on Danny's bed. An Oreo cookie fell out. Not the cause of the odor, but definitely the cause of a few chocolate crumbs in the sheets. She got down on her knees and checked under the bed. She came up with a pair of hockey sticks, sweat socks that produced a different but also unpleasant odor, Danny's missing book report, and a magazine.

Jenny tossed everything aside except the magazine. "Oh, my God. *Playboy*."

Luke looked over her shoulder and smiled. "Danny was reading *Playboy*?"

"I hardly think he was reading it. He probably got it from Christopher's older brother."

"All boys sneak a peek at skin magazines."

"He's only twelve years old," she wailed. "And the worst part is that he hid it from me. What else is he hiding from me? What else isn't he telling me?"

"You're his mother. A boy is not going to tell his mother that he's ogling naked women after the lights are out."

"Danny and I have talked about sex." She got to her feet. "I thought he could talk to me about anything."

"You're making too much of this."

"I am not. I never make too much of things."

Luke grinned. "You always make too much of things. You're passionate and emotional. I love that about you."

The words slipped so easily from his lips that Jenny wasn't sure she had heard him right. Thirteen years of silence, and then an "I love that about you" phrase. As if they had parted friends or lovers just yesterday.

Jenny tossed the magazine into the garbage can. She didn't want to get into a discussion with Luke about sex or anything remotely related to the topic. She pulled open the drawers in Danny's desk and hit pay dirt. With tentative fingers, Jenny pulled out a moldy piece of pepperoni pizza.

Luke made a face. "That was in his drawer?"

"Why, sure. Along with a ruler, a pen, a package of chewing gum, and a batch of Marvel comics. Where else would he keep it?" She dumped the pizza into the trash, picked up the can and walked into the kitchen with it. Dumping everything into a white plastic bag, she tied the two ends into a knot and set it by the back door.

Luke stood in front of the refrigerator, looking at a photograph of Danny at the science fair.

"That's Danny's spaceship," Jenny said. "He has a bit of both of us in him, my penchant for adventure and your love of science. Danny wants to be an astronaut.''

"No kidding. I'm impressed."

"Is that a little fatherly pride I'm hearing?"

"It's a lot of fatherly pride." Luke's eyes softened as he looked at her. "I want to know everything about him, Jenny. I want to go through your scrapbooks, see his school pictures, hear all the funny stories that you hold in your heart. I want you to make him real for me. That boy in the hospital bed seems so cold, so distant. Wake him up for me, Jenny." Luke reached for her hands and squeezed them tightly. "I need to know him."

Jenny searched his face in wonder, noting the vulnerability, the anguish, his feelings exposed for the world to see. It was so unlike the Luke she remembered.

"He wanted to know you, too," she murmured. "I have so much guilt. If only I'd taken him to see you. I was afraid."

"Of me?"

"Of Danny. Afraid he'd love you more than me, want to live with you, want to have the things that you could give him that I couldn't. I was afraid of losing him. That's why I stalled. I didn't want to share. This is all my fault."

"It was an accident."

"There wouldn't have been an accident if I'd taken him to see you."

"It's over, Jenny. You can't punish yourself this way. I have guilt, too. My God, I can't believe I told you to get an abortion."

"Having a child wasn't part of your vision for the future, Luke. But I should have told you to go to hell, that I was having the baby anyway. The truth is, I didn't make a decision one way or the other. I drifted. I debated. I listed my pros and cons until I ran out of paper. You know I could never choose. Well, I didn't choose then. It became too late to have an abortion. So I had him. Then I fell in love with him and knew there had never really been a choice."

Jenny shook her head as she thought about the past. "I've spent my life reacting to things instead of controlling them. You're different. You're in charge. You can make a decision in ten seconds. It takes me ten minutes to figure out if I want bleu cheese dressing or oil and vinegar on my salad. I'm a mess. My life is a mess. Even now, I'm just doing what the doctors say, doing what you say, doing what Alan and Merrilee say. Like I have no mind of my own. Maybe that's why God's taken Danny. He couldn't bear to leave him with such a poor excuse for a mother a minute longer."

"Stop it, Jenny."

"I can't."

"You have to."

"I need to do something, take positive action, change things—"

"Stop."

"I'm out of control. I—"

Luke cut off her words with his mouth, taking her completely by surprise. The kiss was filled with pent-up anger, passion, and memories. Her lips parted involuntarily. His tongue plunged into her mouth. Reason disappeared.

Their bodies came together, face to face, breast to chest, hip to hip, groin to groin. He was hard. She was soft. They fit perfectly together. Only their clothes were in the way.

Jenny pushed off his coat and pulled at his tie. His hands slid up under her sweater, cupping her breasts. He moaned against her lips. She unbuttoned his shirt, running her hands through the thick mat of hair on his chest.

The tactile memories came back. The feel of his muscles. The coarseness of his five o'clock shadow against her face, his fingers teasing her breasts.

His mouth left hers to trail soft, wet kisses along her neck and collarbone. Jenny gasped for air. Her mind threatened to function. She refused to let it. She didn't want to think. She just wanted to feel. And, damn, he felt good.

Jenny pushed Luke's shirt off, ripping a button in her haste. He pulled her sweater over her head and tossed it on the ground. Her bra followed, and he kissed her breasts, working his mouth against her nipples in pure magic. She ran her hands through his hair, down the column of his spine and around to his waist.

Her hands reached for his belt buckle.

He unsnapped her jeans.

Their eyes connected, their breathing heavy.

"Oh, my God," Jenny said. "What am I doing?" She reached frantically for her bra, her sweater. The bra took too much time, so she pulled the sweater haphazardly over her head, taking pleasure in the moment when her face was completely covered. Then the sweater slid down to her shoulders, and she was face-to-face with Luke.

He had pulled on his shirt and slung his tie around his neck. Slowly, he buckled his belt, drawing her eyes to a place where she didn't want to look.

"Bad idea," she said.

"Probably." He shook his head and a small smile crossed his lips. "When I'm with you, I can't think rationally or logically. I can barely remember my own name."

"Even now?"

"Especially now." He pulled on his coat. "Just for the record, Jenny, I don't make decisions any better than you do. The only real decision I made was to spend that summer with you. The rest of my choices were by default. So if anyone's a coward, it's me."

Jenny followed him out of the kitchen and down

the hall to the front door, thinking about his words. Luke had always seemed strong to her, confident, sure of himself to the point of arrogance. With age had come humility, awareness of his own failings. Damn him. She was starting to like him again, and that was the last thing she wanted to have happen.

Luke stopped at the front door. "The desire is still there, isn't it, Jenny?"

"Yes," she whispered. "It's still there. I wish it wasn't."

"So do I."

Denise was playing solitaire and watching "The Late Show with David Letterman" when Luke walked into the bedroom. She wore a sheer black nightgown with spaghetti straps that fell off her shoulders. A candle on the nightstand had burned down to its wick. A bottle of champagne sat in a bucket of water by the bed.

Luke tossed his coat onto the loveseat and sat down on the edge of the bed to take off his shoes.

Denise played a card. "You're late."

"I'm sorry." Luke sighed, dreading an argument. After leaving Jenny's house, he had returned to the hospital, taken another peek at Danny, then spent the rest of the night at his office, holed up with Keith Avery, as they tried to make sense of the medical studies done on coma patients. Five hours of searching had taken them nowhere. There was simply no medical procedure to pull a patient out of a coma.

"Where have you been?" Denise asked.

"At the office."

"I thought you might have been at the hospital."

"I was there for a while."

"How is he?"

"The same."

Silence fell between them. Luke undressed, stripping down to his briefs. He went into the bathroom, brushed his teeth, slapped water on his face, and returned to the bedroom. Denise was still playing cards, and the television blared the annoying sound of laughter.

"Mind if I turn that off?" He reached for the controls.

"As a matter of fact, I do."

"Fine." Luke slid into bed and pulled the covers up to his shoulders. He turned on his side, facing the door to their bedroom. He was tired, weary from too many emotions. He was used to compartmentalizing his feelings, making sense of them. But he couldn't make sense of Danny's condition, or of his overwhelming love for a child he didn't even know.

Nor could he make sense of his passion for Jenny, a woman he had walked away from thirteen years earlier. How could he want her now, when he had put her so successfully out of his mind for so many years?

It was as if a dam had built up in his mind. Danny's accident had opened the floodgates. His feelings were now completely out of control. If Jenny hadn't called a halt earlier, he would have made love to her right there on the kitchen table. And he wasn't a man who did things like that. Spontaneity was not his style.

"I want you to take me to the hospital the next time you go," Denise said. She turned off the television.

Now that the noise was gone, Luke wished it back. Anything was preferable to a discussion with Denise when his thinking was completely muddled.

"Luke, did you hear me?" She rested her head on the back of his shoulders.

"I heard you. Are you sure it fits into your schedule?"

"That isn't fair."

Luke sighed. "We'll go tomorrow."

"Tomorrow is Thanksgiving."

"You always have an excuse."

"It's not an excuse. It's Thanksgiving. Your parents will be here. I asked the Willoughbys to stop by for cocktails before they drive up to Tahoe. We can't slip out and go to the hospital. It would be rude." She paused. "I am trying, Luke. You sprung a kid on me. That takes some getting used to."

He stared at the wall. "You sprung a tubal ligation on me. I'd say we're even."

She didn't say a word for a long moment. "Maybe I could have it undone."

It took a moment for Luke to understand her words. He rolled onto his back. "Would you really do that?"

Denise avoided direct eye contact. "I might. I didn't realize having a child was so important to you."

"I have a child now," Luke said quietly. "A boy. Maybe it would be enough if you could accept him as a part of our family. Can you do that?"

"Of course. I can do anything you want. Anything. I love being your wife. I don't want to lose you."

Luke picked up on her choice of words. Loved being his wife. But did she love him? Or just what he could offer her?

Denise ran her fingernails down his arm. "I wanted to be with you tonight. I wanted us to hold each other, comfort each other. The champagne is warm now, but we can still make love."

Her red hair drifted down against his bare chest. She looked beautiful but cold. At least, he felt cold, and he couldn't imagine drumming up enough energy to make love to her. With Jenny so fresh in his mind, it would be impossible to touch Denise without thinking of Jenny. It wouldn't be fair to either of them. "I'm tired."

Her eyes narrowed at his excuse. "Okay. We have a big day tomorrow anyway."

"Yes."

"It'll be nice to have everyone together."

"Not everyone. Not Danny." He didn't mean to say the words aloud, they just came. Because the thought of Thanksgiving, of pretending to be a happy family without his son, was almost more than Luke could bear.

Denise threw up her hands in frustration. "Good heavens, Luke. It's been just the four of us for the past eight years. You've never complained before. We've always had wonderful holidays."

Because before, the holidays had been an opportunity to bask in his parents' appreciation, to be rewarded for his efforts to please them. Now, he didn't give a damn about what they thought of him or his decisions. He suddenly realized that he had passed over a threshold. He no longer saw himself as the child, but as the father. His relationship with his parents was secondary to his relationship with Danny.

"I never knew I had a son before," he said slowly. "You can't pretend that things are the same, Denise." He looked at her, knowing that she did want to pretend, because she hated to look at anything depressing, refused to even watch the news at night, because she didn't want to be reminded of how harsh the world could be.

"Even if Danny were completely healthy, he wouldn't be sitting at our table for Thanksgiving," she said. "He would be with his mother."

It was a logical point, and Luke was a logical man. He could admit she was right, and he would, if only to end the conversation. The truth was he would rather be at Jenny and Danny's table, not that they would welcome him. In fact, he didn't fit in anywhere, not in Jenny's life, not in his own.

"I don't belong here," Matt said as he looked at his sister's elegant dining room table. Everything was set for a perfect family Thanksgiving, from the china and silver to the tiny Pilgrim napkin holders. Merrilee had even spread red and gold leaves down the center of the table.

"Of course you should be here." Merrilee set the butter dish and olive tray on the table. "We're a family. Families should be together. Now what can I get you to drink? I have some lovely hot apple cider."

Matt grimaced. "How about a beer in a nice cold mug?"

"It's only three o'clock."

"So?"

"I don't want you drunk before dinner."

"That's it. I'm out of here."

Matt turned to leave, but Merrilee stopped him. "You're not going anywhere. I had to go all the way down to your house to stop Alan from throwing you into jail. The least you can do is sit at my table and be polite."

"Alan wasn't going to throw me in jail. GI Joe was just making a point." Matt glared at her. "He's not coming here for dinner, is he?"

"Of course, he is. Alan is going to marry Jenny. He's practically part of the family."

"Shit."

"Watch your language."

"I didn't like him before, and I like him even less now, trying to pin Danny's accident on me. Jesus, what kind of a person does he think I am?"

"Don't make me answer that, Matthew."

"And what the hell does Jenny see in the guy, anyway?"

"Maybe she sees dependability, comfort, companionship. It's about time she settled down and gave Danny a father figure."

Matt snorted his disgust. "Danny can't stand the dude."

"Danny doesn't know what's good for him."

The doorbell rang, and Merrilee pushed Matt toward the family room. "Go in and socialize. Richard's watching a football game."

"Great, another thing I'd love to do, sit around and watch everyone playing what I can't play anymore."

Merrilee ignored him and went to answer the front door. Her father was standing on the doorstep, arms crossed in front of his chest and an expression on his face that told her he'd rather be anywhere else but here.

"Daddy. Come in."

He shuffled past her and paused at the entrance to the dining room. Merrilee waited for a compliment on her exquisite table, but none came. "What do you think?" she asked, determined that someone would appreciate her efforts.

"It's nice."

"Nice? I spent two hours setting the table."

"Your mother could have done it in ten minutes. Had a knack, she did."

Merrilee's joy at the holiday vanished like spit on a hot candle. She could never compete with her mother, at least not in her father's mind. She didn't know why she bothered to try.

"Got any whiskey?" John asked. "I could use a shot."

Merrilee sighed. Great. With both John and Matt drinking, she would be lucky if anyone was sober enough to taste the turkey.

"Coming right up," she said.

Constance entered the room wearing a pair of blue jeans that were ripped at the knees and at the thighs. John raised an eyebrow and muttered something under his breath. Constance sent him a defiant look, which she redirected toward her mother. "I'm going over to Cassie's house for a while. I'll be back for dinner."

"Absolutely not. It's Thanksgiving. Your uncle is in

the family room, and your grandfather is here. You'll spend the day with us, young lady."

"It's only for an hour, Mom. What's the big deal? They're watching some stupid football game. I'm bored."

"No."

Constance flounced out of the room.

"That one's got a mouth on her."

"She's sixteen. Everything is a trial."

John shuffled his feet and picked a speck of lint off his sleeve. He cleared his throat. "Jenny coming?"

"She said she'd try." Merrilee sent him a pointed look. "Have you been to the hospital yet?"

"Your sister doesn't want me there."

"Of course she does."

"Then why doesn't she call and ask me?"

Was that hurt in his voice, disappointment? Merrilee studied his face, but he was a difficult man to read. "She's wrapped up in Danny. She hasn't called anyone. But I'm sure she'd like to see you."

"Where's that whiskey?"

"Dad." He didn't look at her, and Merrilee hesitated. She didn't want to ruin Thanksgiving, but she had to try to get through to him. "After dinner, I'm going to the hospital. Why don't you come with me? We're a family."

"We haven't been a family since your mother died. And your sister, well, she wanted to dance, now she has to pay the piper. I got nothing to say to her."

How about "I love you. I forgive you." Merrilee itched to say the words, but her father looked hard and unreachable. He had so many walls up, she couldn't possibly climb them all.

"How about that whiskey?" John asked. He didn't wait for an answer, just headed into the family room to make himself at home.

Merrilee went to the kitchen and poured herself a brandy. It was going to be a long day.

CHARLES SHERIDAN BOWED HIS HEAD. "LET US GIVE thanks."

Luke obediently closed his eyes, as he'd done every Thanksgiving of his life. His father said his usual prayer, thanking God for food, family, and friends. The words had lost their power over the years, maybe because they were always the same words, nothing new, nothing different.

"Amen," Charles said.

The word was echoed around the table. Luke opened his eyes. He picked up his knife and cut into his piece of turkey. It tasted like sawdust. He chewed, swallowed, and made polite conversation.

The meal seemed to go on for hours. Turkey, stuffing, mashed potatoes, sweet potatoes, corn bread, salad. His stomach revolted at the litany of food items that ran through his head. He set his fork down before he had half finished his meal.

His mother observed his gesture and offered him a brilliant, dazzling smile. He felt like taking a spoonful of mashed potatoes and flinging them in her face. For the first time that day, a smile crossed his lips.

"Denise tells us you're going to be on the cover of *Fortune* magazine," Beverly said. "I am so proud of you."

"You should be proud of Malcolm. He's very good at public relations."

"They're calling you Midas, because everything you touch turns to gold. Your work at McAuley Perkins is consistently praised, and now that you're at Sheri-Tech, the sky is the limit." Beverly exchanged a proud look with Charles. "I knew from the minute he was born, he would be a genius."

"How could he be otherwise with our genes?" Charles asked with a laugh. "There's something to be said for good breeding."

Good breeding? They were talking about him as if he were a horse they were going to run at Golden Gate Fields.

"I knew the day I married Luke that I had the most brilliant husband in the world." Denise looked at Beverly. "I wouldn't have picked him otherwise."

The laughter began again. They were so alike. Luke glanced from Denise to Beverly, saw the same superficial smile, the same sophistication, the same arrogance.

Good God, he had married his mother!

The thought struck him like a blow to the head. Luke felt faint. Why hadn't he seen the resemblance before? Why hadn't he realized that the things he disliked about Denise were the same things he disliked in his mother? Denise wasn't as well educated, but she was just as slick and ambitious, the iron hand in the velvet glove.

Of course, that's why Beverly had encouraged him to marry Denise from Day One. She had obviously seen an ally.

"Luke, I asked you a question."

He looked up in a daze as his father's sharp voice commanded his attention. "What?"

"Do you want to come to Lake Tahoe with us to-morrow? There's plenty of room in the cabin. Should be some great skiing after last week's storm."

Luke shook his head. "I don't think so."

"Why not, Luke? It would be fun," Denise said. "We haven't skied in ages. You know how you love it."

Did he? Or was that just another decision they had all made for him? They were running together in his mind. He was losing himself in his family. Their love surrounded him like quicksand. He wanted to get out, but he couldn't move.

In his mind, he saw Jenny and Danny, holding out a stick, a chance to break free if he dared to take it. But leaving the quicksand meant leaving everything that was familiar, everything that was important to him. Could he walk away from the very people he had spent his life trying to please? Did he have the guts?

"I think we should go, Luke," Denise persisted. "A couple of days in the mountain air will be good for all of us."

Luke set his napkin down on the table. "I can't leave town right now. I think you all know why."

"You promised not to bring that up." Denise sent him an annoyed look. "It's Thanksgiving."

"You can pretend if you want to, Denise. Hell, you can all pretend. But I have a son who's fighting for his life. I'm not going skiing or anywhere else."

Luke pushed back his chair and strode out of the room. Charles set his coffee cup down in the saucer with an irritated clatter. "Damn fool."

"He'll get over this," Denise said with confidence. "He just needs time. After all, Luke has never been all that fond of kids. The reality of having a son is unknown to him. He's just having a midlife crisis."

Charles studied her thoughtfully. "You have a point. But that woman. She—she—" He searched for the right word. "She has some sort of power over him. Years ago, I was afraid he might decide not to go to medical school, after all we'd done for him. Thank God, he came to his senses and walked away from her."

Denise folded her hands in her lap, tense at the mention of the other woman. It was almost easier to ignore the fact that Luke had a son than ignore the fact that he had loved another woman.

"What was she like?" Denise asked, unable to resist the opportunity to learn more about her competition. "Was she pretty?"

"In a frisky puppy sort of way. At least she was then," Charles said grumpily. "I wonder if we could buy her out of Luke's life. I think it'd be worth it. This child will only cause trouble. You should have a son, Denise. Then Luke would be satisfied."

Denise looked down at her plate. She couldn't tell them the truth. Thank God, Luke hadn't said anything. They wouldn't be happy about her decision. They wanted children to carry on the Sheridan name. She had hoped to get around the problem by convincing them that Luke didn't want children or that she was sterile or something, but now—now she was caught neatly in a trap of her own making.

"He's right, Denise." Beverly looked at her with a soft smile. "A baby would be a nice addition to our lives. Just seeing you pregnant would make Luke happy." Beverly paused, turning to her husband. "I'm not happy about this situation, Charles, but I have to admit I'm a little curious about this boy, and I do feel badly for his mother. I know what it's like to have a child, to love him, to be afraid of losing him. I'm afraid of losing Luke—over this boy. What are we going to do?"

"Do?" Charles asked in amazement. "We're not going to do anything. We're going to wait for Luke to come to his senses."

"And what if that doesn't happen?" Beverly asked.

"I'll make it happen," Charles replied.

The housekeeper entered into the dining room with a tray in her hands. "Are we ready for pie?"

Charles muttered under his breath and pushed back his chair. "I need some air."

"I'll come with you." Beverly followed him out of the room.

The housekeeper looked at Denise. "Ma'am?"

Denise shook her head. Left alone, she felt like crying. Her beautiful Thanksgiving dinner was a complete disaster. Damn Luke. And damn that woman for ruining everything. Denise had half a mind to go to the hospital and tell that Jenny to stay the hell out of their lives.

Jenny slipped a pair of earphones onto Danny's head, sticking the padded ends gently into his ears. She turned the volume down to a comfortable listening level and pushed Play. She could faintly hear the sounds of Nirvana pulsing through the Walkman.

It was Danny's favorite tape. She could still see him dancing around the living room like a rock star, playing an imaginary guitar, singing his heart out. God bless him. He had inherited her voice, and musical it was not.

She sat down in the chair next to the bed and studied his still form. He was lying on his back, still connected to the ventilator, because every time the doctor removed it, Danny stopped breathing. The pressure in his head was still there, not going down, not going up.

In other words, Danny was in a holding pattern, like an airplane circling over the airport, waiting for clearance to land. Only the call never came.

Six days of waiting. Six days of hoping. Six days of fear.

Jenny kicked her feet up under her body and

wrapped her arms around her waist. She hummed to herself, trying not to hear the silence. The quiet bothered her, because Danny had always been such a loud kid. Now, there was nothing, a ghost in a hospital bed.

"Jenny?"

She turned around, expecting Luke, but it was Gracie and her niece, Doris. She got up to greet them.

"Oh, my. Oh, my," Gracie said, shaking her head. "He looks so little in that bed." Her eyes filled with tears, and she started to shake. Jenny looked at her with concern. "You don't have to come in, Gracie. This is too much for you."

"No, I'm okay. I can't remember ever seeing Danny so still. He's such a jackrabbit. When he comes to my house, he jumps off the furniture and climbs up the doorways and I don't think he ever actually walks down the steps. How can he lie there so still?"

"I don't know. His body's resting, I guess. One of the doctors said Danny's brain is in hibernation. That when he's healed, he'll wake up, like a bear in winter. I try to hold on to that thought." Jenny put an arm around Gracie's shoulders. "Thank you for coming. It means a lot to me."

"Has he opened his eyes at all?"

Jenny's throat tightened at the simple question. "Not once. The last time I saw him with his eyes open was Friday morning when he left for school. I'm not even sure he knows I'm here."

"Oh, he knows. A boy senses when his mother is close. And the two of you have always been so very close." Gracie opened her black leather purse and pulled out a handkerchief to wipe her eyes.

Jenny felt a rush of emotion at Gracie's words. "Sometimes I think I'm a terrible mother. I make so many mistakes."

Gracie smiled. "He loves you. You love him. That's all that matters."

"We better go, Aunt Gracie," Doris said. "We're supposed to be at Dad's house in fifteen minutes."

"Can I give Danny a kiss?" Gracie asked.

"Of course you can."

Gracie walked over to Danny and kissed him on the forehead. "Get better, young Daniel. I need my checkers partner back. Your mother's too easy." Gracie looked over at Jenny, her blue eyes sharp and wise. "God be with you, child. It's always darkest before the dawn."

"I can't wait for the sun to come up."

"It will. It always does."

"But what if Danny doesn't wake up with the sun?"

Gracie squeezed Jenny's hand hard. "Remember what I told you when Danny had that terrible case of the chicken pox and you lost your temporary job because you had to stay home and take care of him?"

Jenny looked at her for a long moment. "You said there was no greater joy than having a child, no matter how much pain or how many problems they bring with them."

"I think the words still hold true. Good-bye, dear."

"Good-bye."

"Take care, Jenny." Doris paused at the door. "That's the first time I've seen Aunt Gracie so clear about things, especially memories. Maybe seeing Danny is good for her. I'll bring her again, if you don't mind?"

"I'd love it."

"Happy Thanksgiving."

"You too." Jenny couldn't bring herself to say the words. Thanksgiving was a time to give thanks for all the blessings in life. At this moment, there was only one thing she was thankful for, that Danny was still alive, even if that life was barely more than the beat of his heart.

With that thought in mind, Jenny laid her head gently against Danny's chest, just to make sure that his heart was in fact still beating. It was. There was still a chance. She had to believe in his recovery. She had to hang on.

Alan walked into the room, his face somber, his expression concerned. Jenny slowly straightened.

"Hi."

"Hi." He dug his hands into his pockets. "You didn't call me back yesterday."

"I'm sorry. I meant to."

"We need to talk."

Jenny turned away, not wanting to look into Alan's eyes. She felt guilty for having spent the previous day with Luke instead of with Alan. He was beginning to feel like a stranger to her. She couldn't remember why she had started dating him in the first place, why she had thought of marrying him.

The distance between them was as big as the Grand Canyon. Alan was on one side. She was on the other. He wanted to bridge the gap. She wasn't so sure. And that scared her, because Alan was reality and Luke was fantasy.

"Danny looks a little better, don't you think?" she asked, trying to divert their conversation from anything personal. "His color is good."

"Jenny."

"When I clapped my hands next to his ear, I think he moved."

"Jenny, please."

She looked at him. "What? What do you want?"

"Can we go outside? What I have to say to you, I don't want to say in front of Danny."

His words heightened her tension. Goose bumps crept up her spine. She wanted to say no, but Alan had already left the room, and she had no choice but to follow.

Alan didn't stop in the nurses' station but walked down the hall, through the waiting room and out into the atrium. The weather was crisp, the sky partially obscured with clouds. Alan pulled out a chair at one of the tables. Jenny reluctantly sat down.

"What is it?" she asked.

"It's about Matt."

Matt? Thank God. For a moment she thought he was going to tell her he had seen her with Luke, seen her kissing a man she was supposed to hate.

"We located his car in Brenda's garage. The license plate was bent in half. There was a crack in one of the headlights."

Jenny stared at him, unsure where he was headed. "What are you saying?"

"I think Matt was driving the car that hit Danny."

"Merrilee, it's time to eat." Richard stood in the doorway to the kitchen. Merrilee glanced out the window for the hundredth time in the past hour. The cul-de-sac was empty.

"Jenny and Alan aren't here yet," she said, letting the curtain drop.

"Your father is getting sloshed. He's spouting off about Catholics, Clinton, and the right to bear arms. Your brother is sitting in front of the television critiquing every goddamn play the Cowboys make. And Constance is about to rip William's head off."

Merrilee sighed. "All right, I'll put the food on the table."

"Thank God."

Richard left the room without offering to help. Not that she would have allowed it. The kitchen was her domain, and she ran it with single-handed efficiency. With quick, effortless motions, she pulled out the various platters and trays and took them to the dining room.

When she walked into the family room to tell her family dinner was ready, William and Constance were wrestling over the controls to the video game, Richard was reading the newspaper, her father was rambling on about illegal aliens and welfare, and her brother was leaning back on the couch, popping peanuts into his mouth.

No one was making any effort at all to be a family, and it irritated the hell out of her. "Dinner is served," she said.

Twenty minutes later, dinner was over. Her big family meal had been eaten with the same enthusiasm as starving dogs going after one bowl of food. When their plates were empty, they were finished with the celebration.

"Can I go to Cassie's now?" Constance asked, shoving back her chair.

"We haven't had pie."

"I don't want pie, it's fattening."

"Sit down, please."

Constance sighed and sat down with a mutinous expression on her face.

"We've hardly had a chance to talk." Merrilee drew her finger around the edge of her water glass. "Richard. Why don't you tell us about your new ad campaign, the one you've been working so hard on?"

Richard shrugged. "It's a series of ads for a company called Morgan Hunt. They make hunting equipment."

"You mean like guns?" Constance asked. "You're working for a company that makes guns?"

"And what's wrong with that?" John slapped his son-in-law on the shoulder. "Man has a right to protect himself and his family."

"That's disgusting. Uncivilized." Constance thrust her nose in the air.

"Got another beer?" Matt asked Merrilee.

"No."

The conversation fell flat, and Merrilee's gaze drifted over to the two empty spots at the table, one for Jenny, and one for Alan. Although in her mind, she didn't see Alan next to Jenny, but Danny, chomping noisily on his food, hiding his lima beans under the mashed potatoes, and exchanging knock-knock jokes with Matt.

Her heart caught. Her eyes grew misty. She blinked back the emotion, hating when it took her unawares, when she couldn't control it. When her vision cleared, Merrilee realized she was all alone, except for Richard. He was sitting at the other end of the table, his fingers drumming restlessly on the tablecloth, and he was watching her in a way that was very personal, very disturbing.

"I guess we'll have coffee in the family room," she said. "It will be more comfortable there to sit and talk."

"Stop trying so hard to make this a normal day," Richard said. "It's not normal. We're all worried about Danny and Jenny."

"You could hardly tell that from the conversation."

"Everyone's afraid, Merrilee." Richard got up and walked around the table. He sat down in the chair next to hers, recently vacated by William. "We're terrified that Danny's going to die. Admit it, you're afraid, too."

"Of course, I am. He's just a child. It could be William or Constance lying in that bed. I couldn't stand it if anything happened to one of our children." The emotion came again, unexpected, undeterred by her will not to let anyone know how upset she was. "I feel so guilty. That first night when I came home from the hospital, I thanked God it wasn't my child."

The tears ran down her cheeks in a stream. She wanted to stop crying. She was ugly when she cried. The tears continued to flow. Richard pulled her into his arms. It was the first time he had held her in weeks.

"What's happening to us?" she murmured against his sweater. "What's happening to our family?"

22

J ENNY SLAPPED ALAN HARD ACROSS THE CHEEK. IT sounded like a gunshot. "How dare you say such a thing? Matt is my brother. My brother. He wouldn't hurt Danny, not on his life. You're making it up. You want so badly to pin this on someone, you're willing to blame it on my brother, who you've never liked. In fact, you. don't like anybody in my family, except Merrilee. And God knows, she likes you, because you're not—"

"Not what? Or should I say, not who?" Alan's face turned white except for the red mark on his cheek.

Jenny turned away. He put his hand on her arm and pulled her back around.

"Why are you doing this to me?" she asked.

"I'm trying to find out who hurt your son. I should think you'd appreciate that."

"But my brother, Alan? My God, how could you think I'd want to hear that?"

"Matt was drinking heavily Friday night. By his own admission, he has no memory of what took place between the time he left the Acapulco Lounge, just six

264

minutes before the estimated time of Danny's accident, until the next day."

"That doesn't mean anything."

"He still doesn't know where his car is. Fortunately, I was able to locate Brenda, the woman who accompanied him from the bar Friday night. She told me his car was in her garage, and that she didn't think to tell anyone, because she assumed Matt knew where his car was."

Jenny tried to follow his explanation, tried to focus on the facts instead of the panic building in her throat. "Maybe it was Brenda. Maybe she did it."

"She said Matt drove them to her house, that they didn't go to the next bar as planned, because it was too foggy. Brenda said Matt hit the brick wall at the edge of her property as he turned into her driveway."

"Then that explains the damage to the car."

"It's an awfully big coincidence, Jenny."

"I still don't understand. How did Matt get home from Brenda's?"

"Brenda dropped him off on her way to the airport just after six A.M. She had an early morning flight, and she thought he was still too high to drive. Apparently they had continued drinking at her house."

Jenny pulled her arm away from him. She didn't want to talk to Alan, didn't want to hear what he was saying, didn't want to believe a word of it. "Brenda explained it, and I believe her. Someone else hit Danny. Not Matt."

"I wouldn't have told you this if I didn't believe that Matt did it. I've been a cop too long. I know when someone's lying. The guy is guilty as sin. And Brenda is covering up for him. She was probably in the car when they hit Danny."

Jenny clapped her hands over her ears. "Stop. I don't want to listen to this."

"Jenny, you have to face facts." Alan walked toward her. "You can't keep protecting Matt."

"He's my brother," she cried, dropping her hands to her sides. She was so angry her hands clenched in fists, and she thought if Alan tried to touch her, she might just hit him again. Fighting for control, she tried to speak quietly and calmly. "Alan, Matt was with me when Danny was born. He was there when my mother died. He gave me money so I could move out of Merrilee's house. I know that he's changed, that he's filled with self-pity, but I remember the big brother who would do anything for me."

"None of that changes the fact that in this instance Matt might have made a big mistake."

"Might have. You don't know for sure. If you did, he'd be behind bars. And he's not, is he?"

"No."

"Why not?"

"Because I don't have any concrete evidence that he did it," Alan admitted.

Jenny nodded. "That's what I thought. I have to go."

"I'm not trying to frame Matt, just make him own up to his actions—like a man." Alan's expression softened. "Come on, Jenny, cut me some slack. I'm laying out the facts as I see them. Why can't you understand that?"

"Because Matt is my brother. Because love is more important to me than facts. And if you really loved me, you'd never have come to me with this."

"I do love you." Alan stared at her with pain in his eyes. "But you don't love me, do you?"

"I thought I did," she whispered. "I wanted to."

"Jenny, don't. Don't say it."

"Oh, Alan, can't you see how wrong this is? I don't want to hear you talk about Matt. You don't want to hear me talk about us. What's left?"

"A lot of things."

"No. Danny's accident has brought clarity to my

life. I'm not in love with you, Alan, and it wouldn't be fair to pretend otherwise."

"This isn't the time to make big decisions."

Jenny sighed, feeling too emotionally drained to argue. "Fine. Maybe you're right. What about Matt? What are you going to do?"

"Nothing for the moment. I won't stop investigating, Jenny. Whoever did this to Danny deserves to be punished, and they will be punished."

Danny peeked through the leaves of a tree, delighting in his mother's conversation with Alan. "She's breaking up with him. I can't believe she's actually breaking up with him. This is so cool." Danny danced between Alan and Jenny. "You lose, dude," he shouted. Of course, nobody heard him, but it felt good all the same.

"You're certainly a gracious winner, kid," Jacob commented dryly. "Did you ever stop to think this guy might be good for your mom?"

Danny shook his head. "Look at her face. She's relieved." He watched as Jenny walked out of the atrium, leaving Alan alone in the garden.

"Yo, Alan. How does it feel to get dumped?" Danny pulled at Alan's sleeve.

Alan shook his arm and looked around him, as if he sensed he was not alone.

"Hey, kid. You're making me look bad," Jacob said, pointing his thumb to the sky. "The Big Guy doesn't like braggarts."

"What's a braggart?"

"You, right now."

"Oh, well, sorry, but that guy has made my life miserable the last six months, trying to act like my dad."

"Maybe he was trying to help. He is one of the good guys, in case you hadn't noticed."

"He's not my dad."

"Lucky him. You're not exactly the perfect kid, you know."

"Whose fault is that? You're my guardian angel. You're supposed to—you know—make me a good person."

Jacob rolled his eyes and looked up at the heavens. "Why me? Why me?"

Danny laughed. He jumped up in the air, his supernatural leap taking him up to the top of the atrium ceiling. He did a somersault in midair, then a triple twist, landing back on the ground with his hands in the air, like a gymnast sticking a difficult vault.

"Easy, kid. You're starting to have way too much fun. Maybe it's about time you had a reminder."

"A reminder of what?"

Jacob grabbed Danny by the ear.

"Ow, that hurts."

"No, it don't. You can't feel any pain."

Danny's eyes widened as he considered the comment. "You're right. I guess I just remembered that having my ear pulled hurt. My Aunt Merrilee was always pulling me by the ear when Mom wasn't looking. She's got a mean streak in her, I'll tell you."

"Oh, yeah, well look at her now, and look at you."

Danny turned his head and realized they were back in the hospital room. It seemed like a long time since he had drifted out of his body.

Seeing himself now, on the bed, made the pain come back, or at least the memory of the pain. Once again he was reminded that the person he was on earth was gone, maybe forever.

Merrilee pulled a tissue out of her purse and blew her nose. She sounded like a foghorn. Jacob shook his head in disbelief.

"How can a woman who dresses to the nines blow her nose like a bullhorn in a factory?" Jacob asked.

"You should hear her sneeze. Shakes the whole house," Danny replied.

"Hope she doesn't sneeze in here. The last thing you need is a cold."

"What's she doing here anyway? She hates me."

"I don't think so. Listen."

Merrilee licked her lips, looked over her shoulder to determine if she was still alone, then gazed back down at Danny.

"I'm sorry," she whispered. "For all the mean things I said, all the criticism. You're not a bad kid. In fact, sometimes I wish William had your athletic ability, your joy for life. You get that from your mother, I guess. Jenny loves you so much. She can't make it without you. You have to fight this, Danny, fight hard. As hard as you've ever fought for anything in your life."

Merrilee sniffed again and reached out to pat down his cowlick. "They really should comb your hair once in a while."

Danny looked at Jacob and rolled his eyes. "Like anyone cares what I look like."

"Everyone sends you their love, Danny. We miss you. And I'll tell you a secret. If you get well before Christmas, I'll send you to spring training in Phoenix for a whole week. That will be your present. You can even take a friend if you want. You'll love it there. You'll get autographs, see the Giants play. You'll be in heaven."

"Wow! Spring training. Cool."

"You can go to spring training now, Danny. You can ride on the ball if you want to, dance in the stands, blow a breeze through the park so the fielder misjudges the catch. You don't need to be alive to do that," Jacob said.

"It would be more fun if I could go with Christopher."

Jacob stared at him for a long time, and Danny felt his joy drain away. "It's not going to happen, is it?"

"You're still thinking about yourself, Danny.

You've been thinking about yourself since you went looking for your father last week. Haven't you learned anything yet? Open your eyes, kid, look around. Life is about more than just you."

Danny gazed at his Aunt Merrilee, at the boy in the bed, at the tubes going into the boy's arms and down through his nose. His body looked skinny, pale, like a sick person. He remembered how bad he had felt the last time he had the flu. This looked a hundred times worse.

What if Michael was right? What if he was a cripple? His mother would have to take care of him. She would never laugh again. He would be a burden to her and everyone else.

His dad said he would help, but would he really? Luke had walked away before. How could Danny trust him now?

But Danny didn't want to die. He was too scared. Did that mean he was selfish? Probably.

He didn't know what to wish for anymore. Life was too complicated. Heaven was looking better and better all the time.

Matt knocked on Brenda's door. He was glad he had gone home after Merrilee's Thanksgiving nightmare. Brenda's phone message had brought him the first bit of good news he'd had in days.

Brenda opened the door with a wide, welcoming smile. "Hi, Matt. It's great to see you. Come on in. Can I get you something to drink?"

"Yeah, sure."

"Bud?"

"Fine."

Matt stepped into her living room. He looked around at the art deco furniture, the black-framed paintings, the lone bud vase on the coffee table, the black-and-white rug running the length of the living room, and tried to remember the night they had spent together. Nothing looked familiar, but then the only time he would have been here was that Friday night. The last time they had spent the night together had been at his place, and he remembered every last detail of that encounter.

Brenda came back with a bottle of beer. He took a long sip. It felt good, freeing after a stifling day with family. "Boy, was I glad to hear from you," he said.

Her smile faded. "I'm sorry, Matt. I thought you knew your car was in the garage. Otherwise, I would have left you a note."

"Do you know what kind of hell I've been going through the last few days? My nephew was almost killed by a hit-and-run driver, and I'm the number one suspect."

"I'm sorry." She dug her hands into her pockets. They didn't go far in the tight jeans. "How is your nephew?"

"Not good." He set the bottle down on the table, losing his thirst at the memory of Danny. "Can I get my car now?"

"Sure. It's in the garage."

Matt felt an incredible sense of relief when he saw his car, as if a part of his life had been given back to him. But the relief faded when he came around the front. He stopped and stared. Jesus! No wonder Alan thought he was guilty. The license plate was bent, and there was a thick crack in the headlight. "What happened?"

Brenda shrugged. "You hit that low brick wall at the beginning of the driveway when we turned in. I guess you had too much to drink."

Matt shook his head at her understatement. "Too much to drink? I must have been plastered, because I don't remember a thing. Why the hell did you let me drive? And why the hell did you get in the car with me? I could have killed us both."

Brenda swallowed, looking suddenly nervous. "I

wasn't thinking clearly, Matt. Next time, I'll be more careful."

There was something in the way she avoided his eyes, the restless shifting of her feet, that made Matt doubt her statement. Had he hit Danny? Was she hiding the truth from him? But why would she do that? She wouldn't protect him. They had had sex, not a relationship. No, she wouldn't lie to protect him, but she might lie to protect herself.

"Do you want to come in for a while?" Brenda asked. "We could—you know—have some fun. I don't have to go to work until tomorrow morning."

Matt barely registered her words, his mind focused on one thing and one thing only. "I wasn't driving, was I?"

She looked shocked. "Of course you were driving."

"You're lying." He moved forward. Brenda took a hasty step back. "You knew I was drunk. You wouldn't risk your life to let me drive."

"I didn't know you were that drunk. You seemed okay."

"You were behind the wheel Friday night. You're the one who hit Danny!"

"No."

He grabbed her by the shoulders and shook her. "Tell me the truth, dammit. Tell me the truth."

"No! No! I didn't hit Danny." She held up a hand. "Okay, I was driving, but I hit the wall out front. Since you didn't remember, I lied, because I don't have extra money to pay for the damage. But I did not hit your nephew. I swear on the Bible."

Matt stared at her for a long time. "I want to believe you. Because if you were driving, and I was sitting next to you when you ran over Danny, I don't think I could live with myself."

"I didn't hit Danny. I hit a wall. Just a wall. And I will pay for the damage."

"I don't care about the money, Brenda."

"You don't?"

He shook his head. "No."

"Then that's settled." She looked relieved. "Can you stay for a while? I hate spending Thanksgiving alone."

"I can't. I have to see Danny. I should have gone earlier. Now that I know the truth, I can face him and Jenny with a clean conscience."

Jenny put an arm around Merrilee's waist as they stood together next to Danny's bed. "If I could trade places with him, I would," Jenny said.

"You love him that much?"

"Yes. Just as you love your children."

"I do." Merrilee nodded. "I sometimes get so caught up in scolding them I forget how much I love them, how much they mean to me and Richard."

"Speaking of Richard, is everything okay with you two?"

"No."

Jenny raised an eyebrow. "Wow. You really are different tonight. You'd never admit that to me otherwise."

"I don't know what to do, Jenny. He's slipping away."

"You have to fight for him like I'm fighting for Danny. These are the people we love, Merrilee. Look at your nephew. Look at how fragile life is. You can't stand by and let things drift away. They're too precious."

Merrilee glanced over at her and smiled. "You've changed, too."

"How could I not?" She paused. "I'm sorry I didn't come to the house. I just couldn't face Thanksgiving."

"That's okay. I understand." Merrilee paused. "I asked Dad to come here with me. He said no. I'm sorry."

"It's okay. I'm not sure I'd know what to say to him if he did come."

"Funny, I think he's worried about the same thing. I wonder why it's so difficult to talk to the people we love."

Jenny shrugged. "Anyway, you're here. That helps." She cleared her throat. "By the way, Alan came to see me earlier. He thinks Matt was responsible for Danny's accident."

Merrilee sighed. "I wish he hadn't told you that."

"You knew?"

"Yes. Matt honestly doesn't remember a thing, Jenny. I don't know what to say. We both know he's a lousy drunk."

"He makes me so angry. I wish he'd believe in himself again. There's more to life than football."

"I never used to think so." Matt's voice drew their attention to the doorway. "Okay, if I come in?"

"Of course. I'm glad you came." Jenny took his hand and pulled him close. She would not think about Alan's suspicions. Matt was her brother, and she loved him. Right now family was more important than anything else.

"How are you, Jen-Jen?" Matt asked.

"I've had better days."

Matt looked at Danny and shook his head. "Jesus, he looks like shit."

Jenny smiled. "Trust you to put this all in perspective."

Matt turned to her. "I didn't do it, Jenny. I know I didn't. Brenda swears she drove us both to her place, and the only thing we hit was the brick wall in front of her house. I can't prove it. But in my heart, I know I couldn't have hurt Danny. I love this kid."

"I know you do."

Matt rubbed his hand across his eyes. Jenny wanted to comfort him, so she wrapped her arms around his waist and hugged him tightly. As she glanced up, she caught Merrilee watching them with something that looked like envy. After a moment's hesitation, Jenny stepped back and beckoned Merrilee into their circle.

The three of them stood together, holding each other. Jenny hadn't felt this close to her siblings in a long time. She looked past them to Danny and thought she saw a faint smile cross his lips.

"Happy Thanksgiving," she whispered.

"Dad," Danny whispered, tugging on Luke's sleeve. There was no response. Danny glanced over at the clock. It was after midnight, but he didn't care. He dug his fingers into Luke's arm. Luke moaned but didn't open his eyes. At his wit's end, Danny grabbed a strand of Luke's hair and yanked it out.

"Ow!" Luke blearily opened his eyes. "What's going on?"

"You're turning gray, Dad." Danny held up the strand of gray hair between his fingers.

Luke shook his head, obviously trying to wake up. Danny pulled the rocking chair over to the side of the bed and began to rock back and forth, faster and faster, until the chair threatened to collide with the dresser.

"Hey, watch out. You'll wake Denise." Luke glanced over his shoulder to be sure Denise was still sleeping. She was, her eyes covered with a mask of black velvet. He turned back to Danny. "What are you doing here?"

"I came to see you about something important."

"Danny, I don't know if you're real, or if I'm imagining you, but this is crazy. You're a ghost."

"No. I'm not a ghost." Danny tipped his head. "Actually, I'm not sure what I am. Jacob says I'm not an angel, because I'm not dead yet."

"No, you're not. You're lying in a hospital room." Luke shook his head. "I can't believe I'm talking to a hallucination. Do you visit your mother like this?"

Danny suddenly looked pained. "No. Jacob says it's not allowed. I want to though. I miss her. Will you tell her I miss her?"

"Of course. But she won't believe me. How could she? You're in a coma, Danny."

"Do you think I'll make it?"

"I don't know. Will you?" Luke sat up and swung his legs over the side of the bed. "I need a sleeping pill."

"Don't do that, Dad."

Luke hesitated at the tender word. "God, I wish I could really hear you say that."

"Do you?" Danny's eyes searched his face.

"Yes. I want us to be together. I want us to do all the father-son things we're supposed to do."

"Did you put up a basketball hoop yet?"

"This morning."

"Cool. What about baseball? Are you any good?"

Luke frowned. "I always had to play right field."

"Yeah, me, too." Danny smiled in commiseration. "And I strike out a lot. Mom gets so excited when I bat, she jumps up and down in the stands and yells her head off. The other parents think she's nuts. Sometimes, I get embarrassed, but she's kind of cool, you know."

"Yeah, I know," Luke said softly, feeling the same protectiveness toward Jenny that Danny felt.

"That's why I came tonight, in case you've forgotten. Next Friday, a week from tomorrow, is Mom's birthday. I didn't get her a gift."

"She won't be expecting a present, Danny. She just wants you to get well."

"I'm not sure I can."

"Don't say that."

Danny got up from the chair. "Michael and Jacob said I might be paralyzed or retarded even if I wake up. I don't think Mom could handle that."

"I would help her, Danny. We'd do whatever it took to get you well."

"You mean you'd stick around even if I was retarded?"

"Of course. I won't turn my back on you, Danny. That's a promise."

"How do I know you'll keep your promise?"

Luke looked him straight in the eyes. "You'll have to trust me."

Danny nodded. "You're okay, Dad."

"So are you."

"Now, here's what I want you to do," Danny said, and proceeded to tell Luke exactly what to buy Jenny for her birthday.

"That's it?" Luke asked.

"That's it." Danny started to fade away.

"Wait. I want to talk to you some more."

"Jacob says, time's up." On the last word, he vanished.

Luke blinked.

Suddenly Danny appeared again.

"One more thing," Danny said. "Mom broke up with Alan. I thought you might want to know."

23

T HE WEEKEND AFTER THANKSGIVING PASSED quickly with an endless stream of visitors to Danny's hospital room. Jenny held court there, accepting flowers, stuffed animals, comic books, and compact discs. She read Danny stories and told him jokes. She sang to him. Sometimes Danny turned his head. Sometimes his hand jerked back when she pinched him. Other times, there was nothing.

The next week passed more slowly.

Merrilee came and went every day. Richard dropped by in the evenings. Alan checked in before he went on duty. Matt made an appearance at least every other day, and Jenny's friends Gracie and Pru stopped by whenever they could.

Danny's friend Christopher and his other buddies came by after school, solemn and serious. Jenny respected their courage, knowing that it was even more difficult for them to accept the fact that someone their own age could be so close to death. With Danny's accident, the boys had lost some of their innocence.

Christopher, of course, was riddled with guilt over his part in the adventure. Jenny tried to comfort him, to assure him that with or without his help, Danny would have found his way to his father's house. Her words made little difference. Only Danny's recovery would free Christopher from the weight of his guilt.

Seeing the boys and talking to them about school was difficult for Jenny. She had known some of the kids since they'd been born. They reminded her of Danny—their mannerisms, their clothing, the words they used, the tenor of their voices, breaking between childhood and adolescence.

Then there was Luke. He rarely went home. At first, she felt awkward around him, but as time passed, she was grateful for his presence, for the opportunity he offered to escape for a few minutes. And Luke had the inside track with the doctors. He asked questions that didn't even occur to her, and he got answers.

Luke—the man was working his way back into her life, and Jenny didn't know how to stop him. Worse, she didn't really want to stop him.

On Friday afternoon, two weeks after the accident, Jenny paused at the nurses' station and looked into Danny's room through the glass partition. Luke was sitting next to Danny's bed, talking to his son, touching Danny's hands, working his arms and legs with affectionate, loving gestures.

It touched her heart to see them together. Danny would be happy to have his father's undivided attention. She hoped to God that Danny could hear what Luke was saying. It would mean so much to her son.

As she watched the two of them together, she noted how tired Luke looked. His hair was messy, his suit wrinkled. His tie was pulled away at the neck, and he had unbuttoned the top two buttons on his shirt.

The sight of him in such a state brought with it a wave of tenderness. This was the man she had loved. The one who was human, not the one who was rich and powerful and smart as hell, but the one who could be vulnerable.

"He's been here for an hour," the nurse said.

Jenny glanced at her. "Really?"

"Yes. He's different from what I expected. I've met his father," she added.

Jenny nodded in understanding. "So have I."

"But Dr. Sheridan is so sweet with Danny. You're lucky. Well, I'm going off duty now. Have a nice night."

"Thanks." Jenny stepped into the room. Luke looked up and smiled at her.

"Hi."

"Hi yourself. You look like you slept in those clothes."

Luke tilted his head as he considered his attire. "I flew down to L.A. early this morning. I went to talk to another specialist about Danny."

"And?"

Luke walked over to her. "Let's go outside." He put a hand under her elbow and drew her into the hall, away from ICU. "He thinks the longer Danny stays in a coma, the less his chance for recovery."

"It's been two weeks. Is that a long time?"

"Yes."

Jenny took in a deep breath and let it out. He wasn't telling her anything she didn't already know, but hearing the words out loud made them seem more real. "Dr. Lowenstein told me the same thing," she said. "He even mentioned the possibility of moving Danny out of intensive care. I'm afraid if he does that, Danny won't get the attention he needs."

"Don't worry. If they move him into a private room, I'll hire twenty-four-hour, round-the-clock care, with the best nurses available."

"Thank you. I mean that sincerely. I don't know what I would have done without you this past week." She attempted a smile. "Not just your money, but your support. I never expected you to react this way, not after the way we parted."

Luke looked at her with pain in his eyes. "I feel helpless, Jenny. I should be able to do more for you than hold your hand. I can't believe I've spent my entire life studying to be a doctor so I could save lives, and I can't do a damn thing to save my own son."

Jenny studied him thoughtfully, realizing how difficult Danny's accident must be for Luke. Having no medical knowledge herself, she accepted her limitations, but Luke couldn't do that.

"You're doing as much as you can," she said. "That's all you can do. Life is filled with ironies. Sometimes, I get angry and think that God is having a big joke at our expense, but I expect we make our own jokes, by simply believing that we actually have control over our lives."

Luke pulled Jenny to one side of the hall as a woman came out of a room, pushing a little girl in a wheelchair. The girl's right leg was held straight out in a long leg cast. It looked awkward and uncomfortable, but there was a smile on the child's face.

"Want to sign my leg?" she asked Luke.

"Kelly, you don't even know them," the woman said. "I'm sorry. She's determined to break some school record on cast signatures."

Luke grinned. "It's all right. I think I even have a pen." He pulled a pen out of his inside pocket. "Who should I write this to?"

"Kelly Jamison. I'm eight years old today."

"Then I better sign 'Happy Birthday.' "

Luke finished his greeting with a big smile, then handed the pen to Jenny. She added her own words of encouragement, and they stood together as the girl continued down the hallway, racking up signatures.

"That was nice of you," Jenny commented.

Luke stared after the girl with a thoughtful expression.

"Is something wrong?" Jenny asked.

He turned to her with a curious smile. "I just realized that I enjoyed that. I never liked working with patients in medical school. I never knew what to say to make them feel better. I felt inadequate."

"You?" Jenny looked at him in surprise. "Why would you feel that way?"

"I never knew how to relate to people."

"Well, you're certainly great with Danny, and that little girl, too. Maybe you should have gone into pediatrics."

"I never considered anything but biotech. Of course, I'm too old to make such a major change now."

"Oh, come on, Luke. You may have accomplished more in the past ten years than some people have done in their lifetime, but you're still pretty young. If you want to make a change, make one."

"I'll think about my life later—when Danny's better."

Jenny leaned against the wall. She knew it was time to set Luke free from his self-imposed guilt trip. Danny might be his flesh and blood, but he had another family now and a wife to consider.

"If you have to spend more time at home, Luke, I understand," Jenny said finally. "This must be difficult on your wife."

Luke's expression grew tense. "Denise understands this is where I need to be."

"Does she?"

"Well, maybe not."

Jenny tried to be fair. "I'm sure it's not easy for her to accept the fact that you have a son. I don't know how I would feel if I were in her place."

"You? You would joyfully give every bit of love you could to both your husband and his child. I know you, Jenny. You have a big heart."

"A big, foolish heart."

"Say, do you want to get out of here for a while?" Luke asked. "Let's take a drive. Get some fresh air."

A tempting thought. She had begun to know the hospital vending machines better than her own refrigerator. "Where would you want to go?"

"Let's go to San Francisco. We can check out the Christmas tree in Union Square, stop by F.A.O. Schwartz and buy Danny the best Christmas present we can find."

"Danny has expensive taste. Takes after his father."

"The sky's the limit."

Luke took her hand. Jenny felt a tingle at his touch. She hesitated, thinking of Luke's wife, and Alan, who she had promised to at least talk to sometime tonight, and Merrilee, who was expecting her daily call, and . . .

"You're thinking too much," Luke said with a smile. "When did you get into such a bad habit?"

"You must be rubbing off on me. There are so many people I need to keep in touch with."

"Not tonight. Give yourself a break. Come with me."

Three simple words, the same ones she had said to him all those years ago. And he had come. She was crazy for even considering a night out with Luke. Yet, here she stood, with his fingers wrapped around hers, the connection between them stronger now than it had ever been.

Danny would have wanted her to say yes, and so she did.

An hour later, Jenny flung her head all the way back so she could see the top of the fifty-foot Christmas Tree in Union Square. The lights were a dazzling display of color.

"It's magnificent," she said.

"Overkill, I think."

She punched Luke playfully in the shoulder. "Just what I'd expect from a man who has no romance in his soul."

"I have romance in my soul. I can appreciate this moment. In fact, I even have a present for you."

Jenny turned to him in surprise. He dug his hand into his pocket and pulled out a package.

"What's that for?"

"Your birthday is today."

"Oh, my God. I completely forgot." She looked at him in astonishment. "You remembered my birthday after all these years?"

"Actually, I had a little help. Open the box."

Jenny's hands curled around the bright red ribbon on the small white box. "I can't imagine why you'd buy me a present."

"Open it, Jenny. You know you love presents."

Her lips curved into an involuntary smile, and she couldn't help being pleased at the gesture. "You're right. I do love presents."

She pulled off the ribbon and opened the box. Inside was a ceramic angel pin. Jenny gasped at the sight. It was the angel she had seen in the country store up on Skyline Drive. The angel with the backward-turned baseball cap, the mischievous expression, and the budding wings that reminded her of Danny.

"No," she whispered.

"Do you like it?"

She shook her head as tears welled up in her eyes.

"Jenny. I'm sorry. I thought it was what you wanted." Luke pulled her closer as they were jostled by the crowd gathering in Union Square.

Jenny was barely aware of their movement. At that moment, she felt completely alone in the cold, dark night with the winking angel dancing like a firefly in the light of the moon.

Danny, her little angel. Not really, of course, because he wasn't an angel, but a child, an obstinate, impatient, somewhat selfish child, but all hers.

Jenny stared down at the angel pin, at the face, the

tiniest markings on the cheek that looked suspiciously like freckles, and began to cry. The tears flowed easily, effortlessly. Luke pulled her into his arms and held her. He murmured an apology. She didn't hear it. Her fingers traced the face on the pin, over and over again, and finally, she began to feel peace.

She pulled away from Luke to look down at the pin. "It's beautiful."

Luke sent her a wary look. "I can take it back."

"No, you can't take it back." She clutched it to her heart. "It's mine, now."

"I didn't think you liked it."

"I love it. How did you know, Luke? I saw this with Danny a couple of weeks ago. He laughed at me, because I love pins. I make jewelry, you know, and I'm always checking out the competition. But this pin seemed so unique, so different that it captured my imagination. I couldn't stop looking at it."

"I'm glad you like it."

"How did you know?"

Luke looked away, and Jenny wondered at his reaction. He was evading her question, and she didn't understand why. "Luke?"

"How about dinner? Are you hungry?"

"You didn't answer my question."

"Can I buy you dinner anyway?"

"You're being awfully mysterious."

"A man's prerogative."

"I think you've got that backward, but okay." She smiled, suddenly ravenous, hungry for food, for life. A sense of joy filled her soul every time she rubbed her fingers over the angel's face.

"He looks like Danny, doesn't he?" Luke said. "I thought that the first time I saw it."

"He looks like you."

"No, Danny may have my eyes, my hair color, but he's got your soul, and that's the best part of him."

Jenny stood on tiptoe and impulsively kissed Luke

on the mouth. He froze for a moment, then kissed her back. His mouth moved against hers with a passion and need that went way beyond her simple, spontaneous gesture.

Her lips opened under his, and his tongue tasted every inch of her mouth. It was delicious, breathtaking, and hauntingly familiar. Crowds of people moved around them. Horns honked. Cars backfired. People swore, but all Jenny could feel was Luke's arms around her waist, his mouth on hers.

She opened her mouth for air, and Luke kissed the corner of her lips, her cheeks, the sensitive space behind her ears. When he lifted his head to look at her, their breath curled between them, smoky whispers chilled by the night air.

Luke cupped her face with his hands. He studied her with deep concentration, as if he were memorizing the lines of her face, the lines borne of laughter, sadness, and age. Their youthful passion seemed lukewarm compared to what burned between them now. Their emotions were much more complex. With maturity had come pain, sorrow, and the knowledge that this kind of passion was not meant to be taken for granted.

"Jenny, Jenny." He murmured her name. "I can't get you out of my head."

"You have to." She took a deep breath, knowing it was time to end the connection between them. "You're married, Luke. This is wrong. You shouldn't be kissing me; I shouldn't be kissing you. I'm sorry I started this."

Luke dropped his hands. Jenny stepped back, still breathless, but more in control.

"I'm having a hard time remembering that I'm married," Luke said.

"Me, too," she admitted.

"I've been faithful to my wife."

"That's good." She looked away from him, feeling

awkward in the face of such a personal revelation. She didn't want to think about Luke having sex with anyone but her. "Do you want to get something to eat?"

"Denise had an affair last year with a tennis pro," Luke said. "The guy was twenty-two, young, virile."

"Luke, I don't want to hear this. It's your personal business."

"Denise thought I didn't know. I would have had to be stupid not to know. I thought about confronting her, but I didn't want to deal with it. I probably brought it on myself, working long hours, ignoring her."

"This is between you and Denise. I don't think she'd appreciate you telling me about it."

"I know, it's not your problem." Luke turned away.

"I didn't mean it that way." She put a hand on his arm. "I just don't want to come between you, Luke. But I am sorry that things haven't worked out for you."

Luke shrugged. "Why should you be sorry? We make our beds, and we lie in them. If I didn't know that before, I certainly know it now."

Merrilee walked up to the front door of her husband's advertising agency. It was after seven, and Richard was supposed to be meeting a client. She didn't believe it for a second.

At the door, she paused. Through the glass, she could see the door to Richard's office, but nothing else. The conference room was beyond that, so she had no idea if an actual meeting was in progress and if she was about to embarrass the hell out of herself.

Merrilee shook her head, not knowing why she was doing this. After watching her kids shrug off her dinner, rushing to the hospital only to find Jenny gone, then seeing Danny lying in a state so near to death it terrified her, she had found herself driving to Richard's office.

Danny was dying.

The truth finally hit her in the face, shocking her into action. If Danny could die, if his life could be erased so quickly, how could she let her life go on so dismally? How could she keep pretending that things would get better, that Richard would get over his midlife crisis and come back to her? It wasn't going to happen. Not without some help.

Merrilee realized now that she had been fighting the symptoms, not the cause, railing against Richard's late meetings instead of confronting him and acknowledging his unfaithfulness.

Even saying the word to herself was difficult. It meant admitting she had failed, and it wasn't easy for her to face failure. She didn't want to face it now.

Her hand dropped from the doorknob. If she went home, Richard would never know she had come. They could go on pretending to be the perfect couple. What on earth could come of her finding him with some woman? She would have to think about divorce, selling the house, breaking up her children's lives. No, it was absurd.

Merrilee walked back to the elevator and pushed the button. The elevator door opened. She hesitated. After a moment the doors closed without her.

It was Danny's fault. Watching Jenny try desperately to hang on to her son had made Merrilee realize how tenuous a hold they all had on life. Watching her nephew fight for every breath had awakened her to a sense of priority that she had never felt before.

Having the perfect home, being a mother and wife were all she had ever wanted. To an outsider, she had exactly that. But she knew differently. And it hurt. Or maybe it just hurt more now. Since Danny's accident, every emotion, every nerve seemed keener, closely attuned to pain. Two weeks ago, she wouldn't have dreamed of doing this. It was hardly dignified. Still, she had to know the truth.

With strengthened resolve, Merrilee entered the office. She stopped in front of Richard's door, hearing voices—a woman and a man.

Merrilee took a deep breath and flung open the door. Richard jumped up from the couch, hastily buttoning the top two buttons on his shirt.

His twenty-four-year-old secretary, Blair, a gorgeous blonde with big breasts and long legs, also got to her feet. There were two cartons of Chinese food on the coffee table, along with two glasses of wine and an empty bottle.

It didn't take a rocket scientist to know there was more than work going on.

All the nights she had sat alone at home waiting for him raced through her mind. She had been loyal and trusting, and he had played her for a fool.

"My God, Merrilee. What the hell are you doing here?" Richard demanded. Fury was written in every line of his face, along with some other emotion Merrilee didn't have time to define.

"What the hell are you doing with her?" Anger boiled over at Richard's attack. He was in the wrong. She was in the right. Damn him.

"She's my secretary. We're working on a project."

"Like hell you are. You bastard. I'm glad to know you take your marriage vows so seriously."

"You take them seriously enough for both of us. Only the part about keeping your husband happy—"

"Shut up. Shut up. And you—get out." Mortified at Richard's taunt, Merrilee grabbed Blair by the arm and literally threw her out of the office. "Now, you listen to me," she said to Richard. "You've been cheating on me for months. Do you think I'm stupid? You arrogant, son of a bitch—"

"Stop it, Merrilee. You're acting hysterical."

"Hysterical?" she yelled. "You think I'm hysterical?"

Richard took a step back. "Just calm down."

"I don't want to calm down. I want your head on a fucking platter."

Richard's jaw dropped open in astonishment. Merrilee walked over to his desk, picked up his coffee cup and hurled it at his head. Richard ducked, and the cup smashed against the wall.

"Jesus Christ, Merrilee. What are you doing?"

Merrilee gathered all the papers off his desk and dumped them into the trash can.

"Hey, those are important."

She ignored him, pulling out the desk drawers and systematically dumping them out on the floor. It felt good to trash Richard's office. He was ruining her life. Why the hell shouldn't he suffer a little bit?

"Now, Merrilee, let's talk about this—at home," he added. "This is my office. My business."

"Funny, you didn't look like you were conducting business a minute ago." Merrilee headed to the coffee table. The red lipstick around the rim of the wineglass drove her further over the edge. She picked up the glass and tossed the contents into Richard's face. "I think you're the one who needs to cool off."

Richard sputtered, wiping his face with his shirt-sleeve. Before he could recover completely, Merrilee yanked at his trousers and dumped the second glass of wine down his pants. He gasped as the cold liquid hit his skin.

"Goddammit," he shouted. "You're fucking crazy."

"You bet I am. I'm sick and tired of this, Richard. You've been taunting me for months. I won't take it anymore. You want a divorce, you've got one."

The words were out of her mouth before she could even consider the seriousness of what she had said. But as they echoed around the room, some of her anger disappeared, replaced by fear. Richard stared at her in shock.

"A divorce? You want a divorce?"

Merrilee wrapped her arms around her body. "I was hoping you'd get over this midlife crisis, or whatever it is you're going through. Apparently, that's not going to happen. I can't put up with any more of your cheating."

"I didn't think you'd noticed. I was beginning to think you didn't care one way or the other."

"I don't."

"Liar."

His muttered word drew her head up. "I don't care about you. Right now I hate you."

"If you hated me, you wouldn't be here. My God, Merrilee, I've never seen you act like this. You're always so cool, so controlled."

"I'm human, Richard. And I have feelings. How could you do this to me? To us? I loved you. I gave you everything."

"Merrilee . . ." He reached out to touch her. She knocked his hand away.

"Leave me alone. Just leave me alone." She ran out of the office and didn't stop running until she reached her car. With shaky fingers, she slipped the key into the lock and got inside. She made it out of the parking lot and down one block before the tears came. Then she pulled over and cried, long, cleansing tears that had been building up for a lifetime.

24

 ◀◯▶

LUKE PULLED THE CAR INTO THE PARKING LOT OF the Marina Green. It was almost midnight, and the lot was empty, save for a few tourists enjoying a spectacularly clear winter night. Jenny opened her door and got out. Luke followed her down to the sea wall where the waves from the San Francisco Bay lapped against the shore.

Off to their left was the Golden Gate Bridge, red in actual color, but no less breathtaking in the moonlight. In the middle of the bay was Alcatraz Island and somewhere, although he couldn't see it clearly, was Angel Island.

Angel. The word made him glance to the heavens. *Where are you tonight, Danny? Lying in the hospital bed or soaring through the sky with your friend Jacob?*

"This is peaceful," Jenny said, resting her head against his arm. "I love being outside. Danny does, too. From the day I brought him home when he was a baby, as soon as he'd start to cry, I'd take him out on the porch, and he'd shut up faster than an oyster guarding its pearl." She laughed at the memory.

"It's nice to hear you laugh. It's been a long time."

"I feel better tonight. I don't know why. It's strange. Sometimes when I'm away from the hospital, I feel closer to Danny than when I'm there. Isn't that odd?"

Luke shook his head, not trusting himself to speak. He wanted to tell Jenny that he had seen Danny. But saying the words out loud seemed absurd. Danny was in a coma. He was not cavorting around as an angel. Luke didn't believe in angels, or for that matter, in God. At least he hadn't believed—before now.

Looking up into the stars, on a night like this, holding the woman he loved in his arms, Luke began to think all things were possible.

"You're quiet," Jenny said. "Maybe we should go."

"We have time."

"What did your parents say when you told them about Danny?"

He shrugged his shoulders. "Not much."

"Don't try to spare my feelings. I want to know."

Luke didn't know what to say. He didn't want to hurt Jenny any more than he already had, but he couldn't hide the truth from her. She would see right through him. Finally, he said, "My father thinks you're after my money, and my mother thinks that adding a son to my life would complicate things."

"She's right."

"It's my life."

"What about your wife? Does she want children?"

His stomach turned over at the question. He still couldn't believe what Denise had done. "Funny you should ask," he said bitterly. "Denise got a tubal ligation last month without telling me."

Jenny stepped away from him, startled by his words. "She did? Without telling you?"

"That's correct. I found out by accident. She figured she'd just never get pregnant, and that would be that. One of those little ironies you were talking about. I had the chance to be a father to Danny all those years ago. Now he's in intensive care, and I'll probably never have another child. I think you just got the last laugh."

"I'm not laughing."

And she wasn't. She was looking at him with an intensity that was pure Jenny—bold, truthful, honest, and forgiving. He realized it then—she had forgiven him, and for the life of him he couldn't understand why.

"You should be laughing," he said harshly. "I ruined your life."

She did smile then. "Giving me Danny didn't ruin my life. He's the best part of my life. He anchors me, and you know how much I need an anchor."

"I don't know about that. I thought if there was a human being on this earth who could fly, it would be you."

"Me?" she asked in wonder. "I'm a mere mortal, Luke. You were the one who always soared higher than everyone else."

"I didn't soar. I climbed up the ladder, one foot after another, relentlessly on and on and on." He squeezed his eyes shut, feeling incredibly weary. "I couldn't get off. I couldn't stop. Something was pushing me up that ladder, like a hamster that can't get off the damn wheel, even if it kills him."

"What was driving you, Luke?"

"Fear." He opened his eyes and looked at her. "I was terrified that if I stopped, I'd fall into oblivion where no one would care about me." He tried to laugh, because his words sounded dark, lonely, vulnerable. Jenny wasn't buying it.

"You can't be what you aren't, Luke."

"I'm beginning to realize that."

Luke pulled a stand of her hair away from her face. It was a tender, loving gesture. He wanted to have more moments like this, times when he could talk to her about anything and know she wouldn't judge him.

"Jenny?"

She looked at him inquiringly. "Luke?"

He smiled. "What about your dreams? I just realized I don't even know what you do for a living."

"I'm a checkout cashier at McDougal's Market in Half Moon Bay. I've been there seven years now. Talk about a hamster on a wheel. But it pays most of my bills. I work some nights at the Acapulco Lounge serving cocktails, mostly to my brother," she said wryly, "and in my spare time, I make jewelry that I hope will one day make me a rich and famous artisan. Right now, it pretty much just pays for Little League."

Luke looked at her for a long moment, incredibly touched by her matter-of-fact explanation of her life. She made it sound so much easier than he knew it had to be.

"You're something else," he murmured.

"Not really." Her face turned serious. "Your parents were right, Luke. I didn't grow up to be anybody special. Not like you."

"Thank God," he said fervently. "And don't sell yourself short, Jenny. During the last two weeks, you've impressed the hell out of me. You have so much strength and courage. Where did it all come from?"

"Danny," she said simply. "I had a child. I had to take care of him. And I didn't do it alone. Merrilee helped in the beginning, almost too much. And Matt gave me money. I tried not to depend on them, but sometimes I didn't have a choice." She took a deep breath. "Anyway, the past is past, right? Want to see some of my jewelry?"

"I'd love to." Actually, he wanted to take her in his arms and promise that she would never have to struggle for anything again, that he would give her money and a house and a car and anything else she and Danny needed. But he didn't say a word, because he could see the pride in her eyes, and he didn't want her to think that she was anything but a success.

Jenny pulled a necklace out from under her sweater. "I made this piece just before Danny got hurt."

Luke touched the coral-colored shell necklace with a reverent gesture. "It's lovely. Different."

"That's me, different." She shrugged her shoulders. "My friend Pru thinks I should try to sell the jewelry a little more aggressively than at the local art fair. I've been considering it for a while." She shook her head. "I used to think I had so much time to do what I wanted to do. Then this happened, and I realized everything could end in a second." She paused. "Danny helps me collect the shells and rocks. We've been doing it together since he was old enough to walk. I'm not sure I can do it without him. I'm not sure I can fill the couple of orders that I have before Christmas. Oh God, Luke." Her face tightened with fear. "Everything in my life revolves around Danny. How can I lose him?"

"You can't and you won't. Maybe I could help you."

Fear was replaced by amazement. "You, a business tycoon and successful doctor, want to help me look for seashells on the beach?"

"Why not?"

"Why?"

"Because you'd be there." *Because I have a feeling I'd find more on the beach than just seashells. Like a reason for being. Like a love that I thought was gone forever.*

"Luke, I can't—"

"Sh-sh. Don't say it."

"I don't know what you want from me." Jenny looked at him searchingly.

He wanted her love, her passion, everything she had to give, especially her trust. But what he didn't want to do was scare her. It was too soon, too fast, so he said nothing.

"Do you mind if we walk awhile?" Jenny didn't wait for an answer.

They strolled in silence past the St. Francis Yacht Club and the harbor, closer to the lights on the Golden Gate Bridge. After a while, Jenny slipped her arm through his. They stopped at the end of the path, just beneath the bridge, awed by its majesty.

"We're so small, so insignificant," Jenny said.

"I don't know about that. The bridge wouldn't have been built without man's talents."

Jenny smiled at him. "Always so logical. I feel close to you, Luke, as if the years in between were nothing more than a second when we didn't see each other. How can that be? I should hate you."

"You should."

"I don't, and you don't hate me either, even though I never told you about your son."

"As if I could." His voice was husky, filled with emotion. He wanted to stop it, prevent her from seeing how much she affected him, but it was impossible. His senses were filled with the sight of her. He wanted to kiss her again. He wanted it so badly any thought of stopping was beyond his control.

His mouth touched hers, and one kiss turned into two, then three, long, never-ending, mindless moments of passion between two people who had been apart far too long. Her name rang through his head. Jenny. Jenny. Jenny. Her softness washed over him. Her warmth heated his body. He couldn't get enough of her.

Jenny broke away, her face flushed, her lips swollen. "No."

"It's right. Don't fight it. Don't fight us."

"I have to. I'm not a young girl anymore, Luke. I don't believe in fairy tales. And happy endings are beginning to look less and less possible. I've grown up. I've changed. I take responsibility for my actions."

"So do I, Jenny."

"Then you have to see we can't be together. You're with someone else."

"Right now—at this moment—I'm with you, completely, totally."

"Fine, forget about your wife, but I'm involved with Alan."

"Are you?" Luke tipped up her chin and smiled into her eyes. "Are you with him—really with him?"

Jenny licked her lips. "No," she said, honest to the end. "But that's beside the point."

"If you're not with him, then he won't mind if I kiss you."

"Oh, he'll mind all right, and so will your wife."

"I'm going to do it anyway, unless you say no. Are you saying no?"

"No." And she lifted her face to his.

"Mush. I hate mush." Jacob walked along the railing of the Golden Gate Bridge like a trapeze artist.

"Would you move?" Danny said. "I'm trying to see my mom and dad." His eyes widened as the moonlight lit Jenny and Luke like two lovers caught in a spotlight on a dark stage. "Wow. They're really kissing."

Jacob jumped off the railing and put a hand over Danny's eyes. "That's enough for you, my boy. This is definitely not PG-13."

Danny tried to push Jacob's hands away from his face. "Come on, I want to see."

"No way. I'm protecting your morals."

"Tell me what's happening then."

"Use your imagination." Jacob sighed. "Those two are getting ahead of themselves. Looks like they need me right about now."

Danny pulled free of Jacob as the old man leaned over the railing of the bridge. "What are you doing?"

"Bringing 'em to their senses."

"No." Danny grabbed his arm. "I want them to

kiss. I want them to get back together. This is cool."

"Well, I suppose." Jacob tilted his head in thought. "Nah." He leaned over and blew against the water of the bay as if it were a candle on a birthday cake. To Danny's amazement, Jacob's breath created an incredible wave that hit the side of the shore just below where his parents were standing, covering them with a spray of water.

Luke and Jenny broke apart, laughing as they wiped the water out of their eyes. After a moment, they turned and walked back the way they had come.

Jacob laughed with pure delight. "I love that trick. Works every time."

Danny folded his arms in front of his chest, scowling at the old man. Jacob looked a little shame-faced. "It was a joke. Lighten up, kid."

"They were getting together, and you broke 'em up."

"They don't look broken up to me."

Jacob pointed at the couple. Luke and Jenny had stopped and were kissing again.

Danny smiled. "I knew they were still in love."

"Yeah, well, all this mush is making me nauseous," Jacob said. "Come on, I know a place where there's a little more action."

"Wait, something isn't right."

Jacob pulled his arm. Danny clung to the railing with his fingertips, reluctant to leave. Although he wanted to see his parents together, he suddenly realized they were together without him, and they didn't seem to care. "How come they're out here kissing when I'm lying in the hospital?" he asked.

Jacob sighed. "Boy, you aren't happy when they're together, and you're not happy when they're apart. What's it going to take, kid?"

"I want to be with them."

"I don't think they're missing you right about now."

"I guess not." Danny felt incredibly annoyed by that thought.

Jacob rested his arms on the railing of the bridge. "Ever play dominoes, kid?"

"Yeah."

"One action leads to another action. It's the same with life. You make decisions. Things happen. You have to play out your hand. Roll the dice. Go for broke on two outs, full count in the bottom of the ninth. Got it?"

Danny sighed. "You're saying all this is my fault."

"Your life is your fault, Danny boy. When are you going to start taking responsibility for it?"

"I don't have a life at the moment," Danny snapped back, irritated with Jacob and his mother and Luke. "I'm just a kid, you know. I don't know anything."

Jacob grinned at him. "Now that's the smartest thing I've heard you say. I think we're making progress. I might just get promoted after all."

Danny sent him a suspicious look. "What do you have to do to get promoted?"

"I have to right a wrong."

"What wrong?"

Jacob ignored his question. "Come on, we've got work to do."

Danny cast one last lingering look at his parents and then followed Jacob into the heavens.

Saturday morning, Jenny awoke to the sound of pounding on her front door. She looked at the clock on the bedside table and swore. It was seven o'clock in the morning, barely light. What the heck was going on?

She stumbled out of bed, drew her bright floral kimono robe around her T-shirt, and headed for the door. Throwing it open, she said, "This better be good."

"It is." Luke walked in, looking nothing like himself. He was wearing a gray sweatshirt and a faded pair of blue jeans that were actually ripped at the knee. Ripped? Jenny blinked her eyes shut. She must be dreaming.

"Are you ready to go?" Luke asked.

Jenny opened her eyes. He was still there, looking downright proud of himself. He was holding a child's bright orange bucket and a shovel in one hand.

"Go where?" she asked.

"Beachcombing. Seashells, jewelry, you remember," Luke said.

"What's with the bucket? Do you think my business is a game, Luke? A child's toy?" Irritation filled her voice. She was never at her best first thing in the morning, and his incredibly cheerful face made her feel downright angry.

"No. No. I saw it in the store," Luke said hastily. "I thought maybe I could talk you into building another sand castle with me."

"You're crazy. Like I have time to build sand castles. I have to make my bed, pick up the house, stop by the store, and buy some milk. And sometime today, I have to put together two necklaces, send in my registration for the Spring Art Fair, and spend at least eight hours with my son in the hospital." She ran out of steam and leaned against the wall.

"I'll help you, Jenny. We'll spend an hour at the beach so you can pick up your supplies, then we'll divide up your list of things to do."

"I can't just take off for the beach right now. I'm not dressed. I'm not ready."

"You used to be ready for anything."

"Well, I'm not anymore. Okay?" she snapped, running a hand through her tousled hair. "You should have called first. You can't just barge into my life and take over."

"That's what you did to me," Luke said. He stared at her for a long moment, his good humor slowly fading like the air out of a balloon. "I never knew what hit me. You swept me off my feet."

"I couldn't lift you off the ground."

"You did it with your smile, your passion for life. I took that away, didn't I? God, I wish I could give it back to you."

"You can't." Jenny tried to ignore the way he was looking at her. She pulled the sash tighter around her waist, suddenly very aware of her skimpy outfit and the rumpled bed just down the hall. He looked so good this morning, better than a cup of coffee, better than a hot bagel with cream cheese.

Food. She needed food and coffee. Then she could make her list and get organized. But first, she needed to wake up and deal with this man in a logical and rational manner. Logical and rational?

"Oh my God," she said out loud.

"What's wrong now?"

"I just realized—I've turned into you."

Luke smiled. "I was thinking the same thing."

"I don't want to be you."

"I don't want to be me, either."

Jenny put a hand to her head, which was suddenly throbbing with the beginning of a very painful headache. "Luke, go home."

"Not a chance, sweetheart." His smile was back in full force. "We've both changed. That's true. Let's find out who we are now. We'll get your work done, I promise. Just give me an hour. You won't regret it."

"I hate when people say that." Jenny headed for the bedroom. "All right. I'll get dressed. Make me some coffee, okay?"

"Coffee? Uh, Jenny . . ."

Jenny paused in the doorway. "What's wrong now?"

"I don't know how to make coffee. My secretary does it."

She started to laugh softly then with the sheer joy

of feeling good again. Luke looked helplessly charming. God help her. "Then it's about time you learned," she said. "Beans are in the cupboard. Give it your best shot."

"What if I screw up?"

"Then you'll know how the rest of us feel ninety-nine percent of the time."

25

"I MESSED UP," RICHARD SAID AS HE FACED Merrilee across the kitchen counter.

Merrilee wiped down the counter with a sponge. She didn't want to look at him. She didn't want him to see her red, blotchy eyes, didn't want him to know how badly he had hurt her. He hadn't come home last night, for which she had been supremely grateful, but it was now almost seven o'clock on Saturday evening, and she had spent the last eight hours waiting on pins and needles for his arrival.

She knew they would have to talk, make decisions about their marriage. She just didn't know if she was ready.

"Merrilee."

Reluctantly, she turned to look at him. His face was haggard. There was fear in his eyes and that gave her hope.

After a moment, she walked over to the kitchen table and sat down. Richard silently followed.

They sat there like two strangers for almost five minutes. Finally, Richard spoke. "It's not an excuse, but I was lonely, Merrilee. You don't seem to need me in your life."

"What do you mean? Everything I do is for you and the children. I cook your meals. I take care of your house. I hem your goddamned pants. I sew your buttons on, even when sluts like that Blair probably tear them off."

"But you don't love me," Richard said simply. "You used to. I don't know when things changed. One day I realized it had been a month since we'd made love. The next time I looked at the calendar it had been three months, then four. You're so damned independent, you don't need me for anything, not even sex."

"This is not my fault. Don't try to pin it on me."

Merrilee started to rise, but Richard pulled her back down. "We need to talk. We've needed to talk for months."

"You apparently needed more than talk."

"I'm sorry."

Merrilee sent him a look of amazement. "That's supposed to make it better?"

"Nothing can make it better. We're going nowhere, except further apart. I think I've been wanting you to find me like that for months. It seemed the more I rubbed it in your face, the more you denied it was happening. After a while, I figured if you didn't care, why should I?"

"I do care. I love you." Her voice filled with pain, and she knew he could hear it. "I've never loved anyone but you. From the day we met, I've been afraid I wouldn't be good enough. You were the life of the party, everybody's best friend. I was never that, and I couldn't imagine that you'd stay with me. After we had the children, I guess I wasn't as interested in sex as you were, then the longer it was in between, the more doubts I had that I was any good at it."

"Rather than risk being bad, you stopped altogether."

"You found your pleasure elsewhere, so what difference does it make?"

"A lot. I remember how we were that first year we fell in love, necking on your father's couch for hours. We couldn't get enough of each other. What happened to the girl I fell in love with?"

"She grew up, Richard." Merrilee sat back in her chair and crossed her arms. She didn't want to talk about the past, the way she had been as a young girl, the hopes and dreams she had carried in her heart. She had fallen in love with Richard when she was twenty years old. Richard was the one she had clung to when her mother died, just a year after their first meeting.

Now she could barely remember why they had gotten together. He was nothing like that young man, and she was nothing like that young girl.

"You didn't grow up, you grew hard," Richard said. "After your mother died, you became more concerned with controlling everyone's life than just loving them."

"I had to take control. I was the oldest. Jenny was only fifteen years old. She needed me."

"In the beginning, maybe, but not for the past ten years, Merrilee. You know, I work a lot of overtime, most of it legitimately, because you have such high expectations. I've been killing myself trying to live up to your standards. But I can't do it."

"I never told you to work overtime. I just wanted you to have a successful career. And this isn't about my standards, Richard. You cheated on me. I don't know if I can ever forgive you for that."

"I'm sure you can't. Just like you can never forgive Jenny for loving Luke and having Danny out of wedlock, and you can never forgive Matt for not making it in the pros. You're just like your father." He took off his tie and laid it on the table in front of them, a battle line of red silk.

"I'm not like my father," Merrilee said in horror.

"Yes, you are. John is old and isolated, because he can't accept people for what they are. I see you doing it to our children. William is so determined to get good grades, I caught him studying at midnight with a flashlight. He's eleven years old, for God's sake."

Richard's criticism cut through her soul, and Merrilee hated to admit there was even a hint of truth to it. "You're a fine one to talk, Richard. You're not even home with the children. And I love my brother and sister. They don't feel that I'm critical and controlling."

"Don't they? Come on, Merrilee. Lie to me if you want, but don't lie to yourself. And don't you feel the same way about your own father? That what you do is never good enough?"

Merrilee looked away from his eyes. Of course, she did. He was right—at least about John. She would give him that much. But Matt and Jenny were different. They knew she loved them. Didn't they?

"This is not just about me, Richard," Merrilee said forcefully. "You used to listen to me. You used to share things. I can't talk to you anymore. Even when you're physically in the house, mentally you're somewhere else. I've had sole responsibility for the kids for years now, and it's wearing on me, too. Constance is always pushing her limits, testing me, and William is right behind her. You want to talk about pressure, stay home for a few days and deal with your kids."

Richard looked taken aback. "You always look so calm, like you've spent the day painting your fingernails."

"I work every second trying to make it look that way, but it's not, Richard. It's not, dammit." She stood up and began to pace, agitated out of her mind.

"So what do we do now?" Richard asked.

She stopped and stared at him. "I don't know. Do you think we have anything left to save?"

"Do you?"

Merrilee was afraid to say yes, to put her heart on the line, but this was her marriage they were talking about, her life.

"We could go to a counselor," Richard suggested quietly.

A counselor? An outsider? Pour out her troubles to a complete stranger? She would feel like a failure, a misfit. "I don't know if I could do that," she said.

Richard stood up and put his hands on her shoulders. "We have to do something, Merrilee. Unless—unless you want to call it quits?"

Did she? Merrilee leaned against the kitchen counter. She thought about the past seventeen years and knew she had invested too much in this man to just walk away. But how could she ever trust him again? Would she spend the rest of her life wondering if he was working late or with another woman? Was that worse than being alone? She was almost forty years old. She didn't want to start over. And the children. They loved their father.

"Can you give me another chance?" Richard asked.

Merrilee took in a deep breath and let it out. "I'll think about it."

The kitchen door opened and William walked in. "Is it time for dinner, yet?" he asked.

Merrilee sighed. Dinner. Her whole life had changed, but there was still dinner to get on the table.

"In a second," she said. "Why don't you call your sister?"

William sent her a strange look. "Connie? She's not here."

"What do you mean, she's not here?"

"She left with that guy on the motorcycle, about an hour ago. I told her you'd be mad," William said, nodding his head up and down in a knowing manner. "But she said all you cared about was Danny."

"What?" Merrilee ran through the house and opened the front door. The street in front of the house was empty. Fragmented conversations with Constance ran through her mind, the late-night phone calls, the whispers, the makeup.

Richard put his arm around her waist. "She'll be all right."

"I can't believe she's run off like this. Just like Danny," she added, suddenly more frightened than angry. So much could happen to a child. How did a parent let go?

"It's not like Danny at all. It's a Saturday night, and she's a teenager," Richard said.

"And that's supposed to make me feel better? I can't just do nothing." Merrilee strode back in the house. "I'll call her friends. Somebody must know where she went."

Danny looked over at Jacob. "I don't suppose you know where Connie went?"

"I might."

"I can't believe she ran away because of me." Danny walked up the stairs to Constance's bedroom. His Aunt Merrilee was sitting on the bed looking totally depressed. She was holding a piece of paper in her hand, and shaking her head as if she couldn't believe what she was reading.

Jacob muttered something under his breath as he peered over Merrilee's shoulder.

"What does it say?" Danny asked.

"Said she's tired of living in a house where nobody has time for her anymore."

"Because of me?"

"Looks that way. Yep, in fact she mentions you by name."

"Great."

Danny looked up as Richard walked into the room. He paused in the doorway, hands in his pockets. "I've called everyone, Merrilee. No one has seen her or heard from her."

"It's past eleven, Richard. She's not coming back." Merrilee handed him the note. "She's run away."

Richard took the paper from her hand. "Goddammit," he said.

"It's my fault. I shouldn't have spent so much time at the hospital the last two weeks. I should have been here for my daughter."

"It's our fault." He held out his hand. "Come on downstairs. I called Matt. He's trying to track her down."

"Actually it's my fault," Danny said to Jacob as Merrilee and Richard left the room. He sat down at Constance's desk and looked at the photographs she had stuck up on her bulletin board. He had never been super close to Connie. She was older and always bossy, but they had had some fun times over the years. He reached out to move a photograph that was hidden behind another. It was a picture of him and Connie at a birthday party. They were both stuffing cake in their mouths and hamming it up for the camera. He smiled to himself. At least Connie had some guts. Not like William, who never did anything wrong.

He felt bad that she had run away because of him. He rested his chin in his hands. Things were getting complicated. He had just wanted to find his dad, not mess up everyone else's life. He had wanted things to be better, only now they were worse.

"Maybe I should just be dead," he said glumly.

Jacob spun him around in the chair. "You're quitting on me, kid?"

"It would be easier for everyone."

"And maybe easier for you, too."

"I wasn't thinking about myself. Not this time, anyway."

"Good. I can't stand a quitter."

"I just wish I could make everything right. I could do that if I were an angel, a real angel, couldn't I?" Danny asked, suddenly realizing how much more power he would have.

"Yeah, but you'd be dead, kid."

"That's right."

"It's the good with the bad. Balls and strikes. Roses and thorns—"

"I get the picture," Danny said.

"About time. Come on. No point in sitting around here. Your Uncle Matt needs our help. Are you in?"

Danny smiled and gave him a high five in response.

"Jenny, are you in here?" Luke walked through the kitchen into the garage. He stopped in amazement. He had been expecting to see a typical garage, maybe some boxes, a washer, dryer, bicycles, but what he saw was a complete workshop.

There was a workbench filled with shelves and boxes. A hot glue gun sat on the top counter next to a pair of needle-nosed pliers. There were scraps of fabric, gold and silver wires, shells and beads and long strands of thread. Jenny had set up a card table next to the workbench, and there were various pieces of jewelry on display, some obviously finished, others waiting for completion. On the ground next to the table was a stack of boxes, all different sizes, tissue paper, and ribbon.

Jenny looked up as he approached. "Are you back already?"

"Yes. The food's on the table. There wasn't much of a line at this hour."

Jenny glanced down at her watch. "Almost nine. I hadn't realized."

"We've been busy."

"I took up your whole day. I'm sorry."

"Don't be, I enjoyed it."

He watched as Jenny carefully applied what looked like clear glue to the top of a shell. Her movements were carefully controlled, efficient, not a motion wasted.

"What are you doing?" he asked curiously. Although he had helped her collect the shells, he had never really considered what she was going to do with them.

"I'm adding form and substance to the shell. This will dry in a hard pattern, a heart. See?"

Luke bent his head to take a closer look. "It's perfect. You're pretty good at this."

"Practice. After it dries, I'll paint it. I'm trying to develop more complex designs, mixing the gold and silver filigree with the shells to give the jewelry a more expensive look."

Luke moved around to the other side of her. Besides earrings and necklaces, Jenny had made small jewelry boxes out of some type of clay.

"These are nice," he said.

Jenny smiled. "A step above the white cardboard, anyway."

"I'm impressed. I had no idea you were so talented," Luke said. And he was impressed. On the shelves over her workbench, Jenny had a stack of books, some about crafts, others about running a business. This was obviously not a part-time hobby for her. She had invested time, money, and energy into her enterprise.

"It's not such a big deal." Jenny stretched her arms high over her head. She was wearing black leggings and a soft winter white sweater. She looked adorable, sexy, and exhausted. They had had a busy day, finding seashells, running errands, and visiting Danny. He was amazed at her endurance, and the pace that was a part of her daily life.

"You should go home. It's late," Jenny said.

"I should," he agreed. But as he turned to leave, he tripped over a step stool.

Jenny caught him in her arms with a laugh. "Easy."

He hugged her body to steady himself and because it felt so damn good to be close to her.

Her laughter ended abruptly as he turned his face toward hers. Her mouth was just a breath away. It would be so easy to kiss her and so tempting. She had held him at arm's length all day, and he had let her. But now she wasn't moving, and neither was he.

"Luke." She said his name like a plea, but he didn't know if she wanted him to go or to stay.

"One kiss."

She shook her head. "Five," she whispered with a smile."

"Ten"

"Fifteen."

"Jenny, you're negotiating upward."

"Shut up and kiss me."

He lowered his head.

The phone in the kitchen rang. Jenny immediately stepped away. He knew she had to answer it. The hospital could be calling about Danny.

He followed her into the kitchen and leaned against the doorjamb as Jenny picked up the receiver. He watched her face tighten with alarm. Please don't let it be Danny, he prayed.

"What can I do to help, Merrilee?" Jenny asked.

Luke relaxed. Merrilee. Not the hospital. Thank God.

"How long has she been gone?" Jenny looked down at her watch. "It's almost nine."

Luke met her worried eyes. She put a hand over the receiver and whispered, "Connie has run away." Jenny turned her attention back to Merrilee. "I'm on my way. No, I want to come. I love her, too." She hung up the phone.

"Jenny, you've been working all day. You should go to bed."

"I have to look for Connie."

"I'll come with you."

"No." Jenny put a hand out as he tried to protest. "Go home, Luke. This is my family, not yours."

Her words cut him to the quick, and he turned away so she wouldn't see the pain on his face. "Fine." He picked his keys up off the counter and headed for the door.

"Luke, wait. I didn't mean that the way it sounded."

He looked into Jenny's eyes. "You've made it clear you don't want my help. I just don't understand why."

"I don't want to be dependent on you, Luke. For a while you were my whole life, and when you left, I had nothing. I can't risk that again. I won't go into a relationship unless I can be an equal partner."

"We are equal, Jenny, in every way that counts."

"You're rich. I'm not."

"I can give you money, but you give me so much more. This day was perfect, Jenny." He cupped her face with his hands. "We shared our responsibilities, our dreams. We laughed. We argued. We kissed."

"We didn't kiss," she said softly.

"Let me correct that."

Luke touched her mouth with his. He kissed her with a hunger and a need that went beyond anything he had ever felt before. She was his past, his present, and his future. He wanted her to know it, beyond a doubt.

Jenny pulled away, breathless. Her beautiful brown eyes were filled with desire—for him.

"We can't go back to the way we were," she said.

"I don't want to go back. I want to go forward."

"Luke, I can't do this right now. Connie—"

"I know. You have to help your family. Are you sure I can't help?"

"Not this time. But maybe sometime. That's all I can give you right now."

"I'll take it."

Matt walked into the rowdy bar known only as Joe's, located off a rural road in Woodside. It was a popular spot for bikers, not far from the highway but far enough from the highway patrol. The beer was cheap and cold, the music loud, and the air as nicotine rich as a Marlboro cigarette.

He paused inside the front door, checking out the action before committing himself entirely. He had been hit by enough lineman to be able to take a punch, and he had thrown a few in his time, too, but his body was a lot softer than it used to be. Besides that, he was sober. It had been three days since he had had a drink. A record for him.

Shaking his head, Matt moved further into the bar. The only women present were much older than his niece. They all looked old and hard, some dressed in black leather, some in tight jeans, others in miniskirts, but every outfit screamed out the word *sex*.

Matt looked around the room, at every table, at every face. No sign of Connie. Thank God! He could leave.

He tried to turn, but something seemed to be in his way. Mystified, he took a side step. Blocked again. He blinked a few times and tried to clear his vision. There was nothing in front of him but air.

He moved to the side. Again, a force came at him, pushing him down the hall as if he were a piece of paper in front of a fan, helpless to the surge of air that moved him in that direction.

Matt found himself in the hall by the phone and the restrooms. The back door leading out to the parking lot was half open. He heard a scream. He took off down the hall. Another scream, a cry for help. He looked out the door.

Shit!

His niece was pushed up against the wall by some punk with his hand up her shirt. The other hand was in Connie's hair, twisting the strands, yanking them off her scalp. She was crying, trying to hit him with her hands, but she wasn't a big girl, and her efforts were futile.

Matt's first instinct was to grab the kid by the neck and throw him across the parking lot. His second instinct was to find a weapon of some sort. He looked in the hall and saw a mop. It wasn't his first choice, but, what the hell. . . . For added insurance, he grabbed the bucket alongside it.

He ran into the parking lot and tossed the dark, murky water all over the kid's head. The punk gasped and let go of Connie. She paused, shocked.

Matt grabbed her by the arm. "Go on. Get the hell out of here." He pushed the car keys into her trembling fingers as the kid straightened up and came at him.

Matt ducked. The blow landed off his shoulder. He threw his own punch and missed completely, stumbling onto the ground. The punk kicked him in the ribs. Matt groaned and reached for the mop, which suddenly appeared next to him.

Taking the stick, Matt swung it against the kid's legs. The stick broke. The kid didn't.

Damn!

Matt scrambled to his feet.

The kid came at him and swung. The kid's fist never made it to Matt's face. It just stopped, as if it had run into a brick wall.

They stared at each other for a moment, frozen in time. Then the kid reached into his pocket and pulled out a knife. He flicked open the blade.

Matt took a step back. The kid came at him, silently

stalking. The silver blade gleamed in the moonlight. The kid's pace increased. He let out a primal scream and rushed forward.

Matt dropped back like a quarterback, faked to the right, moved to his left. The kid hit the wall with his head and fell to the ground.

Jesus! It actually worked.

A horn honked, and Matt saw Connie waving frantically to him from his car. While the kid was getting up, Matt ran to the car, hopped in the passenger seat and held on as Connie floored it. The car spun around on two wheels, and they sped out of the parking lot.

Two miles down the road, Connie pulled over. She was shaking. Her eyes were filled with tears, and her face was bruised and swollen.

"Oh, God," she said. "You saved my life. He was— he was—"

Matt took Connie in his arms. Black leather pants, midriff top, and pointed boots didn't hide the fact that she was sixteen and terrified. He patted her on the back, reminded of when she had been a little girl, when she had come to her Uncle Matt because her mother didn't understand.

"It's okay. You're okay now," he said.

She cried, heartbreaking sobs. Tonight she had lost her innocence, if not literally then figuratively. She would never be the same. Matt suddenly wished he could go back and beat the kid to a pulp, make him pay for scaring the hell out of a little girl.

Connie sat back, her face streaked with tears and an overabundance of mascara. "I thought he was nice. I thought he was cool. But that place was horrible. Those guys, they all stared at me—"

"Forget it. It's over now."

"How did you find me anyway?"

Matt shook his head, suddenly remembering the strange force that had sent him out the back door. "It was weird. I just knew where you were. I almost left, but I didn't. I couldn't. Something was turning me around, moving me down the hall, like—oh, forget it. I sound like I'm crazy."

"You and me both. I was really stupid tonight."

"You sure were."

She bristled at his comment. "Well, it's not like you've never done anything stupid in your life."

Matt grinned. "You got me there." His smile faded. "Seriously, babe. What were you thinking of—going off with a guy like that to a place like that?"

Connie leaned back against the seat. "I don't know. I just wanted to do something fun."

"Come on. This is your Uncle Mattie, talk to me."

Connie hesitated. "All anyone thinks about is Danny."

"That's probably true."

"Mom doesn't care about me anymore. She doesn't care that Jimmy didn't ask me to the winter dance. And Dad is never around. I think he's having an affair. I hate them both. And I hate William. He's so perfect. It makes me want to puke. Danny—Danny was the only one who ever got into trouble, and now he's—he's . . ." Connie started to sob, so hard her shoulders shook. "He's going to die, and I hate him for it. I mean, I sort of liked him, you know."

Matt smiled sadly as he enfolded her in his arms. "I know what you mean."

She lifted her head. "And I hate myself, because I don't want to visit Danny. I don't want to see him in the hospital. I don't want to think about dying."

"You don't have to."

"I do. Mom says I have to be a grown-up. I don't want to be a grown-up," she wailed, looking pathetic in clothes and makeup that were far too old for her years.

"Neither do I," Matt admitted.

She sniffed, taken by surprise. "But you're old."

Matt laughed and ruffled her hair. "Thanks, kid."

"Well, you are."

And he was, old enough to know better, certainly. The years were passing him by. The glory days were gone. And he had nothing, nothing.

As Matt looked at Connie, he suddenly realized that it wasn't his turn anymore. It was Connie's turn, and Danny's turn, and William's turn. He was a grown-up. It was about time he started acting like one.

"Change places with me, Connie. I'll drive you home."

"Maybe you could just drive off a cliff instead." She scooted past him on the seat.

"I've thought about doing just that, more than once, but I'm not really good with pain, you know?"

She smiled at him.

"And it would be a selfish solution to my problems, running away and letting someone else clean up the mess." He patted her on the leg. "Sometimes you have to take a hit, just so you can keep playing."

Matt looked out at the night sky. There were so many stars out, so much power in the heavens, so much light illuminating everything that had seemed cloudy before. One thing was clear. He didn't want to die. He wanted to live and live right. "Maybe it's time we both gave being a grown-up a chance," he said. "Tell you what. I'll try if you try."

"Are you going to tell my mom about this?"

Matt tilted his head. "Mm-mm. What would be the adult thing to do? Tell your mother? No, I think not."

Connie sighed. "Good."

Matt turned the key in the ignition. "Because you're going to tell her."

26

MERRILEE STRAIGHTENED THE BOOKS ON HER shelf, putting them in alphabetical order. Richard flipped through twenty-five channels on the television set and Jenny sighed as William beat her at yet another computer game. The tension in their house was the same as the tension in Danny's hospital room. There was silence and fear so palpable you could almost touch it.

"That's enough for me," Jenny said to William. "I need a cup of coffee."

"I'll get you one," Merrilee said immediately, heading toward the kitchen. "Do you want one, Richard?"

"No, thanks."

Jenny followed her sister into the kitchen and leaned against the counter as Merrilee poured her a cup of coffee. "I should never have sent Matt alone to that bar," Merrilee declared, handing Jenny the cup.

Jenny met her gaze. "He won't let us down."

"He could be sitting there getting bombed while my daughter is out there alone and—"

"Matt said he was going to stop drinking."

"I'd like to believe him . . ."

"Then do. Matt's changed. Danny's accident has made him take a new look at his life. Something we could all stand to do."

"Tell me about it." Merrilee turned off the coffee-maker and washed out the pot. As she was drying it with a dish towel she looked over at Jenny. "Richard and I are going to see a marriage counselor next week, or as soon as we can get in."

Jenny's mouth dropped open. "You're what?"

"Don't make me repeat it," Merrilee said with a frown. "It was hard enough to say the first time."

"I don't know what to say. Except that I'm glad."

"So you think my marriage needs help, too?"

Jenny hesitated. "Maybe just a tune-up."

"Or a complete makeover." Merrilee tossed the dish towel toward the counter. It fell on the floor. "Damn. I can't do anything right."

Jenny and Merrilee both reached for the towel at the same time, bumping their heads together.

"Ow," Merrilee said, rubbing her forehead.

Jenny looked at her and started to laugh. After a moment, Merrilee joined in. The laughter was a welcome release from all the tension and left them both gasping for breath.

"That felt good," Jenny said.

"I'm sorry." Merrilee looked at her with sudden seriousness.

"About what?"

"Everything."

"I don't think you're responsible for everything, Merrilee. That's been the problem all along," Jenny said gently.

"I tried to control your life. That's why you moved out of the house with Danny, instead of staying here with me. I did the same thing to Matt. I drove him away." Merrilee slid her wedding ring up and down her finger. She glanced down at the glistening diamond and a tear dripped out of her eye and down her cheek.

Jenny wanted to comfort her, but she didn't know this Merrilee, a woman who could admit failure and accept blame.

"And now I've done the same thing to Constance," Merrilee said. "You'd think I would have learned something by now."

"I think you have learned something. We all have. And, hey, it wasn't all your fault. I know I gave you a hard time when I was a teenager. I was so lost without Mom. You had Richard and Matt had football. I think that's why I fell so hard for Luke."

"And you're falling for him again, aren't you?"

Jenny looked away. "I'm trying not to."

"Oh, Jenny. Are we destined to repeat our mistakes?"

"I hope not."

A car door slammed, and Merrilee jumped. She ran to the window and peered out. "It's Matt. And Connie." She yelled for Richard, then rushed out the back door and down the driveway.

Constance and Merrilee stopped abruptly as they got closer, leaving a good three feet between them. Jenny stood back with her hand on William's shoulder. Even Richard lingered behind, instinctively knowing that this was a moment for mother and daughter.

"I'm sorry, Mom," Constance said.

"I'm sorry, too," Merrilee said.

Constance looked at her in astonishment. "You are?"

"I love you," Merrilee said. "Nothing else matters." She held out her arms and Connie ran into them. Mother and daughter embraced so long and so hard that Jenny had to wipe a tear from her eye. Then Richard and William joined in. It was the happiest sight Jenny had seen in a long time.

So much had happened since Danny's accident. So many changes. Was this what it was all about?

Matt walked over and stood next to her.

"You did good," she said, punching him on the arm.

"Aw shucks. Say, did you give Merrilee some Valium or something? I thought at the very least we'd hear about everything Connie has done wrong since her first birthday."

"I think Merrilee finally ran out of breath."

Matt looked at her and nodded. "Haven't we all. I know I'm done whining. Time to move on."

"Do you mean that?"

"Why?"

"I need to go back to work on Monday. They'll let me work part-time, eight to one. I can't afford any more unpaid leave."

Matt looked puzzled. "What do you want me to do?"

"Stay with Danny while I'm at work. I want you to move his legs and arms so his muscles won't atrophy. I want you to talk to him, sing to him, play music, stand on your head, whatever it takes to keep life around him, so close that he wants to reach out and touch it."

Matt's face turned pale at the thought of spending every day in the hospital. "I don't know, Jen-Jen."

"You have to, Matt. I need you. Please, do this for me." She knew it was a struggle for Matt to say yes, that he was wary of hospitals and afraid to make a commitment to anything, even if it was only for five hours a day. But he was the only one available to spend that much time with Danny.

"All right," he said slowly, his eyes meeting hers. "I'll do my best."

"Thank you."

* * *

Four days later, Jenny rushed into ICU after work only to find that Danny was gone. Her first thought was one of horror. Danny had died. They'd moved his body, and no one had called her.

"No! No!" she cried.

"Jenny, it's okay. They had moved him into a private room." Luke's hands gripped her arms. He repeated the words more slowly, breaking through her trance.

"I—I saw the bed, and I thought . . ."

"I'm sorry. They moved him this morning. They have another child coming up from surgery."

"Another child?" Jenny read between the lines. "They've given up, haven't they?"

"No." Luke took her hand and pulled her away from the curious eyes of the nurses. He walked her down the hall, through the double doors, into the main corridor. "Danny's condition is stable. His vital signs are good. In fact . . ." Luke smiled broadly. "They took him off the ventilator last night. He's breathing on his own."

She put a hand to her mouth. "Thank God!"

"He can be cared for just as well in a private room with twenty-four-hour nursing. No one is giving up, especially now. You believe me, don't you?"

"I believe you. I'm sorry."

He hugged her. "Don't be sorry. I would have thought the same thing. Want to see Danny?"

She nodded, and he led her down another hallway to room 307. The room was sparsely decorated, but it had a more personal feel than ICU. Danny was still hooked up to several machines, but his chest moved up and down of its own accord. For that fact alone, she was incredibly grateful.

"He's going to make it, Luke."

"This is a small step, Jenny. And they've left the tubes in, in case he has to be hooked up again."

"That won't happen. He's turned the corner. I can feel it."

An older nurse walked into the room and smiled at Jenny. "I'm Angela Carpenter. I'll be taking care of Danny during the day."

"It's nice to meet you." Jenny shook her hand.

"I've raised six children of my own. He won't lack for care. You have my word."

Jenny walked over to the bed and touched Danny's hand. His skin felt slightly warmer. She pinched him lightly: his hand retracted. It was a slight gesture but a good sign that he felt something. "I feel hopeful for the first time in a long while," she said.

"Why don't we celebrate?" Luke suggested. "Have dinner with me tonight?"

Jenny hesitated, tempted by the offer, but at the same time wary. Luke was creeping back into her life. She was getting used to having him around. What would happen when Danny recovered, when Luke went back to his wife? "I don't think that's a good idea," she said.

His face clouded over. "Why not?"

"I feel guilty."

"Don't. Besides, you still haven't shown me your scrapbooks, your videos of Danny. I won't take no for an answer. I'll pick up a pizza and meet you at your house."

A pizza and home videos didn't sound too alarming. Still—"I saw the newspaper this morning, Luke. There was an article about Sheri-Tech losing out on a potential acquisition. The reporter suggested that your personal life was interfering with your responsibilities as president and CEO."

"Don't worry about it, Jenny. It wasn't that good a deal."

"Really?" She looked deep into his eyes and knew he was lying.

"Okay, I'm a little distracted. But there will be other

companies. Right now I need to be with Danny and with you."

"Your parents must be upset about this negative publicity."

"They'll get over it. And if they don't..." He shrugged. "I'll figure that out later. Are we on for dinner?"

Jenny stared at him, not sure what to make of this new Luke. He had always been pushy and liked to get his own way, but never at the expense of his parents or his reputation. Even their summer fling had been kept away from his friends and family.

"Luke." Jenny put a hand on his arm. "Thirteen years ago when I came to you and told you about Danny, I knew that it would be a problem. I knew that having Danny would be a sacrifice for both of us."

"I didn't sacrifice a damn thing," Luke said. "You did it all."

"Maybe then. But not now. Have you thought about what this is doing to your family, to your career, your position at Sheri-Tech, your wife? Have you, Luke? You have a lot to lose, a lot more than I ever had. It's not too late to walk away."

"I'm not walking away, Jenny. I'm not leaving Danny again. I want you to trust me. I want Danny to trust me. I'll do whatever it takes to make that happen."

"Really? It's easy to say the words."

"What do you want me to do? Just say it, I'll do it."

"No, I won't ask again, not for anything. You have to make your own choices, and I have to make mine."

Luke gave her a grin. "Then make a choice. Dinner or not?"

She threw up her hands in surrender. "All right. You bring the pizza. I'll open a couple of cans of soda."

"Deal."

Luke kissed her impulsively, a warm, personal kiss that lingered on her lips long after his mouth was gone.

"This is starting to become a habit," she murmured.

"A good one, I hope."

"Probably more risky than good. Anyone could walk through that door, including your wife."

"I'll take that chance."

"You know, for a man who never liked to live dangerously, you're walking awfully close to the edge."

"I'm beginning to like it out there. I haven't felt this alive in a long time." Luke kissed her again, and left, but his warmth and his words stayed with her.

A few hours later, Luke arrived home, whistling as he turned the key in the lock. As the sound penetrated his brain, he laughed, breaking the melody. He hadn't whistled in years, hadn't felt so hopeful about the future in a long time.

Danny was making progress. That alone was enough to make him happy, but seeing Jenny, watching her smile, tasting her lips again made him feel like jumping in the air and clicking his heels.

His good mood lasted until he got in the house and saw Denise and his mother sitting in the living room, sipping tea out of fine china cups while a Bach melody played in the background.

"Luke, darling. Look who came to visit," Denise said.

Luke kissed his mother on the cheek, the way he always did. "Mother. It's nice to see you. What brings you north?"

She smiled, but there was worry in her eyes, and he could bet that she had already gotten an earful from Denise. "You, of course. How are you?"

"Fine."

Luke walked over to the bar and poured himself a shot of whiskey.

"I thought we could take your mother to dinner at Max's Café," Denise said. "A lovely big salad would be nice."

"Are you staying overnight, Mother?"

"I thought I'd stay a few days. Anne Howard is having a bridal shower for her daughter on Friday, and I'd hate to drive back and forth."

"Then I can spend time with you tomorrow. I have to go out this evening."

Denise sent him an annoyed look. "Where are you going? To the hospital, again?"

"You know I want to spend as much time as possible with my son."

"And with her," Denise said sharply.

"Oh dear." Beverly looked from one to the other. "I was afraid of this. Luke, we need to talk about your plans for the future."

"My plans?" Luke smiled at the irony of the word. "I don't have any plans, Mother."

"You have to have a plan."

"Why?"

"Because we've already lost Genesys. We can't afford any more missteps."

"It will all work out, Mother."

"You're the president of the company now, the visionary. If you're distracted, the business could blow up in your face, all your father's work down the drain."

"I don't think that will happen," Luke said evenly.

Denise sighed and exchanged a look with Beverly that clearly said, "I told you so."

"Your father wants to talk to you, Luke," Beverly said. "He hasn't been feeling well. I think you should go down tonight. Clear your head. Get your priorities straight."

Luke loosened his tie. "Oh, they're straight, Mother,

And I don't plan on going anywhere right now. You may refuse to acknowledge the fact that you have a grandson, but I won't walk away from him."

"Oh, for heaven's sake," Denise said in frustration. "You don't even know this boy. Please, drop the martyr act. And think about me for a change. There was a nasty little tidbit in the society column this morning about you and your love child. It's not just your reputation that's at stake here."

"I'm sorry, Denise. But I don't give a damn about some gossip columnist's titillating remarks. I intend to do everything I can to help Danny get better and become a part of my life."

Denise rose to her feet, her face as red as her hair. "Don't you mean *our* life, Luke?"

"I can do this with you or without you."

She put a hand to her heart. "You would leave me for him? I'm your wife."

"He doesn't mean that. Tell her you don't mean that," Beverly commanded.

Luke got up and left the room. The silence was deafening.

"He doesn't mean that," Beverly said.

Denise crumpled like a rag doll, slumping onto the sofa, all pretense gone. "I'm afraid he does."

"You have to fight for him, Denise."

"How?"

Beverly sent her a long, pointed look. "Maybe you should think about getting pregnant."

Denise looked away. She absolutely refused to tell Beverly the truth. It wouldn't help, and it could only hurt. Beverly was her ally at the moment. She couldn't afford to lose her support.

"I don't want to trap Luke." Denise stood up and walked over to the mantel. She picked up their wedding picture. Luke looked handsome, strong, arrogant. She looked gorgeous. They also looked young.

"He's changing, Beverly. I see it every day. I don't know him anymore."

"It's this child."

"No, it's more than that. Luke has been different this past year, even before we moved back here. He's been restless, unhappy, and he seems to be searching for something that I can't give him." She turned to Beverly. "Did this ever happen to you and Charles? Did you wake up one day and realize the man you married was gone?"

Beverly looked at her through troubled eyes. "Charles and I have always wanted the same things. Of course, we argue now and then, but it passes. I thought you and Luke were the same way."

"So did I." Denise set the wedding photograph down. "I've been unhappy, too. I want Luke back, the way he was, not the way he is now. I think he's going to leave me."

"Denise, you're getting ahead of yourself. This will blow over."

"When? It's Christmas. We have parties to go to, plans to make, and I can't get Luke away from the damned hospital. Now, everyone is whispering behind my back. I won't stand by and be humiliated. I'll leave first if I have to."

"Don't do anything rash. If you love each other enough, you can get through this."

"Yes, but *do* we love each other enough?"

Beverly sighed. "I suppose only you and Luke can answer that question."

Luke pulled off his dress shoes and threw them into the closet, taking pleasure in the way they landed haphazardly amidst the neatness of his clothes. On impulse, he got up and moved everything around. He mixed up his short-sleeved shirts and his pants, his jeans and his dress shirts, until everything was wrinkled and cluttered.

When he was done, some of his anger had faded. Deep down, he knew that Denise was struggling with the situation. He was her husband, and he owed it to her to try to work things out. It was just so damned difficult now that he had spent time with Jenny.

He loved Jenny. The thought hit him with startling clarity. He loved her, not just the girl he remembered but the woman she was now. He wanted to be with her and Danny, to be a family, to walk on the beach, to drive fast, to live on the edge, because the business of medicine just wasn't enough for him anymore. He wanted to keep it in his life, but he wanted it to be a smaller part of his existence.

But how could he leave Denise? How could he break his marriage vows? A tiny voice inside him mocked his conscience. Denise had broken her vows. She was a beautiful, vain, ambitious woman. That was also clear. At one time she had been the perfect fit, the right hand glove to his left. Now, they were mismatched, an apple and an orange trying to grow on the same tree.

With a sigh, he took off his slacks and traded them for blue jeans, the oldest, most faded pair he could find. Maybe it was his destiny to make mistakes with women, first Jenny, now Denise. When was he going to get the timing right?

It certainly wasn't right now. Although he was looking forward to spending the evening with Jenny, the thought of Danny fighting for his life hung over them like a thick cloud. Speaking of Danny . . .

Luke looked around his bedroom. "Where are you, Danny? Can you hear me? Can you talk to me? I gave your mom your present. She cried. Did you know that? Did you see her, too? I wish we could talk for a long time. You could tell me everything about your life, everything I've missed."

His eyes grew moist as he thought about his son. "I wish I could have seen you when you were a baby," he whispered. "I wish I'd taken you to kindergarten for the first time. Did you know that I cried my eyes out on the first day of school? My mother was horrified. Sheridans love school, you know. I didn't want to leave my parents. My mother told me to be brave, to hold my head high, and to work hard, because they expected a lot out of me."

Luke paused. "I wouldn't have done that to you. I would have held your hand, walked you into the classroom. Come back to me, Danny. I need you. Jenny needs you. We can be a family."

Luke waited, hoping, but the only sound in the room was the clock ticking, second by second, reminding him that time was not on Danny's side.

Danny sat on the roof of Luke's house, listening to his dad's words. He felt incredibly unhappy.

"What's wrong, kid?"

Jacob walked along the edge of the roof, as if it were a balance beam, making a perfectly executed turn at the end.

"My dad is so sad."

"I expect he is."

"How long has it been, anyway?"

"A couple of weeks by human time, a couple of days by ours. But you've been having fun, haven't you?"

"Yeah," Danny admitted. "I liked winter ball. That was cool. And catching a ride on that jet—out of this world. Mom would have loved it. She likes to go fast."

"That she does. I had to save her life once. She took a curve about sixty miles an hour. The wheels spun out, almost went over a cliff."

"No kidding?"

Jacob sent him a dry look. "Would I kid you?"

Danny rolled his eyes. "Yeah."

Jacob laughed and plopped down next to him. "I saved your life, too, you know."

"If you'd saved my life, I wouldn't be here right now."

"I don't mean this last time but when you were five."

"Five?" Danny sent him a skeptical look.

"It's true. You were riding a two-wheeler for the first time. Your mom took you to Bayside Park, remember?"

"I guess. But I don't remember almost dying."

"It was your second time without your mom running alongside you. Your bike was wobbling all over the place. You would have been fine, except a little kid ran across the path. You yanked the wheel, only not far enough. I had to turn it twice more, otherwise your head would have hit the cement wall, instead of the bush."

Danny stared at him in amazement, suddenly remembering the incident with surprising clarity. "Mom said how lucky I was."

"Wasn't luck, it was me." Jacob stuck out his chest proudly. "Saved your hide, I did."

Danny nodded in appreciation. "Cool. So how come you didn't save me from that car?"

"Wasn't my place. I get my orders from above."

Danny sighed. "Can I talk to my dad again?"

"Maybe later. Someone wants to see you." Jacob's face grew serious. "It will take a while to get there. You'll see things that are very important. Watch and listen to what everyone has to say. And no smart talk."

Danny sat up straight, feeling suddenly terrified. "It's God, isn't it? You're taking me to see Him. It's time for me to decide, to make my choice. Or else— He's going to make it for me, isn't He?"

27

"HERE'S DANNY AT EIGHTEEN MONTHS."
Jenny hit the Fast Forward button on
the video as Luke took a bite of pizza.
"See those pudgy cheeks? He looks just like you."

Luke, his mouth full of pizza, expanded his cheeks
even further. Jenny laughed with delight. He loved
seeing her so carefree. It reminded him of when they
first met. Her smile had been missing the last few
weeks. How he wanted to put it back on her face and
make it stay—forever.

"Here's Danny on Halloween. We had a great time.
He smiled cute, and I got all the candy."

Luke squinted his eyes. "Who is he supposed to
be?"

"Toto."

"Excuse me?"

"Toto. From *The Wizard of Oz*."

"You couldn't make him the Scarecrow or the Tin
Man, you had to make him the dog?" Luke looked at
her and shook his head in bewilderment.

"Everybody does those costumes. I wanted Danny
to be different. And he was. Of course, as he got older,

he didn't want to be different, and I had to dress him like all the other little boys in town." Jenny forwarded the tape to Danny's fifth birthday party. "Look at him in his helmet."

"Where is this at?"

"Malibu Grand Prix. I got Danny a race car driver outfit, and took him for a ride on the track in one of those little go-carts. He loved it."

"Not as much as you, I'll bet."

"I admit I had a good time." Her voice dropped a notch. "Every minute with Danny has been the best time of my life. He's a great kid. I wish you could know him, Luke, really know him. He has this wonderful sense of humor, kind of dry, like yours." She tossed him a tender glance, then gazed at the television where Danny's freckled face was frozen in time on the screen. "Danny has a big heart. He cares about everyone. He's always watching out for the little kids at school. He's the best."

"You did a good job raising him."

Jenny stopped the videotape, setting the remote down on the coffee table with a shaky hand. "I can't do this right now."

Luke caught his breath at the pain that flashed in her eyes. "I'm sorry. I shouldn't have asked. Damn. I didn't mean to make you cry."

Jenny took the corner of her long-sleeved sweater and wiped it against her wet eyes. "It doesn't take much to make me cry these days."

Luke nodded in complete understanding, angry that he had asked her to show him the tape. He should have anticipated that seeing Danny alive and happy would only remind her that he was now critically ill.

"You can watch it. I'll make popcorn."

Luke sat back on the couch and stared at the screen. Danny was making a face, fingers in his ears, tongue stuck out, nose wrinkled up like a discarded napkin. Had there ever been a cuter kid?

He started the tape again, feeling incredibly proud of his offspring. This child was part of him. This kid with the missing teeth and the eyes that filled with wonder at each new moment in his life was his son.

For twenty more minutes, Luke watched the tape. He saw a magician make a rabbit come out of a hat on Danny's sixth birthday. Then there was Christmas and Easter, Danny's first soccer game, his baseball play-offs, the Halloween carnival at school, the Winter Concert, where Danny played a horridly distorted version of "Heart and Soul" on the piano.

The tape was filled with joy, smiles, hugs, and laughter. Love. It was everywhere—in Jenny's open arms, in Danny's giggle, in the tender moment when Jenny carried a sleeping Danny upstairs and put him to bed while someone unknown filmed the scene.

Luke's eyes filled with moisture as Jenny tucked the covers around his son's body, tightly, as if she were wrapping him in a warm, safe cocoon. She sat on the edge of Danny's bed and smoothed his hair down with her fingers. Then she kissed his cheek.

Danny blinked his eyes open, his small face framed by Jenny's hair. He smiled up at her. "I love you, Mommy. I'll love you forever."

And Jenny's words, so soft, so fraught with emotion. "I love you, too, forever."

Danny drifted back to sleep. The tape jumped ahead into a hideously loud Easter egg hunt a couple of months later. Luke shut off the video and stared at the dark television set, remembering every word, every image.

It wasn't just Danny that he couldn't forget, it was Jenny, too. Seeing how she had grown over the years, how she had developed from a young, insecure, reckless girl into a loving, caring mother. Obviously, she had struggled, but she had made it work. Jenny had filled his son's life with love, the way she had once filled his. He couldn't have asked for a better woman to mother his child. If only he could have shared their life. If only he hadn't made such a selfish mistake. If only—things could have been different.

Luke got to his feet to go in search of Jenny. In the kitchen, he found a bowl of freshly made popcorn, but the room was empty. He walked down the hall, peeked into Danny's room. Nothing. Finally, he saw her sitting cross-legged on her bed next to a large box.

Her dark hair fell across her face. When she looked up at him, Luke was surprised to see a trail of tears across her skin. He was on the bed next to her, holding her close, before he realized he had even moved.

She was soft in his arms, her breasts spilling against his chest, her head tucked under his chin, her arms wrapped around his waist. His body responded in kind, hardening everywhere they touched, his nerves tingling, his mind moving past comfort to desire.

Luke pushed her away. Jenny looked surprised.

"What's wrong?"

"Nothing. What's all this?" It was everything he could do not to touch her, not to push her back against the pillows and make love to her. Beads of sweat broke out along his brow. "Damn. It's hot in here."

Jenny stared at him for a long moment. "You always used to say that, whenever . . ."

Luke got up and walked out of the bedroom. He grabbed at the first available anchor—the bathroom. There was cold water there, and he splashed it against his face until the heat receded, until he could think clearly again.

When he left the bathroom, Jenny had moved her box of photographs into the living room and was sitting on the floor in front of the coffee table. Luke was pleased by the change in locale.

He sat down on the edge of the couch, picking up

a handful of photos. They were much the same as the videotape, stolen moments in time.

"I'm not much of a scrapbook person," Jenny said with a small smile. "Takes too much organization." She spread her arms open wide. "It's hard to believe this might be all I have left of my son."

"Don't say that. Danny will wake up."

"You sound so confident." Jenny's voice was hushed. "I miss the sound of his voice. I miss his bright, sparkling eyes, his drooping curls. I even miss his temper." Jenny put a hand to her heart. "It hurts right here, down deep. A part of me is gone. I want to see him again, Luke. I want to hold him. I want to tell him I love him, and have him hear me."

Luke didn't say a word, he couldn't. His throat was too tight, his emotions too close to the surface.

"Why did it have to be Danny, Luke? Why couldn't it have been me? I've lived thirty-one years. Danny has only had twelve. Think of how much he's going to miss, the senior prom, high school graduation, college, his first job, his first apartment, his first love affair."

"Jenny, stop."

"Marriage and children. He's barely begun to live, Luke. This is so unfair."

Luke moved from the couch to the floor, putting his fingers against her lips, feeling the heat of her anger and desperation on his skin. "I think whatever happens, Jenny, that Danny will be okay."

Her eyes widened in surprise, confusion. "What—what are you saying?"

Luke shrugged, feeling self-conscious, but this was Jenny he was talking to, a woman who believed in miracles more than he did. "I've seen Danny a couple of times. In my dreams. Actually, it seems like a dream, but I'm awake, and he's there. He talks to me."

"What—what does he say?"

"The first time he came was the night he got hit by the car. Must have been hours after his surgery. He called me Dad." Luke's voice caught in his throat as he fought back an overwhelming rush of emotion. "He told me to visit him in the hospital."

"I don't understand."

"It sounds unbelievable. I feel like an idiot for even mentioning it."

Jenny stared at him for a long moment. "You're lying. You're making this up."

He looked at her in surprise and annoyance. "Why would I make it up?"

"Danny wouldn't talk to you. He'd talk to me. I'm his mother, his best friend." She slugged Luke in the arm so hard he flinched. "You are nobody to him."

"I'm his father."

"Go home, Luke. I don't want you here anymore."

"He talked to me, Jenny. Danny told me what you wanted for your birthday. He told me where to buy it."

Jenny touched the angel pin on her shoulder, her expression growing more bewildered by the minute.

"Danny told me you broke up with Alan. He was actually pretty happy about it," Luke added.

The tension on her face eased slightly as she looked at him. "Danny and Alan were never friends. What else did Danny say? Is he going to recover?"

Luke shook his head. "He said he didn't know."

Jenny shook her head. "This is crazy. Danny is in the hospital in a coma. He is not visiting you in your dreams or anywhere else."

"I can't explain it, Jenny. I can't touch him. I can't feel his body, but I can see him and I can hear his voice. He talks to me."

"Can you see him now?"

"No, and I can't call him up at will. He just appears

out of nowhere. He talks about someone named Jacob, but I never see this person."

"What's Danny wearing in your dream?"

"Blue jeans, a sweatshirt that's really too big for him. Jenny, I can't believe you let him dress like that."

"It's the style."

"And a baseball cap turned backward."

She put a hand to her mouth. "That's what he was wearing when he was hit by the car." She raced over to the hall closet and pulled out Danny's backpack, the one he had had with him the night of the accident. In it were his schoolbooks, and the clothes the hospital had removed from his body. They were cut and torn, but as Jenny held them out to him, Luke could see that they matched the clothes Danny wore in his dreams.

"They're the same."

Jenny sank down on the couch, pressing Danny's sweatshirt against her lips, smelling the scent of her son on the material. "This isn't fair, Luke. I should be the one Danny comes to. I'm his mother. What did I do wrong? Why doesn't he want to see me?"

"It may not be Danny's choice. For all we know, I'm just having some incredibly vivid hallucinations."

Luke drew her into his arms. He stroked her hair, wishing he could comfort her, but all he had were meaningless words.

"I want to go to church," Jenny said abruptly. "I want to pray. I know it's been a long time since I've gone and maybe God's given up on me, but I feel like I need to do this. To throw myself on my knees, to beg for a miracle."

"I'll go with you."

"Really? You don't believe in God."

"I don't know what I believe in anymore."

"I'm sorry I hit you."

Luke tilted his head and smiled down at her. "You owe me a million more punches, Jenny. I'll take everything you've got. Just let me be a part of your life. Maybe I don't deserve it. In fact, I know I don't. Let me stay anyway."

"I couldn't get rid of you even if I wanted to."

"Do you want to?"

After a moment, she shook her head. "No. Danny needs you right now. And so do I." She paused. "I feel guilty about your wife, your family. I don't want to come between you."

"There are a lot of things between us, Jenny. I'd be lying if I said you weren't one of them."

"You can't have fallen out of love with your wife so quickly. Maybe she needs time to adjust."

"Denise doesn't want to adjust. I've asked her twice to go with me to see Danny. She always has a reason why she can't go."

"Maybe she's afraid."

Luke shook his head. "Denise isn't afraid of anything."

The next day Denise walked through the front doors of the hospital and paused in front of the elevators. She took in a deep breath and let it out. Everything looked normal so far, a few white coats, people carrying flowers—but nothing really disgusting, at least not yet.

The elderly man standing next to her began to cough, deep, gasping coughs. She looked at him in alarm. He covered his hand with his mouth, and finally the spasm subsided. When the elevator opened, they both got on.

He began to cough again. The air grew warm, and Denise tried not to breathe too deeply. The last thing she needed was a cold. When the elevator stopped at three, she was relieved to get off.

Room 307, the lady at information had said. Denise walked down the colorful hallways of pediatrics, pleased by the pictures of animals and balloons on the walls. She could do this. She could handle it.

A door opened in front of her. A woman and a man came out. The woman was sobbing. The man was crying, too. They stopped in the middle of the hallway, lost in their grief. Denise's hand tightened on the basket of flowers she was carrying. She stepped around them, trying not to look at them, to feel their pain.

She had a dinner to go to later. She certainly couldn't go with red-rimmed eyes and a stuffy nose. Finally, room 307. She took a deep breath and pushed the door open.

There was a boy lying in a bed, a nurse standing next to him, fiddling with some tube going into his arm.

"Hello," the nurse said.

"Hello. Is that Danny St. Claire?" Denise asked.

"Yes. Are you a friend of the family?"

"You could say that." Denise licked her lips and took a step forward. The room was small, sterile. It had a funny odor to it. As she got closer, she could see Danny's face, and she remembered him, the way he had looked when she had slammed the door in his face. There was no emotion there now, no anger or shock, just blankness. He almost looked dead.

Her stomach churned at the thought. Her heart began to pound, and she felt suddenly hot.

"Are you all right, ma'am?"

"Yes. Fine. How is he?" Her words came out in short bursts. It was all she could do to get them through her tight lips.

"He's better, breathing on his own."

"But he's not awake."

"No." The nurse walked around the bed. "I'll leave you alone for a moment."

Denise swallowed hard, suddenly realizing that this child, this son of Luke's, was practically a vegetable. He was being fed by a tube, and obviously had no control over bodily functions. He might stay like this for a long time. Someone would have to bathe him, sit by him, visit him. She couldn't do it. She couldn't mother this child.

The basket of flowers slipped out of her hand and landed on the floor. She turned blindly toward the door, impatient to leave as quickly as she could. But there was someone blocking her way, a woman. Jenny.

Denise knew it was her, even though she had never seen a photograph, never seen Jenny in person. This woman in faded blue jeans, a white blouse, and a pink sweater, this ridiculously unsuitable woman was breaking up her marriage.

Jenny was pretty. Denise had to give her that. And thin, too. Not voluptuous. Not incredibly sexy, but she could see why Luke was attracted to her. There was a softness about Jenny that made even Denise pause. She wanted to dislike her, but she had a feeling this was not a woman who was easy to hate.

They looked at each other for a long, tense moment. Denise tried to set aside the panic she felt just being in the room with Danny. She didn't want Jenny to see her at a disadvantage. She didn't want Jenny to have the upper hand. Why on earth had she ever come to the hospital? She should have stayed home or gone shopping.

This wasn't her thing. She didn't even visit her friends when they had babies. She waited until they got home and didn't look so ghastly.

"Mrs. Sheridan," Jenny said quietly, "I'm Jenny St. Claire." She held out her hand.

Denise reluctantly took it. "I know who you are. And I'm sorry"—Denise tipped her head toward Danny—"about your child."

"Thank you. I appreciate that."

Another long silence. "You can stay if you want," Jenny said. "I can come back later. I'm here most of the day anyway."

"No. I just brought some flowers." Denise saw Jenny's eyes travel to the bouquet lying on its side on the floor.

Jenny picked them up and set them on the bedside table. "They're lovely."

"I have to go." Denise turned to leave, but Jenny's voice stopped her.

"I don't want anything from Luke," Jenny said. "I don't want to interfere in any way with your family or with your relationship."

Denise sent Jenny a brittle, bitter smile. "It's a little late for those words."

"I do mean them."

"Maybe you do." Denise shrugged. "Unfortunately, you've given Luke something that he desperately wants—a son. I can't do that. I can't compete."

"We don't have to compete. We can work this out."

"You're an idealist, a romantic. That's what Luke likes about you, I'm sure." Denise paused, her eyes tearing in spite of her efforts to maintain control. "I'm not really concerned with what you want. I'm more concerned with what Luke wants, and it's the strangest thing, but I think he wants you."

Denise slipped out of the room, leaving Jenny with something else to think about. Hearing Luke say the words was different from hearing Denise say them. They were more real, more concrete and absolutely more terrifying.

She wasn't sure she was ready to have Luke back in her life. But then Jenny looked at Danny and thought about how happy he would be to have the two of them together.

"It might happen, buddy," she said quietly. "What you wanted most might just happen. But if Luke and I get together, this time it will be on equal terms. He'll need me as much as I need him. We'll both give, and we'll both take. See what you've taught me, Danny? I'm standing up for myself. No more wimpy mom."

She squeezed his hand. "How come you don't talk to me—like you talk to your dad? You're not still mad, are you? Please, Danny, say something. Come back to me, dammit."

28

◄O►

ON FRIDAY MORNING, ALAN AND HIS PARTNER Sue Spencer drove down Jenny's street in their patrol car. Alan pulled over in front of the house just as Jenny walked out the front door. He turned to Sue. "I need five minutes, Spence. Do you mind?"

"Of course not. I'll wait here. Better hurry, looks like she's leaving."

Alan got out of the car and hurried across the street, calling Jenny's name as he did so. She looked up in surprise.

"Alan."

"You're going to work?" he asked, noting her McDougal's Market smock.

"Until one."

"I've called you several times."

"Alan, we've said everything there is to say."

"I can't let you go, Jenny. I won't pursue Matt. I'll drop the case. Whatever you want." Alan heard the desperation in his voice and felt like a fool, but he didn't know what else to do short of throwing himself at her mercy.

346

"I'm sorry, Alan." She smiled at him with big, sad eyes. Pity. God, he hated pity.

"Forget it."

"I didn't mean to hurt you. But I can't pretend to feel something that isn't there. You know I would drive you crazy over the long haul. If you think about it, I've been getting on your nerves for weeks. I'm a messy housekeeper. I can never find my keys and I'm always ten minutes late."

She paused, waiting for him to say something, but he couldn't speak. Deep down, he knew she was right, but time was running out for him. He was beginning to feel like he would never find the right woman, never have a chance to be married or have a family.

"And Danny would light your fuse in a day," Jenny added. "You two never hit it off."

"I tried," he said finally.

"I know you did. And I appreciate everything you've done for me."

"It's that guy, isn't it? All these years, you've been waiting for him to come back. I'm surprised you didn't take Danny to see him years ago. It would have saved everyone a lot of grief."

She paled at his words. "That was cruel, Alan."

He knew he should apologize, but he couldn't. He just stood there and watched her get in her car and drive away.

Sue got out of the patrol car and walked across the street to join him. "Are you okay?"

"Yeah, fine."

"Want to talk?"

"No."

Alan looked at Jenny's house. He had spent some happy times there, and some not so happy times. But her house had always seemed like a home to him, filled with her presence, her joy of life. Now, the doors were locked, and he was on the outside. Where had he gone wrong?

"Love sucks," Sue said.

He reluctantly smiled. "You got that right. Come on, let's get out of here."

As he turned to leave, the garage door opened next door, and Gracie backed her old white Lincoln out of the driveway. Alan stopped and stared as the older woman knocked over trash cans and weaved into the street like a drunken sailor.

"What the hell is she doing?" he asked.

Alan ran to the patrol car, and Sue slipped in next to him. They followed Gracie down the street with the lights on. She drove straight through a stop sign. Alan put on the siren. Gracie ran her car up over the curb, stopping abruptly in front of a tree.

When Alan got to the car, Gracie sent him a blank look as she clutched the steering wheel.

"Are you all right?" Alan opened the door.

"I—I." She put a hand to her temple and rubbed it.

"Did you hit your head, Gracie?"

"No. No, I don't think so."

"You're not supposed to be driving. Where are you going?"

"Going? Why, I'm going to pick up Doris from school. She called and said her ride didn't come, and you know she's such a shy child, she hates to sit alone in the playground."

Alan looked over at Sue.

"Who's Doris?" Sue asked.

"Her thirty-two-year-old niece."

"Oh. I'll call for an ambulance."

"No." Alan shook his head. "That will just scare her. I'll drive her back to the house. It's only a few blocks. We'll get someone to stay with her until we can find Doris."

Sue smiled as she took the car keys from Alan. "Are you going to give her a ticket?"

"Maybe," he growled. "She did break the law."

"She certainly did."

"Slide over, Gracie. Let me take you home," Alan said.

Gracie moved over to the passenger side. "I forgot how much you like to drive, Harold. Next time, I'll remember. Did I tell you how much I love you?"

Alan stared at her and realized that Gracie wasn't seeing him but her deceased husband. "Yeah, you told me."

Gracie put a hand on his arm. "I remember the day we first met. You were so handsome, strong—and so shy," she said with a laugh. "I practically had to beg you to dance. You were afraid you'd step on my feet. I just wanted to be in your arms and dance for the rest of my life. Do you still think I'm as pretty as the day we met?"

Alan looked over at her and smiled. "I think you're prettier."

"You always know the right thing to say."

Alan drove Gracie back to her house, pulled the car into the driveway, and shut off the ignition. He helped her out of the car and up the steps to her house.

When she got to the front door, she turned to him, her eyes suddenly clear. "You're not Harold, you're Alan."

"Yes, ma'am."

Gracie looked over at the car. "Are you borrowing my car?"

"You don't mind, do you?"

"No, of course not."

A cab pulled up in front of the house, and Doris stepped out, her face flushed, her movements hurried. She looked from Gracie to the two police officers and hastened up the drive.

"What's wrong? What's happened?"

"Nothing's happened, dear," Gracie replied. "You're such a worrier. Alan just wants to borrow my car."

"I wonder if I could have a glass of water," Sue interrupted. "I'm thirsty."

"Of course," Gracie said, motioning for Sue to follow her into the house.

Alan looked at Doris. "Gracie was driving." He handed Doris the keys. "I suggest you put these where she can't get to them."

Doris took the keys out of his hand. "I am so sorry. I got delayed at the doctor's office, then my car wouldn't start. I called and told her I'd be right home. I can't imagine what she was thinking."

"She was thinking you were seven years old and needed a ride home from school. Gracie's sick, isn't she?"

Doris nodded, her expression turning sad. "Yes. She has Alzheimer's. That's why I'm living with her now."

"She could have hurt someone, could have hurt herself," Alan said. "You may have to take stronger measures."

"I know. But I can't stand the thought of putting her in a home. When she's clear, she's as sharp as any of us. Think what being in an institution would do to her spirit. No, I can take care of her. I'll just watch her more closely. Is she in trouble? Is she getting a ticket?"

"No, but I want her car taken away, and your keys to be locked or hidden at all times."

"She wouldn't try to drive my car. It has a stick shift."

Sue joined them on the porch. "All set, partner?"

"Yes."

Gracie followed them outside. "Just bring the car

back any time, Alan. I don't drive anymore, you know."

"I know." Alan smiled at her.

"Harold loved that car. It was his prize possession. Kept it clean as a whistle, he did."

Alan looked over at the Lincoln and suddenly frowned. Something wasn't right, and it had nothing to do with the layer of dust on the hood. It was the headlight. The left front headlight.

He felt the blood recede from his face as he was drawn closer to the car. He heard Sue's questioning voice in the background, but he couldn't answer her. The sun danced off the headlight, like a beacon, calling to him.

When he got to the car, he knelt down beside it, saw the broken glass, and closed his eyes.

He felt Sue's hand on his shoulder. After a moment, he turned to look at her and saw the understanding and disbelief in her face.

"What's wrong now?" Doris asked, walking over to join them.

"The headlight is broken."

"So?"

"Have you driven this car lately?"

"Never. No one drives it, at least not until today."

"Gracie." Alan looked over at the woman on the porch. She looked old and frail, suddenly terribly afraid. Gracie knew. Deep down inside, somewhere in the hidden recesses of her mind, she knew, or she suspected. Whether or not she could tell him the truth, he had no idea. And whether or not he could tell her the truth was also in question.

Because this sweet old lady had listened to his problems, had taken care of Jenny and Danny through the early years, had cooked and cleaned and brought over chicken soup when the family was sick. Gracie had been a surrogate mother to Jenny and a grandmother to Danny.

If she had done the unspeakable, how could any of them handle it?

He had to confront her. Still he hesitated, feeling the pressure rise as Doris and Sue stood silently behind him, waiting and watching.

Gracie walked slowly down the steps. She stared at the broken headlight, then looked at Alan.

"Have you been driving, Gracie?"

She looked at him in confusion. "I don't think so."

"Do you know how the headlight got broken?"

"It must have happened when Harold and I went to visit my sister Elizabeth. We were going to stop for ice cream at Ida's place, but it was late, and we decided to just keep going. My sister hates when people are late."

"Do you remember what night that was?" Alan asked, trying to stay calm.

"A few weeks ago, I think. I remember it was foggy, and a deer ran into the road. But Harold said no, it was my imagination. He told me everything was all right. We just kept driving and, well, I guess he forgot to fix the light. Everything is all right, isn't it?"

Alan didn't know what to say. What to do. Everything in his life had been cut and dried, black and white, until this moment. He could hear Jenny's words ringing in his ears. *Sometimes love is more important than the truth.*

But he was an officer of the law, and Gracie had in all probability nearly killed a child. If Danny died, she would be responsible for the death of an innocent boy. How could he let her walk away?

The guilty must be punished. It was his own personal law. And Gracie—Gracie was guilty. She had to be punished.

But how did one punish a seventy-year-old woman with Alzheimer's who had no idea what she had done? Who could possibly benefit from her incarceration? Certainly not Danny, not Jenny, and definitely not Gracie.

Doris looked at him, her face white and tense. "My Aunt Elizabeth died three years ago."

"I know. Take your aunt in the house," Alan said gruffly.

Doris opened her mouth to ask a question, then closed it and did as she was told.

When they were gone, Alan leaned against the hood of the car and bowed his head. "What am I going to do, Spence? What am I going to do?"

"Finish the investigation. Check the skid marks and the glass, analyze the damage. In other words, you're going to do your job," Sue said matter-of-factly.

Alan sighed. "Sometimes I hate this job."

"So do I. She's such a sweet old lady. Do you want me to tell Doris what's happening?"

"Yes, but don't say anything to Gracie, not yet."

"And Jenny?"

"I'll call her at work."

"At least Matt's off the hook."

"Yeah. Looks like I was wrong about him—wrong about a lot of things."

Luke flipped open the desk calendar in front of him. December 20. Five days until Christmas and a month since Danny's accident. So much had changed in four short weeks.

The door to his office opened. Luke looked up, expecting his secretary. His father walked in as if he owned the place.

Luke immediately got to his feet. "Father."

"Had to make me come all the way up here, didn't you?"

"I don't recall asking you to do anything."

Charles sat down in the armchair in front of the desk, although he looked distinctly uncomfortable sitting there. He was used to being in charge, having others jump to obey his wishes, not the other way around.

Luke sat down as well. "Why are you here?"

Charles looked him straight in the eye. "I'm worried about my company. We lost the Genesys deal because of your inattention. Malcolm told me you missed two meetings with them." Charles hit the edge of his desk with his fist. "Dammit, Luke. I gave my life to this company, and I will not stand by and let you run it into the ground."

"It's not my intention to run this company into the ground."

"Then why are you spending all your time at the hospital? You should be taking care of business. I thought you were ready to commit yourself to Sheri-Tech. Isn't that why you came home?"

"Yes. But things have changed."

"Not the important things. You're my son and heir. This company is my legacy to you. I don't understand your attitude."

"I appreciate everything you've done for me," Luke said, "but *my son* is lying in a hospital bed, fighting for his life. And frankly, I don't understand your attitude."

The air bristled between them with tension, distrust and anger. Luke had never confronted his father, never stood up to him, until now.

"I've done everything you wanted me to do," Luke added. "I studied science and math, went to the schools of your choice, majored in the fields you told me to, and worked my way up the ladder of biotech. I've moved into your house, your bedroom, your closets and this company. I have tried so hard to be you. But I'm not you. I can't wear your shoes. They don't fit."

"Luke."

"I can't run Sheri-Tech the way you ran it. I can't live with a woman who doesn't want children. I can't pretend anymore. I'm tired. I'm angry. And I'm afraid."

Charles sat back in his chair, completely taken aback by Luke's outburst. "Afraid—of what?"

"Of losing my son." Luke stood up and paced behind the desk. "I want to know Danny. I want to play catch with him, teach him to drive, and to shave. I want to share my life with this kid, because maybe then I can understand how a father and a son are supposed to love each other. Maybe I can have with Danny what I can't have with you."

Charles' eyes filled with pain at his words. "I've always been a father to you. I don't understand what you're saying."

"Your love came with expectations. I can't meet those expectations anymore, and I'm not going to try. You think I'm destroying Sheri-Tech? It's yours. I'll walk out of here today. Whatever you want."

Charles got to his feet. "I don't want you to leave the company. I want you to run it. I want you to make it more successful than I did."

"I'm not sure I can do that. I'm not sure I want to. I've wasted too much time trying to be someone that I'm not." It was a relief to say the words. Luke felt free and in control.

"You're talking nonsense," Charles said. "You are what you are, and I'm proud of you."

"You should be. I did everything for you. Maybe if I'd had brothers and sisters it would have been different. But it was only me. I was the one to carry on your hopes and your dreams. I've borne that burden my entire life."

Charles reached out his hand to touch Luke's shoulder, but Luke stepped away. Charles's hand fell to his side.

"I wanted the best for you," Charles said quietly. "I still do. If that makes me a bad father, then so be it."

Luke stared at him, feeling the guilt creeping up his spine, but he would not give in. This was his life, not his father's life.

"I didn't say you were a bad father," Luke replied. "Just one with incredibly high expectations."

Charles cleared his throat. "It's not just the boy. It's the woman, too, isn't it?"

"Yes. I love Jenny. I always have. You'd probably like her, too, if you gave her a chance."

"You're married to Denise. You could have a child with her."

At his words, Luke felt an agonizing pain right down to the bottom of his toes. He shook his head. "I can't have a child with her. Denise had a tubal ligation."

"She what? For God's sakes, why?"

"She doesn't want children." Luke sat down in his chair while his father thought about his statement. The tension between them eased. They were no longer shouting at each other. Luke had always thought the truth would drive his father away. In fact, it had brought them closer.

"So, this boy of yours, he's going to be my only grandchild?"

"Ironic, isn't it? And you don't want to see him."

Charles stared at him thoughtfully, then nodded his head. "I do want to see him, Luke. And I want to see him now."

T HE NURSE WAS ADJUSTING DANNY'S IV WHEN
Luke and his father entered the hospital room.
She smiled at them, finished what she was do-
ing, and left.

Luke watched his father walk to the bed. Charles
stared down at Danny, his expression carefully
guarded. He placed his hands on the bedrail, gripping
the bar for support. As Charles studied Danny's face,
he started to sway. Luke rushed forward in alarm.

"Are you all right?" Luke asked.

The color left Charles' face. When he turned to Luke
he looked shell-shocked, as if he had seen a ghost instead of his grandson.

"My God. He looks just like you. That could be you
in that bed. I need to sit down."

Luke helped his father to the chair, poured him a
glass of water from the pitcher by the bed, and
handed it to him. Charles took a drink and wiped his
brow with the back of his hand. "I didn't know. I
didn't imagine that he would look like that."

"He's a part of us, a Sheridan."

"I can see that."

"Can you accept it?"

Charles didn't answer.

"He's also a part of Jenny. Can you accept that, too?"

Charles sent Luke a pained look. "I never disliked her. I just didn't want her for you. I didn't think she was good enough."

"Good enough?" Luke ran a hand through his hair. "You're right she wasn't good enough. She was better. She was her own person, and that's more than I can say for myself. I'll always regret the fact that I walked away from her and from Danny." Luke looked at his son. "I want the best for him, too, Father. But it doesn't have to be what I want, only what he wants."

"What *do* you want, Luke? Do you even know?"

"I'm beginning to. There comes a point when a man has to take a stand. I'm taking a stand."

Charles took in a deep breath and let it out. "And what exactly is your stand?"

"I'm taking a leave of absence from Sheri-Tech, starting immediately."

"How long a leave of absence are we talking about?"

"At least three months."

"That's a long time."

"Right now, I want to be with Danny. After that, we'll see. It's time I made a few changes in my life— for better or worse."

Charles got slowly to his feet. "Believe it or not, Luke, I want you to be happy. I've always wanted that. If you want a leave of absence, take it—with my blessing. We'll work something out." Charles took a last look at Danny. "I must admit, it's kind of nice to know that you're not the last of the Sheridans after all."

"It is, isn't it?" The voice came from behind them. Luke and Charles turned at the same time. Standing in the doorway was Beverly Sheridan, behind her, Denise.

"Mother."

"I had to come, Luke. I had to see him." Beverly stepped forward and put her arm around her husband and her son. When she looked at Danny, her lower lip began to quiver. "So this is Danny."

"Yes, this is Danny." Luke pulled his mother against him, feeling her tremble in his arms. His parents didn't seem nearly as strong or invincible as they had in the past.

"He's beautiful. He's you," Beverly said.

Luke looked over his shoulder to see Denise at the foot of the bed, standing silently, staring at his son, at his parents, at him. She met his gaze, her eyes troubled and sad. For a moment, they connected on a deep and personal level, a place they hadn't met in months, years even.

"I think I understand," she said slowly. "I finally understand." Denise turned to leave.

"Go after her," Beverly urged. "Talk to her. You owe her that much."

Luke strode after Denise. He found her at the end of the corridor by the elevators.

She held up her hand when she saw him. "Don't say anything. Not one word."

"We need to talk."

She shook her head and turned away from him, pushing open the door to the stairwell. Luke ran after her, down one flight, then another, hearing her heels click on the stairs as she ran.

"Denise, wait," he shouted.

He finally caught up with her somewhere between the first and second floors as she stopped to catch her breath. When he approached, she held up a hand, and he saw the tears running down her face in a wash of mascara.

He reached for her. She pulled away. He grabbed her back and yanked her into his arms.

Denise started to cry, and he felt like crying along with her. "It's over," she said. "I've been fighting it for so long, and now I know that it's over."

"Denise—"

She pulled away from him. "Maybe it would have been different if we'd had a child. Then maybe this one wouldn't mean so much to you. I thought about trying to get my tubal ligation reversed. I thought about in vitro fertilization, surrogacy, adoption. Because if I could give you a son, I think I could hold on to you."

"What's done is done. You don't want children. You've made that very clear."

"I made a mistake."

"We've all made mistakes."

"It wouldn't have mattered anyway. Because that boy upstairs reminds you of his mother, and I think . . ." Denise hesitated, her mouth trembling. "I think you're still in love with her."

Luke felt her pain as deeply as his own. "I never wanted to hurt you."

She pulled a tissue out of her purse and blotted her eyes. "You know, for a moment, a horrible moment, I actually wanted that boy to die. I thought if he was gone, we could go back to being the way we were. But that won't happen. Because you've changed, and I have, too. Just tell me one thing, Luke. Did you ever love me?"

"Yes. I still care for you. I just don't know if we can be happy together."

"Care? That's not a very strong emotion, Luke. Certainly not the way you should feel about your wife." She squared her shoulders. "I don't think we can be happy together, either. I want a divorce."

He stared at her, feeling such incredible relief, he didn't know what to say. "Are you sure?" He felt almost obligated to protest, even though he wanted to shout for joy.

"Positive."

And she sounded positive. He tried one last argument. "We can wait, Denise. Everything is crazy right now. We shouldn't be making big decisions."

"I don't want to wait. I don't want to think about it anymore. I came to the hospital the other day." She looked at him steadily. "I saw Danny, and I met Jenny. She's actually nice."

"What did you say to her?"

"Nothing horrible. I realized after I spoke to her that she's perfect for you—at least for the new you, the one who wants a basketball hoop in the driveway, and insists on a real Christmas tree when an artificial one is just as good, and the man who wants to make love on an open air deck for all the world to see." She shook her head. "We could try counseling, but it wouldn't work. The truth is, I don't want to get stuck taking care of that kid for the rest of our lives. He might not get better. He might be that way forever, and I don't think I could handle spending every Sunday in a hospital room." She shrugged. "I'll call Dale as soon as I get home."

Luke stiffened at the mention of their attorney. "You're moving awfully fast."

"Life is short, Luke. Haven't you realized that yet?" She smiled and touched his face in a loving, regretful gesture. "I'm going to make you pay, sweetheart. You're a rich man, and you owe me half. I won't settle for less."

"I'm sure you won't."

She started down the stairs, then paused as she gave him one last look.

"Be happy, Luke."

"You, too," he whispered, but she didn't hear him, because she was already gone.

*   *   *

"Denise is leaving Luke," Beverly said to her husband as they waited in Danny's hospital room. "She's not the type of woman to wait for the other shoe to drop."

Charles shook his head. "I wish we could stop them from making such a big mistake."

"We can't. I don't think we should even try. Luke is a grown-up." She smiled at her husband. "I just realized that. You'd think I would have figured it out earlier."

"Where did the years go?" Charles asked, putting his arm around her waist. "It seems like yesterday when Luke was this age, and we were worrying about him."

"Now, he's taller than you, and we're still worrying. Were we bad parents, Charles? Did we ruin his life by wanting so much for him, by expecting so much?"

"We wanted him to have the best of everything. What's wrong with that?"

"I don't know." Beverly smiled down at Danny and ran her fingers through his cowlick. "This little boy has caused one heck of a lot of trouble, hasn't he?"

"He's a Sheridan. Would you expect anything different?"

"Danny isn't a Sheridan. He's a St. Claire," Jenny said as she walked into the room, holding a teddy bear in front of her chest like a shield. She looked warily from Charles to Beverly. "What are you doing here?"

"We wanted to see our grandchild," Charles said.

"Really? I find that hard to believe."

"That's because you don't know us very well."

"I'd like you both to leave." Jenny felt good after she said the words. She wasn't a näive kid anymore. This was her child, her life, her territory. She wouldn't let them come in and hurt Danny.

"We're sorry about what's happened to your son," Beverly said.

"Thank you." Jenny didn't waver in her stance. Beverly and Charles Sheridan were arrogant and used to getting their own way. She had no idea what they wanted now, but she was not going to let them get it.

Beverly offered her an apologetic smile. "I know you won't believe me, but I'm sorry about the way I treated you all those years ago. I was afraid of your influence, afraid you would take Luke away from us, away from what we wanted for him."

Jenny softened a bit at her explanation. Charles and Beverly didn't look nearly as intimidating as she remembered. "I obviously didn't do that. He left me," she said.

"Not willingly." Beverly nudged her husband.

Jenny set the teddy bear down in the bed next to Danny. "I understand you better now that I have a child. I don't suppose I looked like a great catch at the time. But things are different now. I'm looking to the future, not to the past."

"So are we," Beverly said. "We don't want to interfere in your life. In fact, we'll go now."

Jenny watched them walk to the door with mixed emotions. She didn't want Beverly and Charles back in her life, but then again they were Danny's grandparents. She looked over at her son's face and remembered his endless list of questions about his ancestors, his fascination with family history.

"Wait," she said.

Beverly and Charles looked at her with expectation in their eyes.

"Danny wants to know you. He wants to know Luke. That's all. If you're open to that, I would welcome you into his life."

Beverly smiled at her. "You're very generous, much more than I would have been."

"Just be kind to my son, because I'm a lot older

now, and a lot tougher. And I'll be watching you every second."

Charles laughed at her spirited statement. "And so you should."

Luke entered the room with a look of surprise and wariness, "Is everything all right?"

"Everything is fine," Jenny said.

Beverly kissed him on the cheek. "We'll see you at the house, Luke. You have a handsome son. You should be proud."

"I am proud."

As the door shut behind them, Luke looked over at Jenny. "Are you all right?"

"Still in one piece. Your parents aren't as bad as I remember." She glanced over at Danny. "He certainly seems to have brought about change in a lot of people. I hope that isn't the lesson, Luke. I hope Danny isn't paying the price for our foolishness, that we have to learn something from his—" She couldn't bring herself to say the word. "God wouldn't be that cruel, would he?"

"I hope not."

Luke picked up the teddy bear. "Who's this guy?"

"That's Mack."

"He's missing the fur on his nose."

Her eyes misted over. "Yeah, Danny used to rub that spot with his finger when he went to sleep at night. He finally let it go when he was about nine. I thought he had thrown it away, but today I cleaned his room and found it stuffed in the back of his closet."

Luke tucked the bear in next to Danny's head and moved Danny's arm so that it was wrapped around the bear.

Jenny took a deep breath at the tender sight, trying not to cry. The time for tears was over. Besides, she didn't want to be sad. She had brought the bear to cheer Danny up. Somehow, she hoped Danny would draw comfort from the stuffed animal as he had done on so many nights.

She poured herself a glass of water from the pitcher next to Danny's bed and took a sip. "So, what brought on the family gathering? Did you have to bribe them or sell the next twenty years of your life?"

"I deserved that." Luke smiled at her. "I've made some decisions, Jenny. I'm taking a leave of absence from Sheri-Tech to spend more time with you and Danny."

"What? You can't do that. This was your dream, Luke, to take over your father's company. You can't walk away now."

"It isn't my dream anymore. My dream is you."

His eyes met hers, filled with meaning, promises of a future together. Jenny wanted to believe him, but she was afraid. "You're caught up in all this," she said, waving her hand around the room. "When Danny wakes up, you'll feel differently. You'll blame me. You'll leave me again."

"I won't. You have to trust me, Jenny." He reached for her hands and squeezed them tightly, as if he never wanted to let her go.

"Oh, Luke, I want to trust you. It's difficult."

"I know." He paused. "I'm also getting a divorce."

Her eyes widened in shock. "No. That's not true."

"It is true."

"Your wife will be devastated." She shook her head. "I know how that feels, Luke. I was in her position once, remember? You can't do that to her."

"I'm not leaving her. She's leaving me."

"I can't believe it. This is all my fault."

"No, it's not your fault. The failure of my marriage rests solely with myself and with Denise, not with you or with Danny."

She stared at him in confusion. "This is too much for me to take in. Go home, Luke. Save your marriage.

Save your career. We can't be together. It's too late for us."

Jenny turned toward Danny and clapped her hand over her mouth in horror. "Oh, my God. Look. He's crying."

A tear had formed at the corner of Danny's eye and dripped down his cheek, followed by another, then another.

"Danny. It's all right. I'm here. I love you." Jenny gathered Danny's thin body into her arms. "You're okay. Everything's okay. Wake up, honey. Open your eyes."

The tears came, nothing else but tears, and Jenny's heart broke with each one. "Sh-sh, baby. Don't cry. I'm here for you."

Luke wrapped his arms around both of them. "I'm here, too, Danny, and I'm not leaving, not ever."

Danny opened his eyes wide as Jacob took him through a thick cloud. On the other side was the heaven he had envisioned in his mind, large majestic mountains, green trees, flowers everywhere, the grass so thick it felt like carpet beneath his feet. There were streams and waterfalls, bees buzzing, birds chirping, the scent of wildflowers. It was beautiful and breath-taking. Tears came to his eyes. Tears of wonder and anticipation. The real world seemed far away, a life-time ago.

Danny felt Jacob's hand on his shoulder and savored the strength of the older man's hand. He felt small and afraid in the face of such awesome beauty. He took in a deep breath and let it out.

"Not bad, huh, kid? I'm hoping for a permanent promotion to this place, a nice little cottage with a good view. Yes sirree, that would be the ticket."

"Where are we?"

"The name isn't important. Come on. Your friends are waiting."

Jacob led him around a corner into a patio. There were dozens of people there, all dressed in white robes with gold cords around their waists. Their faces were filled with pleasure, with love. Danny felt instantly welcome.

This place was right. It was home. A woman stepped forward. She smiled at him with the beauty of an angel, and he knew instantly that's who she was—a messenger of God with long, flowing blond hair and eyes as blue as the sea.

"Don't get any ideas, Danny boy. I'm still your guardian angel," Jacob said grumpily. "When people see Isabelle, they always want to dump me."

Isabelle took Danny's hand. "We're here to help you make a very important decision, Danny."

"About whether I'm going to live or not?"

"Yes."

Finally, some answers. But now that the moment of truth had arrived, Danny felt scared. He turned to Jacob. "What's happening?" he asked.

"Just talk to Isabelle," Jacob advised. "Oh, and cross your fingers for luck."

"Cross my fingers? That's all you can offer me?"

Jacob shrugged and faded away.

"Wait, don't leave me here alone," Danny cried.

Isabelle soothed him with one word from her melodious voice. The word was *love*. He looked at her and felt the love, the same emotion he had felt every time he hugged his mother. Isabelle motioned for him to sit on a white wicker chair, so he sat. Two of the other angels stayed with them, standing on either side of him, silently supportive, protective.

"Are you frightened, Danny?"

Danny nodded his head up and down.

"Do you believe in God?"

"I guess. I mean, we don't go to church much, but I always believed there was a God. There is, isn't there?"

"Yes."

"Am I going to die?"

"Life on earth is just part of your overall existence, Danny. What you learn in your life as a human being will help you for the rest of your spiritual existence."

Danny swallowed hard, not really following what she was saying. "Okay."

Isabelle smiled gently. "Think of your life on earth as a school, a place to study, to learn about love, anger, joy, courage, and pain. Each soul has a mission on earth, a reason for being."

"Do I? I mean, did I?"

"You did."

"What was it?"

"When you were born, your parents were split apart. Now at the hour of your death, they have come back together. But they're different now. They realize how fragile human life is. They understand that material things are not as important as love that feeds the soul."

"My mom never had a lot of material things," Danny said. "Just my dad."

"That's true. But your mother let pride and fear stop her from sharing her son with his father. Now, she realizes how much time she wasted being afraid. Your father understands the importance of being truthful with himself and with others. And you—tell me, Danny, what have you learned?"

Danny swallowed hard. "I've learned that I have to be responsible for my actions, that what I do affects more than just me."

"That's good. Anything else?"

Danny thought for a long moment. He suddenly realized that he had learned a lot. He'd learned courage from Michael, who had willingly given up his life so that his parents' lives would be easier. He had learned to accept people the way they were, to understand that his father was just a guy who made mistakes, not some kind of a hero. He had learned that his mother's first priority had always been him, and he had learned that even people like his Aunt Merrilee had a good side.

"I've learned that good things and bad things go together and that the bad stuff makes you appreciate the good stuff even more," Danny said out loud. "Oh yeah, and I've learned patience, because being with Jacob requires the patience of a saint."

Isabelle laughed, a beautiful, joyful sound. "I think you're ready, Danny."

"Ready for what?" he asked, feeling a sense of desperation. "My mom needs me."

"You'll see her again someday. I can promise you that."

"But you can't promise me that I'll live." Danny felt a terrible weight in his stomach. He was going to die. He could feel it. Maybe this was the way it was meant to be, his parents together, without him.

Isabelle waved her hand to the side and the heavens began to roll like a movie on a screen. "Look. Your mother is praying for you."

Down below, Danny saw the earth, a church with a white steeple and bells ringing. He saw beams of light coming from the church up into the heavens. Then he saw inside the church. His mother knelt in prayer. His dad sat next to her, his head bowed.

"That's the third time in a week they've gone to church," Isabelle said. "Your mom prays at night when she's alone in her bed. Your dad says prayers when he's driving to work. We've also heard prayers from Gracie, Matt, even your cousins, Constance and William."

"Will their prayers be answered?"

"They hope so. It's Christmas Eve on earth, a time of miracles."

The screen rolled back, and the heavens returned,

only this time there was a long path leading up to what looked like golden gates. Isabelle brought him to his feet and gently ushered him forward.

"Go forward, Danny. It's time."

30

JENNY WALKED OUT OF THE CHURCH AFTER MIDNIGHT Mass on Christmas Eve and looked up at the heavens. There were so many stars, brilliant lights in the sky. The air was crisp and cold, and she drew her coat around her shoulders.

The last five days had passed so quickly. She had filled the time with work and Christmas preparations, buying presents for Danny to open when he woke up and decorating the tree just the way Danny liked it.

She had tried to stay away from Luke. She still couldn't get used to the idea that he and his wife were getting divorced. But Luke had taken a room at a nearby hotel and true to his promise had spent several hours every day with either her or Danny.

They had played cards, gone shopping together, fought over Luke's desire to pay for everything, and laughed when she had forgotten where she parked her car at the mall.

Luke was different now, more of a man than she remembered, more generous with his emotions. He said it was because of her, that she had given him what no one else could, the freedom to be himself.

They were good for each other. Deep down in her heart, Jenny knew she had never loved anyone else. The few men in between had meant nothing to her. Luke was her soul mate, the one who could hear her thoughts before she said them aloud.

She had found love again, but at what cost? She couldn't lose Danny, not even for Luke. Not her child. "Please, God, don't take my child," she whispered.

Luke caught her by the arm as he made his way through the crowd leaving the church. When they got to the sidewalk, he put his arm around her shoulders, protecting her from the wind that sprang out of nowhere, drawing a chill through their souls that went deeper than the night air. The church bells rang behind them as families left the church, laughing, smiling, carefree.

"It's Christmas Eve, Luke. If there's going to be a miracle, it has to happen tonight."

"Maybe it will."

"I feel so alone," Jenny said, looking around her. "As if a part of me is missing."

"A part of you *is* missing."

"I spent all day with Danny, Luke. I talked to him until I was hoarse. I sang to him, read him his favorite books, told him about all the presents under the tree. He didn't move," she continued, feeling the frustation build within her. "I pinched him so hard I thought I'd hurt him, but nothing, not even a reflex action. I don't know how long I can pretend that he'll be all right."

"Hush."

Jenny looked into his strong, lean face. His eyes were watchful, worried. In his expression she saw the same loneliness, the same fear, the same need.

"I want to go to the beach, Luke."

"Now? It's late. It's cold."

"I don't care. I have to get away from here. I can't

go home tonight. I can't bear to have Christmas without him."

"Then we'll go to the beach."

They walked to his car. Jenny grabbed the keys out of his hand and slid into the driver's side of Luke's Mercedes. "Do you mind?"

Luke smiled at her. "Not yet, but I have a feeling I'm going to."

Jenny drove away from the church, down Highway 1 past the homes and businesses until the only lights on the road came from her headlights, the moon, and the stars. She rolled down the windows, relishing the cold against her skin. Luke wrapped his arms around his chest but didn't say a word. He gripped the side of the car when she took a turn too fast, but remained silent.

Jenny was grateful for his silence. She wanted to feel the speed of the car. The rush got her adrenaline going. Danny was somewhere in the heavens. He was calling out to her. "Mom. Mom." She could almost hear his voice. She had to get to him.

Faster and faster she drove, trying to catch the moon before it went down, before morning came, before another day dawned on her misery.

"Jenny, stop. Stop!" Luke shouted.

Her hands gripped the wheel. She couldn't stop. She had to go forward. Danny was out there. She wanted to hold him, to be with him wherever he was.

"Dammit, stop the car. Are you crazy?"

Luke grabbed the wheel. They wrestled silently. The car swerved against the shoulder, stirring up rocks and pebbles.

"Let go," she cried. "Let go."

"Stop it, Jenny. Danny needs you. He needs you. Stop the car."

The words finally penetrated. Jenny eased her foot off the gas pedal. She pulled the car onto the shoulder of the road and breathed long, deep gasps of air as the panic began to recede.

"What were you trying to do?" Luke demanded.

"I'm sorry. I'm sorry." She stumbled out of the car and fled toward the beach.

Luke followed behind her. He threw a blanket over her shoulders. She tossed it on the sand.

The waves crashed in front of them. She got too close, her feet got wet. It didn't matter. She could walk into the water. She could let herself go under. Maybe then she could find Danny. He was out there somewhere. She knew it.

"Jenny. Don't."

Luke's arms wrapped around her waist.

"Let me go! Let me go!" she shouted.

"No. I will not let you kill yourself."

"Why not? Danny's dead. Why shouldn't I be, too?"

"He's not dead. When he wakes up, he'll need his mother."

"Stop pretending. Stop lying. He's hurt so bad he's never coming back."

"You have to have faith. Believe, Jenny, believe. It's the time for miracles."

"I don't believe in miracles anymore."

"I do. I'll believe in them for both of us. It's a miracle that we're here together right now."

"But Danny's gone. I can't feel him anymore." Jenny turned to face him. She drew Luke's hand to her chest. "There's nothing left in my heart. I feel alone, empty."

"You're not alone."

"I don't feel anything."

"Then feel this."

Luke's mouth came down on hers, forcefully, frantically. His arms came around her body. He crushed her chest against his, until every nerve ending, every taste, every thought was of him.

Jenny went with the kiss, with the touch. The heat of his mouth drove the coldness out of her heart. She wasn't alone anymore. She was with Luke, her first love, the man who had captured her heart and never given it back.

She wanted him as much as he wanted her, more, if that was possible. Luke pulled her shirt apart with shaky, rushed fingers. He broke the clasp on her bra, releasing her breasts, letting her warm flesh spill out on his palms.

"Jenny."

"Don't stop," she murmured when he looked into her eyes. "Don't ever stop."

"I want to love you."

She kissed him on the mouth. "Then love me, here, now. Make the pain go away."

His mouth trailed along her face, down the side of her cheek, her neck. He pushed her shirt off her shoulders, and his mouth grazed her collarbone, dropping to her breasts, caressing the valley, the peak, until she was trembling.

She ran her hands through his hair, holding his head to her breast as he devoured her with an intensity that went beyond anything she had ever felt. His mouth was warm. The heat enveloped her body.

Luke dropped to his knees, pulling her down onto the tumbled blanket she had tossed in the sand. He pulled off his shirt and his pants. She pulled her skirt up and felt a chill. It passed as Luke covered her body with his.

His hands were everywhere, his lips followed in sync. The sound of his breathing took over her thought. The waves pounding the sand echoed their passion. When Luke pushed her legs apart, she was more than ready for him. When he touched her with his fingers, she cried out.

"I want you, Luke," she said. "Inside of me. Close to me."

He entered her with a hoarse cry. The feeling of oneness was so powerful that Jenny caught her breath. He tensed, then pushed in again, harder and deeper, until she felt as if he were touching her soul.

She tightened around him, trembling as her body shook with a release that had been years in coming. Luke collapsed against her, his head coming to rest in the corner between her chin and shoulder. It had been fast, reckless, unbelievably good.

Jenny gripped Luke's back with her hands, rolling her fingers over the tense muscles in his back. She wanted to stay like this forever. Here in his arms she felt whole.

After a moment, Luke rolled over on his side, pulling her to face him. His hand ran down her back, her spine, stopping to linger on the curve of her hip.

"Too fast," he murmured. "I want to make love to you again, slowly, so that it will last forever." He kissed the corner of her mouth.

His words were sweet, tempting. No other man had ever made her feel complete. The years between loving had only heightened the intensity of the love she felt for him. They were no longer kids but adults. They had more to lose but also more to give.

Gradually, the wind picked up, and covered them with a cold, salty mist. Jenny shivered as reality began to intrude. "I'm cold," she said.

Luke looked at her and laughed. "That's because it's December, and this might be California, but I'd hardly call it tropical weather."

"This is where it all started."

"But not where it ends." He paused. "I didn't plan for this to happen, but I'm damn glad it did."

"You didn't plan it?" Jenny smiled. "Thank God!"

"We also didn't use anything, Jenny. No protection."

She looked into his eyes and saw the same awareness of the past and the present and the future. "We've come full circle, haven't we?"

"This time we both know what we want."

"Just not how to get it." She traced his lips with her finger. "Danny," she said, and the sadness seeped back into her mind, into her heart. "Neither one of us knows what's ahead for our son."

"That's the first time you've called him 'our' son." Luke pulled the side of the blanket over them, wrapping them together in a cocoon of love. He kissed her mouth lovingly, longingly.

Jenny stopped his kiss with the palm of her hand. "Are we being selfish? Making love when Danny's sick? Thinking about ourselves?"

"Danny is the reason we're together right now. If his accident has any meaning at all, it has to be this."

"I wonder if he knows." She looked toward the heavens. "I wonder where he is right now."

Danny walked through the gates, down a long, winding path that went on forever. There were flowers everywhere, rich, blooming bulbs of color. Two angels walked by his side. When he paused or faltered, they spurred him on. He didn't know where they were going, only that it seemed to take forever to get there.

Finally, he came to an archway, a garden, and a gazebo. The angels led him to the steps of the gazebo and disappeared. There was someone sitting in the shadows. Danny tried to step forward, but he couldn't move. He knew he should be afraid, but he wasn't. He felt love, not anger, and a sense of welcome.

"Can I come in?" he asked.

"Do you want to?" The voice was deep, tender, the sound of a father's voice.

"I'm not sure," Danny said.

"There is so much ahead of you, a world you have yet to experience. Are you frightened?"

"I was, but I'm not anymore." And Danny realized that he wasn't afraid. He was ready to accept his fate, whatever that might be. "I just wish I could talk to my mom," Danny said.

"Close your eyes and speak to her with your heart."

"Okay." Danny squeezed his eyes tight and tried to see his mother's face. She wasn't smiling. She looked scared and unhappy. He wanted to reassure her that everything would be all right, that he loved her, and that no matter what happened to him, he would always be with her.

When he finally opened his eyes the gazebo had disappeared and in front of him was another long path that disappeared into the clouds.

Danny looked at it for a long moment, then took his first step toward the future.

Jenny arrived at the hospital just after eleven on Christmas morning. The halls were lined with Christmas lights, decorations hanging on every door. The nurses wore Santa caps and the orderlies dressed like elves to cheer up the children.

Jenny smiled and said hello to the people that had become a second family to her. She met Angela Carpenter at the doorway to Danny's room.

"Merry Christmas, Angela." Jenny handed her a small white box. "A little something for you."

"You didn't have to do that."

"I appreciate the care you've given Danny."

"It's a pleasure."

"How is he today?"

"Restless. He's moving a bit more than I've seen him."

Jenny felt a surge of hope. "Maybe there will be a miracle this Christmas."

Angela squeezed her hand. "I hope so."

Jenny walked into Danny's room and sat down in

the chair next to him. "Well, buddy, it's Christmas, and you have a pile of presents waiting for you. Wake up, honey. Please wake up."

Danny didn't move. She leaned her head back. Her mind drifted from Danny to Luke. They had gone back to her house and made love again, making up for lost time, lost hopes. Exhausted, they had fallen asleep just before dawn. She had left Luke sleeping in her bed, in the room next to Danny's.

Danny. How much he had given her. Jenny ran her fingers across the ceramic pin she had worn over her heart since the night Luke had given it to her. Her little angel.

She closed her eyes, not wanting to look at the boy in the bed but to remember the child in her heart. In her mind, she could see his face and hear his voice. His hands reached out to her, and she wanted to grab hold, but she couldn't get to him. He was beyond her reach.

He drifted further away, but his words came clearly to her.

"Don't be afraid, Mom. No matter what happens, I'll always be with you. When you look up in the sky and see a bird that's struggling to fly, that will be me. When you feel a hand on your shoulder or a spider crawl up your arm, that will be me, too, telling you I miss you. I love you, Mom."

"You're breaking my heart," she whispered back. But Danny was gone. It was just a dream. She opened her eyes and looked over at the bed, at the boy lying so still and helpless. Danny's cheeks were now a bright pink, almost red. There was sweat beading along his brow. She stared at him in horror. Something was terribly wrong.

On impulse, she leaned forward and touched his cheek. He was on fire, burning up before her eyes.

"No, no," she screamed.

Angela came running through the door. "What's wrong?"

"He's hot," Jenny said. "Look at his face."

Angela placed the digital thermometer in Danny's ear, punched a button, and withdrew it. Her face turned grim.

"What is it?"

"One hundred four degrees."

Jenny clapped a hand to her mouth, afraid to cry out for fear she would start screaming and never stop.

Danny began to breathe in short, shallow gasps.

Angela called for the doctor. An internist arrived first. He took one look at Danny and rapped out a series of orders. Jenny felt herself being pushed further and further away from her son, until she was standing in the doorway.

She felt a hand on her shoulder. It was Luke.

"What's wrong? What's happening?" he demanded, his voice taut with worry.

"He's hot. He can't breathe. I think he's dying. God, Luke, how can Danny die on Christmas?"

31

F IFTEEN MINUTES LATER, JENNY WALKED INTO THE
hospital chapel and knelt before the altar. She
pressed her hands together in front of her face
and said the prayers that had meant nothing to her
as a child, empty words to recite so her parents would
be happy. Now, each word seemed desperately important.

"Holy Mary, Mother of God . . . You were a mother,
please, don't let them take my son." Jenny sat back
on the pew and turned toward the figure of Jesus.
"Don't take my boy. He's my life. I can't go on without him. I'm not that strong. If this is a test, I've
failed."

She paused. "Take me instead. Let Danny live. He
has so much ahead of him. I know he was a gift to
me. He brought me joy at a moment in my life that
was so bleak. Please, God, don't take that gift away,
not yet."

Jenny's voice broke off. All she could hear was silence.

Luke slipped into the pew beside her. He took her
hand in his. They sat silently for a long moment, two

people irrevocably tied together by their child. His quiet strength gave her hope. Her anxiety faded, replaced by a strange sort of acceptance.

"Is he gone?" she whispered.

"No, Jenny. He's still alive, but he has pneumonia. They put him back on the ventilator and loaded him up with antibiotics. He's weak, and the infection . . ."

"Could kill him."

He cupped her face in his hands and kissed her eyes shut, her nose, her mouth. "Faith, Jenny. You taught me that so long ago. Faith in the impossible."

She opened her eyes. His words were stronger than the expression on his face. He was as scared as she was.

"You taught me logic," she said. "I can see how the numbers add up, Luke. The cards are stacked against Danny. It would take a miracle to bring him back."

"Then we'll ask for one. It's a miracle we're together now, after so many years apart, so many mistakes."

"Maybe that's why Danny is dying. Maybe it's the worst kind of irony, the worst kind of symmetry." Jenny knew her words hurt Luke, but she couldn't stop herself from saying them. "We were happy together last night. We forgot about Danny."

"I didn't forget, and neither did you," Luke said fiercely. "We celebrated the love that made Danny in the first place. Don't give up on me, Jenny. I need you to be strong. I can't do this alone."

He took in a deep breath, and she saw complete desolation in his eyes. He turned away from her, the pulse in his neck beating frantically against his skin. He started to shake, then the tears came, silent and long.

Jenny held him in her arms and cried with him for everything they had had and everything they had lost.

The minutes passed slowly. No one disturbed them.

Finally, spent, Jenny pulled a tissue out of her purse and blew her nose. Luke wiped his eyes with a handkerchief, and together they stood up.

"We'll both be strong—for Danny," Jenny said.

"Yes."

Jenny walked out of the chapel and down the hall to the waiting room. Their families were there. Richard and Merrilee were holding hands on the couch. Constance and William sat stiffly in chairs against the wall. Matt leaned against the doorway, chatting quietly to her friend Pru. Beverly and Charles sat isolated on the far side of the room with a grim-faced Alan. The only people missing were Jenny's father and Luke's wife.

Jenny smiled at each member of the group, and watched as her smile was returned, slowly, reluctantly, hopefully.

"Thank you," she said. "Danny would have liked to see you all here, together. The thing he wanted most in life was a father." She looked at Luke and smiled. "And grandparents." Her gaze turned to Beverly and Charles, then moved on to Merrilee and her family. "And aunts and uncles and cousins," she added. "This is the best Christmas present you could have given Danny."

Merrilee stood up and walked over to her, fighting back tears. "Is there anything we can do, Jenny?"

"You've already done it."

Matt stepped forward and gave her a hug. "The kid's tough. He'll make it."

"I hope so." She studied Matt's clean-shaven, carefully ironed look with a curious eye. "You look like you just came from church."

"I'm going to an AA meeting. They even have them on Christmas Day, you know, to get people through the holiday."

"You might miss the football games."

"I think I'll live."

"I think you will, too." She stood on tiptoe and kissed him on the cheek. "It's good to have my big brother back."

Matt nodded. "Knowing that it could have been me that caused Danny's accident—well, I realized how close I came to destroying everything around me, including myself."

"You didn't do it, Matt. That's what counts."

"But Gracie did. Dear, sweet Gracie. Can you ever forgive her?"

"I already have. It was an accident. She doesn't even know what she did. How can I hate her?" Jenny shrugged. "Besides, it won't bring Danny back."

"You're strong, Jenny, maybe the strongest one of all."

"That's what I keep telling her," Pru said. She gave Jenny a hug. "Hang in there, honey."

"I'm trying."

Pru stepped back and Alan joined them.

"I hope you don't mind," Alan said. "Merrilee called me, and I wanted to come."

"I'm glad you did." She took his hand and squeezed it. "Thank you for everything."

"I'm sorry about Gracie."

"So am I."

Alan twisted his cap in his hands.

"I have to go to work. But I'll be thinking of you and Danny. Good-bye, Jenny." He kissed her on the forehead.

"Good-bye." Jenny wrapped her arms around her waist as Alan left. She stood in the center of the room, surrounded by two families that had been irrevocably changed by the accident. *Danny, look how much you've done for all of us. Come back, honey. Come back to us.* The words flew out of her soul. She hoped somewhere he could hear them.

After a while, Jenny sat down in a chair by the window. The waiting began, hours and hours of hope and fear. As the day went on, visitors came and went. Matt left to go to his AA meeting, then returned, looking better than he had in a long time.

Day turned to dusk, then night. Constance and William fell asleep in their chairs. Richard and Matt played cards. Merrilee stitched a needlepoint, Charles and Beverly read magazines and spoke quietly to each other and to Luke.

At ten, Charles and Beverly left, saying they would be back in the morning. At eleven, Merrilee and Richard decided it was time to take the children home. At midnight, Matt said good-bye.

"Christmas is over." Jenny turned to Luke. "The time for miracles is past." She went into his arms and they sat together on the blue vinyl couch throughout a long, tortuous night. At some point, Jenny drifted to sleep, and her dreams were filled with images of Danny.

She experienced every moment of his life in full color, the moment of his birth, a red, squirming baby who yelled for attention the minute he gasped air. She felt his tiny hand clinging to her finger as he struggled to stand, saw his mouth grimace with determination as he tried to walk, felt his pain when he skinned his knee, and heard his howl of indignation when he saw his own blood for the first time.

There were so many moments to remember, small things that once seemed unimportant, arguments, heated words she wished she could retract. Through it all, she could feel Danny's arms around her neck, his hair brushing against the side of her face as she gave him a piggyback ride. She could hear his tiny snore as he crept into bed with her, afraid of the dark, afraid that morning would never come.

"I love you, Danny." The words echoed around and around in her mind, until there was nothing left but blessed oblivion.

*   *   *

Danny looked at the clouds surrounding him. The path had led to a series of steps, down, then up, then down again. He felt tired, breathless. He had to stop and rest. What was happening to him? He hadn't felt anything for so long that it shocked him to feel something now.

Jacob suddenly appeared next to him, and Danny welcomed him like a long-lost friend.

"I'm scared," Danny said.

"I know."

"It was Christmas. Isabelle showed me the trees, the lights, the presents. I can't believe you're going to let me die on Christmas."

"If it makes you feel any better, it's not Christmas anymore. It's two days past Christmas."

"Then it's over. No miracles for my mother."

Jacob tipped his head to one side. "Personally, I think Christmas miracles are kind of corny."

Danny sighed. "Figures, I'd get stuck with the only angel who doesn't do miracles on Christmas." Danny tried to take a few more steps but felt too winded to go on. "Help me, Jacob."

"That's why I'm here."

"Where am I going? Where are these steps leading? Why do my feet feel so heavy? My arms are like weights. I can barely move them. And it's so hard to breathe."

"You made your choice, didn't you, Danny?"

"Did I? I don't remember."

"The heart speaks even when the mouth is silent." Jacob looked at him for a long moment. "I'll always be with you, Danny. When you're afraid of the dark, look to the sky, and you'll see my light. When you doubt everything that you see, put your hand over your heart, like this, and remember." Jacob took Danny's hand and put it on his chest, covering it with his own. "I'm right there, always."

"Jacob—"

"I'll miss you, kid." He put a hand on Danny's fore-head and slowly ran it down Danny's face, closing his eyes. "Rest. Sleep. Live."

Jenny and Luke sat by Danny's bedside, dressed in hospital gowns and masks to prevent any further spread of infection. It had been two days since the outbreak of pneumonia, two days of fear and anguish, two days of waiting. The rest of the family went on with their lives while Jenny and Luke kept vigil.

Jenny looked over at her son and touched the angel pin on her chest. "Thank you, Danny," she said. "Thank you for this and for giving me back your fa-ther." She leaned over and rested her face against Danny's cheek, feeling the slight warmth of his skin, not nearly as hot as it had been before. For that she was grateful.

"Mom." His voice came tiny, weak, frightened.

Jenny lifted her head. Luke moved around to Dan-ny's other side. They exchanged a long, wordless look, then watched as Danny's eyes began to flutter. His lips moved, but no sound came out.

"Danny," Jenny said. "Wake up." She gave him a little shake with her hands.

Slowly, he opened his eyes. "Mom?"

"I'm here, honey, I'm here."

Danny blinked his eyes, squinting at the harsh light. Jenny couldn't believe what she was seeing. He was waking up. Against all odds, her son was waking up. "Call the doctor, Luke," she cried.

"What's wrong? You're crying, Mom," Danny said.

"I'm happy, so happy you're awake."

"Why? Am I late for school?"

Jenny smiled, then laughed, then cried. She looked over at Luke. He was crying, too. "You're late all right," she said. "But it's okay. Everything's okay."

"You're acting weird." Danny wrinkled his nose as if he had an itch. "What's that smell?"

"You're in the hospital, honey. You were in an accident. Do you remember?"

Danny looked at her blankly. "Am I okay?"

"You're better than you were," Jenny said. "I can't believe you're awake, and I'm talking to you."

Danny tried to lift his hand, but his arm fell back against the bed. "I'm tired."

"Go slow, Danny. We have time, now. Plenty of time." She covered his hand with hers.

"I had this strange dream," Danny murmured. "I met my dad. He came back to us."

Luke stepped up to the bed so Danny could see him. "I'm here, Danny."

Danny's eyes widened. "Dad?" He looked over at his mother. "It's true then?"

Jenny nodded. "Yes, it's true."

Dr. Lowenstein came in and checked Danny's eyes and reflexes. He gave commands to which the boy sleepily responded, moving first his arms then his legs.

Jenny held her breath, afraid to believe that Danny was going to be all right after so many weeks of waiting.

Dr. Lowenstein questioned Danny about his name, his birthday, and what grade he was in. Danny answered every question correctly. Then the doctor looked at Jenny and Luke with an incredulous smile. "Wow," he said.

Luke and Jenny laughed.

"Is that your professional opinion?" Luke asked.

Dr. Lowenstein shook his head in amazement. "He looks good. We'll run a complete set of tests just to make sure, but right now I would have to say that I think he'll make a complete recovery."

"I can't believe it," Jenny said. "Did you hear that, kiddo? You're going to be fine."

"How long have I been here?" Danny asked.

"A while, honey, but you're back now, and that's

all that counts." She pushed down the cowlick at the back of his head. Danny brushed her hand away.

"Aw, Mom," he said.

"I never thought I'd hear you say that again."

Danny frowned. "Did I miss your birthday? I had the best idea for a gift."

"You gave me a gift, Danny."

"I did? What was it?"

Jenny exchanged a tender look with Luke. "It was your father."

"Are you together again?"

"Yes, and we're going to be a family, the three of us," Luke said firmly. "The way it was meant to be."

"I feel like I died and went to heaven," Danny said in utter delight.

Jenny stepped backward and tripped over something. Down at her feet was a baseball. She picked it up. "Danny, your next home run is on me," she read. "Where did this come from?"

Danny took the ball out of Jenny's hand. He looked down at the end of the bed and saw an old man in a baseball uniform, the man from his dream. "Jacob," he whispered.

Jacob tipped his cap at Danny. "Have a nice life, kid."

America Loves Lindsey!

The Timeless Romances of #1 Bestselling Author

Johanna Lindsey

KEEPER OF THE HEART	77493-3/$6.99 US/$8.99 Can
THE MAGIC OF YOU	75629-3/$5.99 US/$6.99 Can
ANGEL	75628-5/$6.99 US/$8.99 Can
PRISONER OF MY DESIRE	75627-7/$6.99 US/$8.99 Can
ONCE A PRINCESS	75625-0/$6.50 US/$8.50 Can
WARRIOR'S WOMAN	75301-4/$6.99 US/$8.99 Can
MAN OF MY DREAMS	75626-9/$6.50 US/$8.50 Can
SURRENDER MY LOVE	76256-0/$6.50 US/$7.50 Can
YOU BELONG TO ME	76258-7/$6.50 US/$7.50 Can
UNTIL FOREVER	76259-5/$6.50 US/$8.50 Can

And Now in Hardcover
LOVE ME FOREVER